Another Sunset

Shakur

Cadmus Publishing
www.cadmuspublishing.com

Published by Cadmus Publishing
www.cadmuspublishing.com
Port Angeles, WA

ISBN: 978-1-63751-257-9

Dedication

To my wife Rhiannon Stepherson, my ZAMZAM WELL, as significant to me as that Well was to Hagar and young Ismael; and to my children: Jared (Never give up), William-Khaliys (Never give in), Lilyth (Never wear out) and Askari (Never set limitations beneath your potential).

I would climb or crumble mountains for them because they have already done so for me.

Holy Qur'an: 52:21

"And those who believe and whose families follow them in faith to them shall we join their families: Nor shall we deprive them (of the fruit) of aught of their works: (Yet) is each individual in pledge for his deeds."

Acknowledgments

I want first to thank Allah (S.W.T.) and His Messengers that brought revelation for the enlightenment of humanity.

There is also Steven Heinz; where did you come from? You are perhaps the most remarkable person I have ever encountered in my life (My wife, of course, being the most extraordinary ... smile). Thank you for your faith and belief in me and the energy and actions that you placed behind that faith and belief. You are truly unbelievable, and we would not be here without you. This is only the beginning, buckle up and hang on. Where we're going, we don't need road skills.

Thanks to my editor Jane Eichwald from Ambler Document Processing. Alvin Jones,(Muhammad) wherever you are, Thank You! You sparked the flame that if God says the same is about to become a bonfire.

My mother and my grandmother, Darlene Stepherson and Velma Hayes. May they rest in peace. They groomed me for life, equipped me with the intestinal fortitude to access the 'Giant within.'

And Brother Aqil Ali (Albert Taylor), Wahiyd (Anthony Hurst), Derrick Lewis, Darius Elam, Baltimore (Calvin Hester), Mario Cockerham, and the "Heckler" Stephen James. YYour brother came in at the end of the journey, but the guidance and inspiration you provided daily during the most challenging time in my life was invaluable. Thank you. You all listened when I needed to talk, spoke when I needed to hear, and read to me when I needed to be read.

Finally, Adrain Lucci Miller, Kewana Santana Grey, and Mr. Karlos Fields, my peers, spiritual advisors, and friends. May God bless you all.

Badness you can get quickly, in quantity: The road is smooth and lies close by. But in front of excellence, the immortal gods have sweat, and long and steep is the way to it and rough at first. But when you come to the top, it is easy, even though it is hard.

—Hesiod 700 B.C.

Table of Contents

Chapter 1

Kenya Wane heard the smooth engine of the Mercedes Benz C250 as it entered the driveway. Subconsciously her eyes followed the lights as they played over the walls in contrasting configurations. Apprehensively she glanced at her digital clock, which read 3:43 a.m. The seconds ticked on mindless of the people that monitored them. The physical and emotional fabric of Kenya's body tensed and shook when the door to her stepfather's vehicle slammed shut. Her young mind desperately tried to grasp some understanding of things transpiring around her. She had cried often, felt too much depression, and held secret meetings with thoughts of death in the private offices of her mind. She was a leap year baby, divinely assigned February 29th. Consequently, March 1st was given to her by default as her birthday. She hated birthdays and time. With both birthdays and time, her body seemed to betray her. She wanted to be inconspicuous and overlooked, but daily her body grew soft, lush, and appealing. She missed her mom and her daddy, especially her dad, who was serving a life sentence behind some deep covert activities that surrounded the Black Panther Movement of the late seventies. She hadn't seen him since she was six. He had flown in from Africa in an attempt to see Aseelah, Kenya's mother, herself, and her baby sister Jamilyah. However, the F.B.I. showed up at Kenya's 6th birthday party through some contingent sources. The ghetto bird brought with it thundering noises and flashing lights. Cars swarmed in from everywhere, shouting and sirens erupted the silence. Aseelah was hysterical; Jamilyah screamed at the top of her young lungs, frightened by all the excitement. Kenya clung to her daddy, held on tight, and cried heavily as female officers tried to separate her from her father's leg. She held on and cried.

"Don't move goddamit, raise your damn hands, and let me see 'em!" the police shouted.

"Daddy No!" Kenya cried.

Manza Wane said, "Lookout, officer, just let me get my baby out of the way. I'm not gonna try anything."

"Go ahead," Director Dennis French said. Manza bent over to speak to his little girl. "Hey nah, quit dripping all this wet stuff on my clothes," he stated in his rich, thick voice, using his hand to wipe her face.

"Don't go, Daddy; I need you to stay."

"Baby, all these people came to take daddy somewhere so he can think. I gotta go. I need you to be a big girl and take care of your mama for me. Can you handle that?" Kenya silently shook her head. He stopped her. "Kenya, what I tell you 'bout sayin' you can't do something. You remember?" Kenya nodded her head. "Now you give daddy a hug and kiss and go to your mama, okay?" Kenya hugged and kissed her daddy, wiped her eyes, and walked towards her mom. She would remember it forever. It was March 1, 2008. Happy Birthday.

Cameras, Reporters, Magazines, and talk shows all wanted an opportunity to speak with Aseelah Wane, the wife of the notorious Manza Wane. November 10, 2008, Aseelah, Kenya, and Jamilyah were headed to the Utah Valley Airport. At 2:45 a.m., they were safe aboard a plane headed to Houston, Texas, a big city to get lost in. Aseelah changed her name to Kimberly Khaliyd. Khaliyd was also given to the girls. Even at the tender age of six, Kenya was brilliant, very sharp, and demur. Her little sister Jamilyah was 2, oblivious to all transpiring around her.

Ironically, to Kenya's surprise, her mother began to bring this white man home. After being subjected to an Afrocentric militant father, it was a twist that was constantly speaking on Malcolm X, Huey P. Newton, the homeland, and the insidious unchecked behavior of the peckerwood, cracker, or blue eye devil. Which she later learned were all synonymous with the white man in her father's line of reasoning. So, to say it was confusing to see her beautiful mother philandering with a white man was a bit of an understatement. Kimberly, at five ft. 4 155 lbs., a solid 34-24-38, caramel-skinned beauty with light brown eyes and engaging personality, wasn't wanting for suitors. When she was seventeen, her classmates went to tour a prison in Chicago. A riot broke out; she was knocked down in the melee and chipped her right front tooth. When she got home, her father was not a man to cut corners with his only little girl. It was not long before he had it fixed and replaced with a gold crown. At thirty-one, she still had it, and she was more voluptuous and radiant than at eighteen when she met Manza.

Mama's friend was introduced as Session Thorn II. He was Aseelah's supervisor at the advertising agency where she worked. Aseelah often noticed the disturbing look in her daughter's eyes. Children give parents the look when they believe that one of the missing parents is perhaps being forgotten and/or replaced. The look that said that no matter what, my mom or dad was not being usurped by the interloper entering my home. Whether a boy or a girl, these struggles happen every day in the house where a parent goes missing for one reason or another. Kenya was no different. It was a night like this when the look had become too accusatory and damning that Aseelah took her oldest child to the side and tried to explain the unexplainable. It all boiled down to, "Mama gotta make a way." At least, that is the way it all sifted out in Kenya's young mind.

Thorn was 5'9", 185 lbs. He had strong aristocratic features; a long-pointed nose, thin lips, and soft brown eyes that matched his receding sandy brown hair. He was friendly but had a peculiar way of looking at things that made Kenya uneasy at times. In 2012 Kimberly married him, becoming Mrs. Kimberly Thorn, sinking deeper incognito. In 2013, Kimberly was with a child; she tried to prevent this, doing everything short of getting her tubes tied. Session's sexual appetite was insatiable, and it seemed as though her smooth, ebony skin was irresistible. She would awake some mornings to find him staring at her as if she were the greatest mystery in the galaxy, in his mind, or so it seemed she could induce world peace just by batting her eyes and walking naked across the continent. He acted like she had the kingdom of heaven between her thighs, and he was determined to find it. He was ridiculous in praising her so, but it was flattering nonetheless to have a man view you in such a way and offer you the world because of it.

On March 1, 2013, Jami, Kenya, and Kimberly were headed to Chuck E. Cheese Pizza, where Kim had arranged to have her daughter's 11th birthday party. While on the 610 Loop, Kim noticed some rowdy youngsta's coming up rapidly from the rear, prompting her to move to the slower right lanes when a gunshot went off. It startled Kim so badly she jerked the wheel, and her car began to tailspin.

"Hold on, girls!" Kim shouted over the screeching rubber and blaring horns of an oncoming 16-wheeler. She struggled desperately to regain control of the obstinate vehicle. The Volvo and other cars were also out of control and, with more significant momentum, slammed into the driver's side door, sending Kimberly and the girls reeling side overside. Precariously, they teetered momentarily before coming to an abrupt stop. Jami, bleeding profusely from a gaping wound in her head, had been flung to the opposite side of the car. Kenya, relatively unscathed, laid awkwardly staring into her mother's moribund blood saturated face; it did not take having a PH.D. in anything to deduce that her mother would never smile down at her again, would never comfort her when the world seemed to be spiraling out of control, would never again hold her and lecture her about the vices of boys with their deviant ways. It was all over; the reality of that sat on her chest like an army of Abram tanks; it was so heavy like spiritual relations, too heavy for a child of eleven. She could not command her lungs to breathe, to sustain her. Each breath was like an act of congress, more challenging than a popsicles survival in the sunshine or an ice cube's chances in an oven. Her mother was dead, she realized, and did the only reasonable thing there was left to do; she passed out—another happy birthday. Sirens wailed in the background, and wreckage was everywhere. Inside, the car phone rang, no one would answer it.

At Chuck E. Cheese, Session called his wife, attempting to discover the hold-up. After twelve rings, he hung up. Turning to the waiting children, he said, "They'll be here shortly," then smiled. They would not be there.

After the accident Session went into temporary withdrawal. He began to drink heavily, experiment with drugs of all temperament, and engaging in activities that were slowly deteriorating him, eating him, changing him, and leaving him unrecognizable from a mental, spiritual, and physical disposition.

Kenya went into shock and would not speak to anyone for two years after her mother's death. Kenya spoke again after numerous doctors, physicians, therapists, and psychologists, thousands of dollars, and hundreds of hours. At thirteen, Kenya was already 5'2", a little over 115 pounds. The woman inside her was impatient, demanding, and screaming for release from her young body; already, she had full breasts with shapely hips and a butt that bordered perfection.

Session often found himself staring at her, marveling at her precocious, overly ripe body. She was simply breathtaking, with flawless, smooth, ebony skin—a xerox copy of her mother, just a darker complexion. The likeness between her and Kimberly was unnerving; the same quiet strength locked in her gold-colored eyes was deeply intoxicating. Kenya missed little, and she knew her inexorable attitude for speaking had infuriated him. She would feel his eyes linger on her as she cooked or cleaned. She had also been awakened on several occasions lately by the creak of the unoiled hinges as the door to her bedroom was open. She would just play possum, as her dad used to say. It frightened her, leaving an ominous feeling deep in her gut.

Two weeks ago, while Kenya showered, he drunkenly stumbled into the bathroom. The door popped open, and she jumped, holding her breath as the heavy sound of his urine drummed into the toilet. Coming to a stop-and-start finish, the toilet flushed for what seemed like twenty minutes; a few moments passed and went to wherever lost moments go. Kenya could see Session's silhouette through the shower curtain; her flesh crawled, and her soul recoiled, watching his hand grip the curtain to snatch it from its rings, and to her horror, he stood there staring at her nakedness, lewdly holding his tumescent beet-red penis.

"Kimberly," he slurred. "You -u ar, are s. -g-goo beautiful." He reached to touch her breast, and Kenya shrunk back against the shower wall to avoid his touch. A knock on the door and the sound of Jami's voice shook him from his lustful illusions.

"Daddy, are you in there?" Jami called out.

"Huh, ah yea baby, daddy 'll be right out, kay!"

"It's the telephone," she said.

He turned his attention back to Kenya, looked somberly at his exposed penis, slightly embarrassed. He fixed his clothes, mumbled something unintelligible, and stumbled out of the bathroom.

Kenya sank to the bottom of the marble tub and cried softly while the warm water ran through her shoulder-length hair and danced a duet with her tears. Growing up was so confusing sometimes.

CHAPTER 2

Kenya glanced at her clock again; 3:50 in the a.m. 7 minutes had raced by since the door of her step-father's car had closed. She laid silently, motionlessly listening for some kind of indication that he was in one of his drunken stupors. She heard nothing.

"God grant me the serenity to accept the things I cannot change ..." Kenya mouthed silently, thinking of things happening around her and happening to her. Her growing aversion for her stepfather; the anxiety and trepidation she felt in his presence. "... Courage to change the things I can ..." she continued. Session made everything about his so-called family look so average, so good. Kenya remembered her daddy telling her once sometimes things that looked good were only the magic of misdirection conjured by the hands of some gifted con man. How she remembered these things, she wasn't sure. But she recalled, "... and the wisdom to know the difference." Kenya drifted' off thinking about Nefertiti. She was an African Queen or something like that. Heard her name on the radio, Lauryn Hill's song.

Session stumbled into the house and stood motionless as his eyes adjusted to the darkness of the living room. A faint light illuminated the threshold to the den from the fishing tank. The air pump could be heard distinctly. The refrigerator hummed its steady rhythm. The Grandfather clock ticked its monotonous lyrics to effectively disrupt the silence to add its two-cents. In his study, he rescued a half bottle of Hennessy, took a long deep pull, and fell into his chair as the liquor burned its way down, settling warmly at the pit of his stomach. Killing the last of the drink, he got to his feet shakily; aided by the wall, he headed towards Kim's room.

The additional weight shifted the bed, and Kenya's eyes popped open immediately. Startled and frightened, she could smell the strong liquor. It blanketed the air, and she felt nauseous. Kenya felt Session's hand begin to stroke her legs through the covers. Cool air rushed in as Session slid underneath blankets. She felt him slide up behind her, and as he did so, she felt the hardness of his penis press against the flimsy material of her nightgown and panties. She thought to herself; this can't be happening. Fright crept through her body like an unwanted cold wind. Her chest tightened, and somewhere deep inside her being, anger bubbled and boiled from wherever anger surfaced and originated from. In the milliseconds that passed, she remembered a book she had read where some similar shit had happened. She could not remember the name. The only difference is that the little girl was white and just laid there and let it happen. Kenya felt him slide the hem of her gown up; his hand slid up her body and squeezed her firm young breast. His other hand rubbed and squeezed her bottom. "Ooh, Kim, you're so beautiful." Kenya closed her eyes and attempted to pretend none of this was happening. But it was! Her mind was saying run, run, run, but her body refused to obey the order. He was pulling at her panties. They tore with what seemed like a loud snap! A snap so loud she was sure all the neighbors heard it and everyone between the San Andreas

Fault and Jupiter. Someone had to be calling the cops, but no one came. She found herself still in her bed alone as he caressed and lifted her leg. His hard insistent tool poked and probed at the gateway to her soul and the core of her being. Pain heightened her senses. He grabbed her hips and pulled her to him as he pushed, the head of his penis penetrated her. She bit back the urge to scream. He moaned and sighed, preparing himself to push further into her. The repulsive smell of alcohol assailed her senses, and her resolve broke. Her body responded, and she screamed, loud! Bolting from the bed, she sprinted for the door, wiping the tears that bleared her vision as she had it open and through it before Session had a clear idea that she was out of the bed. Still, he was quick enough, even in his drunken state, to reach out and snag the back of her gown; it ripped, leaving her completely naked.

"Come here, you little Bitch!" he snarled at her. She ran, not knowing exactly where to, just running. The bathroom offered temporary refuge. After shutting and locking the door, Kenya proceeded through the adjoining door to Jami's room. Once inside, she pulled on some pants and a shirt. "This isn't gonna be as easy as you thought," she said to herself. The hallway door to the bedroom flew open, and Session fell in still naked. Kenya shut and locked her sister's door. Jami, now awake, was a statue frozen in fright. Session was delivering hammer blows to the door. A resounding crack gave warning that it was about to give. Six seconds later, it imploded. Kenya and Jami were already at the front door, frantically working on the locks. As the deadbolt was released, Kenya heard Jami yell, "Leave us alone!"

Grabbing Kenya by her hair, Session put her face next to his. "And just where are you headed off to, Ms. Wane?" He kissed her on the mouth.

She spat in his face. "Let me go, Session!" Jami hit Session on the leg, yelling and crying, trying to free her sister. Session caught her with the back of his hand in the face and sent her sprawling into the kitchen, colliding into the icebox. Kenya slapped him and scratched at his eyes. Session reared back and punched her in the stomach. The impact doubled her over and knocked the wind out of her. He hit her again and again. She crumpled to the floor, disoriented and hurting, the blows completely knocking the fight out of her and renewing her fears. She felt him tugging at her jeans then panties. She was helpless and struggled to find· some oxygen in that big ass room. When she felt the cool air rub her buttocks, her mind registered new fear that she was once again naked. From the corner of her eyes, she saw him standing over her. She thought, at least she tried, then she remembered the book she had read; V.C. Andrews, Darkest Hour.

Session glared voraciously at the young tender dark triangle of hair at the juncture of her thick mahogany thighs. Her skin shined from the light sweat she had worked up. He kneeled between her legs, anxious with anticipation.

Jami wasn't quite sure where she found the strength or the fortitude. Maybe some distant militant gene had kicked in from her ancestors, Cleopatra and Queen N'Zinga. Perhaps it was the same gene that had pushed Harriet Tubman and Sojourner Truth was accelerating the adrenaline in her young body. Maybe she was just scared as hell. She grabbed the biggest butcher knife she could find and headed back into the den. What she saw shocked her at first. Session was between her sister's legs. She was naked beneath him. He was sucking on her chest and pulling on his tally whacker, except it was bigger than the nasty little boys at school displayed. Jami charged him and swung the knife like she was Red Sonja or Xena. She came down with all her might, and the blade cut through the air effortlessly. At the last minute, she closed her eyes, and the knife struck something solid, giving off a sickening sound.

Session saw her too late. All he could do was raise his arm to protect his face. The blade of the knife sunk deep into his arm. He yelled, struck Jami on the chin, and knocked her unconscious. The knife protruded from his forearm in a ghastly manner. Blood ran thick and hot into the carpet on his way to the bathroom. Once there, he wrapped his arm in a towel. After locking the girls in his closet, he headed to the hospital because he needed stitches.

Look, Victor; I have two. One's ten and the other is fourteen. What can I get?" The phone was silent for a few seconds, "Victor, you there, man?"

"Yes, I'm thinking twenty-five thousand for the both of them."

"Hell no. I need at least forty thousand!" Session lamented. "Bring them to me." He paused then asked, "What are they?"

"They're girls! What the hell do you mean what are they?" Session was nervous, in pain, and tired.

"I mean Black, White, and Hispanic ..." A pause, "Other?" he said slowly.

"They're Black! Where do you want me to meet you?" Victor rattled off some directions, and the phone line went dead. He let the girls out and spoke in an apologetic and amiable tone. Blamed everything on the liquor, blah, blah, blah ... it would never happen again. He then told Kenya to cook something to eat for her and her sister. Then promised that he would seek professional help and that things would be better from now on.

"What are we gonna do, Kenya?" that was Jami. They were in the kitchen alone.

"I don't know, Jami. Been thinking about that all night."

"We can't stay here!" her eyes started to water. "Let's call the police."

"If we call the police, they're gonna separate us, put us in some type of foster home, and we'll never see each other. You're all I have left; I can't lose you." Rubbing her stomach, which ached with a dim pain, she bit on her lower lip, "I'm gonna think of something, just give me a minute," she said.

Session was packing his bags; right in the middle of it, he called Intercontinental Airport. "Hello, Inter-Continental Airways," a sweet high-pitched voice chimed in. There was a southern drawl to it.

"Uh, I, I need to catch a flight to Canada fo-for tomorrow a-af- after eight."

"Yes, Sir, would you hold on, please?" He continued to pack quickly and efficiently while music played in the background. "Sir?"

"Yes, I'm here." Session spoke nervously with perspiration covering his clammy skin. He was scared because prison was not where he wanted to end up.

"I have you scheduled for 10:15 p.m., Tuesday. Will that flight do?"

"Yes, Sir," she was polite. "I need some additional information. Please hold while I transfer you." Fifteen minutes later, the dial tone signaled the end of the call.

Chapter 3

Session Thorn II was a prominent businessman and computer analyst hailing from old money and blueblood roots. He worked, although he didn't have to; everyone assumed he was headed for success—the only son of Norman Thorn I, a shipping yard tycoon. The shipping yard was based in New York, and Session prepared all the formats for the computer programs, records, and spreadsheets surrounding Thorn Inc... . He was Vice-President of Operations at the Houston Branch. Kimberly Wane was like a natural disaster that ushered in a new beginning. The type of disaster that is viewed in hindsight as a blessing in disguise because it prompts you to start over from scratch. She was the original text; not some watered-down version of the truth. She was simply irresistible.

When he first noticed her, he was standing in his office window watching all of the administrative assistants leave for the day. It was a group of four women, all moderately dressed in business attire.

However, Kimberly was the type of woman you could put in a nun's habit and still make a man sin. The following day, he called her into his office. He only wanted sex and hadn't figured it would be difficult because women in every division of the company were breaking their necks to let him touch their ass. He was the boss's son, and pussy had always come easy. She drove him crazy with her priceless smooth caramel-hued complexion. She was flawless; hours of tanning beds, sunbathing, or any other means of artificial coloring could not compete with her natural, sensual mocha mix. Her aura made you stop, look, listen. She would sashay with such poise and rhythm. Her diminutive yet prodigious presence drove most men crazy, and he was no exception. He took her out on several occasions. His Dionysian blood boiled to have her, but she couldn't be undone and wouldn't acquiesce to his desires. His intellectual prowess and opulent nature all failed him miserably. He was already neurotic, and her behavior drove him to one of his compulsive acts. He asked her to marry him. A black woman. They flew to Vegas in his father's plane, and Kimberly Wane became Mrs. Kimberly Thorn. The kids didn't bother him; they were part of the package. They made love that night, and Kimberly answered every question Session's soul had ever proffered. Nothing and no one mattered, no one but Kim. He was addicted. His infatuation with this black woman was irrefutable and even to him unexplainable. However, love has never offered more answers than the questions presented. When he and Kim strolled into restaurants, movies, or company gatherings, the smug looks he received from black men never phased him. The man with treasure is never mad at the one without, he'd say to himself.

Shortly after marriage, Session received a summons from his father. On his flight to New York, his apprehension grew.

"Sesh," his father began calmly. "I've received some alarming news." He paused, then leaned back in his chair as it squeaked and groaned from sustaining his weight, all 410 pounds of him. He had massive hands, a barrel chest, and at 60, his hair was untouched by grey. "I trust it's all a huge misunderstanding."

He coughed into his hands, wiped them on his pants, and then rubbed his hands through his hair and over his pitted face. Session began strong as he categorized his thoughts, but they lost strength and momentum as they left his mind and attempted to leave his lips. "What misunderstanding, pop?" he asked weakly.

Mr. Thorn, Sr. stroked his beard repeatedly, then laughed uncontrollably, "Boy, you got gall." A flicker of a grin started at the corner of Sessions mouth, but it was killed before it could reach adolescence or adulthood. No, kilted ... silenced by the death penalty. Which manifested metaphorically in the deafening sound made by Thorn, Sr.'s massive hands, as they made contact on his sturdy office desk. Startled, Session jumped and stumbled backward, meeting the door with his back. "Boy, don't fuck with me!"

Perspiration found a temporary residence on Session's brow. With an effort, he found his voice. "Dad, okay." he paused. "I got married." He smiled.

"Oh." Mr. Thorn was instantly calm again. "Who is she? Did you bring her with you?" His eyes bulged out and feigned as if she was in the office, and he had missed her.

"She's at home, dad," he stated in an exasperated tone.

"Now, isn't that convenient as hell? I hear you done married yourself a nigger girl, boy," he admonished.

"She's a beautiful human being."

Norman Thorn reclined back in his chair and released a burst of sardonic laughter in the thickening atmosphere, then winced at his son's pathetic facial expression. "She's a beautiful human being. Na ain't that a bitch! It seems like just yesterday, I was bouncing you on my knee, and you were running around the house with your cap gun screaming, I killed a nigger daddy. Now it's, she's a beautiful human being. Shit, since we're on the subject of 'beautiful human beings'... you couldn't find any white ones?" It wasn't a question meant to be answered. Norman continued, "Well, never mind. I see that your penis got in the way of your priorities. I've never said you couldn't fuck 'em. Hell, we've been fucking 'em for years. You didn't see George Washington or Thomas Jefferson confusing lust with love. I know, son, the loving is one in a million. I've been there, done that, but we can't lose focus. Rich black men want our women, but rich white men never, I mean never reached back and married a black woman. You'll never find it, let them continue to get rich and abandon theirs. We're not going to do it." He paused to pour himself a drink while his son digested what he had said. "Son, it's alright. I'm not mad at you. You've had your fun. Divorce her, put her up in a nice home, give her an income, and make her your mistress, for Christ's sake!"

Session thought about it. He swore that he could still smell her perfume. His thoughts about their lovemaking the night before gripped him. In that instant, he figured she'd probably go for the house, income, and mistress package. It all seemed logical and rational. Everybody would go for it, but him. Very seldom did life meet you on your terms. Everybody couldn't be happy; life just never allows for everyone to be pleased. Somebody had to go home with their lip stuck out. Yeah, life is like a big ole play, sometimes making you laugh, sometimes making you cry. There was nothing remotely logical or rational about love when cupid hangs that do not disturb sign on your heart.

In an effeminate, almost inaudible whisper, Session said, "And if I don't?"

Norman looked at him incredulously, without ire, he said, "I'll disown you." Father and son stared at each other for what seemed like an interminable period but it was only seconds. Session turned and exited the office. Sometimes the most powerful transactions, the most poignant messages are made in the absence of words. Sometimes silence is louder. Session left thinking that she gave him what was intangible. His dad would never comprehend that.

Life was great until Kimberly was killed. Session was troubled. He turned to drinking, gambling, call girls, and drugs. He lost another job. Plus, psychiatric treatment for Kenya's trauma ate up his savings at an alarming rate. Finally, he fell into debt with a bad company. All of this was something his highly pacified life hadn't prepared him for. He was not mentally conditioned for the adversity knocking at the door. He just simply cracked.

Victor Thi Pierce was originally from Chicago. The bastard child of a Vietnamese woman-child and an American soldier. He was a man of small stature, 120 pounds soaking wet. Characteristically, he wore oversized suits that were a poor attempt to offset his diminutive stature. He wore thick glasses on an elongated face with large eyes and lips but an undersized nose. He was constantly pushing the glasses up his nose. Victor habitually perspired; he sweated even if it was fifty degrees. So, he kept a purple handkerchief to wipe his brow. He owned several clubs, but his money was not in the clubs. Victor dealt in child prostitution, child pornography, black market adoptions, and everything that went along with it. The Greek and Roman Empires established homosexuality and child molestation. The Europeans have historically been recognized as having a natural propensity for incest and other abnormal perversions. Victor understood his history. The turpitude hadn't ceased, just became more secretive and covert. The world was waking up, opening their eyes to the elephant in the room. More than eight hundred thousand corporate tycoons, amiable members of Congress, preferential judges, and sometimes the next-door neighbor with the wife and three kids found Victor's number. They stole away on clandestine rendezvous in wigs, dark shades, and dark vehicles. Business was business. To bake a cake, you had to break a few eggs. Over eight years, he had amassed a small fortune. This last run would put him over the top. He'd marry, have some kids and sip expensive wine on his yacht, which he intended to purchase when things were said and done. Human trafficking, also referred to as the modern-day slave trade, was a complex and multidimensional form of exploitation. It was conducted by organized, sophisticated criminal enterprises, decentralized criminal networks, family members, small businesses, and individuals. Victor's homework had been done well; he was just a cog in the vast wheel—a global epidemic of forced labor generating an estimated 44.3 billion annually. He was determined to get his piece of the American pie by any means necessary. It was big business conducted in dark corners; trafficking took place in factories, fields, brothels, street corners, as child soldiers in private homes, or innumerable other settings hidden behind walls and yet in plain view.

Houston was a candy store of young privileged beautiful youth. A palace of greed and corruption to be gorged upon. He had managed to put a stranglehold on the underground establishment in only a year with brutal efficiency and methodical professional acumen. The small-time filmmakers had been vetted out and taxed according to the proceeds that they brought in. Websites that feed the beast were being monitored and taxed as well. Some years ago, Victor hunted down some of the most prolific computer hackers globally. They could do damn near anything with a computer—find anyone, get into any system, falsify any documents. The government wanted to lock these people away. He, on the other hand, offered them new lives, new benefits, new means, and capabilities. They did not love him or what he did; they did not have to, nor did he expect them to. The world is precisely what it is. Everyday someone rose from their bed to trod off to work for some asshole. Women had bosses that pawed and fucked them for no other reason than he could. Men had employers that were more authoritative than Saddam Hussein, but they endured because everyone wanted to live a certain way at the end of the day. Everyone had a price, from the president of the United States to the nun in the convent. Living is an idea, you unearth the idea, and you could have anyone. Everyone also had fears, dig away the bravado, and underneath it was a shadow lurking in the darkness waiting to be defeated. Everyone also had a weakness ... once that weakness was discovered, whether in a skyscraper or human being, it could be felled. His esoteric instincts for being able to spot and properly relate to the most unscrupulous, incorrigible perverts in the area were impeccable. His prowess in that area had made him millions.

A knock at the door stole his attention from his daily soap opera. "Yes, come on in." Paul swaggered through the door and settled his 350-pound frame into a chair across from his employer. Paul was Victor's trusted friend, and it had been so since starting up the business eight years ago.

"Vatly just pulled up," Paul announced.

"Has he got the merchandise?" Victor asked, wiping his brow and pushing his glasses up before continuing. "Vatly has lost his zeal. He's gotten slow, has he not?"

"Vatly will come through," Paul put in. "He always has. I have faith in his abilities, his dedication."

Another knock. Paul jumped up and opened the door. He and Vatly shook hands. "You look tired, man. You ain't been sleeping?" Paul asked.

"Just stressed, trying to make this deadline. Mr. V.I.C., what do you think?" Vatly pointed at a young Caucasian boy. Victor had already observed the boy.

"Yes, he's beautiful. What's his age?'

"Seven." The boy became fidgety and started to cry.

"Paul," Victor gestured to the boy. "Take him to Yadira." He wiped his brow and pushed at his glasses. "So, Vatly, what's up on the rest of the order? Today is June 5th. On the 21st, we have to have 20 kids ready to be shipped to Thailand. There's a 255-million-dollar closure; 10 boys, five girls ages 13 and under, four girls ages seven and under, and one black infant girl. We're six kids short. I have two girls coming tomorrow evening. After this, you can retire on some island with the natives." He smiled, wiped his brow, removed a cigarette from his case and lit it, then pulled on it deeply. "255 million is a lot of money. Let's get a move on."

"I got it covered, V.I.C." Vatly stood.

But before he could leave, Victor said, "Oh, you were correct. Mr. Thorn did call."

Session was packed. His arm ached. He'd gotten stitches from the wound inflicted by Jami, and the Tylenol threes with Codeine prescribed by the doctor made him sleepy. Session informed the girls that they were going out to eat. He didn't suspect they would be any trouble. Victor was not Session's crowd, fortunately or unfortunately, depending on who was looking. Session knew Vatly because of his new nightlife of girls and gambling. Vatly had mentioned Victor's name at a private gambling shack where Session had lost ten-thousand dollars one night. Session frowned his brow in concentration as he recalled the incident. He tried to remember exactly how the conversation went. They were laughing, drinking, and tooting a little cocaine. "Them yours, man, damn they're cute," Vatly had commented while observing a photo of the girls in Session's wallet haphazardly tossed on the bar.

"Yeah, they're my stepdaughters. Their mother was killed two years ago in a car accident."

"Shit, baby, you keep losing the way you're losing, you're gonna have to sell them." Vatly smiled and laughed. Session looked at him and laughed also. Vatly continued, "Would you ever get that desperate?"

"Desperate?" Session asked. The music was loud. People all over were talking. The drink and cocaine had dulled his senses.

"Yeah, desperate enough to sell them," Vatly said, smiling.

"Sell what?" Session asked. He had lost track of the conversation in his drunken state.

"Sell them." Vatly pointed at the picture still displayed on the bar. Session finally realized what they had been talking about. He looked at Vatly to see if he was still smiling. If it was a joke. Vatly stared intently into Session's eyes. His jocular persona of just a second ago had vanished.

"So?" Vatly asked, dead serious.

"So, what?" Session replied.

"Would you sell them if push came to shove?" Vatly said, insistent on an answer.

"Nah, man, I couldn't do no shit like that."

"Sure, you could," Vatly said. Downed the remainder of his brandy, slapped Session over the back, and laughed. The tension slowly dissipated. Session smiled, downed the rest of his Bloody Mary, and then laughed. Vatly got up and pulled a card from his wallet, "Here."

"What's this?" Session inquired. "The number," Vatly responded.

"What number?"

Vatly grabbed his coat, then said flatly, "You know." The vanilla card just had a number. No name, just a number in the center of the card. After he had lost his damn mind and tried to rape Kenya, he called the number. No one answered, so he hung up. Three minutes after he hung up, his phone rang. "Hello."

"Mr. Thorn, you are ready to do business, yes?" the voice asked. "Yes."

The voice said, "Please hold." Ten minutes later, a man who identified himself as Victor spoke with Session extensively.

The Lincoln cruised smoothly through the mid-day traffic. "You girls okay?" He grinned insidiously, glancing into his rearview mirror and noticing a constable behind him. Immediately checking the speedometer, he wasn't speeding. Nervously glancing behind him once, then twice, the constable stayed behind him for about a mile. Paranoia seized him more possessively with each foot he drove. Kenya noticed her stepfather's condition and looked over her shoulder in the true tradition of money see, monkey do; Jami got on her knees and peered out the back window also.

The officer noticed the two black children in the car with an obviously nervous white male and sounded his siren. Officer Oliver wasn't even interested in the Lincoln. However, the extra cautious behavior of the driver made him suspicious.

Five minutes ago, he called in the license number; it came back clean. Then the two little black girls peeked over the backseat. In the last year, many children had come up missing, but not found dead, just disappeared. The Officer flashed his lights. His instincts were screaming that something wasn't right. Oliver approached the vehicle on the driver's side.

"License and registration, proof of insurance," he rattled off. "Uh, officer, what's the problem?" Session stuttered out.

"Nothing really, sir. This car fits the description of a car that was used in a kidnapping this morning," Oliver answered. He glanced into the backseat at the two girls. "You girls alright?"

"Yes, sir," Kenya said politely. Jami just nodded her head. The officer's instincts told him that something was wrong. Sensing the question, Session stated, "They're my stepdaughters." The officer gave the car one last glance, then looked back at the girls.

"You girls sure you're alright?" he asked. They nodded, 'cool' he thought. Handed Session the paperwork back. "Alright then." He headed back to the car, unable to kill the feeling that something was wrong.

The warehouse looked abandoned. Session glanced at his watch while rounding the first building and headed toward the back as he had been instructed. It was 6:41. The Houston police car parked alongside a Lincoln Navigator and a blue Range Rover instantly spooked him, and he came to a screeching halt. "This just isn't my fucking day," he mumbled to himself. Just as he put the car in reverse, two big Caucasian men from the blue Range Rover motioned for him to come on. With deep apprehension, he shifted back into drive and proceeded on. He could always lie and say he was lost.

Stepping from his car, Session was ushered into the front seat of the Lincoln Navigator. There was a black divider; the back seat occupant could not be seen. "Mr. Thorn, I'm most pleased you could make it." The voice he assumed was Victor's. "Can I see them please?" Session exited the Lincoln, opened his car door, and told the girls to get out. Both girls wore sundresses and sandals. Kenya's effeminate contours could not be concealed nor contained even in a sundress. The only thing that let you know she was still a child was her face and eyes. Session left them standing near the car, and he returned to the Navigator.

"She's not fourteen, Mr. Thorn."

"Here's her birth certificate. I would not lie." The divider cracked slightly, and Session slid him the certificate.

After a moment of silence, Victor said, "And what are you asking?"

"Forty-thousand." Another pause. Victor looked through the tinted window at Kenya. She was a living work of art. Ever attentive, Victor noticed how officer Decker was eyeing her. He was never to indulge in carrying on relations with these kids. Surprisingly, he found himself entertaining thoughts of raising Kenya and marrying her when she was mature and responsible. Crazy for him to even think such a thing, but it was a crazy world he lived in.

"Okay, Mr. Thorn, forty-thousand it is. Wait in your car."

Moments later, the big bodyguard brought Session a black briefcase. Up until receiving the money, Session was nervous as hell. With the money in his possession, he started the car. It sounded like he heard Jami call his name, but he didn't turn around. He was gone ... starting over.

Aboard the plane, Session glanced out the window. Fuck it; it was Kimberly's fault, not his. The wail of a siren shook him from his reverie. The plane was stopping. He looked out the window again, and a string of police cars were headed toward the plane. Minutes later, the doors opened, panic seized him. The black Constable was headed straight towards him. What was his name; Oliver. Session watched him draw his pistol, saw the fire exit the barrel, heard the explosion, and felt his blood saturate his clothing in seconds ... he was dying. Struggling out of his sleep, sweaty and frightened, Session looked around. It was dark, and everyone had fallen asleep listening to the hypnotic hum of the plane's engines. His watch showed 2:15 in the a.m. Canada would be a pleasant change. Yes, a change; that's exactly what he needed.

Kenya held her sister and tried to comfort her. They were in a vast building; they had passed several offices and rooms with beds, tables, and televisions. It was cold because the central cooling unit was not doing any horseplaying. They had been escorted to a room by a police officer, so she had assumed that they were safe. Session had given them up for adoption or something. Jami sniffled and choked on her tears.

"Jami, don't cry. I'm not gonna let anything happen to you. As long as we're together, we can handle anything."

"I'm just scared. I don't understand what's happening."

"Session gave us away to some sort of foster home or adoption place." The locks clicked, and the door opened. A little man in big glasses came in.

"Hello, ladies." He smiled. "Are you girls hungry? I could have anything you want to be cooked."

Kenya just stared at him. "We're fine. What is this place? Who are you?" Kenya asked.

"Where is Session? Why'd he leave us here?" Jami shouted, tears streaming down her face.

"Calm down, little one. No one's gonna hurt you. I'm here to help." The door opened again, and a large woman came in; at least six feet-five inches tall, weighing about two hundred pounds.

"Oh, Yadira, this is Kenya and Jamilyah Wane. Please make them comfortable." Her voice was very soft and feminine to be such a large woman.

"Okay, Mr. Pierce. Come on, ladies." They were led through some corridors, which seemed to lead downward. Yadira opened a door, and at least fifteen children were noisily playing in the room.

"Patty!" Yadira called. "The two I called and told you about." The door closed. Kenya and Jami just observed the room in silence. Kenya was already thinking of a way to get out of there.

CHAPTER 4

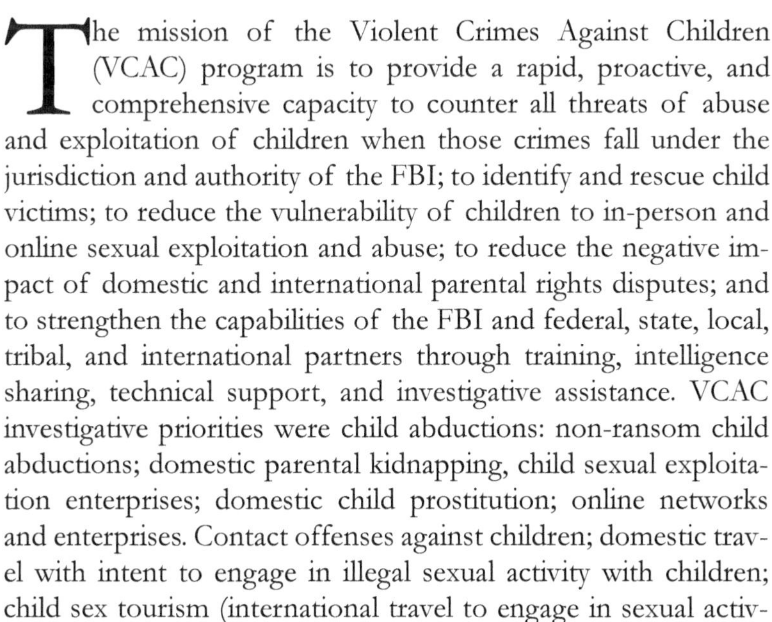

The mission of the Violent Crimes Against Children (VCAC) program is to provide a rapid, proactive, and comprehensive capacity to counter all threats of abuse and exploitation of children when those crimes fall under the jurisdiction and authority of the FBI; to identify and rescue child victims; to reduce the vulnerability of children to in-person and online sexual exploitation and abuse; to reduce the negative impact of domestic and international parental rights disputes; and to strengthen the capabilities of the FBI and federal, state, local, tribal, and international partners through training, intelligence sharing, technical support, and investigative assistance. VCAC investigative priorities were child abductions: non-ransom child abductions; domestic parental kidnapping, child sexual exploitation enterprises; domestic child prostitution; online networks and enterprises. Contact offenses against children; domestic travel with intent to engage in illegal sexual activity with children; child sex tourism (international travel to engage in sexual activity with children); production of child pornography; coercion/ enticement of a minor; trafficking of child pornography; global parental kidnapping; and all crimes against children's violations within the FBI's jurisdiction are investigated in accordance with available resources.

The program's history began while investigating the disappearance of a juvenile in May 1993. FBI special agents from the Baltimore Field Office and detectives from the Prince George's County (Maryland) Police Department identified two suspects who had sexually exploited numerous juveniles over a 25-year period. Investigation into these activities determined that adults were routinely using computers to transmit sexually explicit images to minors and, in some instances, to lure children into engaging in illicit sexual activity. Further investigation and discussion with experts, both within the FBI and in the private sector, revealed that the use of computer telecommunication was rapidly becoming one of the most prevalent techniques by which some sex offenders shared pornographic images of minors and identified and recruited children in sexually illicit relationships. In 1955, based on information developed during this investigation, the Innocent Images National Initiative—initially part of Cyber Division—was created to address the illicit activities of users of commercial and private online services and the Internet.

In 2000, the Crimes Against Children Program in the Criminal Investigative Division. The program continued the efforts of both former iterations, providing centralized coordination and analysis of case information that is national and international in scope, requiring close cooperation, not only among FBI field offices and legal attaches but also with state, local, and international governments.

For Yancy Mordecai, the morning had gone from bad to worse in no time flat. He had been a part of child exploitation investigation for the better part of 20 years. A part of some of the most notorious cases ever seen or heard of. At fifty, he was tired, tired, and more tired. He sat in a room that was cold as an arctic tundra, yet still not as cold as the information pouring in from field agents. There was always something pouring in from undercover intelligence agents planted neck-deep in some nasty sick, perverted operation. The icy slap of reality of the type of perverts that prowled our neighborhoods was something you just could not get your mind around or prepare yourself for. This special task force was formed approximately eight months ago. The FBI's Criminal Investigative Division—of which the VCAC Program is a part—in conjunction with the international Operation Division, has implanted joint operations overseas with governments in some of the top CST (child sex tourism) destination countries in Southeast Asia. Based on the success of these operations, the CST initiative has expanded into selected countries in Latin America. These operations targeted child sex tourists who do not plan their illegal activities from the U.S. but rather seek to procure children once they arrive at their destination. The purpose of these operations is to coordinate with foreign law enforcement to gather evidence against U.S. offenders that is admissible in the U.S. courts, to extradite those offenders back to the U.S. for prosecution. The VCAC program coordinates all efforts with the FBI legal attaches in these countries to provide training, equipment, and logistical support to these joint operations.

For eight months Yancy had been on one of the most elusive trails of child exploitation he had witnessed in many, many years. It was even more covert than Operation Avalanche, which took place in 1999. Avalanche was a major United States investigation of child pornography on the internet launched after the arrest and conviction of Thomas and Janice Reedy. They operated an internet pornography business called Landslide Production in Fort Worth, Texas. It was made public in early August 2001. At the end of Operation Avalanche, there were one hundred arrests made out of 144 suspects. Operation Ore in the United Kingdom followed Operation Snowball in Canada, Operation Pecunia in Germany, Operation Amethyst in Ireland, and Operation Genesis in Switzerland. But Yancy could not forget about Operation Landslide ...

Thomas Reedy was a self-taught computer programmer and entrepreneur located in the Fort Worth, Texas area. He trained and worked as a nurse, but understanding the financial possibilities of the Internet, he set up an adult pornography website that provided a comfortable income. He soon developed a better strategy to provide middleman services for the adult pornography industry. In 1997, he set up Landslide Productions, Inc., which he ran with his wife Janice, who handled bookkeeping for the company. Landslide quickly became an adult pornography empire stretching across three continents, including 300,000 subscribers in 60 countries. Within two years, the company made $10 million and provided the owners a luxurious lifestyle. Landslide provided payment systems for adult webmasters from different countries. The systems were automated; the webmaster could sign up to the system online, and users accessing the website would go through the payment or login system before being granted access. The central systems were AVS for Adult Verification System and Keyz because it operated via the keyz.com domain name owned by Landslide. The AVS System was meant to legally protect the companies from laws against disseminating pornography to minors, as the credit card was used to verify that the user attempting to access a particular website was of legal age to view the website's content. Users could sign up with their credit cards to access affiliated sites, which received 65% of the sign-up fee, while Landslide took the remainder and handled the transaction with the credit card companies.

Landslide Investigation

In April 1999, the United States Postal Inspection Service received an internal complaint through postal inspector Qasiym Serengeti in Texas. Serengeti had received a tip from Clayton Fiver, an acquaintance in Bountiful Utah who provided information about a website advertising child pornography. The image in question was being sourced from a website in Indonesia, which presented the question as to whether the USPIS could legally investigate and prosecute it.

In early 1999, the United States Postal Inspection Service engaged the Dallas Police Department to investigate further whether the image from Indonesia could be prosecuted. As a part of a nationwide initiative funded by the Office of Justice Program's Office of Juvenile Justice and Delinquency Prevention (DJJDP), the United State Department of Justice had announced a grant from the Internet Crimes Against Children Taskforce Program to the Dallas Police Department on January 10, 1990. The purpose of the ICAC was to investigate and prosecute Internet crimes against children.

The court transcriptions from the case against Landslide Productions revealed that the Dallas Police Department had formed a relationship with Microsoft Corporation after the software maker encouraged its technical employees to volunteer their time to better the community they lived. After having confirmed that prosecution would be difficult because the image in question was indeed being sourced from Indonesia, the Dallas Police Department asked its local Microsoft volunteers to assist in investigating the image. Using Web Buddy, a computer program designed to display Internet traffic on geographic maps, the volunteers helped the Dallas police verify that internet traffic related to Clayton Fiver's complaint was passing through the routers of Ft. Worth-based Landslide Productions.

An adult classified section of the Landslide website allegedly included postings offering to trade Landslide-owned Keyz passwords, and illegal child pornography sites were found to be using the Keyz payment system. The U.S. Postal Inspection Service (USPIS) and Dallas police presented their findings to Rhiannon Sepaugh, an Assistant District Attorney in the Dallas/Fort Worth area. They received warrants to search the Landslide business offices and the Reedy home. In August 1999, 45 to 50 law enforcement officials from several agencies conducted a raid on the Landslide business offices in Fort Worth.

The Reedy's Fort Worth residence raid resulted in the confiscation of a home computer, on which computer expert Marcus Vera uncovered business e-mails confirming his knowledge of customers using Reedy's payment system to access child pornography. Sexually explicit images of children were also found on this computer.

Police seized the assets and records of Landslide and arrested Thomas and Janice Reedy. Prosecutors offered Thomas a 20-year prison term and Janice five years if they would plead guilty. Still, the Reedy's refused the plea deal, believing they could not be held legally responsible for the content of third-party websites. Reedy maintained that he had attempted to run a legitimate business, writing software to reduce fraud, reporting illegal sites to the FBI, and cooperating with the ensuing investigations. According to Reedy, he was told by Special Agent Reginald Levi to leave the sites in his index for later analysis.

In January 2000, Thomas Reedy was convicted of trafficking in child pornography through testimony from witnesses, including Lilith Nadera, a UK police officer at SOCA/NS. Based on a prior police investigation in the UK, Nadera identified victims in pictures from a website that used the Landslide payment system. Thomas Reedy was sentenced to 1,335 years in prison, a sentence that was reduced to 180 years on appeal.

The Reedy case led to the creation of a nationwide network of 30 federally funded taskforces to fight Internet crimes against children. In August 2001, Attorney General John Ashcroft and Chief Postal Inspector Kenneth Weaver announced the launch of Operation Avalanche, an operation to gather evidence against users of the Landslide gateway and payment system. The seized database records included 35,000 U.S. subscribers, some of whom were targeted with invitations to purchase child pornography by mail. The Chicago Tribune reported the government also continued to run Reedy's Landslide website for a time as part of the sting. As a result of Operation Avalanche, 100 suspects were arrested following 144 searches in 37 states.

The FBI then passed identities from the database to the police organizations of other countries, including 7,272 names in the UK and 2,329 names to Canada. Initial results of the operation seemed optimistic, as the gateway site and payment system were closed down, and thousands of possible users of child pornography websites were identified for later investigation.

Police conducting Operation Ore in the UK targeted all names for investigation due to the difference in laws between the U.S. and the UK, which allowed for arrest on a charge of incitement to distribute child pornography based solely on the presence of a name in the database, regardless if the card was used—fraudulently or not—for child pornography or other legal adult sites. Law in the UK allows conviction based on incitement to distribute indecent images; as such, the mere presence on the database, regardless of the legality of the sites paid for, was sufficient to warrant prosecution. In all, 3,744 people were arrested, and 1,451 of those convicted. However, a subsequent challenge by those targeted led to an independent reconstruction of the Landslide site and a closer inspection of the database and the payment transactions.

In 2005 and 2007, UK investigative journalist Duncan Campbell wrote a series of articles criticizing police forensic procedures and trial evidence. After obtaining copies of the Landslide hard drives, Campbell publicly identified evidence of massive credit card fraud, including thousands of charges where there was no access to any porn site at all. Campbell stated, "Independent computer expert Jim Bates of Computer Investigations said 'the scale of the fraud, especially hacking, just leaped off the screen.'"

A knock on Yancy Mordecai's door brought him out of his reverie; his eyes momentarily focused on the assortment of papers scattered on his desk like a high-powered microscope. A silent glissando shivered down the keys of his spine. With Herculean effort, Yancy reigned in his free-floating anxiety, rotated his neck to ease his clock spring of psychological tensions. The tap on the door came again. His eyes danced across the new reports about Internet porn coming from Canada, Toronto, and Ontario Provincial Police. Political backlash from operation Snowball. He was flying out to the United Kingdom in an hour. Federally coordinated investigations in the U.S. and Britain were intensifying due to names gleaned from a seized database, resulting in many arrests. In Britain, more than 1,300 people, including 50 police officers. The arrest was only the beginning—reports about white slavery trade, black market child adoptions, more and more, on and on.

The strangeness in the day was easy to perceive but difficult to define. If confusion had been loaves of bread and suspicion had been fish, no miracles would have been required to provide a banquet for the multitudes.

"Come in," Mordecai announced, his baritone deep and piercing.

Lovely entered, shapely, and business-suited.

Her name was Pamela Lovely, and at 31 years of age, she had not outgrown her name.

"The Director's ready," she informed him.

"I'm on my way," he replied.

Lovely turned, sauntered off without another word. The fabric of her business suit stretched across the back of what could only be termed an 'Awesome Ass' tighter than fresh corn roll braids. Yancy experienced a moment of cognitive dissonance: simultaneously holding opposed convictions about the same subject.

CHAPTER 5

It was a windy day, just one of those days that the aroma of frying pork played stowaway and rode the heels of playful breezes. Xavier Masai Dean sat perched on the roof of Southmore apartments and watched life below him shift and move just as the wind did, changing ... constantly changing. This is where he came every day. Here he could witness it all. The projects spread out under him in all its simple complexity, despondent souls, and tired game participants. This was his getaway, where he cogitated in solitude, daydreamed, and confronted reality.

The freeway could be seen from here, the traffic jams, the multitude of projects amid the confusion, the kids running around barefooted with runny noses and happy heads. The most serene part of the day slipped past most people unnoticed and unobserved. Wayward cats ran and dodged the babies while the kiddies dodged their negligent parents. It was crazy. Xavier would come here to think and breathe. Toward the West, at around 6:30, the sun would begin its slow descent behind the I-10 freeway.

Long ago, he had decided this was his Ghetto Sunset. Unlike the movies or the books where the sun would dip behind some magnificent hillside or the ocean. That was an unlikely scene here on the streets of Third Ward. However brief, this was his escape, watching the cars in the distance pass through the sun, and amazingly they did not explode into flames and melt away in the asphalt. Yeah, this was his escape from the madness and surroundings of everyday life.

The insistent horn of a vehicle below filtered into his thoughts. He glanced down in time to see his mom duck inside the crack house. Shaking his head, his attention went to the blue GMC truck blowing the horn. Deshawn stepped into the truck, the driver backed out, and they left.

Back at the crib, he could hear his little sister screaming at the top of her lungs before he reached the door. The apartment was a three-bedroom joint. Section-8 type housing, so it was not much, but it was home. Xavier walked through the door, shut it firmly behind him, and strolled into his sister's room. Vianna was only 5. Her eyes lit up immediately when he came through the door of her room. Sniffling and stuttering, she whined, "Zav-ya ma ... ma ... mama g- g-gone." He swung her into his arms and rubbed his hand over her face to dry the tears.

"Don't sweat it, sweetness, I gotcha covered. I'm gonna have to start calling you cry baby; I see that already." He smiled into her innocent brown eyes.

Vianna smiled back and said in her tiny voice, "Its jus' me and you kid."

Xavier laughed and squeezed her chin. "Yeah, it's just me and you, kid." For the first time he had walked into the house, he smelled red beans cooking and the slight hint of burning rice. Sister in hand, he walked toward the kitchen. "Where dem dollar at Zav-ya?"

"Vi, I'm working on it. I'm working on it." The rice had burned. "Damn," he swore to himself. He took a slice of bread, placed it over the rice, and replaced the top. After running hot water in a pot, he added it to the beans.

"You want a pop, Vi?"

"I wan' two of em." She was bouncing up and down.

Xavier placed her on the table. "Here, Boo." He handed her the popsicle. "Vi, I'm gonna have to kill your mama."

"If I doan kill hur fir," she paused, then added, "she yo mama too."

Xavier was preparing to fry the chicken his mama had taken out to thaw. After getting it on, he and Vi sat in front of the tube to catch Martin.

Xavier had often wondered why in the world his mother had given him a name like Xavier. He was raised in a family of women. His mother had four sisters and one brother. His Uncle Stephen Dean by birth was called Step by everyone. If Xavier had a mentor, it was him. Step did everything hard. As a baby, his uncle would take him everywhere; the local cafes, Muslim Mosque, race tracks, and even meetings with the Disciples. To his understanding, his uncle wasn't affiliated, but being the hustla playa type brotha he was, he entered all types of circles. Step had given his nephew the game, let him get schooled by some of the best con men and hustlers. He had also learned about weapons and self-defense from brothers within the Nation of Islam. Xavier had read more books by age 15 than some people read in a lifetime; mentally feasting on things from Martin Luther King, Jr., Malcolm X, Hannibal, Mansa Musa, Gabriel Prossey, J.A. Rogers, Nat Turner, and more. None of that made him moral, just well-read. Nelli Dean, his mom, was a down woman. She ran into the crumb-type Negroes that turned her on to the glass dragon, which eventually rocked his family. Xavier often contemplated just catching him slipping and toe tagging his ass. However, six years, several ass whuppins and welfare checks later, he had embraced Yahweh ben Yahweh, cleaned up and left her high and dry, and that's the way it is.

Watching the transition from Queen to Fein was hard for him. He had his uncle to lean on until about two years ago. His uncle caught a murder case and was sentenced to life in prison. Practically the weight of everything shifted to his shoulders. Xavier would go to bed with four hundred dollars and wake up broke. Nelli would be gone for three or four days at a time, which forced him to skip school and maintain the upkeep of Vianna. Xavier's money came from dealing in weight; he was careful, meticulous, and methodical. Prison wasn't an option. He never got greedy and was extremely frugal. No one knew what he did, not even Nelli.

After feeding VI, bathing her, and laying with her until she was asleep, ten o'clock had rolled around and Nelli still hadn't returned, which was most uncharacteristic of her. Walking out onto the balcony of the upstairs apartment, he saw Lil' Denise, Deshawn's little sister. She was thirteen or so, a cute little sister with dark skin and hazel eyes. "Dee!" he called. She glanced up and threw up her hands. "Let me holler atcha." She sauntered up the stairs and leaned against the rail next to him.

"What's up, X?" she asked.

"I gotta make a run, and I need a responsible babysitter. I'll tighten you down for doing the deed."

"Give me twenty!" she solicited. "Nah. I'ma break you off ah dime."

"Alright!" she conceded and held out her hand. "It's laying on the table, Lil' Bit." He smiled. "Oh, you just knew I would accept ten, huh?"

"Nah., I didn't just know anything, but outta you," he pointed at apartments 12 and 16. "Keesha and Tay-Tay, one of y'all would have accepted a dime."

Xavier was 5'9", 185, and blessed with straight white teeth. He was a smooth, black, beautiful brother. He smiled at Denise, who was only about 4'7", 110. He glanced at his watch, then looked back at Denise.

"I'll be back about one, if not earlier. There are beans, rice, and chicken on the stove. Pops in the icebox. Vi's already asleep."

They walked into the house together, and he jotted down his cell phone number. "If you need me, here's the four-one-one."

As he shut the door behind him, Denise went to the table to collect her ten dollars. To her surprise, there was a twenty with the words, 'I gotcha covered' written on it. She smiled, looked out the window, and there was Xavier lined up with the window in his Chrysler 300 looking up at the window. When he saw her, he smiled and chunked up the index finger. His uncle once told him that the Muslims in prison here in Texas began doing the one-finger up symbolism to greet other Muslims in the hallways because back in the day, the guards were cracking skulls for any displays of unity and loyalty. In addition to all other Jim Crow laws that were in effect during that time. The Muslims said it meant 'Peace and Blessing.' Placing his cap on his head and slowly letting the window up, he drove off.

Hitting 288, Xavier headed towards Texas Children's Hospital. He placed Charlie Wilson's CD on and relaxed as his voice filtered through the six by nines and twelve's he had installed in his car. The air conditioner cooled the car's interior efficiently as he pushed 65 mph on the freeway. It was June 14th. School was out, and summer was on and popping. He was headed to pick up Shai Montgomery. She worked at the hospital and was a sophomore at the University of Houston. Shai was 5'3", high yellow, 140 pounds, green eyes, with full lips and dimples. She kept her hair short in a Halle Berry type cut, which perfectly fit her face and features. She was not his girlfriend; they were just friends. She had just turned twenty in May. He wouldn't be 18 until July. She had suggested in more ways than one that she liked older men and he was too young.

Xavier and Shai met by chance six months ago. Her car had broken down at the mall, and it just so happened he was parked next to her. When he exited the mall, it was late, about eleven-thirty and dark as an undertaker's pocket; the moon and stars had taken a vacation. Xavier recalled the incident vividly ... He had come to the mall to meet two brothers out of Chicago, whom he had dealt with before. They wanted two kilos for forty thousand. He walked into the TV repair shop with a small portable black and white television. It had been prearranged with Adib. The brothers from Chicago would have an identical TV specially built with a hollow inside, yet it didn't alter the weight.

One TV had dope; the other had money. After switching TV's and quick checks, they departed. It was smooth, calculated, public, and carefully executed. When he exited the mall, he noticed a small Honda Accord with a jazzy yellow hammer frustratingly trying to get the engine to turn over. He had every intention of ignoring her, he had forty thousand dollars on him, and minimal distractions meant minimal risks. Getting into his car, settling the TV in the back, he started the car and backed out of his parking space. Just as he was about to get on the freeway, his conscience got the best of him.

Shai was aggravated as hell. Her phone had died, the car charger for some unexplainable reason had decided to call it quits and no one looked concerned in the least whether she needed help or not. The damn car wouldn't start. Several inconsiderate Negroes had just ignored her and didn't even offer to help. If she were in a Club somewhere, they would be breaking their necks to help her. She could hear them now, "Can I buy you a drink?" Just wanting to help her get drunk, then she would hear the familiar line, "Look out Baby, can I take you home?" Rushing to help her get naked. "Shit," she whispered into the confines of her car. "I knew I should have brought me a car phone charger," she admitted to herself. A light tapping on her window startled her. She laid her head on the steering wheel. The tapping made her look up, and she noticed a young dark-skinned guy smiling greedily at her through the window. Four gold teeth shining brightly, two other light skinned black men stood behind him.

"Open the door!" the dark one shouted.

"What do you want?" Shai asked.

"Money, pussy, whatever you got worth wanting."

Shai was shocked and pissed. "Nigga, you'll smell daffodils in December before you get a whiff of this pussy. So pleaseeee T.Y.A.!"

"Oh yeah, bitch!" The dark one produced a pistol. He pointed the menacing instrument at her and fired a shot that shattered the window. Shai screamed. She was showered with glass and just knew that she was dead. One thing alone fractured that thought. She could hear herself screaming and dead people don't scream.

"Look out KC, five-o coming this way baby. Let's bail!" Black looked into the headlights speeding his way.

"Your lucky day, bitch," he shouted as he ran after his partners. Xavier noticed the three hoodlums around the Honda, heard the gunshot, and silently cursed himself for leaving the girl. They were running away now, apparently seeing his vehicle spooked them. Silently he prayed that she was alright. Before he got out, he pulled his Smith & Wesson 40. Caliber with its infrared sighting from under his seat. It would serve his purpose tonight, because he didn't plan on missing. Getting out of his car, he walked hesitantly toward her car half expecting to see her dead. Relief flooded into him when he noticed her body shaking.

"Look out Lil' Sista, you alright?" She began to touch herself. Tears had ruined her mascara, leaving dark streaks down her sandy brown complexion. Xavier instantly noticed two things, the first being the sheer radiance that the woman exuded, the second being she had not acknowledged his presence yet. Shai was aware of the smooth deep voice; it dulled the inert feeling she was experiencing. She looked up slowly, and only saw a dark silhouette because the lights of the car behind him was hindering her vision. Xavier reached into her car to unlock the door, then squatted in front of her. The car light illuminated the smooth features of his face.

"They're gone, if you'll trust me, I'll take you home. There's a phone in my car, you can call the police and a tow truck." Shai settled her teary-red, blue green eyes on him, and looked directly into his dark brown eyes searchingly, like as if she was trying to find something only his eyes could tell her. He had never seen a black woman with eyes like hers. Never! She slid her feet out of the car, and glass fell from her lap to the ground. Xavier stood and she stood so close to him, that he could feel her. She walked to the passenger side of his car and got in. The interior lights were on and he saw that she made no attempt to pick up the phone. She just laid her head back and closed her eyes. Looking into her car, Xavier grabbed one of her shopping bags and emptied the contents of the glove compartment into the bag, then he collected the rest of her shopping bags, and her purse. He pulled out her wallet and noted the address, Clinton Park, Galena Manor. He knew exactly where that was. Her name was Shai Lynn Montgomery. After loading everything into his car, he got in and picked up the phone and called Sharrard's Towing. After giving the location of the car and its destination, he insured him that he'd take care of him personally. His Rolex read 11:45. Hanging up the phone, he put the car in drive and headed toward Clinton Park.

"Shai, my name is Xavier, most people call me X. Do you want to go to the police or home?" She just stared into the oncoming headlights of passing cars. Ten minutes of silence passed. Xavier put in his Donell Jones CD, and Sped up. "Are you all right physically?" Silence. He was disappointed with himself.

Out of nowhere, almost inaudible, Shai asked, "Why did you come back?"

The phone chimed in.

"Yeah, what's up ... nah." He listened, as Moophisey went on about a Rockets game he had just come from. James Harden played lights out. Eric Gorden & Ryan Anderson backed him up, Corey Brewer and the bench brought 'em back from 19 down, and one of the cheerleaders allegedly chose him.

"Look Moo, I'll head 'round your way tomorrow. Right now, I'm taking care of some business ... Nah, I haven't called Alisha ... look Moo, I gotta let you go, hit me later o-ite, later." He hung up the phone. Shai was looking at him with those eyes, she asked more clearly.

"Why did you come back?"

Sighing heavily and massaging the bridge of his nose with his left thumb and index finger, Xavier said, "Because, I never should have left you."

"So why did you leave?" she asked a little vehemently.

"You know Shai," he began, "I hate excuses, so I'm not going to give you one. I didn't see you breaking your neck asking for help, knowing that your car was broke down."

She didn't say anything for a few seconds. "It would have been gentlemanly of you to offer your help," she said.

"I'm no gentleman."

"Oh, I see."

"Do you?" he asked.

"Do I what?" she replied.

"See," he paused. "See I understand a lot of things, and coming back to check on you wasn't some nonchalant gesture. Black women are so damn fickle, either ignoring, screaming harassment or rape every time a brotha tries to be polite. It's to the point, a brotha don't know what to expect. I came back, because you're somebody else's sister, daughter, maybe even mother. If what goes around comes around, maybe, just maybe someone will look out for my mother or sister one day." He rounded the 610 loop and headed onto Clinton Drive, five minutes later, he pulled up in front of her house.

"Is this you?" She nodded her head. He packed all of her bags to the porch, and left her standing on her porch heading for his car.

"Xavier?"

He looked over his hood from the driver side of his car. "Yeah?"

"I don't think I said thanks." She smiled.

"You didn't, but I should apologize for being late," he said flatly.

"Xavier, the Lord sent you just in time."

"We could look at it that way."

"You're no gentleman, huh?"

He smiled again, "Nah, that's not me."

"That's interesting," she said, "also a first. Thanks." She turned and walked into the house.

About four weeks trailing that episode, he recalled mobbing down to a lil' ole party at the recreation center. Things were already crunk. The music was vibrating the small building. People littered the sidewalk, the parking lot and huddled in hunched little groups smoking chronic, and tight eyed on Hennessey. Ruby was getting in her car as he was getting out of his. She frowned and shot him the finger. Xavier grabbed his dick. They had hated each other since pre-kindergarten. Adib came through the door with two coffee and creamed colored sisters dressed just alike. When he got upon Xavier, he noticed that they were twins. They had front, back and side to side, tall and friendly. Adib was in Levi relax fit pants and a shirt, Houston Rockets cap and MJs on his feet. Xavier was Karl Kani down to his boots.

"Wha's up baby? You rollin' tonight or what?" That was Adib. There were individuals who said they were friends, flaky individuals that got soggy in milk, but Adib was solid.

"Nah homie. Oh, excuse me for being rude. Ladies, this is my boy, Xavier. X they b's the Double Mint Twins." He gave a mischievous toothy grin. They were at least 6'3", made inquiring minds wonder if they had an agent. The sister on the left elbowed him and held out her hand.

"Hey, I'm Tisha, my sister Misha."

"Y'all headed somewhere?" he inquired.

Adib said, "Just 'bout ta go get some drank, so I can thank! You wanna tag, double the pleasure, double the fiz-un." Both of the girls hit him.

"Nah, y'all go ahead. I'ma bounce inside for a few, and see what's jumpin'."

Inside, the local dick teasers and dick pleasers littered the dance floor. There were two sistas dressed square business and had come to put in work. It just so happened the song of their choosing and the dance of their choice was the Harlem Shuffle. The yellow sista wore a blue-green tank top and a matching sarong, while her friend wore a matching outfit yellow in color. Xavier stood transfixed and watched them get their clown on. Lil' red was too fine, with a flat stomach on display. When the song ended, her and her friend headed in Xavier's direction. Alisha waved from across the room; he nodded his head. Red stopped in front of him real close like; he could smell her perfume, her bathwater and nail polish.

"Hey boy." She spoke like they were bff's. The first thing that caught his attention was her eyes. They were the same color as her sarong and he was trying for the life of him to recall where he knew her from, or if he knew her.

"Pam, this is Xavier. Xavier, Pamela," she said. That confirmed that she knew him. Red wasn't the type of sister that a brother forgets.

"Uh, wha's up Red, Pam?" He smiled, and played it off. Pam saved him.

"So, you're the youngsta that saved my cousin huh?" She put her hands on her hips. His mind clicked like chambering a round in a 40. Caliber! Damn, Red cleaned up nice. Must have really had a lot on his mind that day, because I didn't recall her being so well put together.

He choked out, "Yeah, I was in the right place at the right time."

"You just burned off, didn't leave me anyway to contact you. I want to thank you properly and pay you back for the tow truck." She paused and fanned her face with her hand. "Whew, it's smoky in here. Xavier, walk with me outside."

"Bet." Someone from the other side of the room shouted his name, and he spun around to see who it was, however Shai yanked his hand and kept him moving forward. As they exited, Ruby was entering, she scowled and stopped dead in his face. "Punk ass nigga."

"Trash ass bitch," he snapped back. She pushed past him. Shai looked completely nonplussed. Outside, the air was cool and humid. The wind blew and melted Shai's sarong to her legs. They walked to his car, and as he leaned against it, she stood in front of him. "So, Ms. Montgomery, how have you been maintaining?"

"Slow, but steady I guess, how much do I owe you?"

"Owe me for what?"

"For having my car towed to the house."

"Oh, don't sweat it, it ain't nothing." She looked at him with one of those UFL's (Unidentifiable Female Looks). He threw up his hands and said, "Really."

"I'd feel better if you'd let me pay you back."

"Okay, treat me to a movie or something." She laughed or more correctly stated, giggled.

"Boy, how old are you?"

"Seventeen," he replied.

"You're just a baby, plus I'm involved with someone."

"Just a baby." he repeated the words just to see how they tasted. "Now, that's a new one. I wasn't trying to get in your space like that anyway."

"Typical male," she said.

"What's that supposed to mean?" he asked.

"I saw the way you were looking at me. If I got butt ass naked, you're telling me you wouldn't fuck!"

Damn, her directness kind of took him off guard. He tried to recuperate and come back. "What, are you offering?"

"Don't do that Xavier."

"Don't do what?"

"Answer my question with a question. Would you say no?"

"Say no to what?"

"Don't do that shit, Xavier." She put her hands to her hips and stared up at him. Adib rounded the corner.

"Look out X!" he assessed the situation by the look on Shai's face.

"Ah, man if this a bad time, I'll come back." Happy for his distraction, Xavier stopped him and stepped around Shai.

"Nah man, wha's up?" he asked, then introduced him to Shai.

She spoke then turned her attention back to him.

"You got a pen?" he nodded and went inside of the car, retrieved a pen. She removed the cap and wrote her phone number on his chest, in bold numbers on his shirt! A brand-new shirt at that. She handed the pen back and said curtly, "Call me, tonight!" and then walked off.

Adib said, "Whew! Major attitude bro-man." He glanced at her retreating rear end.

"Yeah, major tude in a quality package." Looking at the number on his shirt all he could do was shake his head.

That was six months ago.

Xavier was snapped from his reverie, as the passenger door slammed shut. Shai got into the car in her nursery uniform. The hospital had been her number for two years now.

"Hey' kiddo," she exclaimed. Xavier shot her that cynical glare. "I got cha kiddo," he shot back.

She smiled for the first time that evening. X was sort of a mystery, like the gumbo that you eat with the unique flavor, but you just can't put your finger on the ingredient that makes it taste so damn good. In the six months they'd known each other it seemed as though she knew him no more today than she did when they first met. He was introverted, yet spoke volumes within his silence. He was witty, temporal, yet not so. For his age, he was surprisingly prudent and astute with a utilitarian type attitude toward things. He was conscientious and affable however, his presence alone, his fluid panther like movements gave off the distinct impression you were in the presence of a beautiful, yet dangerous animal. He hadn't done anything to validate her suspicious, but she could feel it. Her boyfriend, Calvin Mack, was wearing her patience thin. He was consistently inconsistent, unreliable and irresponsible. They had been together for four years, and her love, like her patience for him was growing thin like the melting ice in a glass of wine as she got older. Xavier was her homie; someone she could talk to when she was stressed. When he finally called her three days later, she invited him to the movies. And it was there that she said, "We can only be friends X."

He laughed, "Shai, every man is not gonna chase the panties. Some men prefer silver rather than gold; emeralds to diamonds, and salt on their grits instead of sugar."

"So, you don't find me attractive?" she asked.

"Mentally or physically?" was his smooth reply.

She mused momentarily then, "Xavier, don't do that! What kind of answer is that?"

"Why do you need me to confirm what you already know Shai?"

"You're gonna piss me off!"

"Mama always told me that, it's better to be pissed off, then to be pissed on."

She smiled, turned, then hit him in the shoulder. "You're full of shit. What's that gold, silver, nothing?"

"I just understand gold and silver only makes a difference in the eyes of men, because God made 'em both. Diamonds and emeralds to a child are just rocks, we make 'em more important than they really are. Sugar and salt both serve their purpose, but an excess of either is dangerous. You're a beautiful sista, but don't place your value on what men think or you'll end up like the Stock Market and your value will continue to fluctuate."

She reached over and rubbed his head, "You sure you're only seventeen?"

"Seventeen and three fourths."

Six months, and she didn't even know where he lived.

"Shai! Shai!" Pamela shouted. Shai looked over and saw her cousin and coworker running after the car as Xavier was pulling into traffic.

"Hold up X," Shai exclaimed. Xavier touched the brakes, and the Chrysler came to a soft stop.

Pamela looked into the car. "Hey X, can you take me home? My mama isn't answering." Xavier nodded his head and Pam hopped in the back seat. Pulling into the late-night traffic of downtown Houston, Xavier made his way to the freeway. The A/C blew, the car was silent except for the chatter of Pam and Shai.

He heard Shai say, " That nigga is childish. He needs to grow up."

The car got silent then Pam said, "Why you so quiet X?"

"Just listening to the music."

Shai and Pam both looked curiously at each other and asked in unison, "What music?" Because the radio wasn't on.

His eyes focused on the road. Xavier said, "The music in my head." The phone rang. On the second ring Xavier picked up, "Yeah, what's tha deal?"

"Look out X, its Prophet. I need you to come scoop me up cuz. I'm at this party that Romondo and Polley drug me to. I win this bitch, and now these niggas is stressing a whole lot of nothing."

"Who's the woman?" Xavier asked.

There was a pause, "Sapphira."

"Sapphira!" Xavier repeated. "You know better man, where's Mondo and Polley?"

"They eight-sixed this joint 'bout an hour ago."

"Why you didn't go with them?"

Prophet breathed heavily into the phone. "C'mon X, you know ... Sapphira."

"Who's tha cats sweating you?"

Prophet said, "Doc and C. J."

"Where's the party Prophet?" Prophet rattled off some numbers and a neighborhood that Xavier was familiar with. "Give me thirty minutes, hold-down." He hung up the phone.

Both women had been listening to the conversation. Shai asked, "What's jumpin' X?"

"Prophet has got himself into a jam, I gotta go get him."

"Who is Prophet?" that was Pam.

"He's my cousin," Xavier replied.

"Who is Sapphira, Doc's woman?" Shai inquired.

"Nah, its Julian's woman."

"Wait a minute," Pam said. "Prophet and this Doc dude are about to fight over another man's woman?"

"That's right."

"So, where is Julian at?" Shai asked.

"And who is C.J.?" Pam interjected.

"He's bout to fight Julian."

Shai shook her head, "C.J. is about to fight Julian over his woman?"

"It's not really his woman, he's just who she came to the party with."

"So now it's four men about to fight over one woman?" that was Pam.

"Yeah, that's about the size of it."

"Why?" Shai asked.

"Her husband is out of town again," Xavier stated.

Pam said, "Now ain't that a bitch. What's her husband's name?"

"Melvin Brussard."

Pam came again, "And when he's gone, it's may the best man win?"

"Yeah, you got it," Xavier lamented.

"Why?" Shai asked again.

Pam and Xavier looked at each other, then both looked at Shai. Xavier said, "She's 5'1", 140 pounds, creamy, milky and chocolate. Don't have any kids, can't have any kids and loves company.

When her old man leaves its public knowledge. If she shows up at a party, it's usually a fight."

All during the conversation Xavier had corrected his directions and was pushing seventy miles per hour. The Chrysler handled smooth under his touch as he maneuvered expertly in and out of the light traffic. The clock displayed 11:15. He placed his Tupac CD in and Tupac was screaming, 'If I die tonight.'

Pulling up to a house littered with cars, and music pouring out, he stopped, leaned over Shai and removed a 9mm clip from the glove compartment. Then, he reached inside of a hidden compartment on the inside of the front seat and pulled out a solid black 9-mm Glock. It was now 11:43 p.m.

I'm gonna step in, get my boy and step out. Y'all hold down." He pocketed the Glock in the small of his back. The party was in full swing. Julian, Sapphira and C.J. weren't anywhere to be found. Prophet and Doc was into a heated argument. Several brothers were instigating it and pouring gas on a fire.

Prophet was a 6'4", 225-pound high school basketball star. He had just completed his senior year. Colleges everywhere were trying to recruit him. He was ranked number four or five in the nation. Some scouts said he was the most explosive and versatile Point Guard coming out. He wanted to go somewhere he could play point. A lot of colleges were talking about putting him in as a Shooting Guard. His family was pushing him to play with Roderick 'The Rock' Barnes out of Dallas and 'Vail Akbar,' the golden boy from Virginia. Both attended the University of Houston. Named Donovan Tillis at birth, friends and schoolmates started calling him the 'Prophet' his freshman year because his jumper in the clutch was prophetic. If he shot it, every bookie, scout, and onlooker had been conditioned to believe it was already prophesied to go in. Thus, the Prophet was created. Trouble with the laws would hurt his chances in college. Xavier walked over and grabbed his cousin by the shirt.

"C'mon kinfolk, lets bail."

"Nah, cuz, I'm about to put my foot in this nigga's ass. This ass whuppin' he fin'sta get has been prophesied." Prophet swung and connected solidly with the other man's nose. Blood shot everywhere, and Doc, which was on the receiving end collapsed to the floor. Some little fool in a red jogging suit went to digging in his clothes for a gun or knife, it could have been a cell phone or jelly beans; however, Xavier didn't wait to find out. Out of his peripheral vision he caught another guy coming at Prophet, quickly he executed a sidekick to the solo-plex of the guy in the red jogging suit just as he cleared the pistol from its restraints. A forty-ounce bottle was to his right on the table. Xavier grabbed it and hurled it at the other guy connecting him solidly in the forehead, then someone began shooting. The fool in the red jogging suit was sprawled out to his right and the other guy was also on the ground groaning. Prophet was banging it out with some brother. Xavier pulled Prophet out of the commotion, and as they turned to run to the back of the house, the brother that prophet had been fighting grabbed Xavier in a bear hug, Xavier immediately shot his head back, striking his attacker in the nose with the back of his head. The dude dropped Xavier allowing him to spin with lightning speed connecting with an elbow to his jaw. Sirens could be heard in the distance. Grabbing Prophet, they ducked into a bedroom adjoining hall. It was empty, Xavier put a chair under the knob, and then glanced around the room in silent prayer. Bingo, there was a window. Quickly he produced his cellphone, found the call log and swiped his finger across Shai's name.

Shai and Pam heard the gun shot moments ago. People were yelling and bailing for their cars. She and Pam were near panic. The wail of the police sirens were close now. Her phone began to ring, she screamed! Pam put her hand over her mouth. "Girl, shut yo' coward ass up." The phone rang again.

"Answer it Shai!"

"Shit, you answer it," Shai exclaimed. The phone rang again.

"Shai, I'm gonna kick yo' fat yellow ass, if you don't answer your damn phone." Shai picked up the phone. "Hello!" she barked into the phone.

"Hey Shai," Xavier started, before she cut him off.

"Boy!" she whispered. "Don't be calling me, get your ass out here now!"

"That's the problem Shai ..."

"You damn straight it's a problem. You're there, and you're supposed to be here."

"Shai, shut up!" Xavier snapped. "Drive my car to the next street over. Get out of there before the cops come. Drive up and down this back street with the lights off, I'll be there."

Shai started to speak, but the line went dead. "That nigga told me to shut up." As Shai climbed into the driver's side of the car she said, "Shit, he got me fucked up. I'll leave his nigga ass, telling me to shut up."

"Shai!" Pam asserted.

"What!" Shai shouted back at Pam.

"Shut up!" Pam retorted. The Chrysler purred to life effortlessly. Dropping into drive and hitting the gas, the vehicle lurched forward faster than she expected. She headed down Purple Sage seconds before the police arrived. Turning on Trail Bend, she came to the back street, the sign read Eden Brook.

Xavier hung up the phone. Someone was banging on the door. The chair was weakening. Prophet was sprawled out on the bed. Xavier lifted the window, snatched Prophet off the bed and went out the window. Prophet followed. The house was closed in by a wooden fence. He looked over into the adjoining back yard. The back porch light was on, there was no dogs or killer cats waiting to maim and kill them. Shoving Prophet over the fence first, then himself, he made it to the adjoining street. To his surprise, the girls were right there. Shai opened the door and the car light popped on. He noticed at once, again how beautiful Shai was. He shoved Prophet into the backseat, then hopped into the front just in time to see Pam slap Prophet across the back of the head. "Stupid!" she chided.

"Ow! Mama, it was Xavier, not me!" Prophet whined in his inebriated state, then unexpectedly Shai popped Xavier across the back of his head.

"Don't ever tell me to shut up again!" she exclaimed.

Pamela was home safely. Prophet was at the Normandy Inn Motel sleeping it off. He didn't want to go home drunk. Xavier had already called Gail, his aunt and Donovan's mom and explained that he'd stay the night with him. It was 12:55 a.m., when he pulled in front of Shai's pad.

"Nothing rattles you, does it?"

"Nothing never rattles anybody. It's always something that rattles you, not nothing."

"You's a smart ass!" She smiled. "How's school?" he asked.

"Until tonight, I hadn't realized how little I know about you. Six and half months, and I don't even know where you stay. You pop up and disappear, I don't think I like that." Xavier just ignored it all. "How did you do in school this semester?" he asked again. "What's with this mystery shit Xavier, can I know who you are?"

"I'm Xavier Masai Dean, Ghetto Soulja-warrior certified, nothing more, nothing less."

"Cool," she stated in a despondent manner. "That's how you want it, that's how you got it." She exited the car and shut the door. As she walked to her door, he admired her beautiful backside as it stretched to break free from the constricting confines of her uniform. He got out and stood inside the doorway of the car.

"Shai," he called. She spun around. "Is all that you?" he pointed at her butt. She shot him the finger. "Your place or mines?" he asked. She smiled.

"You need me, you got the hook up. There's an appointed time for everything." Getting back into the car he said, "You know how to reach me." The ride home was a quiet one, and full of thought. He picked up the phone and called Tao Sung, and left a message on the machine. Once back into Southmore's parking lot, he could see the kitchen light was still on in his apartment. Inside, Denise was gone. His mother and her smoking partner were washing their pipes for the day. The smell of alcohol permeated the entire room. Xavier went into his room, locked the door behind him and went to bed ready rolled.

Chapter 6

Richmond was the same age as Xavier. He accepted Islam while in the Boys Home in West Texas. Malachi fought hard, preached hard, and partied even harder. At sixteen, he dropped out of high school and went to night school, where he acquired his G.E.D. Outside of Prophet and Adib, Malachi was the only other brother that Xavier trusted and spoke with about his ambitions, dreams and fears.

Malachi was at the Recreation Center with some neighborhood kids. It was the fifteenth of June and the sun was tap dancing on everyone's head.

"As salaamu Alaika, Brother X," Malachi called as he stepped from his car.

"What's up?"

"Nothing but the sky and the ceiling, how you feeling," Xavier chanted. Chante, Keasha and Alisha saw his car pull up, and left the benches headed his way.

"Hey sexy Black," Alisha called out. Xavier looked over his left shoulder, then right, then pointed at himself. "Yeah, I'm talking to you."

"Just trying' to maintain without participating."

"Why haven't you called me?" Alisha Lugo wasn't his girlfriend, but he had made the mistake of accepting her sexual favors under the impression that they both understood the deal. Obviously, she didn't.

"I've been a little tied up. What's on your mind?"

"I just wanted to get together sometime this weekend." He glanced at his watch to break the eye contact.

"Bet," he said nonchalantly. He didn't want to perpetuate the charade, but she was so cute and sexy, not fine, just sexy. There's a difference.

"Where's Prophet at?" Chante asked. Xavier pulled his front pants pockets inside out, then hunched his shoulders, threw his hands in the air. The wind carried the ringing of his phone to his ears.

"What's the deal?" he spoke into the phone. Shai' s sweet voice sang to him.

"Can you come over tonight?" my mama wants to meet you."

"What time?"

"About seven thirty. Mama's cooking and says that it's way past time that she met and conversed with the infamous Xavier Masai Dean." Her giggle wafted across the miles. Xavier could hear a radio in the background, playing 'Me and Mrs. Jones'.

"Yeah, I'm there at seven-thirty. You alright, I haven't heard from you in a couple of days." There was a heavy silence. She sighed, then a thick pause. "Shai?"

"I'm here. Calvin and I had a fight, he came to my job and caused a scene. Dealing with the bullshit has had me stressed. Other than that, I'm peachy king."

Alisha had walked to the car and sat down on the passenger side.

"When you deal with clucks, expect to be embarrassed. You're gonna maintain right?"

"Yeah, come strapped with your appetite kiddo!"

"I gotcha kiddo," he snapped, then hung up the phone. "What's the deal Alisha?"

"Just curious as to where I stand with you," she said softly. The radio was pushing Freddy Jackson's 'You Are My Lady.' Xavier dropped his head and held silent for a second.

"Honestly," he stated. "I believe you'd have more respect for me if I stayed straight up with you. I'm not trying to get emotionally involved with anyone right now. Right now, my feelings are tied up into something I can't even have. What happened between us, just happened. I'm not regretting it, I had more fun than a lil bit, but I shouldn't have started something I was not prepared to finish."

"Well, Xavier, you have my number, you can still use it anytime." She placed emphasis on anytime. To be true she handled it like a real champ, none of that overly dramatized female bullshit. A man can respect that in a woman, hell a man can respect that in anyone. He leaned over and kissed her lightly on the nose, sat back and smiled. She reciprocated his smile.

"Lookout X," Malachi called. "You ready to roll, go take care of that?"

"Yeah, yeah, waiting on you." looking at Alisha, "You girls need a ride somewhere?"

"Nah, we're gonna stay for the dance. You comin'?"

"I ain't promising nothing, but I may swing through here later." She kissed him and jumped out. Malachi got in.

"You called?"

"Yeah, I called and left a message on the machine."

Pulling out of the parking lot, he saw the usual neighborhood hardheads creeping into the park, preparing for the dance. Malachi was more thug, than Muslim. However, being associated with the Muslims kind of offered an extra edge to him. He called it balancing out the good with the bad. Xavier called it faking. Although Xavier disagreed with the way he rolled as far as religion, he stayed neutral. That's between him and the Man. He'd met some solid brothers in Islam, enough to know that Malachi wasn't the norm.

Tao Sung was a Chinese store owner, someone he had become acquainted with some time back. After meeting Shai, he repressed his life, read the writing on the streets as well as in the clouds. It was always there for you to see; some people were just so damn blind. Xavier saw it this way, you don't see Orientals shopping at the mall, so where do they buy their clothes. You don't see them at the white man's bank, so where do they put their money. They had come to his country and established in ten to twenty years what the blacks hadn't accomplished in five hundred. Xavier could respect that. All large sums of money were given to Mr. Sung. He listed Xavier as his employee and every week paid Xavier a regular paycheck, which was Xavier's money anyway. Now it was legitimate, he could just deposit the paycheck every week. Thanks to Mr. Sung's advice, he had made some valuable investments. A year ago, Xavier had hired a financial advisor at Mr. Sung's request. He had stocks in very solid commodities. He had abandoned the dope game when he damn near cost Shai her life, worried about getting the money home safe. It's always time to reevaluate your trade when your priorities get fucked up. The meeting today was to discuss a house in Sugarland, Texas that, Xavier wanted. A six-bedroom, two-hundred and seventy-five-thousand-dollar colonial brick home, with an elaborate swimming pool in the backyard, island kitchen with the works. Malachi knew nothing of Sung and Xavier's business. He came along to receive the valuable teachings. Mr. Sung was a store well of information.

Two years back, Sung's daughter, was attacked in the parking lot of Texas Southern University. He was at Kentucky Fried Chicken on Scott Street, which was right across the street from the parking lot where she was attacked. He sprinted across the street yelling, and the bandits bailed. (Xavier wasn't into no captain save a hoe business, shit just seem to play out that way.) She had been knocked around, sustaining some scrapes and bruises, but nothing that time wouldn't heal. Her keys were still hanging from the door, her purse was gone. Xavier followed her home to assure her safety.

The Orientals have the honor code deal, so Mr. Sung was eternally grateful. Xavier was too young to put his money in the bank, and didn't trust anyone until he met Mr. Sung. They sat and talked for hours, and with Sung's help, he had amassed almost six- hundred thousand dollars. Mr. Sung wanted him to open a business, however, Xavier hadn't decided what he wanted to open yet.

"My little sister's pregnant man," Malachi blurted out. Taking a CD from his pocket and sliding it into the CD player. Some brothers from the house of Yahweh were screaming. "You are not a negro, the world's best kept secret."

"Who's the culprit?" Xavier asked.

"Some nothing 'ass nigga out of South Park. I wanted to bust his ass up, but I don't want to lose my religion. Plus, that won't solve shit."

Xavier laughed. "Man, you ah psyche patient, square bidness, how can you As Salaam Alaikum every brother with a kufi, be Malcolm X half the day, and then Shaft the other half?"

Malachi had pulled a Swisher from his pocket and was licking on it, then stated, "Versatile man." He lit the chronic.

Xavier said, "Versatile my ass. It's called hypocrisy nigga."

Malachi pulled hard on the Swisher and tried to pass it. "Ere." Xavier just looked at him and shook his head. After leaving Mr. Sung's, Malachi asked to be dropped off at the Mosque. He went in brushing his teeth.

At home, Xavier showered and dressed. Vianna was all over him, while he tried to get ready. He slam-dunked her on the bed and she screamed. Nellie was on the couch knocked out; she'd been up for three days.

Vianna was chowing down on some Grandy's chicken, potatoes, corn and biscuits, as soon as she finished, he intended to drop her at his Aunt Rhonda's.

"Zav-ya," Vianna said. "We gone bar-b-que on the nineteenth at the Park?"

"We gonna bar-b-que you!" Xavier said playfully while snatching Vianna from her seat and over his shoulder.

"Noooooo! Zav-ya I don't taste good." She giggled, and tried to wiggle loose while her brother locked the door and toted her down the stairs to the car.

"Yeah, you do," he said.

"Zav-ya, can I drive?" He put her in his lap and gave her the wheel. She looked back at him.

"Girl you better watch the road."

Shortly after that he dropped Vianna off at Rhonda's, then headed for Shai's crib.

The door was opened by a little boy about five years of age. "Who are you?" he demanded. "You're ugly!" he continued. Shai heard him and slapped him across the back of his head.

"Ow mama, I'm sorry."

"Don't apologize to me, apologize to Xavier." Reluctantly he apologized, Xavier was more than surprised. Basically, because he wasn't aware she had a child. The meal was tight, turkey necks and noodles, hot water corn bread and mustard greens. Everybody got their hands dirty eating turkey necks, no shy pride, just straight grub match; finger licking good. Joyce, Shai's mother was nice, Nathan was a little terror on the rampage. Xavier spoke with her mom until nine, while she bathed and put Nathan to bed. Their only disagreement, she was a Dallas Cowboy fan and Xavier was down with the Houston Texans and Tennessee Titans. Joyce excused herself when Shai came from the back room.

Out on the porch, the night was clear, the stars were shinning, and a light breeze neither hot nor cold blew the smell of roses and lilacs that molested the senses. Two cats parlayed in the lawn across the street. Six brothers choked on chronic and sipped some drank. The trees swayed and played their unique melody.

"How come you didn't tell me you had a son?" Shai had on some baggy Tommy Hilfiger jeans and shirt with blue and white Jordan's. On her frame it looked so sexy.

"The same reason I don't know where you live at," she said seriously.

He smiled. "That's a big issue with you huh?" she stared into his eyes. She was on the second step leading to the porch. He was on the ground, which put them just about eye to eye. She looked at him.

"Yes, at first I didn't want in, now I do."

He cocked his head sideways. "In what Shai?" He spoke very slowly and deliberate.

"Inside your yesterdays ... todays ... tomorrows ..." The space and air between them seemed to evaporate. He could feel her breath on his face.

"I see," Xavier said.

Shai responded quickly, "Do you?"

Xavier asked, "Do I what?"

"See." She leaned down to kiss him, and Xavier stepped back.

"Shai, don't play with me, you're still in love with Calvin. I'm no stand in." She had a solemn look on her beautiful face. Those eyes of hers met his, caressed and left a fingerprint on the windows of his soul. Her fingerprints and her voice were like a whisper, barely audible and damn near invisible, yet like gravity had, a way of making its presence felt.

"Calvin's an illusion, his one accomplishment is in the house asleep. I'm tired of the illusions ..." As she spoke, she dismounted the steps to close the gap he had created when he stepped back. "... I'm tired of the games, the false promises, and all the pretty rhetoric void of meaning. I need ..." She touched her chest between her bosom. "... I need something solid, real and reliable. I see all that in you, Xavier." She rubbed the side of his face, and brought her lips to his successfully this time and kissed him ardently. Her perfume was making him heady. When she broke off the kiss, she hugged him. When the embrace broke, she busied herself rubbing the lipstick from his lips.

"Whew!" he smiled. "Can we try that again?" Shai blushed and grinned.

"Yep! Kiddo." They kissed again. It was slow, soft and passionate. When the kiss ended, Xavier licked and smacked his lips.

"What is it?" she asked.

"You didn't brush your teeth girl." Shai's mouth flew open in shock. She swung a right hook at him, and he ducked and grabbed her waist in one fluid motion and swung her over his shoulder.

Shai screamed, "AHHH! Boy put me down!" The brothers on the corner of the street looked around alarmingly. As Xavier placed her back on her feet, Mrs. Montgomery snatched the front door open wide-eyed and disoriented.

"Girl, you alright?"

"Mama, I'm alright. I saw a rat, skunk or something and it startled me."

"Baby, you like to give your poor mama heart attack. Xavier, take care of my baby."

"I got her Mrs. Montgomery." As soon as the door closed, Shai struck Xavier in the stomach, but to her surprise, her fragile fist encountered unyielding muscle that refused to budge under her minimum pressure. She cupped her hands over her mouth and blew into them twice. Xavier popped her supple backside.

"Girl, I was just playing. You taste like turkey necks." He looked at his watch. "I meant to tell you; you were handling those necks."

"You weren't doing that bad yo' damn self. Nice technique," Shai retorted.

He looked at his watch again.

"You gotta go somewhere?" she asked.

"Yeah, I gots to go pick up my little sister from my Aunt Rhonda's. I told her I'd be there at eleven, and it's already ten thirty- seven," he said enroute to the car.

"Can I come?" She wasn't ready to return to her four walls.

"Yeah, come on roll with me, we'll talk. I'll let you know where my aunt lives at." After Shai informed her mother that she was going out, she and Xavier rode the thirty-minute drive to his aunt's house on the North Side.

He swung inside the driveway of a big two-story brick home. Verandas in front and phloxes littered the sidewalk leading up to the front door. Their blue flowers looked beautiful. Shai reached out to touch them and smell their fragrance. There was a turquoise Jaguar posed sideways in the lawn. Xavier rang the doorbell. and the bark of a small dog erupted from somewhere inside the house.

"This is your mother's sister or father's?"

"My mama's oldest sister." The night spoke to those with a little wisdom. It spoke of enchantment and romance, and ordered the stars to go on parade, the moon was there too, bold and low to the earth. The fragrance of Shai's perfume engulfed him, she looked so sexy in her baggy jeans, and shirt and Jordan's. Men's tennis shoes always looked cute on small female feet.

"What's the name of that perfume youz wearing?"

"Sands of Sable, you like it?" He nodded his head, as the locks to the front door started to click. Xavier noticed that the lightning bugs credulously banged their heads against the lit window and being right here, right now, was alright with him. The door swung open and his little sister sprinted into his arms.

"Zav-ya, I missed you. I told Catfish, that you're gonna kick his ass." Vianna covered her mouth with her small hands.

"I told you little ladies don't talk like that, didn't I?" She nodded her head with her hand still over her mouth.

"Be more articulate Vi, okay." She buried her face into his chest and mumbled.

"I gon be more ar-tic-let." He smiled at her innocence. She didn't even know what articulate was. He spoke to Rhonda, and introduced Shai.

"Y'all hungry Masai?" Rhonda inquired.

"Nah Red, we just got our grub on at Shai's place." Vianna was studying Shai conscientiously.

"You must be the one." Rhonda directed at Shai. Shai looked pretty puzzled and smiled.

"What do you mean?" Shai asked politely. Rhonda was nursing a Bud Light, took a sip. "Masai has never, I mean never brought a female home. This isn't his home, but it is his home. In seventeen years, he's never brought a woman here, so I just figured you're the one." Taking another sip of her beer. Shai thoughtfully looked at Xavier, it was something to tuck away for greater deliberation at a later date.

"Maybe, maybe that's what he's trying to say by bringing me here."

"Are you a virgin?" Vianna asked as she completed her analysis.

Xavier and Rhonda both burst into laughter. "Vi, cut that out," Xavier chided.

"Zav-ya, Moophisey said you had to marry a Muslim virgin. She not a virgin."

"How do you know?" Shai shot back. The two women glared at one another. Xavier was astonished to see his baby sister asserting herself at such a young age to this female he had brought into his life.

"So, are you?" Shai responded. That question brought crinkles into Vianna's face. She pondered the question, because her young mind hadn't fully sorted out the accurate meaning for Muslim or virgin. These were only terms she had heard Moophisey use. She looked into her brother's eyes for help, and he gave it. That's what big brothers are for, right? He nodded his head slightly. Vianna smiled, then redirected her attention to Shai.

"Yes!" Vianna said confidently, certain that her big brother had led her straight. She waited for Shai's answer. However, before Shai could say anything, Xavier rescued her also.

After all, that's what soulmates are for. Right?"

"Vi, Shai is a virgin and Muslim also, you are on a physical level." He touched her heart. "Shai's on a mental level." He touched his temple. That seemed to satisfy her curiosity. Thirty minutes later, when they were getting ready to leave, Rhonda asked Shai to come by sometime without her nephew. So, they could talk, Shai agreed to that. They exchanged numbers. SWV was crooning sweetly on the drive back to Shai's place. Vianna was asleep in the back seat probably dreaming of candy lands and Barbie dolls.

"So, what are you going to do tomorrow?" he asked.

"Spending time with you would be very idyllic to me."

"Bet, I'll scoop you and Nate—"

"Nathan," she interrupted. "His name is Nathan not Nate."

"Cool, I'll scoop you and Nathan up at 'bout ten-thirty-eleven o'clock."

"I'll be ready." She kissed him and exited the car. The ride home was filled with many songs, artists which he paid no attention to. He vividly recalled his uncle telling him, that women are the best players in the world, because they take ova a man's whole life and makes him like it. Now that's playin'!

Chapter 7

Sometimes we're given the impression that misery and the ghetto are two individuals. Faithful cohorts determined to cohere no matter what. They perpetuate the conditions that makes us products of the products that determine circumstances and conditions. Conditions that dictate needs and attitudes. Conditions that attribute to personality and character. Even nature finds a way to avoid the streets that are occupied by these faithful cohorts. They flaunt their beauty and create harmonious melodies across the tracks maybe, but on some days nothing but rats, roaches, wayward cats, dogs, ants and mosquitos congregate with the segregated souls living life through a hybrid form of Alzheimer's. We are allowed to view happiness in short stretches, then something always goes sour. It seems we spend our entire life recovering from life. There isn't any pie in the sky or big brass ring. It's all a fabricated illusion developed to make you chase dreams while getting handled by reality. The reality is, that the tears are all real ... the adversity that causes them are even more real.

Xavier was already up before the knocking at the door interrupted his thoughts. He was laying there listening to them, his thoughts that is, and watching two roaches fraternize with one another on the wall. The knocking came again, the sofa squeaked in protest as he got up. Without even checking the peephole, he flipped the dead bolt and swung the large wooden door open.

"Hey boy!" Bernadine shot past him. She had on blue skin tight pants, a black spandex top with Nike written on it, and a pair of black Nike Cross Trainers. Bernadine was his mom's best friend. No one had seen her in a little over two years, since her oldest child got hemmed up by the one-time. Bernadine was jet black, smooth as satin and ugly as sin. Maybe not ugly, just uncommon. She wasn't a zero on a scale of one to ten. She was bowlegged and slightly pigeon toed, fine as hell. She could stop traffic at any angle. When Xavier was fourteen, all his homies thought she was just a fine man, because it was speculated that all that weight sitting in the front of those spandex couldn't be all pussy.

She was changing clothes in his room one night before she and his mom attacked the club. Unknowingly, he burst through the door, and there she stood in some purple panties with lace in the front that allowed him to see her mass of thick black pubic hair. She didn't have on a bra, so her breast hung full and heavy, tipped with big bold black nipples. Her stomach was flat and flawless, no one would have guessed that she had three kids. She neither looked embarrassed or ashamed, nor did she make any attempt to cover herself. Xavier right then and there conceded, that Bernadine was bad for real.

He recalled her grinning then asking, "Do you like what you're looking at little man?" He couldn't remember, but he believed that he nodded the affirmative.

"Well baby you're either comin' in or leavin' out, but you have to shut that door." He proceeded to enter the room, young maybe, but not stupid by a long shot. As the door clicked behind him, she turned her back to him and allowed him to witness her curvaceous ass. After she had wiggled into her skirt Xavier became conscious of his erection tenting in his shorts. Quickly he took a seat on the sofa and put his hat in his lap. His mama walked through the door just as Bernadine slipped into her bra.

"Girl, why are you in here enticing and corrupting my baby?" Nellie walked over and sat next to Xavier rubbing his head cooing. "My poor baby."

Bernadine replied, "As a matter of fact, he's a little man Nellie. He's either going to be exposed to it in real life," she cupped and squeezed her large breast, thus producing the desired effect. "Or the idiot box." She pointed at the small color television. Completely dressed, she headed toward the bathroom to apply her makeup, but she stopped at Xavier's chair, bent over and grabbed Xavier's face in both of her hands and planted a big wet kiss on his lips, then lifted his cap. Nellie noticed the tent in his pants and covered her mouth in feigned awe.

"Girl!" she exclaimed.

Bernadine commented smartly, "At least we know he isn't a damn sissy!"

Xavier came back to the here and now. Bernadine sauntered past him, her butt bouncing a little with every step she took, and it wasn't a jelly shake, just a bounce. It had been two and a half years since she had been around. Rumor was she went home to Louisiana and went back to school. He studied her in his newly acquired maturity, amazed at his own development within the time. He noticed for the first time, that Bernadine wasn't ugly. No, nowhere near it. She had gained some weight, good weight. It was this; she was heavily draped in African features. American men have allowed TV magazines, and racism to define what beauty is. Light, bright and damn near white has always been accepted while the heavily myelinated sisters and brothers were ostracized. Anything too rich in African features was alienated, condemned and deemed unacceptable. She wasn't a La Tavia Roberson or Kelly Rowland from Destiny's Child, nor Kamellah from 702. Her, Janelle Monae, and Jennifer Hudson would never be mistaken for sisters. She had big full lips, high cheek bones and a wide nose, which were positioned just right. She had a beauty, which can only be perceived through the eyes of an intellectual and socially conscious man. Xavier was pleased to know that he had reached that Plateau.

"Where you been Bernadine?" startled by this new baritone in his voice, she paused from digging in her purse.

"Xavier?" she questioned, like she was just now seeing him. "Boy, look at you, listen to you." She hugged him tightly. He smiled, mildly amused. Last time she had seen him, they stood eye to eye at five foot three, now he towered over her. "My little man is no longer little anymore. How old are you now? Wait don't tell me." She did a thing with her fingers. "Oh, okay, seventeen, right? Eighteen in a month?"

He nodded. "So, where you been?" he asked again.

"Baby, I went back to school and completed my hours to get my Bachelor's Degree in Dentistry. I start work at East Loop next week. How have you been doing? You're sure looking good."

"Better than some, worse than others," was his stoical reply. He hugged her again. "I'm proud of you Bernadine." She looked around taking in the ambience of the apartment that she had laughed, cried, fought, and smoked dope in. She inhaled deeply, and exhaled lightly before asking.

"So, X where's your mama?"

"She's asleep, I guess. I didn't hear the door open this morning." She placed her hands around his waist and they walked towards his mother's bedroom. He wanted to ask about K-9, but it brought up bad memories. He didn't want to upset this cheerful reunion with bad memories. K-9 shot two cops while they were sitting in their patrol car. It was the same two cops that were guilty of jumping on brothers in the neighborhood. The same two cops that would have never seen the inside of a courtroom, because in America cops had carte blanche on murder as long as they were black. Many applauded K-9 for acting while doing nothing themselves, it was written in all the newspapers for everyone to see:

Twenty-eight Black People (27 Men and 1 Female) killed by Police Officials, Security Guards, and Self-Appointed "Keepers of the Peace" between January 1, 2012 and March 31, 2012.

28 cases of state sanctioned or justified murder of black people in the first 3 months of 2012 alone have been found (due to under reporting and discriminatory methods of documentation, it is likely that there are more that our research has yet to uncover)

Of the 28 killed people, 18 were definitely unarmed, 2 probably had firearms, 8 were alleged to have non-lethal weapons.

Of the 28 killed people, 11 were innocent of any illegal behavior or behavior that involved a threat to anyone (although the shooters claimed they looked "suspicious").

7 were emotionally disturbed and/or displaying strange behavior.

The remaining 10 were either engaged in illegal or potentially illegal activity, or there was too little info to determine circumstances of their killing. It appears that in all but two of these cases, illegal and/or harmful behavior could have been stopped without the use of lethal force.

He didn't tear up the neighborhood or loot our own stores in his frustrations. He took it to the guilty party. If more black men dispensed street justice when the cops got loose with their morals and pistols it would come to a screeching halt. Either way, that was the last anyone had seen or heard of K-9 and Bernadine until now. It was said that she blamed herself and felt responsible for her oldest son being placed under the jail.

"Nellie get yo' tired ass up!" She hopped on the bed and the box springs started to complain by squeaking and groaning from the additional weight. Nellie rolled over slowly and shot Bernadine the evil eye. "Hey bitch, where yo' black ass been?" Nellie whispered.

"Ran into a nigga with twelve inches of meat and he hospitalized my ass." They laughed together; Xavier left the room. It had been a while since he'd heard his t-lady laugh like that.

❖   ❖   ❖

On television the morning is depicted as such a surreal or serene scene. The sun is always peeking over some immense landscape, ocean or hillside. Birds singing, butterflies dancing to nature's music, while some damn rooster in the background is crowing, and the smell of pork wafted through the air. Xavier didn't walk out on the balcony expecting to see or smell anything but the bacon part of that idyllic scene. It was six-thirty in the morning and the sun was already up. Its rays plastered and laid across his face like a warm wet towel. He took a deep breath of smog-filled air, as the Metro bus roared by taking people to their destination. It was good to be alive. Aaron and Chill sat in front of the complex with old man Clue. Deciding to join them Xavier stuck his hands into his Guess shorts and headed in that direction. The absence of a shirt allowed sun to reflect on the Rolex necklace that shined brilliantly against his dark smooth skin. The two nugget earrings and Rolex watch also caught a healthy dose of sun.

"What's tha deal Mr. Clue, Aaron, Chill?" Chill was just thirteen and sometimes it was impossible to tell. He jumped to his feet, his and Xavier's hands met in a loud clap, then a fancy handshake followed, ending in a dab.

"We just opening up shop early, soliciting ends from friends." Aaron, fifteen, held up his fist and pointed it at Xavier. Xavier followed suit and stretched out his fist until they touched them together, then Aaron said, "Just manifesting our natural inclination to stack, stacks as effortlessly as possible." Xavier smiled, then gave old man Clue some dap. Clue was pushing eighty; thin, wiry, fluid and dangerous. About four years ago, he was disrespected by Cujo, Bobby Fae's boy, six-two, two-hundred fifty pounds. Clue squared off with him and threw six slow ineffective looking punches all to the body, and Cujo folded up like a lawn chair. An old school ass whippin'.

A car stopped in front of them. Chill went to get his serve on. Clue stared up at Xavier with watery dark brown eyes, and cleared his throat.

"You boys know the difference between an 'Uncle Tom' and a 'Jeff Davis'?" All three of them shook their head. "A Tom's, a nigga that thinks white folks is betterin' him and let 'um know it. The Jeff Davis is where a niggah makes white folks think they betterin' him, but know it ain't so."

"What's up with Alisha, X?" Chill asked. Xavier shook his head in a noncommittal fashion.

"Aw, nigga, why ya ass actin' like you ain't diggin' that," Chill shrieked, standing, then pulling a Swisher sweet out of his pocket.

"Yeah, X," Aaron interjected. "Everybody kinda knows she's panting like a bitch in heat behind yo' ass. Ain't no future in frontin', and faking will get ya kilt. Serve her ass playa." Chill started choking on the smoke he produced from the Swisher, laughing between each cough. Old man Clue took a deep pull on the square and expelled a cloud of thick blue smoke.

"You two lil' niggah jus jealous, that X gots ah ghul panting that's worth some'ing, and nuttin' but dope feigns want y'all jive ass."

Chill jumped up. "Bullshit, Clue!" He held up the Swisher. "This my bitch right heah." He pulled hard. "Nah, all bullshit aside, I gotta beat dem ho's off me at school."

"Ya degenerate ass don't go to school!" Xavier exclaimed. "C.L.C. suspended you, and juvenile won't accept you." Aaron was laughing, when Xavier turned on hm.

"Aaron, what happened between you and Peaches?" Aaron sat rigid straight, and his demeanor got serious. "Shit, playa, I'm a thousand-volt live ass nigga. I ain't worried 'bout ah bitch. They just humble a muth-a-fucka, git wit'em and ah nigga gits soft. I live my life a product ready to rumble. Much to harden for a bitch, way too crazy to be humbled."

"It sounds good." That was Xavier. Everyone knew that Aaron had went to school full of the syrup and fell to sleep during a video. While the lights were out, Peaches—or really Tangie Willbacks nicknamed (Peaches), justifiably. Unzipped his pants, pulled out his tally whacker and painted the head with red lipstick. When the lights came on, she screamed, pointed at his exposed phallus with the red head. The noise jolted him awake, although incoherent at first. The other girls in the room were pointing and laughing. He looked down, and saw what they were laughing at, stood up and did an Usain Bolt out of the class, embarrassed as hell.

"Don't play X," Aaron said.

"I thought you wanted to play," Xavier replied.

"Nah playa, T.Y.A. back up those stairs."

Xavier laughed. "Y'all hold it down and walk light." He turned to walk back to the pad, then hesitated and turned his attention to Chill. "Hey baby boy, how many Swishers do you have?" Chill pulled a plastic sack out, which held about a dozen or so Swisher Sweets. "Let me get one."

"Man." Chill gave a pained expression. "You don't even smoke."

"Look lil brotha, can I get a Swisher or do I gotta hire Jesse Jackson to kiss yo' ass fo' I get one." Chill chunked him one.

"Man." Chill's pained expression deepened. "Please, don't neglect or mistreat Mary Jane, cuz she's a down ass bitch. Down like whoa!" For emphasis, he fired up one, pulled hard on it and fell back on the concrete. "I fell in love with her the first time she charged me up ...!" He placed emphasis on charged. "... and I've been high on love ever since!" Xavier shook his head and walked off. It was two minutes after seven. He told Shai that he would pick her up at ten- thirty or eleven. He had plenty of time to shower and lounge. It was June seventeenth.

CHAPTER 8

The club was jumping, Lil Boosie's "I'm Coming Home" was doing a number on the crowd. The lyrics spilled like hot lava into the crowd and infused them with heat. The lights flickered with every color of the rainbow, further inciting an already exuberant and loquacious crowd. Coquettish women, some who were nubile, some who weren't, were on display. Cheap perfume mingled with expensive perfume and together they wrestled with worked up musk as they danced the old dance. A dance that didn't quite predate the calendar, but was close enough. The ladies were in full force in a colorful array too big, too small, and just right mini shirts, skin tights and dresses that looked poured on. It was Tuesday night; ladies get in free until 11:30. It was only a quarter till eleven. Victor stood behind the bar and just watched. No, not watched, but studied the people and absorbed their energy. Paul and Kenneth stood at his right; brick wall stiff. The D.J. was laying it on thick, T.I. was back with "Ain't I" and Rich Boy Quan was feeling 'Some Type of Way.'"

Hypnotize came on, one of Victor's favorites, he nodded his head in time with the beat and sipped his Blue Hawaiian. This was only one of three clubs he owned in Houston, just another spot he used as a front to siphon young talent and potential marks for his game. It was this stage that uncovered some of the sweetest jewels he had come across. The place was jumpin' and getting more exciting by the minute.

Diamond Slim, well really Andrew Guthfield was his name, but no one called him that. Last person who called him by his first and last name was said to have died in his car overdosed on heroin. There was only one problem, that individual had no car; nor did he have a heroin problem. Some people called him Michael Jackson, because he was a helluva character, plus in his youth, he was a helluva performer. At six foot four and only a hundred and seventy pounds, Diamond Slim fit him well. He was monolithic and dogmatic about his theology, ideology or whatever other 'ology' pertinent to his prowess in most areas of life. Most pointedly the female make-up, physically, mentally and spiritually. He was presumptuous, ostentatious and coherent. In essence, he was the epitome of the books and the life that most people only read about. Many people read Iceberg Slim, and Donald Goins, then attempted to imitate what they read. Diamond was the type of brother that made the book believable. Some people wore the title of Pimp like a contemptuous disease. Diamond Slim wore it like an intrepid lion. He made it look natural.

The D.J. screamed, "Ladies, tonight is the night, shake it 'til you break it! Can I get all the ladies to scream, just the real ladies nah!" The building vibrated as the shouts echoed through every brick, every two by four and every piece of sheetrock. "If you got that pussy, say yeeeaaah!" Naomi formerly known as Nijeil, jumped up and led the shouts ahead of all the real women. Diamond Slim sat at his usual table, seven ladies, all lavishly dressed surrounded him. His right-hand man, Sideline Redd stood off to the right with his arms across his massive chest.

Sideline Redd was one of those truly red brotha, red hair, eyebrows and mustache. He had received a life sentence two years ago. Rumor was that they gave him a pardon, because the Governor was touring the unit when a psyche patient maniac Aryan Brotherhood tried to stab the Governor. Redd wasn't trying to be a hero, that wasn't his M.O. The white boy damn near ran him over, missed the Governor, and headed straight at Sideline. They say he yanked the guy's arm off. The governor was so thankful, he pardoned Redd. Other people say that Diamond Slim paid a hundred fifty thousand dollars on a high-power legal team. Nobody really knew and nobody felt comfortable enough to ask. Sideline Redd's mother, when he was a boy had taken him to an old Indian Witch Doctor. The Witch Doctor allegedly performed a ceremony, it was during this ceremony that the witch doctor predicted that Redd would never die by knife or gunshot. His mother and brother presumed he would die of old age and not by manmade devices. Redd didn't really believe all that until he was 17, when he was stabbed in what should have been a fatal wound. Doctors fought for twelve hours in surgery, but still didn't expect for him to survive the night. The police went to notify his mother about the incident at 3:00 in the morning. She shocked the police by cursing them out for waking her up for that 'nonsense,' she called it. Then in an exasperated tone she said. "Shit, that boy ain't gonna die," and slammed the door. The police were dumbfounded.

Redd was told how lucky he was, when he came out of the coma a week later. All the doctors informed him that he was truly blessed. From that point on he believed in the Witch Doctor's prediction. Since then, he'd been stabbed again, shot four times with a nine-millimeter, once with a forty-five automatic, and once with a twelve-gauge shotgun in the stomach at point blank range. Not all at once of course, but at various points of his forty-three years of life. He was still alive, and still minus a colostomy bag.

Diamond Slim had a seven-carat diamond ring on each finger, except for his thumbs. He sat back and analyzed Victor meticulously. Baby doll broke into his thoughts.

"Baby, can we go out somewhere to eat, when we leave this place?" Spinning the ring on his left index finger with his thumb, he said nothing. Tif-girl slapped Babydoll with a napkin playful-ly, "Leave him alone, he's in deep thought, and getting mentally prepared to try and satisfy this monster I'm packing." Everyone at the table laughed. Slim stroked Tif-girl's leg under the table. She was his bottom babe, dove and serpent perfectly mixed. He sat up, when he saw Vatly walk into the club, with a sexy petite auburn-haired gem. Diamond didn't put her a day over eighteen, and he knew women.

"Ladies excuse me," he said in his smooth almost feminine voice. He floated toward the bar with the grace and elegance that was his trade mark. Sideline Redd moved also, except not as gracefully, but like an ominous shadow.

"Victor, this shit is never simple. Hastiness produces mistakes in our line of work, and mistakes are something we can't afford," Vatly whispered over the loud music. He drowned his drink and wiped his mouth.

"These Houston people are not just leaving their toddlers un-attended. So, you know the infants are on lock. I'm taking all the risk, so don't stress me man," Vatly said.

Victor rubbed his brow and adjusted his glasses. "Vatly, I'm understanding." He poured Vatly another drink, and glanced at the auburn beauty seated about ten feet from them. "Look over there Vatly." Vatly followed his eyes. "Leather pants and vest." Diamond was about six feet away and couldn't hear the conversa-tion, because of the music but followed Victor's and Vatly's stares to a very pretty caramel colored sister with shoulder length hair in red leather pants and vest that looked to be in her twenties. She was dancing vigorously, moving everything to the beat of the music. "She just had a baby four months ago and stays alone. A baby girl, eight pounds- two ounces. Tonight, when she goes home, she'll be drunk, tired, and she'll sleep like a log. Why don't you get that little girl for me? That will fill the infant baby girl order." Vatly looked at Victor like he was a damn fool.

"How in the hell am I supposed to get in without waking her or anyone else?" Victor killed his drink, reached out and took Vatly's hand in a firm handshake, then walked off. Vatly looked into his palm and saw a piece of paper and a gold-colored key. He placed his hands on his head and ran them down his face. He ordered another drink, and his date joined him.

"You alright Shane?" she asked. Vatly nodded his head. "Just stressed baby," he said and eyed his objective.

Diamond Slim motioned to Peanut.

"Yeah, what's poppin' Diamond?" Peanut yelled over the music. Diamond leaned into his ear and said some things; Peanut swiveled on his heel and located the sista in question, then looked back at Diamond. "That's Daphane Keye, sweet ain't she?" Peanut stood shaking his head to the beat lusting off the way Daphane shook her considerable assets. He continued, "She just had a baby for this basketball player at the University of Houston ... what's the playa's name, oh Vail Akbar, supposed to be headed to the pros." Diamond thanked him and excused himself. 'My Nigga' by Rich Hommie Quan and YG blasted through the speakers and Daphane went into overdrive.

Vail Akbar was good, really good. A six foot six, two hundred-and thirty-five-pound shooting guard in his sophomore season at the University of Houston. His family was from Virginia, both his mother and father were doctors. His sister was in her first year at Spielman. They knew him, how, he did not know, they just did, and came at him like a nightmare about two months ago. They refused to identify themselves when they presented him with a check for seventy-five thousand dollars to help them abduct his two-month-old daughter. At first, he thought it was just a joke.

"So, you're gonna marry her?" the taller one asked.

"No," he replied.

"What is your family going to think?" the other asked. The more he thought about it, he didn't love Daphane. She had tricked him into this shit anyway, the gold-digging bitch. His emotions played tug-of-war with his morals. His conscious wouldn't let him do it. They gave him a card, just in case he changed his mind. Vail tore the card up. That was two months ago.

    Victor Thi Pierce was a man accustomed to getting what he wanted by any means necessary. When he noticed Daphane six months ago, he wanted that baby. He did the background checks and knew she came from the ghettos on the North Side of Houston. Her father was unknown, and her mother was a career drug addict. An aunt kept her from falling out of school. Daphane was fortunate, black males often use athletic capabilities to escape the ghettos while black females relied on intellect and beauty. Daphane Keye had an abundance of both, however, the latter far superseded the former. For some reason, intellect intimidated black men while extraordinary beauty stimulated. Yes, Daphane had a beauty unequaled by most, and a body most women would kill for. Thus, she had grown accustomed to being pampered and catered to by men of all ages, colors and economic status. Her apartment was paid for by a well-to-do, much older, very married airplane technician. Her college education paid in full by Wilford T. Pratt, an old white man who noticed her at a Houston Rocket's basketball game. He followed her home in a stretch Lexus limousine and introduced himself. At the age of seventy, he offered her twenty thousand dollars to spend a weekend with him on his yacht. Without hesitation Daphane packed and was on her way. Opportunities knocked often at her door, but when Vail Akbar approached her at a sorority party, she fell ... no, collapsed into love. She immediately abandoned her paramours and birth control, and set out to keep Vail permanently. Victor also knew, like everyone else, that Vail Akbar was going to the pros. His mother and father were prominent successful doctors in Virginia. Victor was aware that he had a girlfriend back home that he'd been with since eleventh grade whom he had planned to marry, an illegitimate baby was the last thing Vail wanted. Would Vail sell his soul just to gain the world? Greed and ambition are the greatest compromisers of character. Victor intended to test the fortitude of the young Vail Akbar. He would make things worse for Vail, before he put on his Demi God persona and made things better, he looked at his clock. It was ten thirty-seven in the morning, life was good he thought.

Vail noticed the police car behind him. "Damn!" he shrieked and pulled over to the shoulder. He glanced at his watch. It was 11:00 a.m., and he was on his way home for June 19th, his flight was at eleven forty-five. Already late, this was the last thing that he needed.

The speaker from the police car ordered, "Driver, exit the vehicle."

"Shit!" Vail said under his breath. "Shit! Shit! Shit!" Vail was walking toward the police car, when he noticed the officer inside motioning for him to come to the passenger side. "Maybe this fool wants an autograph," Vail said to himself.

Soon as he opened the door, the officer smiled and said, "Hey kid, catch!" Instantly, a black twirling object came at him, and instinctively he caught it. Vail focused on the object. He felt as though things were moving in slow motion. Recognition of the small caliber pistol he was holding, sent his heart into overdrive. Officer Decker got out of the car and rounded the front of the car with his pistol drawn and pointed directly at Vail. "Get your black ass against the car!" Decker shouted. Vail was too stunned to move, hoping that any second now, someone would jump up and yell April fool's or MTV's you've Been Punked was lurking around the corner. Quickly he realized that this wasn't a joke and he was not likely to get April out of June.

"Now, god dammit!" Decker was yelling. Vail's heart raced, fingers numbed and the gun slipped from his inert hands. Vail felt himself get shoved against the police car and being handcuffed, then pushed into the car. "Looks like you're going to jail kid, for possession of marijuana and carrying a concealed weapon. You have the right to remain silent. Anything you say ...” Vail couldn’t hear anything else, matter of fact, he couldn’t remember what he had heard, and surely couldn’t believe what was happening to him. He thought that he would wake up in a minute, and it would all be just a horrible nightmare, he was sure of it.

The loud slam of a door woke him, and he jumped up with sweat all over his face, glanced at his watch, it was two-fifteen. Taking in his surroundings Vail deduced that it wasn’t a dream.

“Look out Akbar, you got a visit,” the guard shouted. Vail was escorted into an attorney’s booth.

“Hello, Mr. Akbar.” He was greeted by a short, ugly mixed concoction in a suit that was too big, large glasses and protruding front teeth.

“You my lawyer?” Vail asked.

“No, have a seat Mr. Akbar, you and I have business,” Victor stated.

“If you’re not a lawyer, we ain’t got shit to say to one another.”

“Aw, that’s really a shame, I can help you ...” Victor dropped his head and shook it sympathetically, then from nowhere. “How is Daphane and Iyanna?” Now he had Vail’s undivided attention.

“How do you know about them?”

“I come to help you, Vail. I know everything about you, your parents in Virginia, your sister in Spielman, your fiancée Dinetta, and your professional basketball career.”

Vail simply asked, “What do you want?”

“A couple of months ago two gentlemen approached you with a proposition, and you foolishly turned down the offer. So, here’s the new proposition. You give me Daphane’s apartment alarm code, gate code and a key to the apartment. I’ll have you out of here by midnight and on a 2:45 flight to mommy, all charges will be dropped and forgotten about.” Victor wiped his brow and adjusted his glasses.

“You got me fucked up, I can’t get down like that.”

"Quite the contrary Mr. Akbar, I have you fucked just right! I have a gun that was used in a homicide with your fingerprints on it, and all I'm asking for is some cooperation, some gratitude for liberating you from a relationship that you never wanted anyway. Right?"

"I haven't done a muthafuckin' thang and you know it," Vail growled.

"You can tell it to a judge! Life is about judgment and decisions. You now have a choice. If you want to make an omelet, you have to break a few eggs. I'll break you if necessary. Your whole life depends on the decision that you make now! The media will discover that you've been arrested on drugs and weapons charges, and you will be suspended. There was a homicide committed with that pistol and they convict black men daily for crimes that they didn't commit. Do you intend to be the exception?"

Vail dropped his head. "So, I'm damned if I do, and damned if I don't. Why? Who are you?"

"I am an opportunist suggesting you emulate me. I come to help you save your imminent rise to stardom inside of the basketball arena. Do not disappoint your family." Victor rose to leave, gathering his briefcase. "Good day, Mr. Akbar." He was at the door, when Vail called him.

"Hey," with his back to Vail, he smiled.

The Honorable Wilbert Willmont Willow was not all that honorable. He resided over the 230th Judicial District Court of Harris County, Texas. He was of true prominent blue blood lineage. Diminutive in stature, with wide wire-rimmed glasses, in his early fifties, and a Harvard grad, he served for 17 years as a District Attorney before being voted into the position of Judge since then. He was lenient, especially towards blacks and was one of the most favored Circuit Court Judges by the Afro-American Community. Sometimes goodness doesn't come from the heart, it comes as a feeble attempt to break even and balance out the evils committed on the levels of unfair administration of justice that blacks are always left out of. He could have, would have, and should have sought help to correct his illness, but still water runs deep. Wilbert Willmont Willow hated Victor Thi Pierce, however, his perversion made him tolerate Victor. He was simple, weak and pathetic. When he received the call, his mixed feelings surfaced like a crocodile, the bile in his stomach rumbled.

"Hello, yes Victor I can talk."

"I have a very important friend in one of your holding tanks that I need released."

"What are his charges?" Willow inquired.

"There are none. Decker put him there, but before questions arise as to how and why he's there ...?"

"Was he booked in?"

"No," Victor said.

"Alright, I'll take care of it. What is his name?"

"Trey Winters."

"Alright, Victor." The Judge fidgeted a little. "When can I see Yolanda again?"

"Come by tonight. I have something special for you."

Wilbert's forehead broke out in a sweat, and his organ became tumid. "See you tonight then."

CHAPTER 9

Most are comfortable when that dark enigma tacitly places a blanket on the heavens. Sometimes nightfall seems so implicitly final. The way he steps in and steals the daylight, like a kleptomaniac that has serendipitously discovered that he can get away with this robbery eternally. Nights where he has successfully jacked the sky for all her diamonds and tears solemnly fall, slip and slide into obscurity. The divinity of it all negates silly questions like,

"Are you there?"

Vatly was nervous, or was it agitation. Some emotions ran close races, and traveled in close circles which are synonymous some days and antithesis the next. Either emotion would serve the purpose. Victor's little plan was risky, there were too many eyes. Tired and partially drunk, he had been sitting in his car for over an hour. Since he dropped the woman off, he had come into the club with at the town-house apartment. Vatly had been successful thus far because he could think. Knowledge is correct information, whether thought, spoken or written. Wisdom is knowing how and when to use knowledge. Understanding is the receipt of knowledge by the mind as is the unity of knowledge and wisdom. It all must be in organized sequence. Then you embrace a purpose and plan, and develop the power to execute the purpose and plan. Idleness and ignorance play no part in the plan. Make the plan and pursue the purpose. However, insidiously or mendaciously remain diligent. Vatly was good at pursuing his plans.

Daphane was still in the club. Many times, Vatly wanted to just fuck Victor off, he drove him to that point sometimes. Fuck! Fuck! Fuck! Vatly thought as he sat in his car, a black BMW. He blended into the night like a two-tone chameleon. The windows misted as the air conditioner saturated the inside of the vehicle with the coolness of a refrigerator. Vatly tried to recall how he had gotten caught up in all this bullshit; maybe it was right from the start ...

Vatly, or Shane Vatly Muster, was born in East St. Louis. His life was a make-up of unhappy times with short glimpses of happiness, he felt as though he was in a constant state of recovery. He was the product of an interracial marriage; his father was black and his mother was white. His mother was raped and killed when he was seven, and his father, who was already a drunkard and abusive, became even more volatile. He beat Vatly for hours sometimes with a water hose, extension cord, fishing pole or whatever was handy, which caused Vatly to miss weeks of school because of bruises. His father was the type that would fall out in the front yard pissy drunk, and sometimes urinate and defecate on himself leaving Vatly to bathe and put him to bed.

Vatly was only eight at the time his father married another beautiful white woman, Sophia, ten years his junior. Things got better for a while, but he would still come home and beat Vatly like a drum major when the alcohol gripped him. Sophia, his step mom, would try to intervene but when that failed, she would console him afterwards. At thirty-three, Vatly's father was diagnosed with prostate cancer and cirrhosis of the liver. Vatly wasn't quite sure what to feel, relief or anguish, regardless of the facts that be, it was still his father, the only one he knew. With this new revelation his father stayed away from home even more, but when he was home, he was drunk and asleep. Sometime after his fourteenth birthday, Sophia started changing.

He would come home and she would be cooking in just a t-shirt and panties, walking around the house in sheer nightgowns and teddies. She would come home from work and undress right in front of him, while asking about his day at school. Vatly would try not to stare, but she was young and beautiful.

Not long after turning fourteen his father beat him into un-consciousness, and there was no rhyme or reason for it. When he awoke, he was in his bed with Sophia by his side and her warm body wrapped around him. Every night, she would come lay with him and make him talk about everything. She would lay in front of him scooting her butt right into his groin area and he would wrap his arms around her while she talked about her childhood, her mother, losing her first tooth, her first bicycle and boyfriend. At first, she would come in wearing a flimsy nightgown, then only panties. Her breast would mesmerize him giving him an erection that she completely ignored.

On his fifteenth birthday, she gave him a party that all of his friends were invited to. It was nice and memorable. She gave him more than he could imagine. About two the next morning his bed rocked, shifted and squeaked, as Sophia climbed into his cipher, she was naked. Without hesitation she pulled down his shorts and wished him a happy birthday. She loved his chest, stomach and took his penis into her mouth. When she came up, she kissed him on the mouth, brought his hands to her breast and straddled him. Vatly felt himself inside of her body, she was warm, tight and wet. She gyrated and undulated her hips vigorously; the sensation grew, she moaned, and the bed shook with such force that he thought it was going to break. Vatly then felt his seed erupt and surge into her.

Slumping over she fell asleep on top of him with his member still inside of her. This continued for about three months. He asked her to leave with him but she refused, then she informed him that she was pregnant. She tried to convince him that his father would believe it was his; he stayed too drunk to believe anything else. Afraid and paranoid of his father, Vatly packed his stuff and that night walked into his father's room at one in the morning, Sophia was on the right side and his father on the left. Sliding in behind Sophia he pulled her nightgown up to her hips, and Sophia shifted, Vatly placed his hand over her mouth and slid inside of her disregarding the loud snorts of his father. Removing his hand from her mouth, she lifted her leg to give him better access to her awaiting mound of glory. His dad snored on, and didn't even move. When Vatly was finished, he kissed her on the back of the neck and left.

He boarded a cargo train and fell asleep. When he woke up, he was in Louisiana, fifteen, broke, hungry and homeless. The first person Vatly ran into was Pebbles. Pebbles picked him up on the side of the road. A six-foot-two, two hundred- and twenty-five-pound transsexual, with 38C breasts and the plumbing down stairs still intact. He ... she was slightly attractive in that Jerry Springer's I really couldn't tell it was a man kind-of-away. She clothed, housed and fed him.

When he was seventeen, they kidnaped a baby girl from a gro-cery store parking lot, more correctly stated, she kidnapped the little girl. He just stood by and watched dumbfounded. She got fifty thousand dollars for the baby girl and they split the money down the middle. They celebrated and partied, then Pebbles in-troduced him to his first shot of 'b-ussy.' Months went by and he was content with having sex with Pebbles; as long as he was batting and not catching. One night after too much to drink, Peb-bles flipped the script on him. They fought, but Vatly was no match for Pebbles; he was too big and strong. Vatly was knocked unconscious; when he awoke, he was sore all over and barely able to move. Vatly remembered sitting in the shower with a bottle of Hennessy crying like a bitch. The liquor, Tylenol and Valiums numbed the physical pain, but the emotional embarrassment was too sharp to be dulled by anything but time. He was still drinking in the dark when Pebbles returned, she had all kinds of gifts. She turned on the light only to see Vatly sitting there in all black, gloves on and a chrome forty-five in his hand.

"You just thought you were going to bitch me huh?" Vatly asked viciously.

Pebbles trembled and in his overly feminine voice said, "No, daddy ... I had too much, too much weed. Too much alcohol. Please forgive me?"

Vatly gave a sardonic laugh, "Bitch, your ass is dead. Go ahead and run, I won't mind shooting you in the back."

"Vatly, please," Pebbles begged and fell to his knees crying, "I'm so sorry baby."

"I'm going to let you tell it to God, maybe he'll forgive." Vatly pulled the trigger. The forty-five released three deafening barks into the night. Two bullets ripped through Pebbles chest, the third was a facial shot that scattered scull fragments across the room.

Vatly was spreading gasoline all over the house, when a huge white male and short Vietnamese stepped into the living room. Vatly sensed someone in the room and spun around pointing the forty-five at them.

The huge white male had already drawn a three-eighty. "Calm down kid."

"Who the fuck are you?" Vatly asked. The large white man continued to point his pistol at Vatly.

The short one spoke, "I'm Victor Pierce. Pebbles asked me here to meet a friend of hers, which I presume is you or was you." Their eyes both went to what was left of Pebbles on the floor. "However, it seems as though Pebbles ran into some breathing complications. Are you Vatly?"

"Yeah, I'm Vatly."

"Vatly, Paul and I are going to go. I suggest you complete your task at hand." Victor glanced at his watch. "And come with us."

Two-fifteen in the morning, he looked intently at the piece of paper in his hand. 447-227 Apt. #316, twirling the bronze key over and over in his hand, a tap on his window startled him. He looked up and hit the power window. It silently descended.

A mulatto sister leaned into the window with long hair, skinny and wearing cheap perfume. Music vibrated from the club. "Hey baby, you looking for some action?" she said. Vatly shook his head, slowly and deliberately. "I'm just trying to get me a bump. I'll polish ya shit for a little of nothing," she stated.

Vatly's voice was barely audible when he said, "Miss me with the bullshit." Then Daphane walked out of the club sashaying seductively toward a teal green Beamer. The alarm chirped as her keys jingled. The interior light from the car illuminated her features. Vatly thought, damn she's beautiful. The engine purred to life and the lights came on. She backed out and headed towards the exit. He had the address and the gate code. No rush, he needed to know the time she left. No rush, he thought to himself, again. He would give her time to get settled in.

The only reason Vail wanted off the plane before takeoff was because he loved his little girl, He had been there when Daphane gave birth to her, and he was the second person to hold her. He had named her after his grandmother, Iyanna Abiyah Akbar. She was an Akbar and he was going to stay down and protect her. Plus, he was raised better than that.

"Excuse me sir, where are you going?" the airplane attendant asked. He bumped her aside and charged for the exit before they closed the door. Another attendant stood adamantly in the doorway.

"Excuse me sir." He smelled her perfume, it was poison; the same that Daphane wore, and it hit him hard, made him feel sick.

"Look lady, I gotta get off this plane," Vail shot out.

"What's the problem sir?" attendant number one asked. He looked at her name tag; it read Daphanie. Vail shook his head, certain that he was tripping. Attendant number two's perfume assaulted him again.

"Sir ... Sir ... Sir ..." Vail jumped up out of his sleep. Some fat lady was shaking him.

"Sir, last call for flight 213 to Virginia." Vail looked at his watch, it read 2:15 in the morning. He rubbed his eyes and wiped his face. The intercom announced last call for flight 213 to Virginia. With great urgency he rushed to the payphone, and dialed Daphane's number, three rings and a sweet, "Hello," chimed in.

"Daphane, it's me. Get the baby ..."

"Ha! Ha! Ha! Fooled ya huh? Well, knuckle heads and knuckles.

The Daph' s not home right ..." Vail hung up the phone.

Digging into his pocket for his keys Vail raced toward the parking lot, after locating his white Jeep Cherokee, he remembered he had left his luggage. "Fuck it!" His mind was racing as he drove, nothing but the hum of the car broke the silence and interrupted his thoughts. The police, his parents, the prospect of not being able to play pro basketball. "Fuck it all," he murmured to himself. You never truly understand the significance of a child and what they mean to you until you've experienced it yourself.

Vail understood, after the bright lights and shiny things ceased to amaze and impress him, Iyanna would still make him smile. Dad would be upset the most, he knew his mom would fall in love with Iyanna. Key-Key, his girl back home ... the thought lingered in limbo, then got dismissed. Shit, Daphane, wasn't bad, she was beautiful and fine but so damn scandalous. The last thought made him smile and shake his head. By the time he reached the exit, that would take him to Daphane's apartment it was 3:25. He still had about twenty minutes before he was at her doorstep.
***

Showered and refreshed, Daphane was laying down when 3:25 rolled around. She contemplated on calling Vail at home in Virginia, but he had asked her not to do that, he would call her. She had checked her messages and to her surprise he had already called. The phone rang before she could return his call. "Hello." Her sensual voice poured into the receiver of the phone.

"Hey Daph, this is Biron. You got a minute?"

"Biron, didn't I ask you to quit calling me? Take care of your wife and kids. It was fun while it lasted, but it's dead. Been dead for a while now."

"We need to talk Daph. I'm in love with you, and I've invested too much in you. What are you doing tomorrow?"

"None'ya Biron, non'ya damn business. Damn, I'm trying to be nice. Please don't make me get ignorant."

"I've spent almost fifteen thousand dollars on your ass, and I can't get 15 or 20 minutes of your time just to talk."

"I'm not your mistress anymore, or your secret fuck toy. You got fifteen thousand dollars' worth of pussy; you had your fun. I just got fucked and used. It's over, take care of your kids."

"I love you Daphane. I'll do anything for you," he cried into the phone.

"Okay, buy a vowel and put an 'E' on the B-Y-." She hung up the phone. Niggas and flies, was Daphane's thought while dialing Vail's number. It went straight to voice mail.

Vatly was in the house, and his watch read 3:40 a. m. The girl seemed to have dozed off. He stood over the baby girl and picked up his cell phone as he peered down into the crib and dialed a number. It was answered on the first ring.

"Go," Vatly said, and hung up the phone. He leaned over and lifted the infant from the crib, she didn't make a sound. Piece of cake, he thought to himself. The apartment was dark, except for a fish tank in the living room that gave off a dim light. Still quiet, he headed for the door, when BOOM! BOOM! BOOM! The baby jumped, and he rocked her whispering, "Na na baby, don't cry." He stepped back into the shadows of the bathroom. From the bathroom he could see her bedroom and the living room. Vatly eased his forty- five out with a silencer attached, while rocking the baby in the other arm. Daphane's light came on.

"Hold the fuck up!" Daphane yelled. "This better be good." Vatly watched her crawl out of bed in a tank top t-shirt and some bikini panties.

"Damn, that girl isn't a joke," Vatly murmured under his breath.

She jumped into some sweat pants, and walked toward the door. "Who is it?"

"It's me Daph." Her whole demeanor changed, and she opened the door.

"Where's your key baby?" Daphane asked. She hugged him, and standing on her tip-toes, pulled him to her lips.

"I lost ... uh, I mean someone stole my luggage at the airport. How's Iyanna?"

"She's asleep. Ooh baby, I'm glad you're here. I'm a little in need of some T.L.C." Vail looked around nervously.

"Daph. let's go to my place okay. Get Iyanna and let's bail."

"What's wrong?" she asked.

"My place is more private, that's all."

"Okay." They walked to Iyanna's room, right past Vatly, hiding in the shadows. He wasted no time, after they passed him. If they would have turned around, they would have seen him walk out the front door.

When she turned on the light and noticed the empty crib, she screamed. Vail's heart dropped and he spun around and saw the front door standing wide open. Did they leave it open? He couldn't remember. Something caught the light and twinkled about three feet from him and he bent over to pick it up. It was his key. Daphane was still yelling and screaming when Vail tried to grab her, but she broke loose and ran out the front door yelling. Lights came on from everywhere, and people came outside. Vail was still trying to comfort and hold Daphane but she was beyond being comforted.

"My baby Vail, find my baby! My babeeee," she wailed and then fainted.

Vatly drove out of the gates, while the auburn haired beauty held the baby. On West Belfort; several police cars passed them. Vatly was non-committal; neither happy nor sad. Just a paycheck, he told himself with no emotions.

The maintenance man was peeping through Hadie Finley's bedroom window watching her and her husband have sex, while he masturbated. The scream damn near gave him a heart attack. He tucked his equipment away and was headed back to his apartment when the black BMW shot past him and stopped at the gate. For some reason he had the presence of mind to write down the license plate number.

CHAPTER 10

Black folks hated calling the police no matter how rich, how respectable, how sanctified, moral and astute they were. Hated to call our own mothers, fathers, brothers, sisters, sons and daughters if they worked for the law. The antiquities of the soul's feelings were so deeply rooted in the psyche; whether real or imaginary, they existed. The law scrutinized and suspected even the victims. They just made you feel like you would get a ticket for using the wrong vernacular. They would place you under a microscope to see if you took your antibiotics for being black.

Vail called the police anyway. Someone must have called before him, because they got there too damn quick. He was sweaty, fidgety and paranoid. Lights flashed and radios squawked. It was a melee of confusion as the spectator's jockeyed for position. Daphane was awake, crying and holding on to Vail like he was a last chance coupon to get admittance to heaven.

"My baby Vail, Where's my baby?" She was utterly distraught; this was crushing to him because there was no escaping the role he had played in all of this. His guilt was a sea monster devouring him whole, a bucket of acid that ate away his existence piecemeal. It was the type of canyon that you just can't get around and without wings he wasn't going to be able to fly over it. It was the type of thing where you had to wait for someone to construct a bridge, and ...

"Daph baby, we'll get her back, I promise. We'll get her back." Two Houston Police Department officers went through the standard idiom. Everything was routine, standard procedure; no emotions.

Shortly afterwards, a huge man in plain clothes approached them. He introduced himself as Detective Puckett.

"Hey kids, I just want to ask you all a few questions." He stared hard at Vail, like he was trying to remember something, and then glanced back at the notebook and mouthed the name Vail Akbar, then his eyes lit up. "Hey, you're U of H's shooting guard, right?"

Vail gave a halfhearted smile. "Yeah, that's me." "Was she your daughter?" Puckett held a photo.

"Yeah, she's my baby girl." A neighbor had given Daphane some Valiums, a nerve relaxer or something. It was working now; Vail excused himself to put her to bed. When he re-entered the living room, Officer Puckett was checking out all the pictures hanging on the wall. He stopped at a picture of Vail and Daphane. Her hair was dyed blond on the ends in a finger wave.

"She's a beautiful girl. Ya'll planning on tying the knot?"

"Never really discussed it," Vail replied. "Detective, can I get you something to drink?"

"Yes, what do you have?"

Vail looked in Daphane's refrigerator, and then looked back at Puckett. "Well, let's see here." He held up an old clear gallon milk container with some clear liquid in it. "Water?" he smiled.

Puckett grinned and nodded his head, "That's cool."

Vail liked what he saw in Officer Puckett's eyes. Plus, he knew the only way he would find Iyanna was by being straight up.

"Detective Puckett," he began shakily, but gaining strength with every word. "I gotta trust you, if I expect to get my baby back. No one knows what I'm about to tell you. I may have to serve some time my damn self, but you have to promise me you'll get my baby back." Vail told him everything, as to how the man approached him, offered him money, and that he refused. The police officer framing and arresting him, although he could not remember the police officer's name. He told him about the visit, and described the man. His knowledge of everything about him; the threats about the murder and drug charges. All he wanted was the gate code and alarm code, then all the charges were dropped. Puckett listened intently, took a few notes. It was 4:41 in the morning when they finally ended their conversation.

"Vail, I'm going to do what I can. I appreciate your honesty. They put you between a rock and a hard spot. I only fault you in hesitating to get here. I've been looking for some type of crack in this case; you've given me a lot of insight. Help me, I'll help you, and when you go to the pros, send me a ticket sometimes." Puckett extended his hand, and Vail shook it.

"That's a bet."

"I'm going to run down that arrest record, find out who the arresting officer was and your visitor." After Puckett left, Vail locked the door and called his parents and explained to them about Daphane and his daughter being kidnapped. He left out all that other stuff, and just explained that he was comforting his baby's mama. Last thing he did was say a prayer, and then got into bed beside Daphane. He held her tight, and he found comfort in her warmth.

Victor thought that he'd sell his off-spring for the bright lights and shiny things. He had gotten comfortable and careless, and let Vail see his face. That was his second mistake; his first, was misjudging Vail's character. Money wasn't everything to everyone. Some black men had gained a little more consciousness, things had changed, and he cursed himself for hesitating.

CHAPTER 11

Living in the ghetto around dilapidated buildings, and misguided adolescence, you can hear the music. All you have to do is listen and you can hear it. The streets will sing to you a song so beautiful that it's difficult to ignore. The birds chirp a different song in the daytime and some nights, the vociferous crickets hit poignant notes that's undaunted by the wail of sirens, drum of a helicopter or explosion of gun fire. It's understood, that they are all different instruments orchestrated with uncanny precision in the same symphony. On nights like these, even the mosquitos won't bite. They just sit on your skin and listen. It's all volatile, yet tacit to all in attendance. Everyone just listens to the enchantment of Ghetto Romance. Kids with the wicked jump shots witness these things in all its splendor, it's where their magic comes from.

The crack sizzled as it melted on the stained-glass pipe. Nellie looked around slightly paranoid, before she leaned the pipe sideways and flicked the lighter back and forth over the stem of the pipe. The flame licked hungrily at the glass concoction. Her eyes widened like silver dollars as she watched the bowl fill with white smoke, inhaling deeply, she held her nose to push the smoke to her brain for the purpose of maximizing the euphoric feeling that was coming upon her. It gripped and held her momentarily. Hastily, she rose and paced to the window, looked out, and then back to the table. The plate she had been using was now empty, still she slid her index finger across the plate in search of any crumbs, powder or dust that would aid and assist in elevating and sustaining her high. It was 8:45 in the morning. Bernadine had left forty minutes ago. Xavier was on the roof again. it was his ritual. He was so distant lately. Nellie knew her drug addiction hurt her oldest child. She vividly recalled a stashed away memory, it was hidden well, locked up in the deep recesses of her mind. Nellie grabbed it for a second, then a minute, it made her smile. Before cocaine, things were different, good. Xavier was born in the late July blistering heat, even the birds were catching heat strokes. Nellie had just turned fifteen and was determined to keep the baby no matter what. Being the third child of five, it was difficult to find solace and peace. She was neither fast nor promiscuous, it was just one man, one time. God had already laid the foundation; Xavier was destined to be born. Nellie never truly blamed her mom, she had to work, had to provide; no ifs, ands or buts about it. She wasn't blessed with the luxury of monitoring her children twenty-four seven. The love was there, some days so thick that you could view it, put it in a jar and save it for a rainy day. After she conceived Xavier, felt him begin to grow inside of her, eat from her, drink from her, live with and through her, she became more tranquil. Sometimes, the one thing in life that will give us peace is the life you contribute to bringing it into existence. She would rub her swollen belly, talking to her unborn child and express her goals, fantasies and fears. For once in her life, she had something, someone to love her unconditionally. She couldn't outgrow him and be forced to give him away. Nellie's mother was furious with her at first, but soon conceded and supported her. That's what some mama's do; accept the things they cannot change; concede and support.

He was seven pounds, four ounces, dark as midnight and simply beautiful; they grew together. Nellie held down solid productive jobs, but nothing was as lucrative as the game. So, she abandoned the nine-to-fives and sold weed and sherm before the introduction of crack cocaine dropped on black communities like Hiroshima. Where do the good times go, when they are gone? It would be something God could be questioned about some day; it's a valid question. Once, she fell short, everyone kind of abandoned her except Rhonda, Nellie's oldest sister, pretty even keel as well. She could probably teach Solomon a thing or two. When Nellie's mom passed away, the pin came out of the wheel. She was the fulcrum, the centrifugal force. Looking down from the heavens, Nellie knew it was hurting her mama to see how her children had forgotten the most important lesson she tried to relay; the importance of family. She'll probably spank all of them, when and if they get there, for forgetting what was supposed to be remembered ... where you come from.

Xavier loved her, this she acknowledged. He had given and taken plenty of ass whippings on her behalf. However, her capricious behavior had made him distant. His first priority now was Vianna. Nellie was gonna quit smoking, she told herself again. The door opened and Xavier walked in.

"Mornin' mama." He spoke without making eye contact.

"Mornin' baby. You hungry? I could whip you and Vi up something."

"Nah, I'm cool. Where's Bernadine?" Xavier inquired. "She left, went to go talk to a lawyer about K-nine." Xavier switched stations. "Step hasn't written?"

"Nah, I haven't heard from him."

"Did you shoot him the money I gave you?"

She dropped her head and he knew right away, that it wasn't a good sign.

"Mama," he continued, "I try to trust you a little. He's your brother and he's on lock. You could have sent him something, its hell being broke in the penitentiary."

"Something came up Xavier, I needed the money for something." "Don't sweat it, it's on me. You're selfish though."

"Xavier," she called, as he headed for his room. "Xavier!"

He turned around and threw his chin and hands in the air with a frown etched into his face. "Wha' sup?"

"I'm sorry baby," Nellie stated in an apologetic voice.

"Yeah, don't sweat it." He went into his room to shower and get dressed. He had sent a separate hundred-dollar money order the day he gave her the money; he was nobody's fool. However, it saddened him to deliberately give her money to send up in smoke just to keep her from turning tricks. He couldn't just say "here, go buy you some dope." Nawl, he couldn't pop it like that. So at least once a week he gave her grocery money, utility bill money and phone bill money. If the ends justified the means, then it suited him. She stayed close to home, didn't turn tricks, and to his knowledge never had. He never intended to put her in a situation where she was desperate. He'd like to believe she would never stoop that low, but crack cocaine was a rogue element of astronomical proportions. He peeked inside Vianna's room; she was sprawled awkwardly on her bed sound asleep.

"Vi, get ya narrow butt up if you're coming with me." She rolled over and looked at him. "Lookout pip squeak," he called. "Wash your face, brush ya grill and let's· get ready to bounce." Vianna rose up and was rubbing her eyes.

"Zav-va, I'm hone-ree. Can I hav som pop tarts?"

"Yeah, yeah, yeah. I bought you some new clothes and tennis shoes, check'em out." He closed her door and left to handle up.

"Mama, you like my new clothes?" Vi was asking. She had on a sundress with black leggings and expensive white sandals. On her little baby body, it was cute. A Houston Rockets cap was cocked ace- deuce and her pony tails and barrettes stuck out of the sides. She wolfed down her pop tarts and O.J., and they were ready to go.

"Where you headed Xavier?" Nellie asked.

"I'm going to scoop up Shai, maybe mall hop and parley for a couple of hours. Then I was gonna swing back through and let her meet you if time don't run short on me."

"Take care of my baby."

Instead of Xavier answering, Vianna did. "I'm gon take care of him mama." She grabbed his hand and dragged him out the door.

It was a beautiful day out; the sun was making a bold statement to all who questioned his dominion over the day. It was June seventeenth, the trees and flowers competed for attention by brilliantly displaying all colors in the spectrum. Even the birds were feeling daring; they were landing extremely close and even observed curiously for several seconds. Chill and Aaron had started a domino game out front that had drawn a helluva fan club, people gathered eagerly around the table to watch. Chill and Aaron were playing Clue and Stank, from where Xavier stood, he heard Clue shout.

"Three lil girls from New Orleans, two wearin' dresses, one wearing jeans. Dats fifdeen!"

"Same thang he took, you thank I'm lying. Take a look!" Aaron started.

"Tint the windows on that truck. I told Clue; I was in there tryin' to fuck!" Chill growled.

Then Stank's scratchy voice fell into play, "Tender loins ... beef steak ... and gravy."

The table fell silent for a few, then Clue crunk it up again. "Bolts and screws make a bicycle move."

Aaron was right there and screamed, "Hit rocks, I swear dey is. Bolt da doors, there's a thief in the house."

Another silence, then Stank dominoed with five. "Fifth Ward, Texas, a bunch Negroes and a few Mexicans." Laughter erupted from the table as someone washed the dishes. Xavier and Vianna had reached the bottom of the stairs. His alarm chirped as he un-locked the passenger side door on his Chrysler. Without warning the heat jumped out and caught him and Vi with Muhammad Ali, and Roy Jones Jr's, two piece. It was still jumping around capping and boasting, it was the baddest when they recovered. Deshawn stepped from her apartment wearing an emerald green Nike spandex body suit that looked poured on. All erogenous parts of her body were visibly standing out. Deshawn was twen-ty-six, everyone except Xavier called her Honey. First, because of her complexion, second because honey is the sweetest natural substance known to man. Deshawn ran a close race, sometimes the bees got confused. If Hugh Hefner saw her, he'd break his damn neck trying to sign her, even from the grave. She floated over to Xavier, taking in the scene, then nailed him with those beautiful hazel eyes.

"Hey X, how's it hangin'?" She looked him over. He had on red and white True Religion shorts and shirt. Red and White Jor-dan's and a Houston Rocket's cap. A nugget earring in each ear and a diamond in the left. Gold Rolex watch, Rolex necklace. He was clean to the bone. Unbeknownst to many, Honey was in her last year of Medical School, and was about to begin her residency at Herman Hospital. She was ghetto fabulous, but not ghetto stranded.

"He's hangin' to the left." Xavier smiled. Honey was only 4'11" which added to her appeal.

"When are you going to let me test drive your vehicle?" she asked seductively, while she rubbed the car but stared between his legs, then walking her eyes up his torso to finally make eye contact.

Xavier smiled, then adjusted his cap, "Deshawn, it's a danger-ous ride, bad breaks, suspension's shot, and the alignment is off. It kinda pulls to the left, and I don't want you to wreck me or yourself before you get your Ph.D."

"That's sweet of you, but I'm willing to take my chances." She glanced over his shoulder, which made him turn around, quickly jarring his memory. She had been dating this Crip named Solo, he was stupid. Xavier was afraid of no man, he was always careful, an ounce of prevention was better than a pound of a cure.

Honey said, "I forgot you're just a baby. Maybe you're not ready to handle a real woman. Maybe I intimidate you, you're always so calm, so cool, I thought maybe ..." She put her hands on her hips and looked him dead in the eyes. "... maybe you could handle the girls ..." Her eyes went to her breast and jutting nipples, "... and mama." Her eyes fell between her legs, as she placed emphasis on mama. Xavier could testify that Deshawn's Bermuda triangle was looking fatter than a government check, threatening to lose anyone who ventured near it. The offer was almost irresistible, almost. 'Ounce of prevention ...'

"Deshawn, I'll have to kill that nigga of yours. No matter how much my little head says go, my big head is saying no. I'm not quite ready to kill or be killed for a piece of ass, no matter how good it is. Maybe if the circumstances were different."

She smiled, and respected that or so it seemed; with women one could never tell.

"I have to go, X. You're right, that's why I cut for you, you're always in control. Any other nigga would have jumped. Fuck the wife, kids and consequences." She turned and walked away from him. When she reached her door, she turned with a mischievous grin on her face.

"It was hard though, wasn't it ...?" She paused. Xavier looked amused. She continued, "... your decision?"

Simultaneously, he nodded, smiled and said, "Very."

She tapped her butt, "It's always yours." Then she disappeared into the house.

Xavier sat inside the car with Vianna and turned on the music. A blue GMC truck pulled up, bumping UGK a little harder than his Kevin Gates. Solo was driving, six thugs were in the back of the truck, the horn sounded and Deshawn came out wearing a yellow sundress and sandals. When she passed him, they shared a quick knowing glance at each other.

"Vi, baby, you ready to roll?" She nodded her head talking to her imaginary friend on his cell phone. Vianna was exuberantly loquacious on the ride to Shai's place. She had a million and one questions, yadda, yadda, yadda. Xavier tried to feed her mind. He didn't neglect her inquiries, he answered them, or tried to, navigating the car expertly through the morning traffic of 288 wasn't extremely busy. He applied pressure to the accelerator and the car lurched forward. The speedometer climbed, 55 ... 65 ... 75 ... John Legend serenaded them through the speakers. Vianna was hypnotized by the scenery as they whizzed through traffic, and his mind was a constant influx of images. He exited Clinton Drive off of the 610 Loop, then rode down Fidelity and made a right on Bolden. Taking Bolden to Bank Drive, then off of Bank to 7th street, Shai's crib was the fourth house from Bank Drive. Vianna removed John legend and put in Megan Trainer. Her CD lyrics spilt into the car just as Xavier killed the engine. Another car entering the driveway caught Xavier's attention. A light skinned brother exited the vehicle. same height and build as Xavier.

He nodded his head and spoke. He was polite. "What's up, bro- man?"

Xavier nodded, no smile, just a nod. "Devin." He extended his hand.

"Xavier." They shook hands. Devin was about to say something when a black Nissan truck pulled up sitting on triple gold Dayton's. The words Calvin Mack air brushed on the sides. Something like eighteens pushing Gucci Mane. Xavier looked at his watch, 10:30. He thought to himself, if anyone else drives up, I'm leaving. The loud music from Calvin's truck brought Shai out, she made a frantic motion with her hand and Calvin killed his engine and the loud music also.

Shai said through her teeth, "I've told you about that shit!" Then did a complete 180. "Hi, D, what's up, X, Hey, Vi." She hugged Devin then Xavier, quickly introducing Devin as her cousin from Louisiana.

"Lookout Shai, let me holler at you." That was Calvin.

She shot him a look that could have melted Superman. "Hold up boy! Xavier give me a few minutes, please." She went from she- demon to Nubian princess in the blink of an eye. Her tone of voice was sugar sweet, cotton soft; very feminine and alluring.

"Nathan and I are ready. El fooley-o don't want anything."

Devin invited X and Vianna inside. Fifteen minutes later Shai came in looking agitated as hell.

"Whew!" Negros can be the most bothersome creatures on the planet."

"You look sexy when you're upset." That was Xavier.

Shai ran her fingers through her hair and sighed heavily. "Flattery will get you everywhere."

"I'm banking on that." He smiled.

"Oh, were you now?" She ran her tongue over her lips, then bit down on the bottom lip.

"Y'all· must go to school for that," Xavier said, then imitated her. They both laughed. She looked good in an off-white Guess jumper with black muscle shirt underneath; her earrings, lipstick, belt and sandals were a blackberry color.

"You ready to jet?"

"Been ready, I started to leave ya ass," Xavier said sardonically.

"Now, I know you're just talking. You've been watching this ass ..." She turned and pointed. "... too hard to leave it anywhere."

"I've been watching it because it's funny shaped." He smiled.

She slapped him on the shoulder.

Vianna had seen enough. "Let go, Zav-ya."

"Nathan!" Shai called. "I'm finta go, boy."

Fifteen minutes into the drive, Shai asked, "Where are we headed?"

"I was going to take you by the clubhouse, then maybe mall hopping. After that, I was gonna take you to meet my t-lady."

"So, you're one of those Muslims?"

"No."

"You're a Christian?"

"Nope."

"You're one of those satanic worshipping brothas, are you?"

"Last time I checked I wasn't."

"So, what are you then, Xavier?" Shai asked in a mildly exasperated tone. Xavier looked straight ahead. Mary J. Blige husky voice filled the void of silence.

He said, "I'm searching."

She looked at him waiting on him to continue. When she saw he had no intention of pressing forward she asked, "Searching for what, religion?"

"Nah, searching for God, the truth, been lied to so much, just trying to sort out the truth from the lies." Shai's attention was stolen by Nathan jumping up and down in the backseat. Shai shot him one of her she-demon looks.

"Boy, sit yo' ass down before I tear it off the bone." Nathan sunk into the seat; his eyes misted; she hurt his feelings. It was a beautiful day and Shai was looking out of the window when her thoughts were interrupted by Vianna's sweet voice singing along with Future and Kelly Rowland's "Never End."

CHAPTER 12

Bug eye and Gus were from Detroit. At least that's what they told everyone, we believed them. A brother really didn't have the ends to be hiring private investigators and running background checks. They talked like they were from Detroit, walked like they were from Detroit, even looked like black men that could be from Detroit. So ...

They had told tall tales in a short period of time. Distributed priceless wisdom camouflaged in humor and little white lies. Every ghetto had characters that fit this profile. That's how life writes its story. Everything must be in its proper place. All characters accounted for; life makes sense of itself that way. Bug eye earned the nickname honestly. He was five feet tall with a slim wiry frame pushing fifty-two. He told everyone that he and Redd Foxx were third cousins. They resembled each other in no way, fashion or form. Gus was a six-foot paper sack brown, pretty boy. They capped about the infamous stunts and cons they played and perfected on the Detroit strip. Popping trunks and pulling stunts since they were teenagers.

In sixty-five, they both, received draft notes for Vietnam. Bug eye opted to run, became a high power grifter and put away some serious cash. In sixty-eight, he was arrested for avoiding duty and given a choice; he could report or go to prison. Bug eye selected the penitentiary. He told them, "I'd rather be scared and alive, than brave and dead. Tell Uncle Sam to kiss my scary black ass." Gus went and looked just as out of place as any black man fighting in a white man's war. He was hit with some shrapnel in seventy and lost both his legs at the knee. Gus returned broken mentally, physically and spiritually. In seventy-two when Bug eye was released from prison, he heard about his home boy and went to his mama's house to see him. The house was abandoned. All the regulars said she had passed six months prior and Gus was placed in a Veteran Hospital. It took three months for Bug eye to find Gus. When he did, he was shocked to see Gus filthy and smelling like stale piss and cigarettes. He was disoriented with a forlorn look in his eyes. He was only twenty-five, but looked forty. Bug eye was unsure at first so he spoke slow and careful. "Hey Gus baby, don't look like you're in a healthy mood." Gus looked up from his cold cup of coffee, recognition registered in his face. Bug eye stated slowly, "Looks like you and me the same height now nigga!"

Gus looked at his legs, then his stumpy friend and smiled through dry, cracked lips, "I still look better," Gus whispered. His eyes moistened.

"I would hug ya homie but yo' ass stank fo' real."

"Convict," Gus uttered, they laughed.

"They don't bury scary men. They bury dead men, my daddy told me." Bug eye handed Gus a deck of cards. "Let me see if you're still lucky as hell."

Gus had never believed in luck, only skill. He said more animatedly, "Luck only helps a nigguh over a ditch if he jumps hard enough." He dealt the cards, although he was rusty, his skill in manipulating the cards was still sharp. Bug trained eyes watched him put the ace of spades at the bottom of the deck, show it and at the last-minute move it. The move would have gone unnoticed by the untrained eye, but this was Bug Eye! They weren't big for nothing. God had intended for him to see a black ant, on a black night, on a black rock. Bug eye checked Gus out and two months later they were headed to Houston, Texas.

When the car rounded into the Club House Apartments, or the Jail House Apartments coined Club House by Gus, kids were walking around snotty nosed and barefoot. young brothers congregated here and there. Bug eye and Gus were in a crowd of youngsta's. From what Xavier could tell, they were shootin' dice. Gus saw the silver Chrysler pull up and hollered gleefully, "Oh, oh, oh heahs my boy, heahs ah young jack with plenty of trades!" The other fellas looked and acknowledged Xavier. Some he recognized, others he did not.

"Mama, can me and Vi go play at the swings?" Nathan cried out.

Shai looked at Vi and Xavier, he nodded his head.

"Don't get dirty Nathan," she shouted after him, he was gone. Vianna stopped to give Bug eye and Gus a hug and kiss. Since Xavier chose not to acknowledge his biological father and his uncle was on lock, Gus and Bug eye had sort of filled the void, giving him that old wisdom he needed. As they exited the car, Bug eye and Gus met him, "Good to see you X. Wha' cha been up to?"

As he answered, he bent over and hugged Gus in his wheel chair. "Just been maintaining without complaining, doing a bunch of sucka duckin' and watching ghetto sunsets. What's tha deal with you two cats?"

"Just been thinking long thoughts and praying even longer prayers. Who's your shortie?" Gus asked.

"Oh, this is Shai Montgomery." He turned to Shai, "This is David Hayes, aka Bug eye." He pointed, "And Nicholas Spade, aka Gus."

She extended her hand to each. "Mr. Hayes, Mr. Spade." Gus was sipping from his beer when she said that, he choked, spit and beer went all over his lap. Bug eye laughed and so did Xavier. Shai looked perplexed.

Gus gathered himself and said, "Chile, please, just call us Gus and Bug eye." He feigned nervousness and glanced over his shoulder, "Gus" he touched his chest, "and Bug eye." He pointed at Bug eye. "Nothing but police and bill collectors use our last names. Peoples ah, lose respect fo' us theys heah you disrespect us like that." Shai was observing Bug eye's diminutive stature. He caught her studying him. He looked at her, "Don't try it honey, I ain't never been whooped by a real female. Couple of homosexuals got with my ass but never a real female." Gus and Xavier started laughing.

Shai smiled, "Mr... . I mean Bug eye, I wasn't—"

"Yeah, you was," he cut in. "I saw you sizing me up."

"You sho'·look like Halle Berry wit yo' hair like that. Them yo' eyes or store bought?" That was Gus.

"There mines, everything on me is natural," she said, addressing his eyes' bold unbashful appraisal of her breasts.

Bug eye said, "Yeah yous a purdy lil ol thang."

Gus rubbed his beard, then, "Well X, this must be the one you wanna lock up wit. Been knowing you four years, you ain't never brought a female around us. You gonna marry her?"

Xavier smiled, "Sho' nuff pops, as soon as she signs the prenuptial. All black American women are scandalous." Shai hit him on the shoulder.

"Lookout Gus and Bug, y'all gon shit or get off the pot!?" Everyone looked at this big youngsta in the center of the group. There was eight of them; the big one gave Shai more than a passing glance, Xavier ignored it. He recognized three of the eight from school; Pee-Wee; Junebug and Tweety. Kindle walked over to the group and spoke to Xavier. Kindle was Alisha's half-sister; same daddy, different mamas. The two women looked each other over, then turned their attention to the gambling.

Bug eye was on the dice, "Boy, you begged for this ass whoopin'." He rolled and caught a four. Gus bet that Bug eye would roll ten or four before he rolled seven or eleven, the bet was accepted. Bug eye romanced the dice, "Come on baby, let's go money hunting y'all!" He rolled a nine. "I ain't mad atcha, daddy needs a new pair of shoes. How they come to the pond?" He rolled, they landed on six. He held the dice up to Shai, "Blow on these for luck sweetie." Shai looked at Xavier, then Bug eye, then at everyone staring at her. "C'mon honey, your gon make me late." Shai leaned over and blew on the dice. "Oooh weee! X, you gotta call it, even if it hurts." He shook them and as he rolled, "X, how do they come to the pond?"

Xavier said, "Two by two pops." As if it were controlled by remote the dice stopped on twenty-two.

Just then some young boys started tussling. Xavier looked up; Shai had already taken off in a trot. Nathan was fighting two other boys in the complex. "Nathan," Shai yelled with Xavier right behind her. Shai yanked the two boys off her son, "You little muthafucka's, get off my baby!"

A woman yelled across the parking lot, "Bitch, don't touch my son!" Xavier recognized the voice of Baba. Her husband, Boo, and sister, Tangie, were in close pursuit.

Shai held Nathan who had tears in his eyes, no bruises, just dirty. Shai looked at the woman. "Bitch, who you calling bitch? Get your nasty ass children, that's what you do."

"Oh no! I know that bitch didn't just call you a bitch, Baba!" Tangie yelled. "Yo' high yellow ass just took a high price ass whoopin' off lay-a-way. Didn't she, Baba?"

"Damn sho' did!" Baba replied.

Xavier stepped in front of Shai, "You know, Nakia …" That was Baba's real name, "… two on one isn't fair. Big as your boys are they can handle little man one on one." This made Shai look at Xavier like he had lost his damn mind. She imagined she had only thought it, but when Xavier looked at her, she realized that he had actually said it.

The twist of the conversation made Boo step in. "Come on, X, you know my boys, either one of them can whoop that little sissy's ass."

"Well," Xavier said, "I got a hundred dollars that says he'll whoop either one of them one on one."

Shai couldn't believe what she was hearing. She turned to leave but Gus and Bug eye held her still. "What?" she asked.

"Just chill, chile. Xavier knows what he's doing," Gus said.

Boo hesitated; the older kids were placing bets on Boo's bigger son. Tyrell was about seven, a little bigger than Nathan, more ghetto raised, but it didn't mean more heart. Xavier was betting that Nathan had his mother's heart and fire.

"Alright," Boo said, "that's a bet."

Xavier turned his attention to Nathan, squatted down in front of him, looking into his eyes. He tried to determine if the look in his eyes was fear or anger. Xavier decided it was neither, just a little confusion.

Shai said, "I'm not going to let him do this Xavier."

Xavier looked at her, then turned his attention back to Nathan. "Nathan, you know how to fight?" he asked. Nathan nodded his head.

"Are you scared?"

Nathan looked at the other boy with his daddy. "No. I'm not scared of nothing, Xavier."

"That's good. Since those two dudes over there tried to double team you and I don't think it was fair, me and your mama want you to kick his butt. Can you handle that?" Nathan nodded his head. "Good. I know you can do it, Nate, he's bigger but you have a bigger heart." He touched the young man's chest. "You ready?" Nathan nodded his head again. Reluctantly Shai released his shoulders.

The boys scuffed and tussled for a good fifteen minutes. Neither gave up, neither lost. Boo and Baba in their ignorance thought it was actually about winning and losing. When two boys of that age fight who can really tell who won or lost unless one started crying and quit. Both boys were exhausted, Xavier separated the two boys, scuffed up and dirty. He walked both boys to Nakia breathing hard. He handed Nakia the hundred, smiled "Ya boy is the real deal Holyfield. Just like his t-lady." She smiled.

Xavier and Nathan walked back toward Shai. She wanted to baby her baby, but Bug eye and Gus stepped in guessing her intentions. "Lil Champ!" Bug eye shouted.

Gus fell in with Bug eye and Xavier. They play boxed and dusted him off. Xavier said, "Damn, Nathan, I didn't know you were that tough. Man, teach me a move or two." Nathan smiled. Vianna stood next to Shai. They understood it was a male thing.

After another uneventful hour they left. Shai had been quiet ever since the incident, talking sparingly. Nathan was asleep, Vianna on her way. "What's wrong, Shai?" he asked.

"Just listening to the music," she replied curtly.

The radio wasn't playing but he understood. It was one of his little idiosyncrasies. "What cha listening to?"

Shai looked at him quizzically, "What?"

"You say you're listening to the music, what song's playing?" Shai looked out of her window, "Betty Wright 'No Pain, No Gain'."

"You're upset?" Xavier asked.

"Yes, I am, Xavier, you turn my son into a gladiator to entertain and amuse your friends."

"So, you believe that was my modus operandi, huh?"

"Your what?" she asked.

"My M.O., my motive," he explained.

"Yes, some egotistical male bullshit, and I'm not with it. I'm trying to raise him better than that."

"I'm sorry that's how you took it ..." He paused. "Nathan is a little boy. Hopefully one day he'll be a little man. You babying him isn't going to do anything but make him dependent on a mother who's not going to always be there. You're not going to do anything but hurt him, and you in the long run. Shai you're a good mother, but the best thing you can do for Nathan is let him be a little boy. All little boys fight, tussle, and rough house. The ones who get pacified, spoiled and babied are on Jerry Springer and Oxygen looking prettier than you. I just did what I would have done for my own son, if I had one. I apologize if I offended you or overstepped my boundaries."

Shai glanced back at her baby sleeping contently in the back seat. Then thought on the incident and smiled as she recalled how her smaller son had held his own with the older bigger boy. "He did alright, didn't he?" she asked.

Xavier smiled. "Yeah, little man surprised me. He held his own, a future Jundillah, a young Soulja."

"It ain't easy," she said.

"That's what Tupac said," he replied.

Nathan had gotten dirty so Shai wanted to take him home, get him cleaned up. It was a little past one, the sun was still blazing, all clouds M.I.A. The plans had changed, but it was all good. They stopped by Churches Chicken to get some grub. Xavier hadn't eaten anything since last night, his stomach lurched and practiced Kungfu with his intestines. The aroma of fried chicken was doing cartwheels and half gainers. Vianna started bouncing up and down, she loved chicken. Shai was standing close to Xavier, sharing his space intimately. Vianna boldly inserted herself between the two of them. Ruby was at the checkout counter and turned her lips up and frowned. There was a freckled face boy at the register, they gave the boy their order. Ruby continued to frown at Xavier as he and Shai went to take a seat waiting for their order to get ready.

"That's the girl from the party, right?" Shai asked.

"What party?" Xavier asked.

"About five months ago."

"Damn! you really went back. Yeah, that's my Ruby."

"What did you do to her?"

"I haven't done Nathaniel to her. We've gone to school together since Pre-K. She has never said a word to me. We've never liked each other. We've had at least one class together since Pre-k and she just can't stand me." Their number was called, Xavier got up to get it.

Ruby handed him the trays. "I hope you choke," Ruby stated venomously.

"If I do, you better trip on your breath, break your neck and beat me to hell," Xavier retorted.

"If I was a man, I'd kick ya ass," Ruby shot at him.

"Yeah, yeah and if you had a radio in ya ass we'd hear music every time you farted?" Xavier grabbed their tray and left her standing there. When he returned, Shai was staring out the window, lost in her own thoughts. "Can I come in?"

"Huh?" she asked.

"Just want to come inside whatever world you had drifted off to." She smiled; her eyes sparkled. They started eating, Vianna and Nathan argued over certain pieces of chicken. "Where's your father, Xavier?"

"I don't know, he never looked for me, so I never looked for him. We have an understanding, an unspoken contract."

"You not knowing him doesn't bother you?"

"Nah, I have too many other things on my mind to be worried about that."

Her eyes misted. "My daddy was killed by some police officer in L.A. for nothing. In the newspaper they spelled his name wrong, called him Nate, his name was Nathan." Her son looked up at hearing the name. "Some days I really miss him."

Xavier grabbed her hand, "I'm sorry to hear that Shai." His phone went off, he looked at the number, ignored it and ate some more chicken.

"Xavier, what do you do?"

He hesitated for a second. "Work for this Oriental Store owner, why?"

"Your seventeen, new car, Rolex watch, Rolex necklace, always clean. Just makes a girl wonder." She trailed off, then, "Wonder what she's getting into."

"What, are we getting into Shai? I'm still trying to understand last night. Was that it or will there be more later on? Where do I fit in, if I fit in at all?"

Xavier knew he was in love with Shai, had been for almost two months. He didn't want to push though. He thought she loved Calvin but last night had reopened that optimistic window in his heart. "I think you'd be good for me ..." She looked out the window speaking softly, "... good to me. I just have to deal with

Nathan's father, our relationship has been dead. He's always using my, our son, as a reason to see me. That'll get old to whoever I'm involved with, you know."

"Calvin is his daddy." He rubbed her arms.

"Yes, no matter how much I want him to go away he won't. As long as he chooses to participate in Nathan's life, he'll be a thorn in my side." Xavier nodded his understanding.

Women really got the rawest deal in life. The double standard, the forced responsibility. They had babies before they were ready, forced to nurse them. To get emotionally involved with something growing inside of you is tacit. If you reject it, you're a cold heartless bitch. If you give it up for adoption, you go through life counting birthdays of a baby you will never see, always remembering. You keep it, you are a single mom, no win. Men just drop sperm like heat seeking missiles altering and changing other people's lives, their reality, and just walking away free to change another life within the next twenty-four hours. There are no repercussions for most men, just new faces and new doorways. Animals show more responsible behavior than most civilized human males.

They left Churches and took Nathan home. Xavier, Shai, and Vianna talked all the way to his crib. As he turned off of Scott onto Southmore street, a Metro bus rumbled past them. Turning into the big open driveway of Southmore Apartments he noticed that everyone was in full force. Lil' Chill, Aaron and Dink stood against the back wall in the shade, drinking and smoking. Kids ran here and there. Solo's truck was parked in Xavier's normal parking space, so he parked directly in front of Deshawn's house. When he exited the car, he noticed Prophet standing in front of his crib with Ke-Ke.

"X, you wanna go ball at McGregor?" Prophet asked.

"Got damn, X-man, is this you?" Lil Chill had slid up on the side of Shai. Shai smiled at him; Aaron had also seen her get out of the car.

"Excuse me lil mama, is this ya man? Cuz if not."

Xavier cut him off, "I'ma 'bout to test you niggas boxing game." Aaron threw his hands in the air in surrender.

"Down, Butch! Down, Boy!" Shai laughed, Lil Chill shouted, "Boy, I'm ah giant killer!" He started shadow boxing the air, from the looks of things he was winning.

Prophet had descended the stairs extending his hand to Shai, "How you doing?" he said. "I'm Prophet, Xavier's cousin and future NBA Star."

Shai remembered him. She shook his hand, replying smartly, "Shai, Xavier's friend, mother of one, junior in college, business major."

Prophet looked at Xavier, "I like her cuz."

"Yeah, she's my potna!" That was Xavier. "Shai this is Aaron and Chill." She shook their hands but Lil Chill wouldn't let her hand go. "Damn your hands are soft, Shai. The way you look I needs a potna like you."

"When you turn twenty-one, give a girl ah ring," Shai said coyly.

"This heahs the New Millennium, I can arrange to be twenty-one tomorrow if it's convenient for you." Again, Shai smiled.

Solo came out of Deshawn's apartment and slammed the door. Since they were in front of Deshawn's pad Solo came right past Chill and rudely shoved past him, knocking Lil Chill into Shai. Chill spun around speaking before he had a chance to see who had shoved him. "Better watch that shit man!"

Solo spun around, "What you say, little nigga. Fuck you!"

Chill's pride wouldn't let him back down. "Nah, hook ass nigga, fuck with me."

Solo went at Lil Chill, Dink who was standing on the wall went at Solo. "Don't fuck with my little brother, homie," Dink said.

"I'll fuck with you," Solo shot out.

"I can't say whatcha ain't gonna do, but I can say whatcha won't do long." Dink and Solo were about the same height and weight, just as they squared off Deshawn came out.

"Go home Solo, quit messing with folks!" she yelled.

Solo reached into his back and pulled out a 9-mm Glock. People in the parking lot scrambled for cover, yelling. Shai jumped into the car. Chill, Aaron and Dink all got ghost. The nine started singing, he was shooting in the air, and yelling. The noise ceased; you could hear a rat piss on cotton. "You niggas got me fucked up. I will peel ah niggas cap back!" Everyone was still ducking and hiding except Xavier, he was still leaning on his car with Vianna wrapped around his leg. "So, you G'ed up like that my Nigga?" Xavier remained silent, both men locked in a deadly stare. Solo trained the gun on Xavier. "Just me and you heah my nigga, God ain't gonna intervene." The gun clicked on an empty chamber.

Deshawn yelled at him again, he switched clips and shot at her. The bullet shattered the window, Deshawn screamed. Solo then redirected his attention to Xavier.

"Oh, I guess you live playa, Happy C-day."

Xavier picked up Vianna, motioned to Shai and headed up the stairs. Prophet followed closely behind Shai. The GMC ignition turned over, gravel shot from under the tires and barked as they roared out of the parking lot. Bernadine and Nellie met them at the doorway galvanized into action by the gunfire.

"Xavier what happened?" That was Bernadine.

"Vianna, you alright," Nellie asked.

"Yeah mama, but Zav-ya is pissed off." She cupped her hand over her mouth. Xavier had left them all standing in the living room and disappeared into his room. Five minutes later he came out and headed for the door. Nellie and Bernadine cut him off and grabbed him. Nellie held him tight, "Baby, where are you going? Bernadine, lock that damn door."

Quietly and calmly, Xavier said, "Mama let me go."

"Calm down Xavier baby." Vianna walked over and hugged his leg. Bernadine was rubbing his arm. Nellie started crying and hitting him in the chest, "Boy you can't leave me and Vi, you can't! Can't! You just can't just go do something stupid and let these white folks take you away from us!" Her little fist pounded on his chest. Vianna had also started crying and was hugging his leg. He gathered his mama's hands and hugged her. She spoke in between sobs, "Baby, you're all I have that's keeping me up. I can't lose you behind some bullshit." Shai was taken aback by the whole scene. Seconds multiplied and became minutes, allowing calmness to creep in like coolness to a hot meal.

Prophet finally spoke, "She right cuz, just hold down and stay up."

"Mama," Xavier held his hand out to Shai and she walked to him.

"This is Shai Lynn Montgomery. Shai, this my t-lady, Nellie Dean and my surrogate aunt Bernadine Watkins."

Bernadine spoke as Nellie wiped her face, examining Shai for a moment.

"She's cute Xavier, how are you Shai?" asked Nellie.

"I'm alright Ms. Dean," Shai responded.

"I'm going to the piz-ark and ball til I fall," Prophet announced. Nellie appraised her son. I have to borrow the car. Me and Bernadine gonna go pick up some things to cook for June 19th. I won't be no more than two hours. I'll drop Prophet off too." He dug into his pocket and tossed her the keys; she shut and locked the door behind her.

'One Life to Live' was going off. The credits rolled up the screen. He looked at Shai and said, "Welcome to the Ward." She sat next to him on the sofa. The Guess jumper rose on her legs exposing some smooth yellow thigh.

"Are you alright?" she asked.

He nodded his head, "As well as to be expected under the conditions. Just don't appreciate him pointing the gun at me, then my little sister next to me to."

"You should have gotten into the car," she chided.

"For what? He's shooting in the air. I'm not moved or impressed."

Shai switched directions. "Your mom is pretty; you favor her a lot."

"So, you calling me pretty."

She smiled, "Yeah, you're a pretty S.B.T."

"S.B.T., what is that?"

"Pretty sexy black thing." She leaned in to kiss him, pushed her tongue into his mouth, got on her knees so she could be over him. The kiss deepened, became more amorous, urgent, then reluctantly she broke the kiss. "Xavier, you can touch me," she-prompted sensually. Xavier dropped his head and sighed, realized that his hands, like rusty hinges, were frozen at his sides. Shai's lithe body audaciously straddled Xavier, his hand rounded her tiny waist, squeezed her lusciously full backside. She was soft, her tongue expensive Cognac that intoxicated him. She screwed and rubbed herself against his growing erection, abandoning her comfort zone, invading his. Shai didn't know what had gotten into her. There was an ache not to be denied, a burning in her loins determined to be quenched. She was soooo hot, she'd never been so hot before. She could feel the hardness of his throbbing member. He had pushed the jumper off her shoulders, his hand felt like fire burning every place he touched. Exposing her silk mauve bra, Xavier unsnapped it and paused. Sweat misted his forehead, his breathing was ragged. He whispered, "You're beautiful." Her breasts were crested with dark nipples that contrasted with her light complexion. Her bosom was like two prodigious golden pyramids capped with deep rich chocolate; ripe and pendulous. They were the heavy matured breasts given to a woman whose body had experienced the life-giving process. Her skin was satiny smooth, silky soft, warm and supple. Her touch was feverish and everywhere she touched, his skin celebrated. The oxygen in the room paced and waited because for long seconds neither breathed.

Xavier cupped and manipulated her tender breasts, squeezed the taut nipples and Shai broke the kiss and sighed, "Oh God, I don't know what I'm doing." Before dipping his head to take her nipple into his mouth he looked into her glassy iridescent eyes glistening like priceless opals. Shai arched her back as intense pleasure shot through her body. She would have fell out of his lap and onto the floor if he hadn't held her. Shai felt a fluttery sensation in her lower stomach; it had been about four months since she'd been touched, her body was in need of the attention he provided. Xavier stood and she wrapped her legs around his narrow waist. She felt the muscles in his arms stiffen and tighten as his hands went under her butt and accepted her weight. His tongue probed her mouth, she caught it and sucked on it. He carried her to his room kicking the door shut behind him, and lowered her to the floor. Still locked in a deep kiss she stepped out of the jumper leaving her naked except for her French cut mauve silk panties. Xavier was on fire by this time. He kicked his shoes off while she worked on the button to his shorts. Naked except for his boxers, he stood in front of her, bent over to lick her chin and then sucked on it. Running his tongue down her throat, between the valleys of her breast. Slowly he eased to his knees in front of her licking her navel and kneaded the flesh of her butt. Burying his face in the silky forest at the bottom of her belly he inhaled deeply through the sheer fabric of her panties, palming both halves of her ass firmly and lifting her into the air as he stood up and laid her across the bed. Pulling at her panties, she lifted her hips so they could slip over her butt. Xavier took another few seconds to absorb her beauty. The dark hair at the juncture between her legs was neatly trimmed.

Slipping out of his shorts, she watched in anticipation as his swollen member stood at attention. Shai knew the one thing that would put him at ease. Xavier leaned over her and found her lips, kissed her softly, passionately, so much passion. Shai felt the thick knob of his chocolate rod knock on the doors to her soul. She relaxed her vaginal muscles and opened herself to him. It wasn't a straight shot, she was tight; he pushed, she wiggled and squirmed beneath him as he gained deep entrance into her body. She moaned, "Oh ... oh, mmm." Her hands left his chest and went above her head to grasp hold of the bed board. "Damn ... oh ... uh." Her legs stiffened, which forced him to pullout some. She was trying to control how deep he penetrated her sensitive tenderness. Shai enjoyed Xavier's movement in and out of her body. He had nice length and girth, and she felt him deep, wanted him deeper. She knew he wanted to dig deep but the pleasure for the moment was here, her climax was coming, she squeezed her eyes shut, and bit down on her lips to keep from screaming. Their sweaty bodies were dancing the dance when she exploded. "Mm, oh shit." She sighed. He lifted her leg and surged in hard and deep, it was unexpected and Shai gasped loudly, and breathlessly mouthed, "Ugh ... mmm." Writhing under him she reached her hands to the back of his head and shoulders pulling him to her lips in a driving unyielding kiss that went far beyond anything Xavier had experienced before. While digging her hips into the mattress, scooting up and away from him she buried her tongue deep into his mouth while he buried his persistent tool deep inside of her. He surged again and she said his name almost as a plea, "Ugh, Xavier ... oooh." Licking her ear he drove the tip of his tongue deep into its convolutions, then lifted her other leg and drove home again, "Oh ... baby ... wait." And she climaxed again. "Shhhit ... Ummm." Shai's nails raked his back clutching the skin of his shoulder blades. Finally, she felt his seed burn its way through her. Laying there panting, she felt him begin to soften within her soft vaginal walls. Before he rolled over and slipped out of her, subconsciously she ran her hand between her legs and touched herself. "Goodness, boy ... I've never been like this." She turned on her side to face him and was pleased when he faced her, and even more pleased when he caressed her wide hip and full buttocks.

His breathing was still irregular. "I could get use to this, being with you every day. You make me feel so complete, Shai." They started kissing, Shai reached between his legs until she found what she was looking for, stroking him, and he started to rise in the name of Shai. She straddled him, reached back to position him at her doorway and she slid back onto him. Xavier felt himself slide into her warm sweetness, moaned and grabbed her waist. She made love her way, this time, slow and easy, instead of sitting up, she leaned over and slid back and forth over him. He sucked on her dark nipple, matched her rhythm, Shai was working up on another orgasm, it was a big one this time. Her insides started tingling, throbbing, contracting and relaxing. She was in a position where she could control the penetration, the rhythm, she worked him. "What's my name, Xavier?" she asked.

Her question made him open his eyes, they locked stares, her breast swayed back and forth seductively. "Shai," he whispered. His muscle jumped twice inside of her then erupted. That's what she was waiting for, as he started to soften, she sat straight up and plunged down completely on his penis, in his less rigid state it didn't dig as deep. Xavier cupped the velvety halves of her bottom, guiding her to the final moment of rapture. She felt his body arch beneath her gyrating his pelvis, lifting her higher with the ease of a thoroughbred stallion. His breathing ragged ... hers in soft pants, their bodies in exquisite harmony ...

"Umm, oh, Xavier," Cried Shai as she felt blood making explosions through her body. "Ahhh," she cried out in release, feeling as if a strange spiritual intoxication had taken control of her ... her eyelids closed tightly as a kaleidoscope, swirling, eddying appeared to dance before her eyes. She fell in exhaustion to his chest.

Shai did not realize she had fallen asleep until she woke up. Xavier was up and dressed, sitting down on the bed woke her up. "What time is it?" she asked.

"Four-thirty."

"What time is your mama coming back?"

"She left about two, so I expect her back any minute now. You want to shower?"

"Yeah, I'd like that," she replied.

He handed her the orange juice he had been drinking. She drained the glass, he leaned over and kissed her. "The bathroom's right there." He pointed and rose to leave.

"Wait, my clothes, face towel, soap."

"I folded your clothes there," he pointed, "on the chair behind you. Towels and soap in the cabinet."

Shai climbed out of bed naked, unashamed. His eyes fell to her jiggling breasts, the stock of well-trimmed hair between her legs. As she passed him, she tipped toed to kiss him then said,

"Quit staring boy." Still, he watched her round bottom bounce as she sashayed into the bathroom.

While in the shower, Shai touched herself, reminisced about her and Xavier's lovemaking. No man had made her feel the way he had; her experience was limited to two men excluding Xavier. Both older and neither had done what he had. She spent four years with Calvin and rarely experienced an orgasm. Today in less than two hours, she had three. "I could love him," she said to herself, then smiled.

Xavier was gone when she got out of the shower, Ms. Dean still had not returned. There was cocoa butter on his dresser, which she used it to lotion down. He had other toiletries which she noticed, and while she dressed, she examined them and the pictures stuck in his mirror of him and an older woman she assumed was his grandma. Him and his sister in one, another one of him and six guys, she recognized Prophet. There were bills on his table, which she ignored. She opened his drawers which were a mess to her relief, women hated men that were too clean; boxers in one, t-shirts in another. The one to the farthest right had a big gun in it. She lifted it, pointed it at herself in the mirror. "Bang," she mouthed. She heard the front door open and close. Returning the gun, she went inside of her purse and grabbed her make-up case.

Xavier walked in with a bag; he had a large bag of Cheetos, two big gulp orange crushes, and two pints of ice cream; Tin Roof and White Almond. "I didn't know what you'd want, so I grabbed my favorites."

She grabbed the white almond ice cream, "Where's my spoon?" "In the kitchen with all the other eating utensils."

She batted her eyes and made her voice sound thick as molasses, just as sweet.

"Can you go get me a spoon?" "Yeah baby."

Xavier grabbed the ice cream, the bag of goodies and went into the front room. Shai heard the T.V. come on. Her watch displayed that it was five o'clock. She finished putting on her make-up and joined him in the living room. He was watching X-Men;

her ice cream was on the end of the table with a spoon sticking out of it. Bare footed she padded across the carpet sat down and put her feet in his lap while eating her ice cream. "Does all this mean your mines now, or was it just something for you to do?" Shai asked.

"What do you think it means?" Xavier replied.

"Don't do that Xavier," Shai snapped.

"Do what?"

"Answer my question with a question. I don't want to be your potna, I want to be your woman."

Xavier said nonchalantly, "So it is said, so it is written, so it shall be done." Shai smiled and leaned over to feed him some ice cream. Some missed his mouth, it started to drip down his chin.

"I'll get it," she shouted happily. She jumped up and kneeled between his legs, ran her tongue up his chin, then sucked his bottom lip. "Damn boy, you taste good." She smiled at him lavishly. He leaned into her and they started kissing heatedly. She broke the kiss, "Oh!" waving her hand in front of her face like a fan. "We can't start that again."

The door knob twisted; keys jingled. Shai jumped up and sat beside Xavier. The door opened, Vianna and Nellie filed in with bags in hand. Bernadine followed also toting bags. Xavier looked at his watch and Nellie launched into an explanation. "We lost my damn wallet baby, we back tracked trying to figure out where we left it."

"We my ass, your ass ain't French," Bernadine snapped coming from the kitchen, "you lost yo' damn wallet lusting after that young ass boy." Bernadine had read the paper on the way to the house and there was a headline on the same boy she and Nellie had seen at the Stop-N-Go.

"What boy?" Xavier asked.

"Vail Akbar, you know him?" Bernadine asked.

"I heard Prophet talking about him, seen him play a couple of times. He's raw, gets too cocky sometimes, forces some shots but he's holding it down."

Shai said, "I've seen him around school. Everyone thought he was going into the NBA draft this year and come out early."

"He surprised a lot of people by staying. How many sophomores do you know lead the nation in scoring, then stay in college?" Xavier added.

"You know his baby was kidnapped last night, well this morning," Nellie stated.

Xavier looked surprised. "Naw, where you hear that?"

"It's in the paper," Bernadine said, holding it up. "You want it?"

"I'll get it in a few. So, my mama's lusting after twenty-year-old ballers?"

"I had to pick that ho's tongue off the ground."

"You's ah damn lie, I just thought he was cute. He was gawking at yo' fat ass, not my narrow one."

Bernadine got serious. "I ain't fat Nellie, and don't start no shit won't be no shit." Shai started laughing.

Nellie plopped down on the sofa next to Xavier and stretched out across him until her head fell into Shai's lap. "I love that car," she said.

"Nellie get off ya ass and help me put this shit up," Bernadine yelled.

"Do you want me to help you Ms. Dean?" Shai asked.

"Call me Nellie or mama Shai, and no baby, me and that old stank got it." Vianna came out of the kitchen and sat between her brother and Shai. Xavier just smiled.

Shai took in her surroundings, she felt happy here. Maybe love is simply identifying with an object or a person so strongly they became eternally connected to you. Or maybe it's a self-hypnosis where subject and master become the same. Believe what you wish about the mystery and power of love, there is one truth concerning the remedy for its pain which cannot be argued, time. She realized she had been nurturing these feelings for Xavier for close to four months. These feelings were not sudden, but suppressed. The more time she spent with him, the more she realized the experiences with Calvin were not a lesson in love. For far too long she had been smiling that smile. That's what confused hearts do ... you know. they hope when there is none, smiling that smile. Sometimes reality sets in slow like rigor mortis, stiffens you before you notice it's happening. Shai kissed Vianna on the cheek.

Vianna spun, wiped her face. "Quit it," she asked more than demanded.

"Give that to your brother please," Shai stated in a cajoling manner.

Vi looked up at Xavier. He leaned over and put his finger on his cheek, she kissed it. Then kissed her on the lips, "and give that to Shai." She looked at Shai, then back at Xavier, then back at Shai. Finally, she got to her feet and kissed Shai on the lips. Xavier snatched Vi by her waist into his lap. She screamed as he tickled her. "And these are for you Boo-Boo." He started placing kisses all over her face.

CHAPTER 13

Freshly promoted Detective Darrel Puckett looked like he had eaten a doughnut a minute for the past couple of years. He was a big man, six foot five and three hundred pounds. He sat at his desk going over the reports from last night, or this morning rather. Twenty- two witness statements all stating that they had seen nothing. The cursor on his computer blinked, he sipped his cold coffee and leaned back in his chair, it squeaked and groaned in protest as his weight punished the feeble inanimate object. People shuffled back and forth around him; his thoughts were focused. He had been in the library archives all morning. His day had begun at three in the morning with calls to the Federal Bureau of Investigation requesting the National Missing Person File of children and infants from 2005 to 2015. They e-mailed him a detailed printout listing cities, states, names and years. It covered all states, detailed who had been found alive, dead and still missing; he took extensive notes from the spreadsheets. There were seven states that gradually caught his attention with a significant rise in kidnappings. In 2005-2006, in Louisiana forty-two children were reported missing, then in 2007-2008, sixty-five children were reported kidnapped. Then in 2009-2010 the numbers dropped back to the low forties. That was interesting and unusual to Puckett, a one-year rise; other states followed the pattern, but if you were not specifically looking, this pattern would not seem strange. It all seemed to originate in Louisiana. Many of the children were eventually located and returned to their families. A great number of children were found dead or were still missing. There was detailed psychological evaluations done on several of the children, the pattern was random. Then in June 2009, Washington D.C. had the same scenario. The Washington Post had run an article in November of 2009 about a set of twins that were abducted from a suburban home. The parents, Mr. and Mrs. Robert Ashley, were out at the town. The maid, Yadira Holmes, was reportedly knocked unconscious. She and the parents were thoroughly investigated; no indictments were issued. The Ashley twins had never been found. In July of 2010, two little boys showed up in Virginia that were kidnapped from Washington. Their stories completely baffled the authorities. It was different states and in different years which made it hard to trace. In Detroit, Michigan, August of 2011, a husband and wife, James and Jenise Witiker were killed while camping in their Winnebago with their two daughters; Shamira twelve and Yolanda ten. Local authorities discovered the badly decomposed bodies late August of 2011. The children were nowhere to be found. Other children were abducted, some eventually located, most still missing. There was a rough time line beginning to form, all places visited were large cities: Seattle, Miami and Sacramento. In Phoenix, July of 2015, only a year ago, one police man injured and another one killed while investigating the kidnapping of a preschool teacher, Sheila Penock, and two of her preschoolers, Valerie Johnson and Amber Ambrose. Apparently, they had received an anonymous phone call reporting something unusual was happening at 5152 Burbank, a three-story brownstone. The caller said there was crying and screaming the night before. According to Officer Drew Decker, the surviving officer, they knocked and when no one answered they went inside; upon entering, gunshots exploded. Neighbors said a tall blonde and a male fled the scene in a white BMW. Officer Clifford Day was D.O.A., the pre-school teacher was decomposing in the basement, and Valerie Johnson and Amber Ambrose were not found.

Puckett left the computer station despondent and exhausted. It was 3:00 p.m., ten hours later. He needed to type a summary report to his supervisor but that would have to wait. He also needed to call Washington Police Department and try to locate Yadira Holmes. Then there was Officer Decker in Phoenix. He jotted down notes in his little notebook, notes that instructed him to contact some of the parents of the surviving children; also get the names of the psychiatrist that that had evaluated those children. He made notes to get police reports and investigation packages for the Ashley family, Witiker murders and a detailed history of Sheila Penock.

Back at his desk, he was mentally sorting things out in his head. "They're about to move again," he said to himself staring at the calendar on his desk. He began to shift through the witness statements again, maybe he missed something. Thirty minutes later he froze, and read carefully. Marshall Curry stated that he saw a black BMW that he'd never seen before leaving the apartments when he heard the girl scream. When the girl screamed, he wrote down the license plate number. Puckett thought about the white BMW that fled the scene in Phoenix; maybe it was just coincidence. Marshall was widowed, 65 years old Caucasian, maintenance man. Claimed he was returning from fixing a busted pipe. Puckett jotted down Marshall's name, number and address in his miniature notebook, then he picked up the phone, "Hello, Becky ..., yes its Puckett. I need you to run a plate for me ... get back at me ASAP." He made several other calls, explained he was working on a case that may be related. They all agreed to call back and fax reports; his last call was to Phoenix. "Hello, Phoenix Police Department?"

A banal nasal voice chanted, "Yes."

"This is Detective Puckett with the Houston Police Department. I'm investigating a case down here and uh ..." he shuffled through some papers, "Terry Vantz has agreed to send me the Penock case file, he referred me to you for assisting me in locating Officer Drew Decker."

"Can I call you back Detective uh ...?"

"Puckett," he interjected.

"Give me your information and I'll e-mail you the information in an hour."

"Okay, thanks." He relayed his information and hung up. A Seattle family had acquiesced to see him and allow him to see their son and his psychiatrist. He booked a ten o'clock flight to Seattle, then he had to fly to Sacramento and speak with two other psychiatrists who had been given permission by the parents to talk with him. He looked at his watch, six twenty-three. He had four hours til his flight. The phone rang, "Detective Puckett," he said into the phone.

"Puc that plate that you gave me belongs to a Shane Vattil Muster, African-American male, age twenty-six, five foot ten inches tall and one hundred ninety-five pounds. Date of birth, May 10, 1970, St. Louis. No priors, no tickets, current address is 1510 Stuebner, Spring, Texas 77373. Is that all?"

"Becky, how long that plate been registered in Texas?" "August 16, 2014."

"Thank you, Becky." When he was leaving, he told Cathy to send everything to his phone.

Something just wasn't right. He had just come from booking; there was nothing, not a grunion. No arrest record, transcripts, fingerprints, nothing on Vail Akbar/ According to the computers he never passed through these walls. Tired and frustrated he stormed out of the Police Department and hopped into his Buick La Sable. Two days ago, Darrell Puckett was promoted to Detective and assigned to this case. He was forty years old, twice married, twice divorced, three kids; two from the first marriage and one from the second. His oldest two children were in Toronto. Puckett was pretty much even keel; he had learned from the job that courage and cowardice were interchangeable. Both catered to different spaces and different times. He had learned there is no use factoring in emotions in any equation because emotions were capricious. Nothing in life is completely what it seems, there are no absolutes. Every pretense brings with it a certain amount of truth. Truth was there was a war going on inside of him about what Vail had told him and what he was finding. The kid knew he would be able to verify whether or not he had been arrested or not. Why lie? No Vail was on the up and, someone had gone through great lengths to erase any record of Vail's arrest. His old man had once told him, "You cannot pull the lion's tongue with yo' head in his mouth." His instincts were telling him that he was about to pull the lion's tongue with his head in its mouth.

Puckett did not believe in God, not the way everyone else did. He did believe there was a supreme being, that this being had set life up in a network of predestined blessings, all you had to do was make the right decisions. All the praying hoopla was a waste of time. He could come out of church after four hours of worship get in a car accident and die. No, the man had given everyone five senses, you make the right decisions it had already been decided what would happen. If Puckett decided this, Bam! There's a blessing, if he decided that, oh well. Life was not about prayers; it was about decisions. The way his mind worked, if he pursued this case he could be killed. If he retired tomorrow, he may live longer. Decisions.

Traffic was congested, cars ebbed along at snail's pace. Puckett's mind was in a foot race chasing ideas. He glanced at the newspaper sitting in the passenger seat. He had bought it on the way to his office. Headlined in bold print was 'Infant Baby Kidnapped.' June 17th at approximately 3:00 a.m. at the townhouse apartments in Southwest Houston, infant baby belonging to Daphane Keye and U of H's basketball sensation Vail Akbar was abducted while mother slept, no forced entry. No suspects have been named, disappearance totals sixteen in the last year yadda, yadda, yadda. Any information please contact 1-800-222-TIPS. There was a family photo of Vail, Daphane and Iyanna.

❖   ❖   ❖

Vail's mother and father were not as upset as he had expected they would be. He had not been back to Daphane's since leaving at 7:30 this morning. Her girlfriend Chiquita, her mom and aunt had come over even before the sun came up. Amid all the conversation, he made his exodus. All morning long he had been at the gym running horses and shooting the rock. Escaping reality by entertaining thoughts of taking his team to the final four, then winning it all this coming season. He had a shot, but he would have to elevate his game even more. Everyone was looking at the guard Donovan Tillis, nicknamed Prophet. He was like number seven or eight in the country coming out of high school. Vail had attended several of his games at Galena Park High School, the kid was something else. Media had speculated he would jump straight to the pros, if they all allowed it, but his mother said he had to go to college. She taught girls basketball at the middle school. Word was he was going to Houston, with a guard like that to help him out they could shake shit up. The NBA draft was in twelve days, he was tempted to enter the draft but reason one to stay was he wanted to improve his ball handling skills; he could be a six-foot six-inch point guard entering the draft. Better ball handling would lift his stock; small forward, shooting guard or point. Being able to play three positions would ensure him a lottery pick with his twenty-six-point average. Galena Park opened their doors at the gym at 12:30 to 6:30 p.m. on Monday, Wednesday, and Friday. Today was Wednesday, the seventeenth, but too much was happening today. Friday was June 19th and he doubted it would be open. He just wanted to holler at Prophet and see what his intentions were.

A mother pushing her baby into a store across the street instantly catapulted his thoughts to Iyanna. The whole situation was fucked up; someone blew a horn behind him. The light had turned green, but he had not noticed it because his mind was focused on speaking with Daphane alone. Those men knew him because of her not the other way around. They had seen her somewhere, but where? Pulling into Stop-N-Go, a clean Chrysler 300 pulled into the space beside him. A cute slim black sista exited the driver side with a little girl in close pursuit. A darker sista, that immediately brought to mind the Commodores song 'Brick House,' exited the passenger side wearing blue spandex pants and a black spandex tank top. She looked at him and waved; he waved back. From the front seat he dialed Daphane's number. "Hello?" It was a female, but not Daphane.

"Let me holla at Daph," Vail said into the phone.

"And who the hell is this?"

He hated ignorant people, but the world is full of them. "This is Vail." There was a pause, the phone clanked down ... he heard voices in the background.

"Vail, where the hell are you?" Daphane asked vehemently.

He ignored her attitude. Guilt had an uncanny way of finding the most arrogant man and humbling him. "Daph, how are you holding up baby?"

She heard the humility, the concern and the pain in his voice. She was weak behind Vail, had been since she met him. Her voice softened. "I'm hurting Vail, I need you here with me. I can't handle all this bullshit alone." She began to cry.

"Daph, I haven't abandoned you. I'm just thinking you know ... trying to find some answers. Pack you a bag, we're going to chill at my place. I'm not trying to shun your people, but I don't want to be around anyone but you. Can we manage that?"

She sniffled, cleared her throat. "What time will you be here?"

Vail checked his watch, it was four-thirty. "Look for me a little after five, okay?"

There was a pause, "Vail ... you know that I love you, right?"

"Yeah Daph, I know." The line was silent. "I'm on my way, so get ready." He hung up the phone. Looking up, he noticed the Chrysler was gone. A female's wallet looking lost and alone was on the blacktop. Exiting his vehicle, he leaned over and picked it up. When he opened it, there was a driver's license belonging to Nellie Dean, a Lone Star Card, social security card and some other whatnots. Vail threw the wallet on the dashboard, sat behind the wheel and started the engine. He was tired, it felt like someone had placed a ton of bricks on his conscious, feeling sorry for himself seemed reasonable, his emotions vacillated between bad and worse. His mama once told him that the fruit of silence is prayer, the fruit of prayer is faith, the fruit of faith is love, the fruit of love is service, and the fruit of service is peace. He smiled to himself thinking about his mama. When mama is not available, her teachings and unconditional love are reflected upon. The need to purge himself of his guilt was running rampant, he needed to find his child. Vail pulled into traffic beside a black BMW, a mulatto looking brother was waiting at the light, they made eye contact. The light changed and Vail turned left, the black BMW kept straight. Had Vail looked in his rearview mirror, he would have seen the Chrysler 300 return to Stop- N-Go.

"Daphane, don't forget to call baby." That was Daphane's aunt.

Vail was taking all her stuff to his jeep.

"When you comin' back?" That was her mama.

"I'm not sure ma, you have to ask Vail." That was Daphane. Her anemic and anorexic looking mother turned bulging glassy eyes on Vail.

"Ms. Keye, we'll be back when the media quits houndin' me. When things settle a bit, people know me, so this story is real juicy. Daph will call you and keep you posted."

She sucked her tongue to the bridge of her mouth and made a popping sound while placing her hands on her waist. "Just give me your address and number, I'll come by and check on my baby," Ms. Keye said acerbically.

"Mama, Vail doesn't give out his address or phone number," Daphane interjected.

"That's bullshit!" she exploded. "I want to be able to check on you."

Daphane's aunt restrained her sister. "Baby, call us okay."

Daphane kissed her aunt then her mom. Vail was already in the jeep with the engine running when she got in. Tupac's 'It

Ain't Easy' was playing. Ten minutes into the ride she turned the radio off. "What are we going to do, Vail?"

He looked at her and then back at the road. "What do you mean?" he asked.

"If we don't get Iyanna back?"

"We'll cross that bridge when we get there. Until then, just pray and stay optimistic, we'll get her back." Daphane looked beautiful even without makeup on. "Is that what you wore when you spoke with the reporter?" She had on a sheer white silk pants suit, the kind that you could see the panties if they were of a dark colored material. He had assessed that she had worn simple white panties, because he could not see them.

Daphane glanced down at herself. "Yes, I decided on this, you like?"

He nodded his head, "It's classy, showing your true beauty minus all the accessories, extensions and additives." She smiled. Vail had checked Daphane about the weaves, nails, eyes and pounds of make-up over the sixteen months he had been with her, she made monumental changes for him. When he met her, she was thoroughly brainwashed; fake hair, fake nails, fake eyes and a fake ass attitude. She was a natural beauty that had turned herself into a natural disaster; she was very bellicose, vulgar and vain. What made him stick around was the front, back and side to side, then the sex was unbelievable, plus she was intelligent. The more he dug away what was not her, the more he enjoyed what was her. A lot of sisters had made false adaption to please and satisfy the false desires of confused black men. In sixteen months, she had done a complete One-eighty. Her eating habits changed, she rarely drank anymore, never cursed in front of him and her clubbing had been reduced to a minimum. As Vail drove, he thought about all this. She stared out the window and he stared at her sitting there, and for the first time he acknowledged that change. Was a woman really a reflection of her man, or is that just a colorful but empty rhetoric? Vail never drank, rarely cursed and was a vegetarian. Either way she had left the little girl somewhere in time to become the woman of this second, this minute, and this hour ... the woman she thought he wanted. Daphane had been growing and either he forgot to, did not want to, or just failed to see it happening. How could those that see so well be so blind? If he made it to Heaven, it's a question he would ask God, it is a valid question. Black men are such shallow creatures, always running; escaping one problem just to allow another one to find him. Always in the mirror ... you know, the problems always staring at you. Adversity has a way of drawing attention to itself and a habit of demanding profound responses to unanswered whys, an untamed ego had been the root of his problem; ego and arrogance are merely toys in the hands of men parading as children. the tools of accomplished men are those of purpose and direction. Sometimes it is beneficial to listen to the voices ... the voices that tell tales of misery as well as tell of joys. We're always trying to make them hush, forced solitude is not like voluntary solitude until you learn how to volunteer. All day he had been thinking about if he would stay, if they did not find Iyanna. Oh yeah, this ordeal had knocked on all the doors of his emotions. Emotions that weren't even supposed to be home answered and filled out witness statements. For a long, time he had been convincing himself that Daphane was only a vessel that brought forth the precious cargo that he loved so much. Until today, he was too afraid, too fragile, too shallow or too selfish to admit even to himself, that he loved Daphane. To him that was a sad revelation, not that he loved Daphane, but that he had lied even to himself. Who can you trust when even 'self' is deceiving you? The epiphany was poignant.

Daphane felt Vail's eyes on her. She looked at him and noticed the tears in his eyes as he refocused on the road. She had never known Vail to show any emotion outside lust. He started to speak; his voice steady but thick with emotions. "This may sound crazy, but I hadn't really looked ... hadn't seen ... you know." She scooted close to him and rubbed his leg. "Until today, I never looked at you like I should have. Losing Iyanna made me think about losing you ... you're the mother of my only child and I've never even told you I love you. Haven't done anything but use you to gratify myself ... and—" He ran his hand over his face. "... and that's some selfish shit. Daph, you ought to know that I love ... I love you." He finally looked at her and tears ran down her face. Vail held up his hand and Daphane took a firm hold of it, he pulled her closer to him.

"I know you figured Iyanna was the only thing keeping me around, but I'm letting you know that the woman that you are today is what kept me here, and I'll be here as long as you want me."

She kissed him and he damn near had a wreck. "I loved you, Vail, from the first time I saw you."

Fifteen minutes later, they exited 288. "Where are we going?" she asked.

"I'm going to drop by the gym and pick up some things then drop that off." He nodded to the wallet on the dashboard. Daphane noticed it for the first time.

"Who does it belong to?"

"Some woman dropped it at the Stop-N-Go. I'm just going to return it." Daphane picked it up and examined it.

Less than twenty minutes after leaving the gym, Vail pulled into Southmore's large parking lot. He spotted the Chrysler. From where it was parked, he assumed twenty-three was the apartment. A honey colored sista, twice more stunning than Daphane in black Polo jeans and shirt with Jordans stood with a younger skinnier version of herself. When he got upon them, he noticed at once, that they both had hazel eyes. "Excuse me, you know the owner of this here?" Indicating the Chrysler. The younger one spoke first.

"Who are you?"

The oldest said, "Ah that's Xavier's why. What's up?"

He was about to address the older sister, when the younger one must have felt she was about to get ignored and jumped in again, "My name is Denise, this is my sister Deshawn, now who are you?"

Deshawn placed his face, and answered for him. "Vail Akbar."

Denise looked at her sister, "You know him?"

Deshawn directed her comment to Vail. "You look different in person, you're the basketball player, right?"

He smiled, "The one and only."

"I also attend U of H, I've never seen you, except at the games."

"What do you want with X?" Denise inquired.

Vail held up the wallet, "I believe one of his relatives dropped this. I just wanted to return it."

"Xavier stays-in twenty-seven," Deshawn said.

"I appreciate it," Vail said. "Maybe I'll see you around." He smiled.

"Maybe," Deshawn said insouciantly.

Vail looked at his watch, 6:45. He ran up the stairs and knocked on the door. He heard talking and music coming from inside, he knocked again. A jazzy ass yellow bone with the prettiest Vanessa L. Williams blue-green eyes he had ever seen answered the door. "Y'all are crazy ..." She was talking to someone inside the house. The aroma of fried fish danced on the breeze and had a brief introduction with his senses.

"Hi, is Ms. Dean here?"

Shai turned into the house. "Nellie, you have company."

Nellie came to the door and stood next to Shai. She looked up; a partial yelp left her lips. "Bernadine! Here he goes right here, the boys part bloodhound."

Bernadine was at the door in seconds. "Baby, are you stalking my friend." She grinned coquettishly. "Or me?" They both started laughing. There was the faintest hint of alcohol on her breath.

"No, ma'am. I was just returning this wallet you must have lost."

"Girl, he's athletic, gorgeous and honest," Nellie stated. She took her wallet and tried to usher him in. "C'mon in, baby, Xavier will be back any minute, he'd love to meet you."

"Thank you, but I have someone waiting for me ..." Before he could finish, Bernadine and Nellie had pushed past him onto the balcony. They waved at Daphane and motioned for her to come up. Vail was helpless, the two women had successfully taken over. The jeep engine died, Daphane stepped out in her pants suit looking elegant as hell. She finally looked like a junior at T.S.U. majoring in finance. Within the last ten minutes, he had met three extremely beautiful women, but was proud of his Daph. She climbed the stairs with one of those quizzical, but serious looks. The two older women read the look on Daphane's face and instantly remembered the newspaper. "Y'all come on in," Bernadine said. Introductions were made, they expressed their regrets about their loss and their prayers were with them and their daughter. Nellie offered them something to eat, they declined. She fixed them two plates anyway and wrapped them in foil; it was fried fish, macaroni and cheese, scalloped potatoes, broccoli with cheese and Jiffy cornbread.

Vail and Daphane had been there fifteen minutes, when the front door opened. Vail saw the stocky, shorter dark-skinned brother register recognition upon seeing Vail. He was followed by a taller mocha colored brother with a basketball in his hand, which he recognized. The darker brother spoke, "Wha'up Vail?" He extended his hand. Vail accepted it and spoke, then addressed Prophet.

"So, you're Prophet?" he asked.

"And you're the Golden Boy, Vail Akbar," Prophet said.

"The one and only. I wanted to come bend your ear at the G.P.H. gymnasium today, but my day has been kind of hectic."

"What's on your mind, cuz?" Prophet asked.

The room had grown silent, Xavier was sitting on the arm of the sofa next to Shai listening. "I was just thinking you and I, with Roderick in the middle could bring it all home, if you signed with the city."

"Roderick's coming back?" Xavier asked. He was Roderick 'The Rock' Barnes, six foot eleven inches, two-hundred-eighty pounds, all power plus. He was a junior this year also.

"Yeah, when I told him I was staying, he also decided to stick around. He also believes we can win with your handles and ball savvy."

"I was already going to sign playa, so I could represent this 'H', but talking to you and knowing that I'm wanted, really solidifies the deal for me, cuz." They slapped and shook hands.

"Just get me season passes, when you hit the pros," Xavier exclaimed.

Daphane thanked Nellie for the plates, said good-byes to Bernadine and Shai, who promised to hook up when all the drama cleared up. Solo's blue GMC blocked Vail in. To avoid any drama, Nellie went to ask him to move it. He came out, saw Vail in the jeep, did a double take and froze.

"Hey nigga, you Vail Akbar, right?" "In the flesh!" Vail sang.

Solo actually started jumping up and down. "Nigga, that game against Purdue, where you hit forty-one points won me a truck. I gave up fifteen by halftime, I was calling yo' ass all kinds of bitches cause y'all were down by eight. Yo' ass only had six points on three for ten shooting. This hook ass Columbian put his truck up for another 500 dollars cash." Everyone in attendance listened as he reiterated the story. "I was gonna jack his bitch ass, if I lost anyway. Man, second half you hit foe treys in a row. That nigga, 'The Rock' got crunk too. That second half you had to have a lucky rabbit foot up yo' ass cuz you couldn't miss for shit. When y'all jumped that fifteen, that nigga ass was sick." They talked for another five minutes before Honey sauntered up. Her and Solo got into the truck and peeled off. Vail and Daphane left also, it was ten after eight.

Vail headed toward his apartment in Jersey Village. When they entered the expressway, Daphane said, "Good thing you found that wallet and Nellie gave you this food because I wasn't cooking for your butt tonight."

"I would've gotten something to eat at my other girl's crib."

"What other girls?" she asked incredulously.

"Wendy's or Luby's. Both of 'em can cook," he said factitiously.

"That's all they can do is cook!" she said smartly.

"They were nice people, ole Xavier's a good character, isn't he?"

"He's cute too," she said jokingly.

"You laugh, but what's her name ... Shai was holding something." She hit him.

"Holding what?"

"Holdin' down Xavier's attention the way you were holding down mines, baby."

"Eewww ... good answer." They laughed; the detour had relaxed the tension.

Showered and well fed by Nellie's charitable offering, Daphane called her mom and aunt as promised. Afterward she got comfortable in a transparent yellow camisole with matching French cut panties. The nipples of her mango sized breasts jutted forward ostensively and the lush fullness of her ass pulled the thin fabric tight into the juncture between her legs, making her fleshly sex and mass of vaginal hair look too heavy for the flimsy material to hold. The yellow complimented her caramel-coated skin beautifully. He curbed his lascivious intentions. "Come here, baby." He pulled her closer. She turned on her side and threw her thick thigh on his, scooted up so her pouty sex rested on his legs. Vail was immediately aware of her warmth.

"I believe someone was watching you while you were pregnant." A fleeting look of panic crossed her face. It passed so swiftly Vail thought he imagined it. "I just don't believe this was random."

"But I haven't been associating with anyone."

"I need you to remember all the clubs, malls, grocery stores, etc... . that you visited. I'm going to check some things out tomorrow." They stayed up and compiled a list together. It was after twelve when the conversation died and light petting evolved, graduated and then produced the fruits of its labor. Their lovemaking was different Daphane noticed, from start to finish. It was slow, passionate and intense. Almost as if it were choreographed by the perfect hands of the heavens.

For some reason, Vail was thinking about the Titanic, the ship. The unsinkable one, that God sunk with a piece of ice. Seems God is ever present, ready and eager to laugh at the arrogance of man. Unsinkable, should have tried to convince the Creator. Vail replayed the visit he had with Victor, recalled his narcissistic ostensible attitude. He drifted off to sleep drunk off sex, comparing Victor to the Titanic. Why? His foggy conscious mind asked his incisive subconscious mind. Right before sleep kicked in the doors, the similitude registered lucidly. One thought to be unsinkable, the other thinks to be unsinkable, arrogance. Maybe God would laugh again sometime soon.

CHAPTER 14

Kennybrew had been a judge in three different states. At sixty-five he was still in good shape. A gregarious man by nature, who spent the majority of his time with his grandchildren at his two-story brick home in Northshore. Nicely trimmed hedges adorned his yard, Hibiscus and alyssums neatly lining the front drive. Two bicycles and a big wheel where in the driveway. Two little girls and a young boy were in bathing suits playing with the water hose; yelling, running, screaming and just being kids.

All the way over here, Puckett had been digesting all the events of the day. The reality of it all percolated and marinated. He parked his car on the side of the road outside of the house, exited and briskly walked to the front door. He rang the doorbell, chimes echoed through the house. Thirty seconds later, Judge Kennybrew came to the door in maroon cotton shorts, a shirt and patent leather house shoes.

"Judge, how are you doing?" Puckett asked.

"I'm alright, son, come on in and get out of the heat. Can I get you something to wet your whistle?"

"No sir, just wanted to run some things by you. Can't even stay long, two more stops to make and a plane to catch. Then I still have to pack."

"Okay, c'mon in my study, we'll converse."

For the next ten minutes Puckett ran down briefly what he had stumbled on. "I believe it's the same people, same pattern. That's what's making it difficult to believe it's arbitrary."

Kennybrew had been around, seasoned by time and experience. He was a very cognizant individual and most of his knowledge was empirical. "Well, Darrell," Judge Kennybrew began, scratching his salt and pepper beard, "From what you've just told me, it sounds like you're dealing with a sex trafficking enterprise, which will include human trafficking. I have a really good friend from my days in Chicago. An FBI Special Agent named Yancy Mordecai. He works with the Violent Crimes Against Children (VCAC). He has dealt with some of the nastiest cases in America and abroad."

Puckett sipped from his glass of ginger ale. Allowed his observant brown eyes to patrol the tasteful decor of Kennybrew's study.

"So, you've seen something of this nature before?" Puckett asked.

"Oh, yes?" His eyes rolled back into his head slightly accessing memories safely stored away.

"Yes, son, ya see ... a while back, there was a scandal, maybe forty years ago. Had to do with some Vietnam Vets, they had been raping and killing several under-aged Vietnamese girls, young girls about eight years old or so. It was a bunch of 'em involved." Kennybrew sipped from a crystal glass with some ginger ale in it. "Well, seems when, when two of them boys got back to the states ... what were their names." He paused, squinting his eyes and tapped his head in an attempt to remember. "One of them was Vincent Grubar. Damn, what was the other boy's name ... Sydney something. ·Anyway, they came back to America with an affixation for young flesh, started kidnapping young children; selling little black boys to the Klan and little white girls to sick perverted men. Human trafficking is enormous business. They launched into pornography too. You'd be surprised at some of the sick people walking around you. Anyway, he was busted, sentenced to life in prison."

"How was he busted?"

"Oh, this is going to kill ya. While Sydney was over there in Nam, he raped a twelve-year-old girl. She got pregnant; he thought he had trained her and broke her in. Well, he brought her with him to the states, thirteen years old. She knew what he was up to, waited for just the right time and reported him to the police, she testified in court about everything."

"Where's Sydney now?" Puckett was enthralled.

"Back then prison wasn't the place for child molesters. His trial drew a lot of publicity. About two years after his imprisonment, he was sodomized. They say, he killed himself, but you know how it is."

Puckett sat back and mused for a few seconds, admired the Judge's study; solid oak book shelves, dark mahogany desk, leather sofa, black lacquer end tables and at least three hundred books. "Judge, where was this at?"

Kennybrew thought for a few seconds, "Chicago, the Windy City."

"What ever happened to the girl and the baby?"

"Don't know. Never really checked into it, probably went back home."

"So," Puckett said slowly, "you believe this is what I'm looking at?"

"That's what it looks like to me, but I'm an old man. One year away from the life expectancy age of the Blackman. I could be wrong." Kennybrew smiled, then got serious. "Darrell, you be careful with this one, there are usually some powerful influential people involved in this. Sick perverted people yes, but influential also." That made Puckett remember Vail being arrested, yet no arrest record. He briefly told Kennybrew about that.

"Yeah, watch yourself son, they hide or bury the arrest record by just slipping him in the back door. Don't book him in, just slide him in there. However, a judge would have to authorize his release. You know the saying, 'Easy to get in, hard to get out'."

"So, I'm dealing with at least one bad cop—."

"And one bad judge." Kennybrew finished the sentence for him."

Puckett thanked Kennybrew and got up to leave. The yells and screams of the children playing in the yard filtered through his thoughts. He had just reached his car, the judge called him. "Darrell!"

"Yeah?"

"Pierce!" Kennybrew shouted.

"Huh?" Puckett was lost.

"Sydney Pierce, that was his name." He paused, "I'll give Mordecai a call."

Puckett smiled. "You're not quite ready for the grave yet, old man, and thanks. I'll be waiting on his call."

Marshall Curry was an old school cat. Thoroughly weathered, thoroughly cynical and thoroughly sanctimonious. Every sentence was laced with Jeees-us, gawd this or lawd that! Puckett thought that the man had been snatched from a Richard Pryor movie. Several times he strayed away from the topic of the conversation. Began to get excited and actually started to preach! Puckett smiled on his way to Shane Muster's home remembering the theatrical episode.

"Yes, lawd jeees-us I saw that car, but you know Matthew twenty-seven and thiticce-twoooo says; 'and as they came out.'" He deftly slurred and pronounced his words. Reminded Puckett of Richard Pryor in 'Which Way Is Up?' *"They," he continued, "found a man of Cyrene, Simon by name: him they compelled to bear his cross. The commitment of the Christian journey. The commitment I make is between me and my gawd! The commitment you make is between you and your gawd! So, I can't look at you, and presume to know what you are going through, what you should be doing, where you should be doing it or who you should be doing it with. I mind my own business!* Where gawd put me or what he tells me to do, or how he chooses to use me, it's not your business. So, mind your own business!" He paused, took a drink of water and wiped his face with a towel that forgot about being ice white years ago.

"So," he continued, "when that purdy black automobile eased by me at three some'ing in the morning that's what I was doing, *minding my own business!*" It took twenty minutes for Marshall to tell him he didn't see the driver of the car.

The drive to Spring was a lengthy drive, thick traffic but not congested. Puckett was listening to 1540 AM. The Isley Brothers had just sung 'Voyage to Atlantis.' Now Al Jarreau was crooning 'just the Two of Us.' The sun had gone down, night was stepping quietly upon the scene as always, solemn and nonchalantly, Stuebner Street was a suburban street, well taken care of homes, impeccable lawns, nice cars ... you know, nothing too shabby, nothing too fancy. Shane Muster's home was moderate, painted yellow and white. A teal green Ford Excursion was parked beside the black BMW. Puckett pulled in behind the BMW and killed the engine. He carefully surveyed the yard, the area surrounding the house; for some reason he was apprehensive. Maybe because Clifford Day was killed investigating a house with a white BMW. Puckett reached the front door, there was dance music coming from inside the house. He pushed the little white button and chimes started. When he released the button, the chimes stopped. He waited, pushed again, while in the process of pushing it the door swung open. The screen door stood between Puckett and a precocious auburn haired, blue-eyed beauty chewing gum abstemiously. Puckett presumed she was no more than seventeen, but her eyes held experience, mischief and some pain. She was petite and diminutive, wearing a diaphanous orange blouse with orange bikini top underneath. The blouse was tucked inside some orange leather shorts that were unbuttoned to reveal the front of her orange bikini bottoms. Her tanned skin looked luminous in all the orange. She wore a dark color lipstick and some mascara, simple. If she desired to look sexy, she was most definitely efficacious.

"Yes, can I help you?" she spoke.

"Yes, I'm looking for Shane Muster." He fished inside his pocket and produced his H.P.D. detective identification. "I'm Detective Puckett."

She popped her gum, "Okay, come on in copper." She smiled. "I'll get Shane. Can I get you something to drink, Spumante, or Chardonnay?" She looked over her shoulder to see if he was still behind her. She smiled again, and said, "Kool-Aid, apple juice."

"No thanks, uh ..."

"Shamira Muster, Mr. Puckett. I'm Shane's wife."

"Well, no thanks, Mrs. Muster."

"Please have a seat, I'll be right back." She picked up something off a glass boutique and tossed it to Puckett and was gone. Puckett caught the remote; there was an 80-inch color T.V. on step aerobics. The volume was all the way up, he hit the volume and the dance music slowly died.

"Shamira, turn that back up! I'm not through with my workout." This female voice came from a room to his right. When the volume didn't return to the T.V., the voice entered the room cursing, but froze when she saw the huge black man standing in the living room.

"How are you?" Puckett asked.

"I'm fine, who are you?" she asked.

"Police. Darrell Puckett, who are you?"

"Yolanda, Shamira's my sister." She too was beautiful; her hair was more strawberry blonde than auburn, she had the same aqueous blue eyes and she looked about fifteen or so, he guessed. All resemblances to her sister stopped there. Yolanda was voluptuous with full lips. Shamira's skin only looked tanned, Yolanda had a tawny complexion. Minus the blond hair and blue eyes, she could have been black. She wore a leotard that outlined her young effeminate features.

"Hello, Detective Puckett," Vatly said.

Puckett turned around. Shane was similar to Yolanda, a mulatto brother about five feet ten, one hundred ninety pounds. Vatly extended his hand and they shook hands. "How can I help you?"

"Mr. Muster, your car was seen leaving some apartments on the Southwest side of Houston where there was a kidnapping. I'm investigating all vehicles seen in the vicinity, but wasn't a resident." Vatly sat on the sofa next to Yolanda who had already made herself comfortable, they sat close.

"And when was this, Mr. Puckett?" Vatly asked.

Viscerally, Puckett's instincts said that Shane felt like this was a game. "The morning of June 17th at approximately 3:45 a.m."

"Oh yes," he laughed. "You mean the town house apartments. Mr. Puckett, that wasn't me, that was Shamira."

"Shamira, you mean Mrs. Muster."

"Yes," Vatly said. As if on cue or rehearsed, Shamira walked into the room. Puckett turned his attention to her.

"Mrs. Muster, you were at the town house apartments this morning about 3:45?" She grinned salaciously. Nodded her head.

"Why?" Puckett asked.

She stood behind Vatly and started rubbing his shoulders. "I met someone at the club. We talked, had some drinks at his place."

Puckett shook his head as if he hadn't heard what he knew he had just heard. "I thought you were married to Mr. Muster."

"She is." That was Vatly.

"And you don't mind her having an affair?"

"She said they talked and had some drinks. That's not an affair."

"But even that's cool with you, you encourage this?"

"No."

"You don't discourage it either?"

"No, Detective Puckett. Shamira's a very vivacious, very sexual and carnal woman. She has even expressed her attraction to you, which I will not attempt to stop if she chooses to pursue it. I forgive her for her sexual escapades and she in turn forgives me for mines. We have an understanding relationship."

Puckett was utterly flabbergasted and momentarily at a loss for words. Finally, he looked at her, "So who were you seeing?

"Ladezma Rios, apartment thirty-two."

Puckett's ride home did nothing to kill his feelings about the mendacious character of the Muster clan. The ambivalence he was feeling could only be cured with answers. He started to check out Rios but he figured it would be futile. He had to pack and a plane to catch.

CHAPTER 15

The house had been designed by a Greek architect in the late forties. A three-story brick structure. The basement, cellar and storm shelter were magnificently constructed into corridors and four massive departments. The house sat on four acres of land surrounded by a cultivated wooded area with a maze of short cuts and trails. The neighboring homes in either direction, were at least a third of a mile away. There was a barn that housed horses, a chicken coop, cows and pigs. The homes of Sugar Land had been ideal because of their spacing and privacy. Surveillance cameras were mounted to large poles. A room with ten monitors received feedback from the cameras. It was a task getting within seventy-five yards of the property without being detected. In between the house and the wooded barrier stood a huge tent with a transparent roof. Inside was an assortment of games, toys and recreational equipment. On the far East side of the house was a huge swimming pool and small shacks. Extensive research and money had been invested into acquiring this particular home and renovating it to satisfaction.

Kenya stood staring out the window of the library. The same library where directly below her children of all ages were kept. The same room where Victor sat and listened to her like he really gave a damn. Truth had crystallized solidly in her mind early on that this place and these people did not represent a foster home or adoption agency. Last night they had brought in a baby girl and a crib into Yadira's room across from hers. It was a strange arrangement the way things happened in this house; Kenya just observed silently. Initially she and her sister were separated, it was this that motivated the conversation between her and Victor, as everyone called him. Kenya did not like the way they were dressed either. Always in tight, skimpy, nasty clothing that made her feel naked and self-conscious. Patty had given her some hot pink pants that hugged every centimeter of her like a second skin. Uncomfortably they stuck in her butt when she walked, and she always found herself consciously waiting for opportunities to pull the uncomfortable outfit out of unwanted places. A lot changed after their talk in the library.

"You asked to speak with me Kenya?"

"Uh ... yes, sir, I ... they took my little sister. They separated us."

He stared at her transfixed and frozen. "Kenya, I want you to call me Victor, please. Are you comfortable here, have you had any trouble?"

Kenya thought about his question and just decided to be honest. Hell in her line of reasoning, it couldn't get any worse. Could it? "Mr. Victor ..."

He cut her off, "No Kenya, just call me Victor, please. I would like for you and I to be friends."

"Victor," she began unsteadily, "I need my little sister with me, she's the most important thing to me." She watched Victor's eyes travel over her young body. His eyes lingering at several places for several seconds. They had given them only tight t-shirts, no bras, so her nipples protruded lewdly through the tight cotton t-shirt. "I just want us to have the same room, please."

"Is that all?" Victor inquired affably.

Kenya looked puzzled, thought for a second. "Could you please get us some decent clothes, it's embarrassing wearing stuff like this." She indicated the lack of material.

Victor once again glanced at her, this time soaking up her flawless golden-brown skin. "Kenya, are you a virgin ... you know, are you sexually active?" Kenya was stunned by the question, no one had ever asked her something like that. Victor continued, "You are a very beautiful, very desirable child in a woman's body. Are you not aware of that?"

Kenya stared at him unbelievingly, briefly recalled the incident with her stepfather. "No sir, I'm not sexually active." she answered demurely.

Victor got up and walked his squat little frame to the window, stared out contemplating. "Kenya you are an intelligent girl. I am certain you have guessed that this is no foster home. I wish to trust you, offer you security and freedom, make this home, your home. If you give it half a chance, you will like it here. You will not be treated as the other children, I will give you and your sister your own room, your own clothes. But you must, I must trust you." He walked over and stood in front of her, kneeled and placed his hands on her knees. "Can I trust you, Kenya?"

"Can I trust you?" she asked.

Victor smiled, "Yes, Kenya, you can trust me." He grabbed her hands and stood her up, they were about the same height. He observed her clothing and physique. "You're most definitely correct, these clothes are not befitting a young Queen." He smiled, pushed his glasses up on his nose. "Would you like to go shopping?"

She hesitated momentarily. "You're going to take us shopping?" she said incredulously.

"No sweetheart, I'm going to take you shopping, you may purchase as many things as you wish for your sister."

"Why?" Kenya asked.

"Why what?"

"Why are you being so nice to me, all the other girls have been here longer?"

"You are beautiful Kenya, very precious and very special. I'm not trying to buy your affections, but I am trying to build a trusting relationship with you. You are not them! All this," he spun indicating the Big House, "can be yours if I trust you. I could give you to the authorities, the police, but I guarantee you they will split you and your sister up. You do not wish for that to happen, right?"

"If we stay here, you'll keep me and my sister together?"

"Yes Kenya, I promise."

"Okay." She gave Victor a half-hearted smile, just a fraction of her brilliance and damn near fried the man like bacon in a skillet.

"I'll send Patty up with some proper attire and we'll leave at six. Okay?"

"Alright. Thank you, Victor."

"Anything for you sweetheart, anything."

Out the window Kenya watched the blue range rover pull into the gates half a mile away. It was just a blue speck gradually getting bigger. There were also two fifteen passenger vans parked in the driveway. She, and Jami had been here a little over a week. Their room was on the third floor overlooking the pool. Next to them were two freckled face twin sisters about her age named Tisha and Tiara Holmes. They were skinny with dark brown hair. Two other girls about her age stayed in the basement rooms, named Valerie and Amber. The clothes did not seem to bother them. Valerie preferred to walk around in t-shirt and panties, not bothering to dress unless going to one of her dates as she called it or out to the tent. All except Amber wore heavy makeup and basically ignored the younger kids that ran around.

Tisha had asked Kenya. "Damn, how old are you?"

"I need a damn cigarette," Tiara stated. "Do you smoke?" Kenya shook her head.

"How old are you?" Tisha asked again.

"I'm fourteen," Kenya replied.

"You're about to be fifteen, right?" Tiara asked.

"No," Kenya said. "I just turned fourteen in March."

"Damn, you have some big titties to be fourteen," Valarie said cynically.

"A big butt too!" Tisha interjected.

Tiara palmed her orange size bumps, "Mine are growing, most men like big titties." She giggled. Amber remained silent and stared at the television.

"When you start fucking?" Valarie asked emphatically.

The bluntness and nature of the question immobilized Kenya for a nanosecond. She answered hesitantly and hoarsely, "I'm too young for anything like that."

The trio busted into a sardonic laughter. "You're bullshittin' right?" Tisha asked in her cynical tone.

"You've never had your pot stirred!" Tiara asked unbelieving-ly. The three girls giggled as if they had a secret. "They're going to love you," Valarie said.

"Who's gonna love me?" Kenya asked.

"The filthy, dirty old men who molest and rape us." That was Amber.

"Shut the fuck up Amber, you're the only one who's not with the program," Valarie exclaimed harshly.

The twins looked at each other and in unison rolled their skin-ny necks, snapped their fingers and sang, "Get with the program baby —"

"—Or the program will get with you." Valarie finished. Amber was cute, she had long blonde hair with dark eyes.

Tiara said arrogantly, "We're the forbidden fruit, men love to taste us instead of their wrinkled, tired ass wives."

"Yep!" Valerie retorted. "The innocence, they love to be in control and teach us. It hurts at first, but a lot of fun afterward. You'll get with the program Kenya. I've been sexually active since I was eight."

"Me too," Tisha piped in.

"Me three," Tiara sang. The trio started laughing.

"I'm not getting down like that until I'm grown and married." That was Kenya.

"We are grown," Tiara retorted.

"No! You just think you're grown. Victor has just screwed y'alls head up," Amber stated acerbically.

"I'm gonna go steal some cigarettes from Patty. Y'all comin'?" Tiara whined.

Children ran here and there, yelling, screaming and playing. Valerie, Tisha and Tiara had left. Jami came from the big tent looking discontent and somber. Kenya asked Amber, "Are there always this many kids here?"

"No, we've been in Sugarland about a year. Normally it's just the regulars. Me, Shamira, Yolanda, Valerie, Tisha, Tiara and Dominique. Then Timothy, Vance and Jerald. Babies come and go real quick, it's never been this crowded."

"What is everyone doing here?" Jami asked.

"Victor sells children to people who can't have them, either here in the United States or to other countries. Some girls and boys are just used to satisfy nasty old men and women."

"How long have you been here?" Kenya asked. "Since I was five or six."

Jami looked at her big sister, "Kenya, are they going to sell us?"

"We're not stayin' here; we're getting out of here some kind of way," Kenya stated vehemently.

"Good luck," Amber said skeptically.

When Kenya was moved into the Big House and was given different clothes, the other girls jealousy grew fangs, they shunned her except for Amber. Through Amber she began to get esoteric understanding of her surroundings. Yadira was a teacher, The

Teacher. Initially it was difficult to believe Victor was capable of all this she had heard. However, if seeing was believing, she was in no position to deny what she saw daily. Amber was fond of Yadira; said she cried a lot when she thought no one was looking.

The library door opened. Yadira was holding the little baby that had come that morning. "Kenya, have you seen the twins?"

"No ma'am."

"Would you mind watching the baby for a second? I have to find them."

"Yes ma'am, I'll watch her. Why don't you check the horse barn?"

Yadira handed Kenya the baby, "What's her name?" Kenya asked.

"Huh ... um, oh Camilla," Yadira said hurriedly as she raced from the room.

"Hey baby, where your mama at? I know whoever she is, she's worried about you, huh?"

"So, you're what the big fuss is all about." Kenya spun around to face the male voice. Her back was to the door and had not heard him enter the room. "Yes," he thought out loud, "you're definitely a jewel. How are you, Kenya?"

"Who are you?" Kenya asked with mild irritation in her voice as she held the baby over her shoulder. He was a light skinned brother, around sixteen or seventeen, she guessed. Kenya was wearing a sundress with an assortment of colors. Her hair had grown past her shoulders and she had braided it into two long pony tails.

He walked upon her and stared into her golden colored eyes. "Lawd, what are you doing here!" he said.

"Who are you?" she demanded. Familiarity with the place had brought forth fortitude and assertiveness.

"Jerald, and you're Kenya, right?" He looked at the baby. "Oh, and little Iyanna Akbar."

Puzzled, Kenya said, "Yadira said her name was Camilla."

Jerald laughed, "That's the name they gave her. Her mama named her Iyanna."

"You know her mama?"

"Nope, jus read about it in the paper," he said in an insouciant manner.

"Why are you here?" Kenya asked.

"Is there any other place I should be?"

"Where are your parents?"

"Victor and Patty are my parents."

"They're your jailers!"

"Now ain't that a bitch, if they're my jailers what are they to you?" Kenya stared at his sardonic grin. "Difference is I'm not fooling myself. Plus, you could just leave, but you don't. I'm here because they won't let me leave. You're here because you're afraid to leave."

"Victor has made several promises to us, I'm waiting to collect, simple as that." He walked around her like you would a new car on a showroom floor. "You're only fourteen?"

Being here had given Kenya a glimpse of her feminine powers. She had sat many hours prudently listening to the twins and Valarie anecdotal sexual experiences. She had come to a slow realization that most, if not all women had an advantage over most, if not all men. She was learning how to tap into that well that gave her the edge. "Why?" she grinned. "Am I too much for my age?"

Her response surprised him. "Ah ... yeah ... a little."

"What's little about anything on me?" she teased.

"Nothing from what I can see, do I get to see more?"

"Now that," she said emphatically, "will depend on your behavior."

"Mmm ... hmm. I see."

"Where's the paper you read about Iyanna at?"

"It's in my room, you wanna check it out?"

"If you can handle that."

He walked behind her and lifted the hem of her dress. Kenya cringed and fought the urge to jerk away. He studied her curvaceous buttocks sheathed in her cotton panties, shook his head, and released the hem of the dress as he patted her gently on the butt. "Yes Ms. Kenya, I can definitely handle that."

He was headed out of the door when she had succeeded in curbing her anger, not her fear anymore, anger. She said coyly, "Next time why don't you ask me can you do that. It's much more exciting with permission, isn't it? Or are you accustom to stealin' what you want?"

Jerald laughed, "Sho' ya right, my bad. Just promise me you won't say no, if I ask."

"Promises are made to be broken, bring me the paper, please."

Jerald shut the door. Kenya breathed a heavy sigh of relief. "That was easier than I thought it would be Iyanna. If I can help get you back to your mama I will."

Kenya did not want to upset the balance of her and Jami's reality, but she had learned a lot, but not enough. Amber told her that sooner or later Victor would want something in return for all his kindness. He had never been this nice to anyone. Amber was only thirteen, yet, her experience, knowledge and wisdom by far outreached her years. She was not a child anymore, rarely laughed, rarely talked and eighty-five percent of the time when she did say something it was serious. Slowly she opened up to Kenya, they would talk for hours.

Twenty minutes later, Yadira came back to collect Iyanna. Kenya headed toward the kitchen, when in route she heard an argument taking place in Victor's study. "So, you're not going to ship Jami along with the order?" Patty asked icily.

"No, I am not, I promised Kenya they would stay together. It's a promise I intend to keep," Victor stated.

"I've told you once before she should be in the basement room with the others. She hasn't earned the privilege to move around as she does."

"When did you start making decisions such as that?"

"You're a fool, Victor. That little beauty queen will never, I mean never accept you. The minute you give her wings she will fly. It may be ten years from now, but-I guarantee you she will fly."

"Are you through Patty?"

"Please listen to me Victor. Put 'em in the basement, ship them Sunday with the rest. Make a clean break and let's move on."

"Patty, they stay with me, this is a dead issue."

"You're getting old, comfortable and sloppy."

"And you're beginning to annoy me." He waved his hand. "Do what you are paid to do."

"Oh," she said, "Vatly called, a detective named Puckett came to see him. His car was seen leaving the apartment that the baby was taken from. The same cop called Phoenix looking for Yadira and Decker. One of Decker's old acquaintances informed him of that.

Last but not least, golden boy did not get on the plane to Virginia. He's talking with the cop, and they're looking for his arrest record. So, they can find out who arrested him, released and visited him. All this came from Decker this morning while you were out riding horses with your little Princess." Patty stormed out of the room. Kenya held her position, listened as Victor got on the phone. The details of the conversation were lost to her.

Kenya had heard enough and decided to fall to the kitchen and get something to eat. She walked in on Vance and Dominique fondling each other. They jumped and straightened their clothes. Vance was like Jerald, a boy toy for rich, lonely old women. Dominique was Yadira's only biological child for Paul. Paul was the only reason Yadira and Dominique were here. They were a happy family until Paul got mixed up with Victor, she was madly in love with him then. The choice was either split her family up or just let this run its course, then return to being a normal family. Women routinely compromised their values and beliefs, lowered their standards to follow their hearts; allowing irrational and illogical emotions to take center stage over logic and common sense.

CHAPTER 16

Victor had called a meeting, it was ten thirty p.m. All present were Paul, Kenneth, Timothy, Vatly, Officer Decker, Yadira and Patty. Timothy and Kenneth were only twenty-one but both had been specially trained since their abduction to kill. They were proficient, remorseless and dangerous. Victor sat in his large leather recliner in his normal oversized suit.

"Alright Vatly, what happened?" Victor asked.

Vatly gave a short account of the incident that took place at the girls' apartment. Described and emphasized that all would have gone smoothly if the boy had not showed up. Then he described Officer Puckett, what had taken place in his house. The alibi that he gave, he wasn't overly concerned.

"The cop called Phoenix looking for me," Decker said. "For him to even know about me he had to do some digging. Vanderbilt up in Washington called me and said that a Houston Detective called asking for information about the Ashley case. Also inquired as to the whereabouts of Yadira Holmes. Sooner or later, he's going to trace Yadira to this city, he's also going to trace me to this city."

Victor looked frustrated, "How can he know so much?"

"All I can tell you Victor is after he spoke to Vail, he checked the computer for an arrest record and didn't find one, then started doing his homework. He's getting help from a former Chicago prosecutor by the name of Kennybrew. He reached out to Yancy Mordecai with FBI's VCAC. You know Mordecai's reputation, and I'm sure you remember the fiasco 10 years back concerning special agent Qasiym Serengeti.

"Former Special Agent Serengeti," Victor corrected hatefully. "Yeah, be that as it may, Mordecai's unconventional. He trained Serengeti, and despite Serengeti's shameful ousting he and Mordecai are still tight.

"So, what are you saying?"

"Involving one is like involving the other."

Victor thought for a moment, "For now the Houston Detective is our only threat, right?"

"Yes, sir."

"I anticipate we'll be long gone before FBI Bureaucracy can assemble a task force that will focus on us."

"It's the money," Patty said knowingly.

"What are you talking about?" Vatly asked. He didn't know that Victor had went with more money trying to bribe the kids. He would have strongly disagreed with that method. Just from what he knew he would not have come at them like that.

Patty explained, "Victor offered him seventy-five thousand for the baby. The boy turned it down, any common sense whatsoever would have told you if he turns down that much money for a baby you thought he didn't want, just leave him alone." Everyone was listening to Patty. "But no, you set him up, send him to jail and make him give up his baby for his freedom. You fucked him and he's lying dead to fuck you back, you better hope he doesn't have a bigger dick because he's lying dead to hurt you far worse than you hurt him."

Seething in anger, Victor's voice was a low growl. "Please Patty don't play with explosives, you may hurt yourself." The room was quiet, tension thick as wet concrete.

"Where is he now?" Paul asked.

Decker dropped his head and shook it. "Caught a flight tonight." "To Washington?" Yadira asked in panicky voice.

Decker shook his head, "Seattle. When he leaves there, he's going to Sacramento."

"He knows about Seattle and Sacramento," Vatly said incredulously.

"Let's just smoke the fool." That was Timothy.

"Who the fuck is this guy, Columbo?" Victor exclaimed. "Do you know exactly why he flew out?"

"No, I spoke with his secretary; she said he's due back eleven o'clock on the eighteenth. She wouldn't disclose the nature of his business." Decker explained.

"You said he checked the computer for an arrest record, can he trace it back to us?" Victor's voice and demeanor were calm.

"No, but he can find Willow."

"How? We used a fake name."

"Willow had to sign a release. If Puckett snaps, he'll just run a record of everyone that was released that day. Cross reference it with address and priors, when you find the name with no priors and no address, you have the fake name and who released him."

Vatly said, "If he knows about those other states then it's safe to assume he also knows about Detroit; Shamiria and Yolanda."

Patty jumped out of silence, "He was at your house, he met them. He didn't show any signs of knowing them?"

Decker interjected, "I don't think Puckett has the case file just yet. Or he didn't have them when he talked to Vatly. He will have them soon, if not already. I'm certain there will be old photos of Shamiria, Yolanda, the twins and Yadira. It's been eight years, whether or not he can identify them from childhood photo's is anyone's guess."

"I told you to change their damn names," Patty cried. "He doesn't have to recognize their faces. Shit he knows their names.

All he has to do is recognize one of their names. You never listen Victor."

Victor ignored her, "Timothy, Kenneth locate Willow and put him to sleep. It's time we start tying up loose ends. Vail also, he can identify Decker and myself. When the cop gets off that plane tomorrow night, make him a memory."

Patty said, "Victor let's just pull up. They win this time, let's just go."

Victor lost his composure, his last nerve snapped! He slammed his hands on top of his desk and shoved his papers to the floor. Then hoisting the small color television, he threw it at Patty. It fell short and exploded into sparks and flames upon hitting the floor. "Fuck that! Kenneth, kill that Bitch!" Without hesitation Kenneth pulled his Walter P-K from his coat.

"Wait Kenneth!" Paul yelled. He stood in front of Patty, who had cringed and started crying. "Victor," Paul said calmly. "Let's not go there. Please. Stay rational."

Victor adjusted his glasses, wiped the sweat from his face. "Alright! Alright!" Kenneth still had his gun drawn, Victor waved his hand downward and Kenneth lowered the gun. He sat down, steepled his fingers under his chin and spoke slowly. "Upon completion of this deal everyone in this room is getting five hundred thousand dollars and a plane ticket anywhere in the world. Five hundred thousand dollars!" he said emphatically. "The twenty-first is only three days away. Can we hold this shit together until then? After the twenty-first, I don't care where you go." He turned to Patty, "I am quite sorry Patty, but your constant complaining has become tritefully monotonous, we're all pressured. Decker, Kenneth, Tim take care of Willow, Vail and that damn cop."

After everyone had left, Victor walked up to Kenya's room, listened to the door. The T.V. was still on; he knocked. Kenya opened the door in a blue nightgown he had bought her, it was very modest, stopping at her knees. He noticed that she slept in her bra. "Hello beautiful."

Kenya was surprised to see him. "Hello Victor."

"Is your sister asleep?"

"Yes."

"Can I speak with you briefly?"

She stepped aside and allowed him to enter the room. What Kenya liked about this place was although she was only fourteen, they treated her like an adult, not as a child. Victor seated himself in a chair across from her bed. "What are you watching?"

"The Rock, with Nicholas Cage and Sean Connery."

"Oh, yes, I've seen it. Kenya, I come to tell you, we will be leaving in four days, been kind of thinking about Brazil. Are you coming?"

"Do I have a choice?"

Victor laughed softly, "Some days you are such a child, then some days so much a woman. Kenya, there is always a choice."

She decided to try out some of the things Amber had told her about. Her feminine qualities that could drive a man crazy. She left her bed and sauntered over to Victor and stood in front of him, called up every ounce of courage she had and sat in his lap. "I want to stay with you Victor." She hugged him and rested her head on his chest. Felt his arm circle her waist and his hand rest on her hip. "I know you'll always take care of me." Victor was utterly overwhelmed, felt himself begin to get an erection and jumped up out of the chair. Kenya fell clumsily to the floor. "Ow!" she exclaimed.

Victor was ashamed, "I'm sorry Kenya, I just remembered something. I must go. And yes, I will always take care of you." Victor backed out and shut the door. Still on the floor Kenya laughed, and couldn't wait to tell Amber. Two minutes later there was another knock on the door, she thought Victor had come back and swung the door open.

Jerald stood there frowning. "What was he doing here?" he said angrily.

Kenya noticed his tone. "He wanted to talk to me."

"Yeah whatever!" He pushed past her into her room.

"Jerald I'm about to go to bed, you gotta leave."

"I bet you didn't tell that to Victor!" he said viciously.

"You're not Victor," she replied curtly.

"What the hell is that supposed to mean?"

"He's a man, you're just a boy. If I ask him to take me out right now, he will. You can't or won't … you're afraid of him."

Jerald pushed Kenya against the wall and placed his forearm between her chin and chest. "Watch your mouth Kenya, I only fear God and that's only because I can't see Him. I'm going to show you just how much of a man I am." He mashed his lips roughly against hers while his other hand went to the hem of her nightgown. Spreading her legs with his knees he rubbed her vagina through her panties. When he removed his mouth from hers Kenya said calmly and frigidly, "There you go stealing again." Her comment shocked him, he was expecting tears, pleading and fear. Her voice was neither tipped with anger or fear. It was laced with some unidentifiable substance. Jerald stepped away from her. Kenya walked toward him slowly, seductively her hips swung in a subtle yet presumptuous rhythm. Her golden colored eyes caught the light at a crazy angle, they looked like miniature fireballs glowing amber red with each step she took towards him. Jerald stepped backwards until his back hit the wall. Kenya stepped right upon him; her breast rested on his chest. Her words were capped with cyanide when she spoke, low and effusively. "If you knew who my mom and dad was, you wouldn't fuck with me like that. For the last four years I've been going through hell, I'm tired. I'm nobody's victim, you ever touch me again without my consent I'll kill you." A loud clap of thunder shook the house, Jerald's heart jumped. Kenya asked softly, "Are you going to apologize?"

He took a deep breath. "I'm sorry Kenya, I was out of line."

Still in her polite but serious manner, "Just ask Jerald. Be polite, like this … Jerald will you kiss me?" she asked. Jerald looked totally perplexed. Kenya smiled, more of a demand this time, she said, "Kiss me." Their lips met in agreement this time. His tongue explored her mouth while his hands caressed her hips. When the kiss ended Kenya said, "So much nicer when both parties are in agreement, isn't it?" Jerald nodded his head. "Victor wants me for himself, what are you going to do about it?"

"Find a way to get us out of here," he said hoarsely.

"Sounds good to me," she whispered, sweetly.

While lying in bed waiting for sleep, thinking about her beautiful mother, and her resilient father, she smiled. Adversity always demanded profound responses. Adversity is like fire to gold, it's that extreme heat of pressure that boils or brings out all the impurities, leaving the purest, rawest finished products. She could not just run to the cops; they would place her in a foster home and separate her from her sister. Tears trickled down her cheek and landed on her pillow, pain was not the cause of her tears. Maybe all butterflies cried when they stepped from their cocoons.

Chapter 17

They played cards until ten, then Xavier and Shai went outside. He took her up to the roof, his office. He stood behind her with his arm encircling her. Isis hung high in the sky; her milky white light bathed them clean. Shai had a heavenly scent, he absorbed it all or tried to. Some things in life just fall into place and instantly felt normal. "You come up here a lot?" she inquired.

"Yeah, this is where I get my peace and solitude, a lot of answers too."

"What answers?"

"Just when life feels like it's bearing down on me from all sides and this yoke feels like it's too heavy to bear, I come up here and vent my frustration, my anger, my pain." A cool breeze passed them and Shai shivered. "Here I can shed tears that only God can see. Up here my soul convinces me that I'm better than some, worse than others."

Shai turned to face him; his hand rested on the rise of her butt. "I guess I've felt like that before. Is this like running away?"

Xavier smiled. "Thought about it myself a time or two, but Moses went to the top of the mountain, Jesus went to the top of the mountain and Mohammad went up to the mountain. Were they running?"

"So, this is your mountain?" Shai whispered in one of those unconditionally understanding tones that only women can create.

"Sho-nuff, this is where I pray and think, look for answers." "I never knew you could be like this."

He grinned. "Be like what?"

"So easy to be with, so easy to talk to. I've just never felt so comfortable with anyone." All that talk about answers, Shai thought her panties were trying to find the answer, but it wasn't up the crack of her behind. So, she reached back and pulled them out, wiggled her hips.

"Did you get it?" Xavier asked facetiously.

Mildly embarrassed, she laughed and buried her face in his chest. "See that's what I mean, I would have never done that in front of anyone else."

"I'm honored, but next time tell me, I'll hunt 'em down." They both laughed.

She put her hands in her pockets. "I'm really liking this, Xavier, being with you. I'm tired of seasonal relationships, can we make this work?"

Xavier spun, now his back was to her. She put her hands into his front pockets and laid her face on his back. "Are you patient, Shai?"

She thought the question was out of place but responded placidly, "Yes."

"Good. Shai, I know you want to be number one, but right now I have to get my t-lady straight. She's my number one priority. So many women get upset when men say that, but I've never started something I couldn't finish. I intend on getting her off drugs and outta this ghetto."

"What about your life, Xavier?"

"How can I live when I know she's killing herself? Shai, a lot of brothas hide their feelings, then wonder how come their women don't understand them. I'm not askin' you to read my mind. Today being with you was like something out of a dream. This may sound crazy but I've been in love with you since you were bold enough to write your number on my brand-new shirt." He turned back to face her. "Sometimes the same winds that pushed you into my life, will enter into a conspiracy with the night and pull you away. This isn't forever, I just need some time and understanding."

"I'll wait, be patient and help if I can. I'll give you all that I have, if you give me all that I need." She paused, "How come you're just now telling me how you feel?"

He gave her a knowing stoical stare, "C'mon, get off the horse playing, you were wrapped up in Calvin."

"I stopped being intimate with Calvin over four months ago. Do you know why?"

"Post-traumatic stress syndrome," he said playfully.

"Seriously!" she snapped.

"Naw, why?" he asked.

"Because of you. I needed to see you without any distractions."

"Did you see me?"

"I'm still looking."

"Oh ... I see."

"Do you?" she asked.

"Yeah, I do." He found her full soft supple lips, tasted her thoroughly. Then somebody below screamed, loud!

Nellie, Vianna and Bernadine were standing on the balcony. When Xavier and Shai joined them, they saw Solo and Dink had gotten back into it, a miniature crowd had formed. A pearl white Cadillac Escalade sitting on chrome blades pulled into the parking lot. Adib and Moophisey exited the vehicle in matching baby blue silk suits. A minute into the fight, Dink started getting his ass whupped. Two of Solo's cohorts were playing cheerleaders. When Dink fell, Chill tried to offer some assistance when the other crips caught him and started whupping up on him. Aaron jumped in and was dropped by the third member of the trio. "Xavier do something!" Nellie shouted. He hit the stairs three at a time. The deafening roar of a pistol grip erupted repeatedly. Silence located everyone in the parking lot.

"Cut this shit out!" That was Adib.

Dink was folded up and bleeding badly. Chill and Aaron had gotten touched up pretty good too. Xavier walked over to Chill and picked him up. "Ya o-ite lil homie?"

"Yeah," he coughed, "just need ta fire some'ing up, conversate with my bitch!" He looked at Aaron, "What 'bout you, lil' hustler?"

"Just embarrassed man, that's about it," Aaron said.

"What's up X?" Adib asked.

"I'm 'bout to taste some of this drama juice these niggas passin' out, it smells like Kool-Aid to me."

"Handle ya business baby, I gotcha covered," Adib assured him. Vianna was jumping up and down, "Awww, you gon get it. Zav- ya pissed off," she sang.

Nellie yelled, "Baby leave that shit alone!"

Solo was laughing, "That's right crack monsta, you better call his punk ass."

"Xavier, kick his ass!" she recanted.

Shai stared at Nellie and Vianna, she was naturally afraid that Xavier would get hurt. She had just witnessed Solo dismantle Dink, who was a lot larger than Xavier. Solo had height and bulk. Deshawn, Denise and their mother watched from their doorstep; the parking lot was packed. Xavier pulled off his shirt and looked up at Shai. She was looking all scared, she just didn't realize this was nothing spectacular, just another day in the hood. He took a hundred-dollar bill from his pocket and held it up at her. She leaned, squinted her eyes trying to understand, then smiled and nodded her head, he put his cell phone on top of it. He pointed at the trio, "Y'all line that shit up."

Chill hollered at him, "Handle up X-man."

Xavier turned and winked, "Anything else would be uncivilized."

Solo told the other two to stay back, "I got this cuz." Solo wasted no time, he swung three that Xavier avoided by just backing up. Solo threw three more; a straight right, straight left and then a right hook. Xavier weaved left, then right, then bobbed under the hook and caught Solo with a solid right hook to the kidney, then straight left directly to Solo's chin which immediately sat him on his ass. From the balcony Nellie, Bernadine and Shai all said in unison, "Damn!"

Xavier stood back, "Get yo' bitch ass up. That's fo Chill and Aaron." Solo got up slowly, shook his head, yelled and ran at Xavier throwing a wild right hook. Xavier went to one knee and threw a six-inch left hook to Solo's right thigh, then his left thigh. Solo buckled, grabbed Xavier's shoulders and tried to lift him up. Xavier hit him in the nuts, Solo folded over and fell. "That's for disrespectin' my mama. Y'all better help him up before I stomp his ass."

The bigger of the two ran at him. He was quick, caught Xavier over the eye and on his cheek. Xavier made a low growl, executed a three-hundred-and-sixty-degree spin and connected solidly to the man's jaw with his elbow. The impact was loud, the man fell to the ground unconscious, his jaw broken.

Bernadine said, "That boy is bad!"

Nellie was quiet, shocked! Solo was back on his feet. He came at Xavier with more anger and determination. Xavier blocked four or five licks thrown, then shot his hand out with lightning speed and slapped Solo. The skin on skin echoed throughout the parking lot. Solo could not believe he had just been slapped. He ran at Xavier, Xavier braced, turned and shot his foot out between Solo's chin and chest. The force of him running into the kick lifted him off his feet and elevated him. He landed on his back with a loud thud. "That's for pointing that damn gun at me."

Xavier turned to the last brother, he threw his hands in the air, "You win today playa."

"Load ya boyz up and get' em out o here."

Deshawn walked out to him. As he approached his car, the blue truck sped off. Adib and Moophisey pulled deeper into the parking lot. "You alright youngsta, that was some shit right out of a Wesley Snipes movie." That was Deshawn.

Xavier laughed, felt Shai step to his side in one of those females possessively-claiming- type-moves. You ever see two beautiful women who automatically acknowledge the others physical strength. There's an esoteric telepathic conversation: *'You tight?'*

'Yeah, you tight too.'

'You got him.'

'Yeah, I got him.'

'Cool.'

Deshawn spoke, "How are you? I'm Honey."

Shai spoke, "Shai." She put her arm around Xavier's waist.

Deshawn smiled, "I should have known more than good character was behind your discipline and self-restraint. Every man has to eat." She looked Shai over, "And it seems as though your appetites being taken care of. I shot my shot sista, but he turned me down. From one woman to another, you got a good one, hold on to him."

Shai 's grip tightened, "I intend to."

The telepathic conversation jumped into play again when Shai and Deshawn met eyes again: *'You got him.'*

'Yeah, I got him.'

"Cool.'

"You looked good baby-boy, I'm impressed." That was Adib. Vianna ran and jumped on Moophisey, "Zav-ya found a virgin."

Everybody laughed. Shai was introduced to Moophisey. "Man, where y'all been?" Xavier asked.

"They had a black Expo at the Hofheinz Pavillion, Sister Souljah, Brenda Perryman, Donna Richardson, Mocha Lee—"

"They fine as hell X, Donna and Mocha!" Adib cut Moophisey off. "—and Dr. Ro," Moophisey completed.

"Moo wanted to mob, so we dressed to impress and bailed up in there. A lot of sista's, Blackman you should have—" He noticed the look on Shai's face and cut his thought short. Moo had been working with Xavier since he was eight or so. He was in his thirties, taught self-defense classes at the mosque. He balled his fist and placed it beneath his chin while crossing his other arm across his body. This was his signature gesture. "You was slow and sloppy on that spin, X."

"Aww man it worked Moo!"

"But he could have grabbed you, then what?"

"Adib's gonna sound the alarm again."

"Damn skippy!" Adib announced, everybody laughed. Dink walked over and hugged Xavier, "Preciate it, X-man."

"You know how we do it, Dink."

After about thirty minutes of affable conversation Xavier said he had to get Shai home. He threw her the keys and hopped in on the passenger side. The Cadillac Escalade pulled out with Bernadine inside. They agreed to drop her off on Rosedale and Ennis. Shai pulled out in the other direction, "Honey's pretty."

"I'll tell her you said so."

Shai just laughed. "You're silly, boy, are you going to teach Nathan all that?"

"Not until I teach him that fighting is a last resort. When nothing else will do, then get physical."

"When you kicked that boy, I thought you had broken his neck."

"It scared me too, I work on that shit with punching bags and sparring partners. This was the first time it was just all the way real. I kicked him harder than I intended to because he ran into it, I don't want no murder cases."

"Were you scared?"

"All confrontations are scary."

"Will I see you tomorrow?"

"If the good Lord blesses you to open your eyes, and me likewise, we'll hook up."

"How 'bout a movie?" she asked excitedly.

"Bet, look for me 'round five or so."

After leaving Shai's, Xavier rode out to Baytown. It was late but he just wanted to ride. Called his homie AJ and told him to meet him at J.D. Walker Park. It had been months since he had seen AJ. When he got there, AJ's six-four Impala was sitting on three wheels. It was painted in swirls of dark reds, light reds and pinks. It was a nasty ride with vanilla insides and convertible top. Gold plated eighty-threes finished the look. Xavier took the Swisher out of the glove compartment that Chill had given him. They talked about that three percent of something that was better than a hundred percent of nothing.

CHAPTER 18

Today is June eighteenth, seven thirty-five on 1-oh-1 The Bus. This is David D. Today's forecast is clear sunny skies, highs in the nineties. Right now, it's forty-five degrees in Seattle, and forty-eight here at 1-oh-1 The Bus. Number one in classical soul and today's R & B." The radio was on but Puckett was not listening. His mind was on the call ...

The call came late enough to catch him sleeping. The lights were off, the television was on. The whetstone of exhaustion had sharpened the edges of his disgruntled disposition. His muscles, like his mind were tired and restless. Moment by moment he felt like Quasimodo, the high-living hunchback of Notre Dame—perhaps not as ugly as that poor wretch but not a fraction as nimble.

The windows were closed, though the curtains stood open, casually inviting the night into the room. Thunderous explosions bungeed from black skies that roiled menacingly and lent unto man apocalyptic speculations. The thunder resembled the great guns of battleships providing cover fire for invading troops. Hard hollow explosions echoed along the skies chased by a light show that would make old man July Fourth envious.

The call came from Special Agent Yancy Mordecai. He was trapped in Britain. FBI bureaucratic bullshit would prevent the fast action necessary to make a difference in his case. However, he had the name of a person who would help, if Puckett welcomed his help.

The name given was Qasiym Askari Serengeti.

The name was known because of Candance Hanemauer, a native of Tamasco, Norway, kidnapped at age eight and moved in an international white slave craze. Candance was fortunate, whereas many women and children were ushered into poor countries and forced into sexual bondage of some form, harsh labor, surrogate motherhood or death. Others landed into the harems and stables of millionaires. Candance landed on a farm in Northern Montana to the care of the elderly.

A gift from their son who had amassed millions moving drugs between countries. His name was Louis Driskell. His reach touched cartels in Mexico, Mafia in Italy, organizations in Columbia and Bolivia and other various organizations. His parents were old, always wanted a daughter, he provided them one.

Candance grew up normal, loved and taken care of, well educated and she loved her adopted parents. In school her best friend was Fajr Serengeti. Fajr rebelled against her Islamic upbringing, was fascinated by the streets and the two-legged animals that patrolled them.

When Fajr was eighteen she overdosed on heroin. Her brother Qasiym Serengeti was home from the Marines. When Fajr recovered, twenty-one people associated with Fajr's supplier had been murdered. Police had absolutely no leads. Fajr told Candance that no one but Qasiym would do something like that.

When Candance was twenty-one Louis Driskell was murdered. Later the home of his parents was burned to the ground, leaving them for dead. Candance and Fajr were taken prisoner. For 18 months they were fed drugs and raped repeatedly.

Police investigators along with FBI task forces yielded nothing. But for 18 months bodies showed up. Drug dealers, mafia heads, organized criminals and their businesses were burned to the ground. Initially just men, then women. Finally, two children of a highly positioned corrupt politician.

Suddenly Fajr Serengeti and Candance Hanemauer turned up at a hospital in Mexico. Firestorms fell on the head of FBI Agent Qasiym Serengeti. It was speculated that he was the person behind the slew of murders. There was circumstantial evidence, but nothing concrete.

A witness came forth and was subsequently murdered under strange circumstances. Qasiym was quietly released. For years afterward he cared for his sister, and fell in love with Candance. Then tried to kill him, who, no one can say. He killed four but was left for dead along with his dead sister and a dead Candance.

It was only by a miracle of God alone that he survived.

Darrel left a message on Qasiym's phone. He'd take help from Shaitan himself right about now.

Darrell Puckett was on his way to Fahiym Ali's office, the psychiatrist of Charles Boyd, an eleven-year-old boy that was seven at the time of his abduction in December 2002. Then in May he was dumped over a bridge at midnight and expected to drown. Charles survived the fall and swam to shore. Last night Cathy emailed him all the case files that had been sent to him. The sleep on the plane was good, plus he had grabbed a couple hours in his hotel room. Most of his morning had been spent at the Seattle Police Department. Time was of an essence because he had a twelve o'clock flight out of Seattle to Sacramento.

The reports from Louisiana were the vaguest. From Washington he received photos of Yadira Holmes, fingerprints and mugshots. There were also photos of the Ashley family, statements from the parents. Yadira was a raven-haired amazon. Her vitals listed her as six foot-five, a hundred and ninety pounds.

He had attempted to locate her through the computer, however all attempts had been futile. She was no longer in Washington, it seemed as though she had just disappeared. There were records stating that she was married to Paul Holmes. Puckett traced Paul to Dayton, Texas. He had a blue Range Rover registered in his name. Occupation was listed at a club called the Tanqueray on the Southwest side of Houston. Puckett figured Yadira had to be with him.

The Detroit case file displayed a black man and a white woman with two little girls. The report read that James and Jenise Witiker were camping with their daughters; Shamiria and Yolanda Witiker.

When the local authorities found their thirty-two-foot Winnebago, the bodies of James and Jenise had been decomposing for seventy-two hours. James and Jenise had sustained fatal gunshot wounds to the head with a large caliber pistol. Their two daughters; Shamiria, twelve, and Yolanda, ten, were missing. Case unsolved. Puckett studied the photos; they were five years old. The mother and the oldest daughter had on orange shirts the father and youngest daughter wore aqua blue. The youngest daughter was definitely his, the oldest was most likely from a previous relationship. Something about the mother looked so familiar, he just could not put his finger on it. He put the photos inside of his attaché case.

In the first report from Phoenix, it was a detailed background check done in 2015 about Shelia Penock; Age: 24, Occupation: Preschool Teacher. Shelia was reportedly by family very gregarious and fun hearted. She frequented the local clubs and lead an active night life. Her boyfriend told Detectives that the clubs she visited the most was the Tanqueray and the Mistique. Puckett stopped. "The Tangueray," he said to himself. For the next fifteen minutes, he backtracked through the files. He knew he had just recently read across this name. He finally located what he was looking for; Paul Holmes worked at a club called the Tangueray. Too much of a coincidence, is not a coincidence. Two clubs called the Tangueray, Yadira being in Washington and Houston.

He made a note to check Phoenix real estate archives to see who had owned the Tangueray. There is a connection, he thought. Shane Muster is also in Houston. He recalled the white BMW leaving the scene in Washington. "I'm missing something, what though?" He thought out loud. Puckett rubbed his eyes, massaged his temples and picked up the last folder. Clifford Day was shot and killed on July 17, while investigating the disappearance of Shelia Penock, Valerie Johnson and Amber Ambrose. Clifford and Drew Decker shortly after they entered the residence, gunfire erupted. Day, 37 was shot and killed. Decker only sustained superficial injuries. Suspects fled in a white BMW. He continued to scan the report looking for a current address on Officer Decker. His eyes almost fell from their sockets when he saw a Houston address as Decker's present place of residence.

The ride to Fahiym Ali's office was filled with questions. The kind of questions that you knew deep down in your heart and soul you already had the answers for. His old friend Judge Kennybrew had schooled him a long time ago. Two principal objects stand in the way of solving a puzzle; two little knowledge and too little patience. Sometimes courage took precedence over both. They were not stupid, everything they had done was all too random, no one could have guessed it. People all over the world move businesses, change states but retain the same name so not changing the name of a club is not unusual. Obviously, they never expected anyone to narrow things down so close. If not for Vail telling him they offered him seventy-five thousand, he would have never gone the route he had. Seventy-five thousand dollars meant big business.

The visit with Fahiym had been successful. Charles recognized the photos of Yadira, no one else rang a bell. Charles said he had been sexually assaulted several times by different men. Kennybrew was right. By twelve-thirty Puckett was on his way to Sacramento. On the plane he called Vail.

Vail was still in the bed when his phone rang. He rolled over, yawned, stretched and his eyes fell on the digital alarm clock on his nightstand. Twelve forty-one, he smelled potatoes cooking and music was playing in the living room. Vail picked the phone up on the second ring. He and Daphane both answered at the same time; him from the bedroom, Daphane from the kitchen. "Hello." They both sang simultaneously.

"Vail?" Puckett asked.

"Yeah, who's this?" Vail asked sleepily.

"This is Puckett, where's Daphane?"

"I'm right here, what is it, you found Iyanna?"

"No, but I'm close, real close. Daphane what clubs do you go to?"

The question seemed odd to her. "Why?"

"Daphane this is important, please work with me ... okay?"

"Alright," she said despondently.

"What clubs?" he repeated. Vail just listened intently.

"Uh ... Carringtons, Mainevent ... um and Limelight, D Bar, V- live, Grooves."

"So, you have never been to a club called Tangueray?"

"Oh! Yes, but it's small, nothing spectacular, so I don't go there much. Is that what Officer Decker wanted?" The phone line hissed noisily. Puckett went rigid, apprehension eased into his voice.

"Decker called you?" He almost whispered into the phone. Vail detected the change in his voice.

Daphane said, "No, he left a message and number with my aunt for me to call him."

"Damn! How long has it been since you spoke with him?"

"What's up Detective Puckett?" Vail asked.

"I thought you were coming with him. That's what he told me."

"How long ago Daphane?" Puckett demanded.

"About thirty-five or forty minutes ago."

"Where are you Detective Puckett and what the fucks goin' on man?"

"I'm on a plane headed for Sacramento." His voice dropped an octave. "Vail, Decker's the cop, you gotta get outta there now!" The exigent nature of his voice was unmistakable.

"Detective, no one but you have this address."

"I gave him the address," Daphane said quietly. "What's going on?"

"Vail get out of there! Write this number down." Vail jumped out of bed. "Shit, I gotta find a pen."

"What's the number, I'll remember it," Daphane demanded.

"You certain?" Puckett asked.

"I'm a finance major, what's the number?"

"Puckett relayed the number and informed them to call him when they relocated.

"Hurry up Vail!" Puckett hung up.

Daphane ran into the bedroom, she was already dressed in sweat pants and a t-shirt. "What's going on Vail?"

"Get'cha shit and lets bail, we'll talk later."

"What is it Vail?" she yelled.

He ignored her, grabbed his wallet and keys. She yelled at him, near tears, "Where are we going?" Vail grabbed her hand and headed for the front door, he unlocked it and set the alarm. Daphane pulled away, "Wait!" She ran into the kitchen, turned off all the pilots on the electrical stove, gathered her purse and joined Vail. As they stepped from the West end of the breezeway, two white men were coming up the sidewalk; they had not noticed Vail or Daphane. Daphane quickly snatched Vail back into the breezeway, "Shit, it's him!"

"Who?" Vail asked, confused as hell now. Vail's apartment was in a breezeway with an East and West entrance. Daphane pulled him to the East exit where escape was possible.

Once on the freeway Vail asked, "How do you know those guys?"

"I only knew one, well recognized one." She hesitated and started crying. In between sobs and sniffles she explained that when she was six or seven months pregnant, he approached her, offering to adopt her baby for seventy-five thousand dollars. He would have all the paperwork drew up. "He told me you have a girl back home that you're engaged to. That if I really loved you, I would get rid of the baby because it would only hurt your career. He told me I was wrong for trapping you into a relationship with me." Her tears were a waterfall now. "I almost did it Vail ... because I wanted you ... to ... happy. At first, I wanted you by any means necessary, then I started loving you more than I loved myself and I only ... wanted you ... if ... if you were happy." Vail pulled over to the shoulder of the road and put his blinkers on. "They told me to speak with you about it, but I was afraid you'd want the money ... not me and the baby."

Vail pulled her into his arms and kissed her forcefully and tasted her salty tears, her running nose made a mess of them both. Wiping her face with his shirt, he said, "Don't worry about it baby."

"I couldn't do it Vail, I never thought I could hold you ... so she would be all I had left of you. I couldn't give away the gift you had given me; now they've taken her."

"Naw, they only borrowed her, 'cause they gots to unass her. Gotta give her back!"

"I'm so sorry Vail."

"For what? You haven't done anything wrong except put snot on my shirt, but you alright." He smiled. She rewarded his support with a smile, and a ferocious hug.

CHAPTER 19

Everyone in America is either searching for God or hiding from Him. They are trying to fill that spiritual hole, hush or satisfy that insistent urge to find a niche in this paradoxical ecosystem. Many times, the thorough whippings issued out by life are as ambiguous as the writings on the walls, that is only deciphered through unpredictable vicissitude or Einstein-like sagaciousness. Everyone's hoping or praying that if tomorrow comes they are a part of it, but time cheats us and makes us victims of circumstances, someone else's heaven becomes another man's hell. Interchangeable roads are so absolute, emasculating some, invigorating others. It's a waiting game whose essence is patience, life's so volatile. The todays of someone else could someday be your tomorrow, and the yesterday's forgotten will become the now's that are impossible to forget.

Victor woke up exhausted, drained by nightmares. He fought diligently with eerie images. Voices from his childhood with tentacles that held him under a viscous substance. His bed was soaking wet from perspiration and urine. He had a migraine headache that no medication to this point had mitigated the pain. Victor prayed silently for the first time since his mother killed herself nine years ago. There was a lot to be done before the twenty-first. He had already been on the phone with his connections in Saigon and Thailand. A barge would dock on the ship channel at midnight Sunday. The money would be exchanged there, the children loaded on to the boat, all drugged to ensure silence.

Images flashed past him as the twelve o'clock news played. Victor was only mildly interested, preoccupied by his thoughts. He had not heard from Decker this morning about Vail and Judge Willow. It should not be much longer now. Sunlight streamed through the blue curtains making the whole room blue. A familiar looking house on the news caught his attention, Victor leaned forward and turned the volume up. The news reporter described the scene. *"This morning around 8:00 a.m., the bodies of fifty-five-year-old district court Judge Wilbert Wilmont Willow and an Afro-American female identified as Ava Cynthia Brimha, age thirty-three was shot to death while in her car at 301 San Jacinto. Ava Brimha, alias Tif-girl has been identified as a prostitute from the southwest side of Houston. Police are baffled by the double homicide because it's apparent that robbery was not the motive. Detective Terry Vantz has gone as far as to say it was a professional hit. Back to you Tim."*

"We have Katherine standing in front of Judge Willow's home in Kingwood, where fire fighters have been fighting a blaze since ten this morning. Katherine."

"Yes Tim, the trucks have been on top of this blaze since ten and it's now under control. As of yet authorities are not certain what started the fire and whether or not anyone was inside. Neighbors have been questioned but they all reported seeing nothing unusual before the fire started."

Victor sat back in his chair. Picked up the phone and dialed the number. The phone was answered on the second ring. "Yeah?"

"Have they taken care of Vail and the girls?"

"Uh ... no, there was ... uh a problem."

"What type of problem?"

"The boy had another apartment no one knew about. I left a message with the girl's aunt last night when I left your place, told her to have her niece call me, it was important ... Victor she just called me about twenty minutes ago."

Victor's watch had a quarter after twelve, "So they're on their way now?"

"Yeah, they're on it," Decker said.

"Cool, just let me know when it's taken care of." He paused. "Decker who was the prostitute with Willow?"

"Just a street girl, nothing major. You're not getting paranoid, are you?"

"No, no, no, there has already been far too many mistakes. Precaution is mandatory from this point on. A philosopher said, if something can go wrong, it will. I forgot his name." He sipped from his drink. "Find out a little more about the girl."

"I'm on it," Decker snapped.

The strong drink had desensitized his throbbing headache, numbed all the conflicting emotions. His focus was on securing and closing his final deal. Maybe he would move to Jamaica and try to get his groove back. Antigua, St. Lucia, the Bahamas were all options. Kenya and Jami would like it in St. Lucia. Buy some ocean front property. A knock on the door interrupted his thoughts. "Come on."

Yadira came into the sunlit room, "Hey, Victor, you got a minute?"

"Yes, Yadira, what is on your mind?"

"Victor, I wanted to go ahead, send Dominique and the twins to my father's in Mexico. That's where Paul and I are headed once we leave here."

"Why so early Yadira?"

"Victor, I've never lied to you. Lately, I've been real nervous with the cop calling Washington and all I'd just feel a lot more comfortable if my only child was out of the picture."

Victor dropped his head considering whether or not to allow the twins to leave.

"Dominique can leave, let me get back with you about the twins, okay?"

She hugged him tightly, "Okay, thank you, Victor." Victor walked to the wet bar, poured himself a drink. Checked his watch, time was ticking.

Patty's hormones were raging. Slowly she rubbed her aching, throbbing clitoris through her bikini panties. It felt good, but she needed more, squirming and gyrating her hips on her hand she moaned and fire bolted through her. Patty was thirty-five, born Lovisa Heidarsdottir in Akureyri Iceland. She changed her name after leaving Chicago. Lovisa Heidarsdottir was arrested for indecency with a minor. A private tutor for a prominent Chicago family, at twenty-six she allegedly became pregnant by their fourteen-year-old son. Allegedly, because the baby could have easily been the husband's; that is how the fourteen-year-old got in her panties from jump street. He became aware of the affair between her and his father, threatened to tell his mother. He blackmailed her and outlined the terms; all he wanted was her and he would not say a word. The son eventually became jealous and possessive, wanted his father out of the picture. The problem was the father was just as far gone behind Patty. She was the typical blonde bombshell minus the Bazookalicious breasts. Her eyes were of a violet color and that is strange for a blonde. Yeah, Patty was beautiful, maybe that was the problem. She was also a preacher's daughter, maybe that was a problem. Maybe! The son confronted the father and they fought. The father was furious she had slept with his son, the wife called the police. Patty was arrested for indecency with a minor but denied it ever happened. To her surprise he also denied it and implicated his father. The father denied the allegations and so did Patty. However, she was pregnant so the family dropped the charges ... the wife feared discovering that the unborn child could belong to her husband despite all his denials. The husband's fears were just as great.

She was alone in America, had been staying with the family while she attended school, a foreign exchange program. Now she was pregnant, damn near broke and alone. Deportation was also a possibility. She started frequenting night clubs; drinking and drugs offered temporary relief. Seven months onto her pregnancy she met Pebbles. Pebbles was a homosexual; he befriended her, took her in and introduced her to Victor Pierce.

The body next to Patty felt her moving, and reached over and slid his hand inside of her panties, she was wet. He disappeared beneath the blankets. Patty felt her panties being pulled down her slim legs. She gasped and arched her hips in pleasure as he slid his tongue deep inside her sensitive passage, then moved up to skillfully manipulate her clit. She writhed and gyrated her hips, ran her hands through his curly hair. "Oh ... oh ... ahhh," she moaned sensually. She beckoned him up with her hands, found his lips and tasted herself on his tongue. "Mmm ... fuck me!" she mouthed huskily. "Please, just fuck me." She felt him position himself, lift her knees into the air, felt his hard insistent organ slide into her silky haven with powerful urgent intensity. "Yes ... mmm." Her hands palmed his firm butt and guided him at a feverish, consistent rhythm. "Oh, gawd that's it ..." The bed squeaked and sweat dripped from his face. He reared up so that he was on his knees, placed both pillows under her ass, put his thumb over her clit. Applying a little pressure and jerked it back and forth while he continued to rotate his hips, plunging his rod into her yielding soft vaginal walls. She dug her nails into the sheets, bit her bottom lip and had a stiff orgasm. "Mmmm ..." Ten seconds later she felt the warmth of his essence rush into her heated sex. "Lord, that was heavenly." She sighed breathlessly.

He found her lips and kissed her deeply. "I love you," he said into her ear.

"I love you too," she replied.

"What time is it?" he asked.

"A little after twelve."

"Are you going to be alright?" His voice full of concern.

"Yes. Now, I'll be alright, but just to play it safe, I better get me one for the road."

His soft organ was still resting inside of her, she rolled him onto his back. He slipped from her grasp, slowly descended southward. His eyes rolled to the back of his head as she took him into her warm inviting mouth.

While Patty showered, her lover left. She contemplated what she could do to hurt Victor. They say hell has no fury like a woman scorned. "The little ugly bastard." Patty was washing the soap from her long golden tresses when she heard the bathroom door open. Cool air rushed in and played tag with her nipples. "I thought you had gone." she said with her eyes closed under the showerhead.

"Gone where?" Victor said.

Hearing Victor's voice startled her, her eyes shot open and viewed him through the glass partition. "What the fuck are you doing here, Victor?" Patty asked angrily.

"I come to speak with you." Pulling the door open.

Patty stood before him naked only a matter of seconds before she reached for a towel and questioned acerbically. "Do you like what you see?"

Victor soaked up her tanned flawless skin. The mass of un-tamed golden hair that dressed her house. Her perky, just-the-right-size breasts. "Yes indeed. You do such a thorough job of masking your beauty. Why? You are exquisite!"

She slipped past him, grabbed her thick yellow robe next to her thin flimsy white one and draped it over her nakedness. "What do you want?"

Victor looked like a lost child for a minute. Patty was at least four inches taller than him and his diminutive stature made things seem trivial sometimes.

"Oh ... yes, the twins, do you think they're ready to leave?"

"What do you mean leave?"

"Yadira wants to send them to her father in Mexico."

Patty looked at him like he was the dumbest man on earth. released a harsh sardonic chuckle. "You're serious, right?" He nodded. "Victor, you turned them into little sluts, what the fuck do you mean, are they ready. Ready for what?"

"Trustworthiness, or do you recommend elimination?"

"Just give them a dick and they're satisfied. Yeah, they're ready."

"What do you suggest, Patty."

"Oh! Whoa, now you want my suggestion. Are you certain I won't get killed for giving it?"

"I apologized for that impulsive act, did I not?"

Patty walked to her bedroom window, "Yadira wants them, huh?" She turned again to face Victor, he nodded. "Well, they love Yadira, if she stressed the importance of their silence once they leave here, then let them go. They'll never hurt Yadira."

"Alright then." He paused. "Can I see you again?" He motioned his index finger back and forth, indicating for her to open her robe.

She frowned, shook her head. "I can't do that, Victor."

"Oh, but you will," he stated soundly. Again, he motioned and reluctantly Patty opened her robe. "Can I take you to dinner to make it up to you for my behavior lately?"

"Thanks, but no thanks," she said blithely.

"So it is," he replied, and left the room.

Patty smiled to herself, "That's what you get for being an asshole. Had you been nice, I may have felt sorry for your ugly ass." She looked at herself in the full-length mirror, opened the robe to inventory the merchandise. She met her eyes in the mirror and shook her head.

When the plane touched down in Sacramento at 3:30 p.m., Puckett immediately made reservations to fly back to Houston. While at the airport he cancelled all of his appointments. His mind was focused on one thing, getting back to Houston ASAP. Vail had communicated their new whereabouts. He relaxed a little, at least they were alright. The airport was a cornucopia of activity, busy and boisterous. His flight was not until four-fifteen, he had a good forty- five minutes to kill. He found a cozy corner in the coffee shop and started to go over the files again, running different theories and scenarios through his head. What confused him the most was the profile on Yadira Holmes. According to her file, she was thirty-eight with a Bachelor's degree from UCLA. A teacher certified by the board of education. Why? She just didn't fit. He picked up the pictures of Sheila Penock, Valarie Johnson and Amber Ambrose. The photo of the Witiker family also sat on the table. His eyes rested on the mother in the orange shirt and sea blue eyes, her auburn-colored hair and he clicked. She looked just like Ms. Muster. What was her name? He flipped open his notebook. Shamiria Muster! He opened the file, Janise Witiker. "Damn!" His eyes continued to browse, until they rested on the name Shamiria Witiker. Puckett stared at the little girl in instant recognition, he had been in the same house as these girls.

❖   ❖   ❖

"Hello," Kennybrew spoke into the phone. "It's them, Judge."

"Darrell?"

"Yeah, it's me."

"Son, where are you?"

"In Sacramento, the girls that came up missing in Detroit, I found them. They're living in Spring, Texas, with the brotha that kidnapped the Akbar baby."

"What are you going to do? Do you want me to dispatch a patrol car to that address?"

"Naw, I'm on my way. Can you have the warrant for his arrest ready for me when I touch down?"

"Alright, I'll have that for you. Darrell there was a judge killed this morning. I remembered our conversation son. On a hunch I ran a check. On the seventeenth of June he released a black male by the name Trey Winters."

"So, what's up?" he asked vivaciously.

"Trey Winters don't exist."

"So, he released Vail, now he's dead," Puckett said slowly.

"That's right. Another thing, after he was killed this morning I made some calls. In '68 Judge Wilbert Wilmont Willow was a lawyer in Chicago. He represented Cydney Pierce."

"This shit goes deep, huh?"

"Already."

"Thanks Judge, I'll be there about nineish. At least that's when my plane will land."

"Later then." The Judge hung up.

CHAPTER 20

Sung and Xavier sat inside the cool realtor's office, signing the documents that closed the deal on a two-story, six-bedroom house. The house was located on the Southside of Sugarland.

"Well, my boy, it's yours, you want to ride out and walk through it again? It'll look different now that it actually belongs to you."

"Yeah, let's mov'dat way." Xavier smiled, looked at the keys in his hands, it felt like gold. This had been a busy morning. He purchased ten thousand dollars' worth of Arm and Hammer Baking Soda stocks. His financial advisors were two sisters, Etana and Abiyah Stepherson. They were going to help him start a cellular phone company. In his time alone he had cogitated on a talent show. In his mind the idea was huge; announce a ten-thousand-dollar reward to the best group. Have every major newspaper run it. Call all the radio stations and let them broadcast it. A two-hundred-dollar entry fee. Rent the George R. Brown Convention Center or the Hofheinz Pavilion. Call it the Mac-a-tac-talent-feast! Charge twenty- five dollars for tickets, contact certain record labels and solicit representatives to attend, so winners or contestants would have the opportunity to be signed to a record label. He even considered making it a two- or three-day extravaganza. Solicit colleges to perform the Greek show and put up flyers announcing a five-hundred-dollar reward for bikini contest. The possibilities were endless. Groups and women from all over the state. If three hundred groups entered, that's sixty thousand dollars. Two thousand tickets at twenty-five a ticket is fifty thousand dollars. After the first year, the next year would be huge. Kite, Mink, Vibe, Ebony, Jet and media coverage; when he was dead and gone there would be the Mac-a- tac-talent-feast to testify that he was here.

Sugarland was not far, it offered privacy and beautiful homes including the one that Xavier had just bought. Sung patted him on the back, "So, Xavier, will she like it?"

"Yeah, Sung, she's gonna love it." The house was yellow brick, two story with marble floors in the kitchen and bathroom. There was a winding stairwell made from solid oak. The master bedroom was almost bigger than the living room and bedroom combined at home. There were four bathrooms, an island kitchen and a pool out back.

"What are you going to do with six bedrooms?"

"My mama's young, after she eighty-sixes the drug habit, she might meet a brotha worthwhile and have a couple more kids, you never know."

"She could meet a down ass Oriental." Sung laughed.

Xavier lifted his left eyebrow, "You try to mac on my t-lady and I'm gone test yo' skills."

"X, I know some shit that when you wake up, your clothes will be out of style."

"You better quit reading those Chinese Comics, that shit only works in the movies. That reminds me, how come Orientals supposed to have originated Martial Arts, but in the movies Chuck Norris and Van Damme are always kicking they ass?"

Sung chuckled. "I'm curious how your people win all the track meets, dunk basketballs and let flat foot white cops in dress shoes run you down?"

"Just the way the world is, Tao, black folks hollerin' racism, white folks sceamin' reverse racism and Chinese people yellin' sideways racism, only in America, man. When the white man gets me down, I turn on the tube and watch boxing ... white guys can't box." They shared some friendly laughter.

Sung's disposition changed, he became serious. "Xavier, are you going to go to college when you graduate next year?"

Xavier mused momentarily. The sun was up, but dark clouds littered the sky. The trees swayed; leaves rustled; it was peaceful and tranquil. "I haven't really thought about it. I know I should, but I'm tired of school, tired of Texas, wanna move around. I got places to go, people to see, a million calls to make, I kinda wanna ball, parley for a minute. Just let loose and forget for a second, can you feel me?" Xavier released a heavy sigh. "I ain't happy here, but I smile because I rather be here than nowhere. I want to scuba dive, water ski, go parasailing and shit, meet Beyonce Knowles and Halle Berry."

"You want autograph?" Sung asked jokingly.

"Hell naw, just want to shake hands and say hi, simple shit man."

"You still can go to college."

"And major in what?"

"Anything, I've never told you anything wrong. Get a business degree, just think about it."

Xavier and Sung had driven in separate cars; he had to pick Shai up. They were going to see a movie at Eastway Cinema off I-10 freeway. He wasn't overly concerned with the movies, he just wanted to be with her. He continued to think on Tao's advice about college. Yeah, he'd go, but not in the states. Africa, China, maybe even Hawaii, anywhere that will present something new. Shai would like that, if she's still around. He had never been in a serious relationship, never had time. Just watching the masses, it was easier to fail than to succeed. According to his watch it was three forty- three. He picked up the phone and dialed the seven digits.

"Hello." It was the young sharp voice of Nathan.

"Nathan, what's up, lil soulja?"

"Nothin', just chillin', you wanna talk to mama?"

"You know who this is, lil playa?"

"Yeah, this Xavier."

"Yeah, baby boy, let me holla at your moms." He heard Nathan yell in the background as the phone dropped noisily on the table.

A breathless Shai answered the phone. "Hey Boo-Boo."

"What's up yellow bone?"

"Don't get cursed out today boy." Her voice turned into liquid sex. "Thanks for the card and flowers. They came this morning, the words in the card were beautiful, are they yours?"

"Yeah, you inspired me to give Maya Angelo and Iyanla Vanzant a run for their money. What are you doing?"

"It was really sweet of you Xavier, touched me deeply."

"How deeply?"

"All the way to the bottom."

"What are you doing?" he asked again.

"Just stepped out of the water."

"So, you're in your birthday suit?"

"No. Nude, naked, in the buff, my birthday suit didn't have such beautiful accessories."

Xavier laughed. "Girl you throwed off. I just wanted to hear your voice; let you know that I'm on my way."

"Alright, I'll be ready. Thanks Again Xavier."

"Don't sweat it baby girl, chivalry's not dead yet. Later."

"Bye Boo." The phone went flat.

Xavier had gone to a florist and had a floral arrangement placed in a basket and a card he purchased at Walgreens. They had a machine where you could put your own words in it. He spoke from the heart:

Shai, I don't know where you've been, I apologize I couldn't be there with you. I'm not even sure where you're headed ... but

I'm comfortable with the knowledge that we'll be together. I apologize I can't change the world, however feeling the way I do about you, I'll make the sacrifices and necessary changes to hold on to you forever and always.

Shai, don't let me scare you when I tell you the similitude of your presence to me is synonymous with the presence of the sun to the earth.

Vital! You are my consistently persistent sunrise.

My beginning!

My Silently nonchalant, yet proverbial Ghetto Sunset.

My Conclusion!

Staying up Always,

Xavier Dean

Xavier was not even certain what motivated the gesture, just seemed appropriate. So much hitting and splitting going on these days, he just wanted to do something that said I'm here for the duration with undeniable, irrefutable and irrevocable clarity. 'Actions speak louder than words' was the cliche' that reverberated clamorously through his mind, body and soul.

Shai looked radiant. She wore some beige DKNY slacks that had that loose but snug look to them. A see-through Jill Stuart beige blouse that allowed you to see her beautiful butter colored complexion. Her flat stomach, the naval ring and black bikini bra. She wore black earrings, black belt and black Chanel slides. Her fingernails and toenails were a smoky grey. The shirt set off the whole outfit. Xavier originally dressed to meet the real estate agent. He wore tan Versace slacks and a short sleeve shirt with white leather vest and white leather belt. Some ostrich skin boots. His Rolex watch, necklace and earrings.

"You look good," Shai said, giving him a nice kiss at the door.

"You're looking very sexy your damn self," he told her. "Have I told you how beautiful you are?"

"No, not yet." She smiled.

"I will." He smiled back.

"Damn X, when you clean up, you clean up! Aunt Joyce come look at Xavier!" That was Pam, Shai's cousin.

"Let me get the camera," Shai said.

"You look real nice baby," Mrs. Joyce said.

"Thank you, Mrs. Joyce," Xavier responded.

"Mama, take some pictures." Shai handed her mama the camera. After taking about fifteen flicks, they left for the movies.

The movie was alright. Shai enjoyed it. There was a jocular euphoric atmosphere throughout the entire evening. The movie ended at eight and Xavier took her to the Olive Garden to eat. He opened the door for Shai. "I thought you wasn't a gentleman," she said sarcastically.

"Gentleman is a European word. Black folks, African men have never been misogynistic people. We have always treated our women with dignity and respect. Gentleman is a misnomer. Don't place an act as ancient as common courtesy, respect and decency under a name that derives from Greek and Roman homosexuality."

"What's mis ... misogy?" She couldn't pronounce the word.

The waiter approached their table. "Ma'am, sir; are you ready to order?"

"Yes," Xavier said, then looked at Shai.

She frowned at the menu, "What's Arroz de Coco?"

The waiter said, "It's rice with tomatoes, chilies and coconut milk."

She wrinkled up her nose, looked at Xavier and he shook his head. She looked over the menu again. "Why don't you order Xavier?"

The waiter was an older brother, he turned his attention to Xavier. "Ah ... give us two Peixe a Lumbo, one Kurma with rice and a Diced Tomato Salad. For dessert, give us the Akwadu."

"What would you like to drink?"

"Apple cider with lemon."

The waiter left and Shai asked, "What was all that?"

"The Peixe a Lumbo is shrimp and fish stew. The Kurma is Quick chicken curry. You know what tomato salad is, Akwadu is a banana-coconut cake. It has rum in it, so that's the only liquor you'll get. We're not over twenty-one." He smiled.

"You bring all your girlfriends here?"

"Naw, I usually just take 'em to a movie, McDonald's and ..." He stopped and smiled.

"And what?" she asked.

Xavier was tempted to throw in the other 'M,' but prudence suggested otherwise. "And back to their mama's." He glanced around thoughtfully. "My grandma use to bring me up here before she passed. Use to tell me she's gonna find me another granddaddy." He smiled at the memory. "So now I come here every year of her birthday."

Shai asked solemnly, "Is today her birthday?"

"Naw ..." he paused, "... it's our birthday. Our first date as a couple."

"You be tripping me out sometimes because of your intensity."

"That's what happens when you're raised by intense people. My aunts ..." He shook his head, "... very, very intense women, all of them. Being raised by them has truly made me sympathetic to the female plight. I've watched so many guys use, misuse and abuse them. Seen the tears, I believe being a part of their lives has made me a cut-above."

"What about your mother?"

He smiled, his eyes veered off and stared at something that didn't exist. "I'm just a male version of the woman she use to be. When you see me, you see her in her most magnified, intense and extreme form. Raw, uncut and X-rated." He smiled at that non-existent spot, then his eyes fell into synergism with hers. "She's like PG-13 and I'm the exact same movie but with the NC-17 rating. Can you feel, me?"

She nodded her head, "Just can't believe you sat under my nose for six months and I didn't know you."

"Be's that way sometime. I heard a song once, he said 'we tried to talk but the words kept getting in the way'." The waiter came with their meal, they ate and talked. Her junior year was coming up, getting her own place was discussed. Kindergarten for Nathan. It was a pleasant evening.

In Galena Manor at Shai's home Xavier leaned on his car with Shai between his legs. "Have I ever told you how beautiful you are?"

She mused and feigned deep thought. "No, you've never told me."

"Oh, I thought I had."

"No. You can tell me now."

"I just told you."

"No, you didn't, you were asking a question."

He laughed, "O'ite." He looked into her eyes, "Shai you are the most beautiful woman in the world to me. Your eyes, lips and these holes in your face," he put his fingers inside her dimples, "I could disappear inside of you."

She smiled and hugged him tightly. "I had a really nice time. It's been a minute since I just let go and relaxed. You surprised me for a youngsta. There were a lot of attractive females at the movies and the restaurant. A lot were admiring you and not once did you look toward them. Not once, I thought that was tight. Made me feel special, I had your undivided attention all night long."

Xavier rubbed her chin with his index finger and thumb. "Shai, I'm not color blind. I'm hip that the grass isn't greener somewhere else. I'm here to tend to my own lawn, perfecting my gardening skillz!"

She started bouncing up and down, "Ewww, I wish I could be with you tonight. That's why I need my own place."

"I could get us a nice hotel room. Not a motel, a hotel."

"I can't as long as I'm under my mother's roof. I'm gonna respect her home by coming in at a respectable hour."

"I can dig it." They talked until eleven and decided to call it a night.

"Where you headed, Mr. Dean?" she asked.

He looked up at the sky, "To the East, the place of light and the cradle of mysteries."

"That better mean to ya damn house, because I'm gonna call."

He threw up his hands, "You win lil mama, home it is." He patted her on the ass and sent her toward her front door. "Call me now." He held up his cell phone.

"Tomorrow's the nineteenth, y'all get ready. We gonna kick it at Clinton Park."

"Bet, we'll be there with bells on," he said. Shai disappeared inside the house. Xavier hopped in his load and turned a few corners.

Pulling onto Southmore from Scott Street, Xavier saw Solo's truck at the Rib Hut. It's a bar-b-que place sitting right on the corner of Southmore and Scott. He pulled beneath his apartment window and killed the engine. It was eleven thirty and he had been ripping and running all day long but he wasn't really fatigued. Dink was nursing a bottle of Old E and bar-b-queing for Juneteenth. Some hood rats and gold diggers littered the parking lot with some scrubs vying for their attention. He mounted the stairs two at a time, turned the knob, it was locked. Pulling his keys from his pocket and unlocking the door he frowned, the house smelled like crack. Two women and a derelict looking brother sat around the kitchen table wide-eyed and paranoid looking. "Where's my T at?" he asked.

One of the females asked, "You're Nellie's son?" She took in his immaculate attire.

"Yeah, where's she at?" he replied.

The other female said, "She stepped out a minute ago." Just then a fusillade of automatic gunfire erupted, loud and persistent. The two women yelled and the man fell to the floor. The gunfire stopped as abruptly as it started. There was yelling and screaming outside. Xavier bolted out the door, his mother, his main concern. Standing on the balcony people had gathered at the entrance to the apartments.

Denise came around the corner with Chill. She was crying, "X- man she got shot! She got Shot!"

Xavier's heart immediately fell to his feet. His mother at the forefront of his thoughts, he flew down the stairs. "Who? My mama?" he yelled.

"Naw, Honey. Some niggas did a drive-by gunning for Solo, they got Honey too." Xavier broke into a Tyson Gaye sprint for the Rib Hut. People were gathered around gawking, blood was everywhere, glass all over the ground. Holes were in Solo's truck and Honey was laid out on the concrete. Solo was several feet away.

"Move the fuck outta the way!" he yelled. Kneeling over her he touched her neck. People were yelling not to move her. Ignoring them he pulled her into his lap, there was so much blood. "Deshawn! Deshawn!" he shouted. He touched her cheek, her blood soaked into his expensive clothing.

She opened her eyes, tears flowed freely, "Xavier ..." She winced in pain, "... what are you doing in heaven?" She tried to smile.

"You're not in heaven yet," he said weakly.

She touched his lips and smeared her blood on them. "How ... come you never call me Honey?" She winced again.

"Because you're more than honey. Honey's an unthinking natural substance. You're Deshawn."

"I ..." Her voice broke, she trembled. "... I ... d ... don't wanna d ... di ... die, Xavier.

"You're not gonna die, I got cha!" He picked her up.

Her mother was by his side yelling and crying. Denise was hysterical. "Xavier help her, please help her!"

Nellie appeared at his side. "Mama, get my keys out of my pocket and go open my car." Nellie did as she was told. When he got to the car, he laid Deshawn in the backseat. "I'm not waiting on ah damn ambulance. Deshawn keep talkin' to me, please."

"I don't want to die," she cried.

"You're not going to die, so quit sayin' that shit." He turned to her mother, "Mrs. Lowe, I need you to get yourself together, get in the backseat and keep Deshawn talkin'."

"Okay Xavier, okay."

Xavier sped out of the driveway. He maneuvered the vehicle expertly through traffic at an alarming pace. It took him approximately fifteen minutes to reach St. Joseph's Hospital. The ambulance had just reached the scene in Third Ward when Xavier was pulling into the emergency room. The Chrysler screeched to a halt, bystanders all looked at the car. Xavier quickly but smoothly removed Deshawn from the car. She winced and cried, "Oh Xavier, I'm hurting." Her voice barely audible.

"I know baby, just hold on, whatever you do just hold on." The doors automatically opened and he rushed through the door. "Lookout!" he shouted. "I need a doctor!" Two nurses rushed to his side, yelled at someone and a brother produced a gurney. Xavier laid Deshawn down. A doctor appeared at his side and started barking orders, nurses were taking vital signs.

He listened as if detached, she held his hand. "I'm scared, but not afraid does that make sense?"

He leaned into her ear and whispered, "Yeah, it does, hold on baby I need my own personal doctor so you can't check out."

She looked at his clothes. "I messed up your clothes."

"Naw ghul, I bought 'em like this. I'm startin' a new trend." She smiled, winced and closed her eyes.

Deshawn stayed in surgery for five hours. Bullets had ripped through her legs. One through her left clavicle. One bullet ripped under her rib cage just missing the kidney. Doctor Isaiah Thomas said she lost a lot of blood, explained to Xavier it was a risk but gutsy chance he took moving her. However, about fifteen minutes had made all the difference in the world. Dr. Thomas listened as Xavier explained that whenever death is trying to make a deal with you it's difficult to think, just gotta follow your instincts.

Deshawn was placed in the I.C.U. She was placid. It was four twenty-three in the a.m., but coffee stimulated he was up. Shai called him at one, wishing she could be there with him. Deshawn was in critical condition but was expected to pull through. He stood over her while her mother stepped out. His clothes ruined, attitude somber and despondent. He said, "You know Deshawn, I know you can hear me." Tears rolled slowly down his face and his nose instantly stopped up. He sniffled, "I have this re-oc-curring reality, losses that are so final. I figure it's about fighting from the cradle to the grave, even when you got one foot in, and one foot out, it's about fightin' to survive. It isn't the strong that always survive. Sometimes it's just the ones who want it the most. I'm finsta bail, but I'll be back and when I get back, I wanna see those hazel jewels looking at me, look at them." He kissed his two fingers and put them on her lips. He and Mrs. Lowe left; she would ride back in her car.

His car smelled like blood. June 19th had stepped up on the scene witness to all the drama that had taken place. The ride home was silent, what was there to say? Words would have just gotten in the way; some emotions are silent. Police had spoken with them, Solo was D.O.A., Doctor said he never had a chance. Hearing that Solo was dead did not move Xavier and he hated feeling that way. Every life was precious. His thoughts went to Solo's mom, whoever, wherever she was. At five-oh-one the parking lot was deserted. Strange huh? But that's how it is sometimes. Life only offers you highs in intervals, then it's gonna knock you on your ass. Some people get up and move on, some never recover. Strange huh?

CHAPTER 21

Kenneth and Timothy were not expecting Detective Puckett until after eleven. So they were in no hurry, while they inventoried his home thoroughly and put everything back as they found it. Finally, they wired some explosives to his answering machine. When he played back his messages it would trigger the device, see-you later- bye! Kenneth found a Klondike bar in the fridge and munched on it slowly, no hurry, they took their time.

Puckett stepped from the plane at eight forty-five. A deluge of people flooded from every direction. Mild pandemonium as the intercom squawked announcing late flights, delays and final calls. Next to Puckett an obese lady traipsed past him smelling like cheap perfume and cigarette smoke. Moving through the crowd someone touched him on the butt. He turned around casually, too many people around him to pinpoint the culprit. There was an old lady pushing sixty or pulling seventy with a guilty crooked toothless smile. Puckett displayed his own awkward looking grin and moved on. At the luggage rack, he collected his bags and headed for the exit. He wanted to stop by to check on Vail and Daphane at a LaQuinta off I-10. Some angered mom was giving her son a show-out-ass- whuppin'. Two females stood near the payphones clinging to one another kissing ardently. Another woman scolded her man for staring at the buttocks of this white female in some white transparent Jodhpur-like pants. Her outfit left very little to the imagination. Women are certified lunatics Puckett thought to himself. How in the hell was he not supposed to look at that! Oh well.

In the parking lot it was a humid warm night. Yellow cabs littered the lot, even a couple of limos with chauffeurs. Some chaste looking sisters walking with some chauvinistic looking brothers, figures. Some things are just inextricable, the way we perceive people are one of them. He was tired, cranky and kind of wished he was still a patrolman, so he could stop some white males for nothing! Just enact some revenge for some of the brothas who are stopped every day, just for being black.

"Darrell!"

Puckett spun casually and noticed Big Anthony was approaching him. They played football together in high school. Vigorously they embraced each other, "What's happening D, you alright?" Anthony said enthusiastically.

"Yeah, just tired but outside of that, I'm living."

"That's good man. I just recognized you and wanted to holla. I gotta jet to pick up the wife and kids."

"Alright, it was good seeing you Ant."

"Yeah, take care baby."

Puckett drove to Kennybrew's house to get the warrant for Shane Muster's arrest. He wanted to wait until morning, but time was of the essence. If they killed Judge Willow and he was quite certain they were going to try for Vail and Daphane. It appeared as though they were trying to clean up. Traffic was light and moved rapidly. An accident had taken place but one monkey did not stop the show. Forty minutes later he pulled in front of Kennybrew's home, lights shone through the windows. Across the street a dog barked noisily. At the porch a loquacious cricket went silent as he depressed the little white button that sounded the chimes inside the house. Light bugs on gullible missions attacked the light bulb with tenacity and vigor. Mrs. Kennybrew swung the heavy door open on its well-oiled hinges. She was a woman of Creole' decent with long beautiful salt and pepper hair that cascaded down her back. She smiled exposing two open face golds and pretty, straight teeth. "Hello, Darrell." The Creole' accent was sweet and inviting.

"Hello, Sabrina, where's your husband?"

"He's in his study, been waiting on you. Are you hungry?"

At the mentioning of food his stomach started making vulgar sounds. He hadn't eaten a decent meal in almost three days. Everything he'd been into up to this point had essentially suspended his appetite. "Yes, ma'am I'm famished."

She smiled, "Good, c'mon I'll tighten you up."

He joined Judge Kennybrew in the study, who was watching Young and the Restless, that had been taped by Sabrina while he was at work. In his lap was a bowl full of cashews, in his hand was a glass of Chablis. "Hey son, how was your flight?"

"Exhausting, you got the warrant?"

"I'm old, not senile Darrell. It's on my desk, get yourself something to drink." Puckett poured himself a tall glass of Chablis and downed the glass, then poured himself another.

"That rough, huh?" Kennybrew asked.

"Just been a long day, too long." Sabrina entered the room with a large plate of smothered steak, rice cabbage and garlic bread, The aroma was hardy and blotted out the strong smell of potpourri.

"How are you going to handle this?"

Puckett finished chewing, took a drink. "I called the chief, explained everything I got. They're supposed to be watching Decker, and before I leave here, he wants me to call some patrolmen to meet me at Shane Muster's home."

"You think he's going to talk?"

"When he sees he's faced with a double homicide and kidnapping, I expect him to cooperate."

Judge Kennybrew rubbed his beard thoughtfully. "And what about the girls?"

"Shamiria and Yolanda?"

The judge nodded.

"I don't know."

"Just be careful, because after you arrest one of theirs, it's going to be hot!"

"I gotcha," Puckett said.

The knock-on Shane Muster's door seemed louder than he intended. A long fifteen seconds ebbed by, this time he rang the doorbell. The BMW set in the driveway. Two patrol cars and four officers had accompanied him. The door swung open and Shane stood there. "Shane Muster, we have a warrant for your arrest."

"What! For what?" Vatly exclaimed.

"For the murder of James and Jenise Witiker, and the kidnapping of Shamiria and Yolanda Witiker."

Vatly started laughing. "You must have lost your Rabbit ass mi ..." His insult was cut short. Staley spurred him in the gut. "Ugh!" Staley was a hot shot cop headed for the NBA, but ironically ended up with the HPD ... you figure it out. Vatly folded over, the other cops handcuffed him and put him into the backseat. The officers went through the house with a fine-tooth comb. The sisters were gone, as a matter of fact; there was not a trace of them; clothes, shoes, nothing.

There must have been a mad scientist deep inside the halls of the C.I.A. that thought of 'interrogation rooms.' Everything has to be scientifically sound. The room size, temperature, location of the table and acoustics. Everything theorized and hypothesized to cause claustrophobic responsiveness. The cheap seats, cheap table, cheap tape recorder and cops in expensive looking cheap suits. Then there is the mirror. The only thing in the room that costs a little change and you are watching it while they are watching you and you know it. They, the police of course, make sure you are facing the mirror. Why? There is some deep-rooted psychological reason, that's why. Viewing yourself, however intrepid, fretful, fearful or pathetic, you are facing the number one jury, 'Self.' It's difficult to lie confidently to the number one jury, unless you have plenty of practice.

This is where Vatly was at. He wasn't particularly worried, but it's extremely difficult to be completely without some anxiety, some apprehension. Not a lot, just some. He stared at the mirror trying to imagine the faces behind the glass—like the man constantly grabbing his privates. He is not just checking; he knows it is there. The authoritative scent clung to the air. The air in a police station has an identity of its own, just like a funeral home or hospital. Nobody ever walks into a funeral home and thinks they're in a bakery. Never.

"Where are they?" That was Puckett.

"Where are who?" Vatly replied innocently.

"This is just a big game to you, isn't it?"

Vatly shook his head, "Chess is a game, and monopoly is a game. Getting drug from my bed, assaulted and hauled down here because of your delusions isn't a game, it's embarrassing."

"So, I'm having delusions, right?" He rubbed his eyes. "Shamiria said Yolanda are delusions!"

"Who?" Vatly asked.

Puckett stood up; his menacing form loomed over Vatly. He raised his voice. "You sick sonavabitch, you know who I'm talking about, your wife! And her sister." Two more plainclothesmen entered me room.

Vatly responded, "My what? I'm not even married, never have been." He looked at the other two cops, "He needs some help, or some rest, one or the other, maybe both."

Puckett understood that he was being made to look like a fool. He tried a different approach. "So are Paul and Yadira figments of my imagination also?" His fixed gaze hard and unwavering, looking for any signs of recognition at the mentioning of those names.

Inwardly Vatly's heart plummeted, outwardly he was stolid and stoic. "Well ..." Vatly said as he looked left over his shoulder, "... it all depends ..." he continued as he looked right over his right shoulder, then pushed his chair back and peered under the table before meeting Puckett's icy stare "... are they in the room with us ... right ... now?" Vatly finished in slow deliberate words.

Puckett dropped his head and hissed, "Your ass is mines, you know this right?

Vatly sat straight back in his chair bulged his eyes and puckered his lips. His voice was high and effeminate when he spoke. "Now that's an intriguing thought."

The black plainclothesman snickered brazenly. Puckett gave him the ice grill.

The other officer spoke to Vatly. "Your neighbor has reported two females coming and going from your home quite frequently. Who are they?"

"Oh, that's my girlfriend and her cousin, Sherina and Phashunda."

"Where are they?" the officer inquired. Vatly gave them their address.

Puckett stood off in the corner and like his fresh cup of coffee, he was silently steaming. He lumbered toward Vatly, leaned over the table so that their faces were close, eye contact locked in. "I'm gonna bury this little scheme of yours. I'm gonna huff and puff and blow your house down, then put you away for a long, long time."

Vatly made a skeptical smirk, leaned across the table so that their noses were only inches apart. He dropped his voice to a whisper, "You're not going to fuck with me. I got a lawyer so raw I wanted to suck his daddy's dick, and in a couple of days, you're going to bring a written apology to my doorstep. And I'm going to forgive you ... because I know that's what God would want me to do. Then we're going to eat porridge and sleep in the same bed." Instantly, the table flipped and all three hundred pounds plus went at Vatly. The officers tried to restrain Puckett. Vatly scrambled backwards, and fell heavily to the floor. The door was flung open and several other officers assisted in restraining Puckett. Other officers escorted Vatly from the room. Vatly soliloquized the word, 'bye' and blew Puckett a kiss.

"Captain I'm telling you he's lying. I know what the fuck I saw," Puckett exclaimed angrily.

"Puckett what you're saying you saw and what we're finding are two different things." It was a little after ten, Puckett's eyes were bloodshot from a combination of stress and exhaustion. A slim white detective entered the Captain's office.

"We have the girls," he said.

"Bring them in," the Captain barked.

Three minutes later Sherina and Phashunda were escorted into the room. They both immediately looked at Puckett and like synchronized watches or swimmers they smiled and spoke to him with ease and eerie familiarity. Sherina was an auburn-haired beauty with dark green eyes. Phashunda was a strawberry-blonde with freckles and dark brown eyes. The Captain held up the photo of the Witiker children and there was a resemblance. The Captain eyed Puckett who was shaking his head. The one called Sherina had on the same outfit that she had on when he met her.

"It isn't them," Puckett said shakily. The Captain said, "I know but ..."

"I mean these are not the girls I met two days ago," Puckett interrupted, exasperated beyond explanation. The Captain looked at the two ladies, "Do you, well it's obvious you know him. Where did you meet Detective Puckett?"

"At Vatly's on Tuesday. He was investigating a kidnapping."

"Is Vatly, Shane's nickname?" the Captain asked.

"Yes sir." They spoke with the Captain for several minutes, not missing a beat.

Vatly was released, nothing could be substantiated. Puckett headed for home after an exhausting day. His discontentment and the events of the night had him doubting himself. Were those the girls he met? Lights flashed by him and he continued to recede further and further down the tunnel of uncertainty. He had seen them once, it all seemed so distant now, even scary because there is no instant replay or rewind for him to view the situation and pinpoint with certainty what he suspected in his heart. Pausing life and scrutinizing the details and every minute aspect before continuing to the next frame was not a luxury offered to him. So, his drive home was spent attempting to rethink and recall every word, phrase and gesture.

There was a bootleg near his place, he stopped by and picked up some bourbon. Saw some young brothers on the corner, instantly knew they were drug dealers. He pulled in front of them and the younger of the two approached the car. "You have any weed?" Puckett asked.

"Naw playa, that's Banana with all the chronic."

"Look, can I get you to run and buy me one?" "One what, ol school? One nick, dyme, or dub?"

"Just one joint," Puckett said.

The youngsta laughed. "It's been a while since ya bought some chronic huh, ol school?"

"Yeah, you can say that."

"Aw fuck it, heah, old school." He dug into his pocket and tossed Puckett a joint. "It's my personal, but I'll get anotha. Go 'head and getcha blow on. Watch out fo' tha five-oh!"

Puckett smiled for the first time that day. "I'll do that, you do the same."

"Sheeit Pop, I'm part blood hound. I can smell 'em comin' a mile 'way."

Puckett smiled again and drove away. "Sho you can." He looked at the joint and started to feel guilty, then hunched his shoulders. Shit, even the president got his blow on sometimes. Tonight, this joint was therapeutic.

CHAPTER 22

Diamond Slim read the newspaper in his plush condo. Denise Williams plea-bargained with love to quit making a fool of her on the eight tracks he was listening to. Diamond Slims' impeccable taste had designed his condo to near perfection. Beautiful things always made him feel tranquil. His ladies paraded around half-naked in his lush apartment. In his opinion it is difficult to be aggravated, frustrated or depressed when you are surrounded by half-naked beautiful women. His philosophy was the best anger management treatment to date, that's how come those biblical characters stayed so cool. They had harems of beautiful women. He had painted his apartment in eight shades of blue: Royal Hawaiian Blue, Midnight blue, heavenly blue, Scandinavian sky blue, Royal blue mist, Empress blue, Cornflower blue and Federal Indigo blue. The ceiling had been painted a dusk red-orange imitating a sunset. Green ivory plants littered the entire apartment. His train of thought led him to surround himself with things he figured would bring balance.

The blue represented the water, which represents the moral nature of man, cleanliness and his ability to communicate. Water is synonymous with justice. The green plants represented earth. The color green itself meant fertility, life, youth, and prosperity. Earth, like water is one of the four cardinal elements symbolizing man's material vision and insight. Material needs and knowledge, his fortitude. The reddish color in the sky represented fire which symbolizes wisdom because fire breaks down matter to its elementary and original substance. So does wisdom allow one to see behind the apparently obvious with prudence and temperance. His father had been a mason, tried to lace him up properly, but every man has to choose his own path. His own square to travel on.

Diamond Slim was in deep meticulous thought, had been since learning of Tif-girl's death. He felt responsible because it was him who put Tif-girl in the Judge's company. The Judge turned out to be a store well of information. It is believed that you can fool some of the people most of the time. Most of the people some of the time, but never all of the people all of the time. Diamond's original interest with Victor Pierce was purely territorial. He could smell the man's craft, wanted to know his competition inside and out. Then he realized that Victor's trade had a twist and posed no threat to his livelihood. Either way he was content to just chill. His code of ethics didn't allow him to run to the pig for any reason. He would mind his own business, but knowledge was power and he knew that was all that mattered. Judge Willow had been so easy to manipulate. After two blissful nuts he was deliriously happy, pouring out his heart and soul. Victor had three clubs in Houston all registered under Paul Holmes. Paul had a home in Dayton, but was seldom there. Victor lived in Sugarland. Sideline Redd had followed Paul once. Their Henchman was Vatly who resided in Spring. Diamond Slim knew—but those who see, do not know, and those who know, do not tell. Who was he going to tell anyway? However, now they had made it personal. Killing Tif-girl was not cool at all, and revenge is like the sweetest joy next to getting pussy. Tomorrow was June the nineteenth. The fourth of July was coming early in Houston.

Dollarbill sat across from Diamond Slim, Big Cash, Redd Dirt, Kilo and Whodini who stood at attention and listened. Dollarbill was a street hustler who believed he was destined to play con, smoke chronic, drive fancy cars, wear fancy clothes and consummate illicit relationships with beautiful women. Unfortunately, all this was preconceived in the mind of man without first consorting with the blueprint of God. Dollarbill was thirty when he lost his leg racing motorcycles in Portland, Oregon. He was doing a hundred and ten when this lady unexpectedly opened her car door. The door went through his leg like a hot knife through butter. The impact threw him fifteen feet into the air and landed him in a coma for three months. When he woke up, he had not only lost his leg, he was minus the attitude, minus the arrogance. The Bible has a saying that Diamond Slim believed, 'He who exalts himself will be humbled, and he who is humble, will be exalted.' Dollarbill had burned more than his share of people in Portland, so his younger brother Big Cash flew him to Houston, Fifth Ward. At forty-one Cash had sired ten children by seven different women. He religiously played dominoes, cards and drank Chivas Regal. The only deviation from this routine was Sunday church three times a year: Christmas, Mother's Day and Easter Sunday.

Dollarbill and his group were notorious for handling their business. They were better than David Copperfield at making people disappear. They plotted and planned well into the night. When they departed everyone understood what was expected of them.

CHAPTER 23

It was Patty's idea to bring the girls in. Sherrhonda and Tabitha were actors, long time acquaintances of Victor. Some years prior he had met them at a strip joint. As one could imagine they became friends, he financed their modeling and acting education. To them, they did not look anything like Shamiria and Yolanda, but to strangers looking at childhood photos, make-up and dye beats the world. Right now, Shamiria and Yolonda were in Brazil, soaking up sun in very small bikinis on white sandy beaches, drinking two-hundred-dollar bottle Dom Perignon and Château d' d'Yquem and looking for mates with radical political views.

"So, how did it go?" Decker asked Victor from his phone.

"Vatly's here now, from the looks of things all went well."

"Tim and Kenneth told me that they wired the cop's answering machine with explosives. When he plays messages back ... kaboom!"

"I've spoken with them."

"What about Vail?" Victor inquired. He showed no emotions but he wanted Vail dead for defying him and proving him wrong. He was supposed to be on that damn plane.

"Can't find him," Decker replied. "There's an unmarked police car a couple blocks down from my house. I think that detective has them watching me. He must be hiding them."

"What about the hooker?" Victor questioned. Decker excused himself from the phone, when he returned Victor heard papers rattling.

"Okay, Ava Brimha, age 33, born and raised in Houston. Attended Aldine High School, graduated in '81. She has had a dozen or so arrests for prostitution. Went to prison twice in '90, she just stopped getting in trouble. Apparently, she hooked up with an Andrew Guthfield. He's noted as being a pimp, which didn't come from police records because he doesn't have one. Uh ... let me see, he's called Diamond Slim. Stays on the Southwest side and has a little muscle but he's laid back, not really a threat."

"Who's determining that?" Victor hissed on the phone.

"Determining what?" Decker asked.

"Determining who's a threat and who isn't."

"Victor, I was jus ..."

"Don't," Victor interjected.

Decker picked up on the thread of agitation in his voice. "Yeah, you right," he conceded.

"What are the chances that the Judge told her something and she in turn told him something?" The phone went silent for a few seconds.

"Uh ... I'm not sure Vic. There is that possibility."

"It's just uncharacteristic of Willow to initiate a relationship with a prostitute considering his taste. However, maybe she initiated the relationship with him. Then I would have to ask myself, why?" Victor's methodical mind was actively churning.

"I don't know Vic." He paused. "Could just be a coincidence. Willow may have had many perversions."

"Alright Decker, get some rest, I would like for you to find Vail. I want him."

Time was moving slow on purpose because there were things to be done. The surveillance technicians were meandering about trying to stay out of Victor's way. He was uncharacteristically on edge, something everyone in the house had noticed. Paul and Yadira walked into his office with Dominique on their heels. She was not that pretty, and that was strange because Paul and Yadira were both handsome people. She was not ugly either though, and had inherited Yadira's stout figure; big legs, attractive hips, luscious breasts and backside.

"Paul, do you know Andrew Guthfield?" Victor asked.

Paul's brow wrinkled in thought as he mused, he was shaking his head when Victor added, "They call him Diamond Slim."

"Yeah, I know of him, He comes to the Tangueray at least once a week."

"Any day in particular?" Victor inquired.

Paul thought for a second, "Wednesday, no Tuesdays."

Victor thought about it, Tuesday was the day he visited the Tangueray. "Paul, I think we have a problem."

Vatly was in the kitchen when Dominique rounded the corner that led to Victor's study. She wore a pink tennis skirt that put her big legs on display. Innocently she walked to attack the frig. "Nuh, nuh, nuh," was his response to her precious cargo saddled at her waist.

"Do you have a problem?" was her tart inquiry.

"Yeah, I can't figure out for the life of me how you got all that ass for a white girl. I would say it's Atavistic, but I doubt it."

She smiled, "Vatly you're crazy. You've been knowing me since I was what, fourteen or fifteen, now you want to comment on my behind?"

"I've always been in awe of it, wanted to touch it. You were just too young." He walked up behind her, squeezed her buttocks, that melded like velvet sheets in his hands.

"So now I'm not too young anymore?"

His other hand rose to cup her full right breast. It was biddable and pliant, melted and molded into his fingers. "Doesn't feel like it," he whispered into her ear.

"Quit it Vatly!" She glanced around nervously. "My mother and father are right around the corner," she whispered back.

"Let me taste it, Dominique!"

"Taste what?" He groped his erection so she could see. "Vatly stop!"

"Look at what you've done to me!"

Dominique said sheepishly, "We can't Vatly, we're gonna get caught."

"No, we won't, come here." He pulled her to him, expertly he began sucking on her ear, while his nimble fingers caressed her fleshy distended sex through her panties. Half by force, half willingly she allowed herself to be maneuvered into the storage closet. There she glanced through the wooden doors that were made like Venetian blinds. Without losing rhythm, or wasting precious time he dropped to his knees taking her panties down with him. Hesitantly she stepped out of them fighting the butterflies doing kamikaze runs in her stomach. Vatly moaned upon encountering her tuft of black hair glistening heavily and releasing a sultry musk.

"Vatly ... Please ... no we can't. Pleas ...oh." "Shhh." He put his mouth on her thick folds.

"Ooooh!" She closed her eyes and entwined her fingers in his hair. "Uh ... mmm."

Vatly slowly manipulated her button with gentle but urgent strokes from his tongue. Her knees buckled forcing her to brace herself by putting both hands on the shelves on either side of her. Expertly he inserted two fingers into her warmth and she gasped, felt her legs buckle again from the mind scrambling orgasm she was having. Her and Vance petted and played, but she hadn't gone all the way just yet. All this was new and extremely overwhelming. Still swooning from her first orgasm, Dominique was a little slow to react to Vatly's urgent kisses, slow to the realization that it was her own sex she tasted on his lips. Someone entered the kitchen.

"Dominique!" It was Vance. In the closet Vatly freed her breasts and sucked on them feverishly, while his other freed his swollen member. "Can I have it, Dominique?" he asked breathlessly.

Over his shoulder she watched Vance pillage the cabinet and the ice box through the venetian doors. "Yes!" she said as she found his lips. His hands were all over her, kneading painfully her soft luscious butt. She felt his large member rub against her naked thigh, bump against the malleable doors. Fear shook her from her delirious state. "No Vatly!" There was panic in her whispered tones.

He licked her neck, "Why not?" He looked into her eyes.

She seemed embarrassed when she mumbled, "I'm a virgin."

"You're eighteen now. Let me Dominique, it'll only hurt a second. The rest is pure pleasure." He stroked her knob sending electric shock of pleasure through her body.

"Okay, please take it easy." Vatly grabbed her full buttock, dipped his hips and penetrated her. She was tight, yet wet and took half of him in. She gasped and winced, "Ugh!" In the kitchen Vance spun around.

"Vance, have you seen my baby, she's not in her room?" Yadira said as she walked into the kitchen. Dominique buried her face in Vatly's chest to conceal her sobs of pleasure. Vatly made slow steady thrusts into her giving body.

"Naw Yadira, I was looking for her myself."

"Ah! Ah! Ah!" she whispered into his chest as his thrust became more urgent.

"Alright then, if you see her, tell her to find me."

Her orgasm hit harder than a mule's kick. She bit into Vatly's flesh to stifle a scream. Vatly in turn dug his fingers into her plump ass, dug deep to stifle his own orgasmic scream. Dominique felt the throbbing vibrations of his member deep inside her.

"I got you, Yadira," Vance called out.

Vatly looked into Dominique's eyes, "You okay?" Sweat had matted her hair to her forehead. Affectionately he brushed it out of her face. She nodded and dropped her head, afraid to meet his eyes. With his index finger he lifted her chin, kissed her lips, and dabbed the sweat from her face with his shirt. After fixing his clothes, he opened a jug of bottled water and saturated a dish rag, knelt before her and lifted her skirt to wash and wipe her clean.

"Will I see you before I leave?" she asked tensely.

"I wish you'd leave with me Dominique, but you're afraid, I know."

"Tomorrow night I'm leaving for Cancun, Mexico. You could easily decide to be on that plane."

"Call me tonight. We'll talk." He looked through the venetian blinds. It was clear. "Can I keep these?" He held up her panties. She nodded, blushed and smiled. Hastily he exited the closet, headed toward the hallway. After composing herself, Dominique headed in the opposite direction, she floated on the helium of her emotions.

They say Cleopatra was irresistibly beautiful beyond reason. Some say she was a god that descended from heaven to live among us. It sounds farfetched but it's reported that she was charismatic, enchanting and bewitching to a degree bordering astronomical proportions.

Kenya passed Vatly in the hallway headed for the pool wearing a slightly risqué open face and open back black bathing suit, with a thin white sarong that looked as though it would turn into cellophane if any perspiration hit it. Yadira had put her hair in finger waves and sculptured to her head and she wore some blackberry-colored lipstick. Vatly's eyes bulged, it looked like he was headed for a seizure or aneurysm. He stumbled on some lint in the carpet and caught himself awkwardly with the wall. There is a difference between looking, lusting and admiring. Vatly simply looked, admired and noticed things Stevie Wonder could not have missed. He noticed the sleek smooth contours of her young curvaceous body, coated in deep rich mahogany colored skin without flaw, wrinkle, mark or sag. As she drew abreast of him, then continued past him without a glance in his direction, Vatly witnessed the lily sway of her unconfined proud pretties. The whiffy fragrance of some light high dollar perfume mixed with a ripe young woman's smell. Then a lavishly bouncy behind whose three-corner perk and wobble was sensational enough that it could hypnotize the pope out of his saintly gown. He was still just looking in one direction and walking in the other when he collided with Jami. "Ow!" She fell.

"Oh, I'm sorry, lil bit, you alright?"

"I'm fine." Vatly helped her to her feet. She also had on a black bathing suit similar to the one the older girl had been wearing, but a lot more material than its counterpart. The presence of Jami confused him because of most of the children he had brought. This one wasn't familiar. The other one was around Jerald's age he speculated, maybe even Jerald's little piece of game. Vatly squatted down, Jami was now taller than him.

"What's your name sweetheart?"

Jami studied the stranger, he looked nice and only the second black person she had seen outside of Jerald. "Jamiljah Khaliyd, everybody calls me Jami."

He thought, Khaliyd did not ring a bell. "What are you doing here?"

"Mr. Victor is going to adopt us."

"Us, you're not alone?"

"No, it's me and my sister, Kenya."

Kenya, he thought, "Did she go to the pool?"

Jami nodded her head. "Jami, how old is your sister?"

Jami smiled, "She's fourteen."

Vatly lost his balance and almost fell. Jami caught his hand and helped him right himself. "You serious, she's fourteen?" Jami nodded.

"How old are you?"

"I'm ten."

"You're going to the pool, right?"

"Yes."

"Alright then, I'll be seeing you." Jami trotted down the hall. Vatly was curious as to how those two beautiful girls got here. Victor had neglected to even tell him about Kenya. Women that possessed a beauty such as hers never failed in life. Men like Victor, himself, even the average man wouldn't allow her to fail. Only fourteen, he shook his head in denial. Although neither of them spoke, he was certain that she was pleasant and without guile. He also believed she was unaware of just how beautiful she was.

Patty traipsed from the living room with her angelic angular features that contrasted with her canny violet-colored eyes. She wore a large dour dress which was customary of her. There was a friendship here that baffled most, but it existed. Upon seeing each other they launched directly into the little game they played with each other. "Hit sho hot tonite mommuh," Vatly said.

"Zactly whut I wuz thinkin' poppuh. Bein hankerin' wit dis heah all dey," was Patty's reply.

"Reckon ifen' we git nekkid, son't fuh som ice hit'll help?"

"Ifen' you thank hit'll help. I do declare, wheah you bein'?"

"Don't matta I heah."

"I son't fuh you."

"I heah," Vatly said. Then, "Whut you doin' out heah? Why ain't you got de chilluns in de bed and you in deah wid'em wheah you belong wid awl dis goin awn?"

"Jus und'de im'pres'son I'd search de house fuh cool place and gi' und hit on de accounta you wasn't heah."

"I heah!" They laughed and embraced one another. "You're getting good," he told Patty.

"You're getting better," she replied.

He changed direction to walk with her to the kitchen. "Your face is filling out, you getting fat on me?"

"Never ask a woman about her weight."

"Patty I just saw this little goddess come down the hall. Who is she?"

Patty smiled, "You don't know? That's compliments of you, Shane." He looked puzzled. "You met her father, gave him the number, told him to call." Shane was trying to remember what Blackman had he given the number to. "Session Thorn," Patty said, reading his expression and supplying the answer. Vatly made a low mewing sound then focused on Patty's astute violet windows. She just nodded her head, no smile, just a nod. "She's Victor's little prize possession. He actually believes he can keep her to himself."

Vatly read Patty's expression and tone. "You don't like her, do you? Is she jaded and incorrigible like the twins and Valerie?"

They stopped at the patio door looking out at the pool; Sherrhonda, Tabitha, Vance, Dominique, Jami and Kenya were around the pool. Kenya sat alone staring into the inexorable night. Jami played at the shallow end with Dominique. Patty looked at Vatly, "No. Not by a long shot. She's sweet, respectful and demure. I tried to hate her, to be mean to her ..." She dropped her head and shook it. "... I was envious, not of her beauty, but the innocence hidden inside it. Have you seen her eyes?"

Vatly shook his head. "They're gold."

She continued, "Not brown or hazel, gold. She looks at you and you just melt. Never seen anything like it Shane."

"She passed by me and made me feel counterfeit as hell," Vatly stated.

"Shane," Patty's voice sounded distant, "God put his hands on that child. Tried to show you a piece of heaven. I can't fathom how fate brought her here, but my female intuition has been telling me it's time to go. May just be a whim, but between me and you, she doesn't belong in our company ... isn't going to stay in our company. I can feel it. Sun's been shining too long on Victor, clouds have already come, thunder is on the way, then it's going to rain."

Vatly stared out of the window, listening in earnest. He stuck his hands in his pockets and felt Dominique's panties. His eyes left Kenya and swiveled onto Dominique. He squeezed the panties. "What are you going to do, help her get out of here?"

Their friendship was solid, Patty trusted Vatly completely. "Shane, I'm pregnant."

He looked at her, she grinned sheepishly and buried her face into her hands. Vatly grabbed her thin waist, rubbed her still flat stomach. "Who? Nah, I don't want to know. Are you happy?"

She nodded her head. "That's why I have to play it safe. I'm leaving before the rain gets here. I suggest you do the same, maybe Cancun, Mexico." She looked at him knowingly. Before he could speak, she put her finger to his lips. "You've watched her grow up. I've seen it in your eyes, she's old enough now Shane."

He just smiled and hugged her. "What about the money?" he asked.

"I've been saving money eight years for a rainy day. I won't gamble with my child's life or mine anymore."

"Where?"

"Back home to Akureyri, Iceland."

Chapter 24

The stars overhead were like tiny silver lilies stitched onto a purple canopy. A yellow hot harvest moon had risen, the moon-bright trees swayed in the warm breeze. It was a hot summer night; the pools thermostat made the water and wet bodies alike steam. Phil Collins played on the radio, his lyrics filtering into Kenya's daydreams while she sat on the lounge chair and counted stars, then the rustling leaves. She distracted herself by trying to decipher the different fragrances and aromas that crossed her senses. Jami had insisted they go swimming; however, it seems as though that same sentiment was shared by many. Just one of those nights. Victor had purchased her bathing suit for $325.00. She had never paid so much for so little, but he loved it. Jami liked it; it was beautiful. She noticed Jerald step from the house; he was handsome, and had avoided her all day, not that she was looking for him. It is extremely difficult to live in the same house and not see each other, unless ... "Hello beautiful," he said. He had never seen her in lipstick and her hair, whoa! Her golden eyes caught him, pulled him, questioned him; her perfume worked him like a masseuse, relaxed him.

"Hey Jerald," she replied, her dulcet tones touching nerves. She caught him grinning like a Mako shark. Driving his eyes two miles an hour up her ebony limbs. He sat at the foot of the lounge chair, sipped his drink and handed it to Kenya. "What is this?" she asked as she took the cup. It had an alcoholic minty smell.

"It's Julep, taste it."

She tasted it, "Mmm ... this is good. What did you say it was?"

"Julep, it's a mint sweet drink, has a little liquor in it, not much though."

Kenya took several more sips from the glass. It was really sweet and minty with a little tang to it.

"I saw Iyanna' s father and mother today."

Hearing this instantly piqued her interest. "How? Where?"

"Old Vic's got his dogs looking for them, kinda sore Vail went to the cops. They're hiding out now. Vic can't find 'em."

"And you did?" Kenya asked skeptically.

He started rubbing her feet, ankles, calves; her skin was soft like warm water, he got his hands wet. "Yeah, I did. Vic is stupid, common sense led me to him. Vail is a college basketball star. He gave an interview to Sport Source about a year ago. Said when he's depressed, he likes to shoot around. He said when anxiety and apprehension's pulling at him, his relief is the basketball court. The rims, nets, lines, and wooden floor talk to him and relieves all his tension, pain and uncertainty. In his world, he's the king. He told all this to the interviewer."

His hands had roamed higher and Kenya stopped him. "Jerald."

His eyes met hers, "Okay, anyway, I just figured he had a lot on his mind, so I drove down to the University he attends, hung around the gym. They walked right past me. I followed them back to their hotel." Kenya's golden eyes flickered like orange flames in excitement. "Do you want to tell them something?" he asked.

"You're going to deliver a message to them for me?"

"Yeah, just write a note. I'll give it to them when I can. Don't give em' this address Kenya, they'll run to the cops and that'll fuck shit up."

"Alright," was her dulcet reply.

"Hello Kenya." A butter-colored brother stood with his hand extended. Jerald and Kenya looked up at him.

"I'm Vatly."

Politely she shook his hand. Vatly took the cup from Jerald's hand. "Mmm-num this is hitting, who hooked this up?"

"Patty," Jerald said.

Vatly looked down into Kenya's eyes. He thought Patty had exaggerated, but she had not, her eyes were remarkable. "How do you fit into all this ...?" She swept her hand across the land-scape, "... madness disguised as sanity?"

Vatly was taken aback, exactly how do you answer a question like that. "I suppose I'm nutty as a pecan orchard, what's your excuse?"

"I'm a victim of circumstance."

He eyed her suspiciously. "You don't look like a victim to me."

"And you don't look, nutty as a pecan orchard."

"Looks can be deceiving," Vatly retorted.

"Remember, you said it," she replied candidly.

Jerald watched Victor, Kenneth and Tim approaching them from the house. Mariah Carey's 'Vision of Love' played on the radio. Dominique sat on the steps of the pool looking dreamily at Vatly. Vance sat in a lawn chair staring at Dominique, his ad-ulation for her etched into his features and tattooed in his eyes. Yadira who had come out earlier sat with Jami and the twins. Sherrhonda and Tabitha spoke with a member of the surveil-lance team.

"I cut for your style Kenya," Jerald heard Vatly say.

"Your cha-lin technique isn't bad either." That solicited a smile from Vatly. Kenya smiled back, showing pretty even white teeth. Jerald wanted to puke, retch, regurgitate. His hatred blazed silently as if all the graphite rods had been pulled out of his acid reactor. He rose to leave. "Where you going?" That was Kenya.

"Uh ... I'm ... I'm just finsta move around. I'll get back atcha later."

"Don't forget Jerald." Her mellifluous; manna, butterscotch, taffy coated tones delivered body blows to his alter ego. He smiled, "I gotcha beautiful." And stepped off.

Victor, Kenneth and Timothy came abreast Vatly and Kenya. Hellos exchanged. Victor wore a grey jogging suit and Jordan's. "Kenya, may I have a dance?" Vatly boldly asked.

Her feeble protest was for naught. He grabbed her hand and pulled her to her feet. "I really don't want to."

"Of course, you do." Vatly insisted. All 4 One 'Cry No More' was playing. Paul and Yadira danced alongside Dominique and Vance. After pestering her for fifteen minutes, Vance finally got her consent. He didn't know what was the problem, but she had been remote and aloof tonight. He held her tight. Tabitha snagged Victor and Sherrhonda danced with both Kenneth and Timothy; one in front, one in back.

... you fell so deep in love. It was like a fairytale that somehow came true ..., the song played. Vatly held Kenya at a safe distance. She was only fourteen and that made a difference to him. He came at her from an avuncular standpoint. Even to him it seemed absurd, here he was a kleptomaniac; running around stealing folks' children but his morals would not allow him to lust or sleep with a fourteen-year-old. Maybe that's worse than the Christian that gets holy and baptized every Sunday morning, then gets pissy drunk and pugnacious Sunday night. A hypocrite is a hypocrite and the world's full of them ... *heartache you had; you gave your very best ...*

I'm not going to bite you, Kenya."

"That remains to be seen," she said insouciantly.

... you don't have to cry no more ...

"I'm not here to hurt you, there's not any kryptonite in my pocket."

... I'm what you're looking for, no more lonely nights, wipe the tears from your eyes ...

"You're not here to help or protect me either. That's the problem, you're just here minus the keys in your pocket taking up space and oxygen. My mama told me right fo' she passed, if you're not a part of the solution, you're part of the problem ..."

... you don't have to cry no more ...

"... I don't need any more problems." She did not speak rudely, just matter of factly.

... I'll never leave you lonely ...

Vatly glanced over his shoulder and saw two things. First, Victor's limpid eyes feasted on Kenya's ripe young body. His infatuation was conspicuous. Secondly, Dominique's midnight blue diamonds found him and asked a million questions. She had changed into a modest empress blue two piece. He winked at her and she smiled. Vatly thought about what Patty had said. Now a fourteen-year-old girl was checking him. Maybe it was time to cut this scene short, the masquerade had exhausted itself.

"You're beautiful and smart," he said almost incredulously.

"You thought I was a nincompoop!"

"Nah, just hadn't rated you as high as I should."

"Looks can be deceiving," she stated candidly.

"Remember you said it," he retorted smartly.

The night waned gradually. He did get around to dancing with Dominique and even talked Victor into letting him take Kenya and Jami to Slitterbaum for the nineteenth. Victor trusted Vatly, even Kenya. Kenya even asked him to come along, he declined gracefully. He was going to send Timothy along, then changed his mind. Timothy had better things to do. Kenya thanked Vatly for getting them out of the house. His reply was, "Just trying to be one of the good guys."

And hers was, "Slitterbaum doesn't make you a good guy, just a guy trying to do a good deed. There's a difference."

CHAPTER 25

Exactly what is it about life that you love? You can have as much time as you like to think about it, it is a broad question. Someone got famous for saying an object in motion tends to stay in motion; and for every action, there is an equal and opposite reaction.

Common sense cannot be common sense, because everyone does not have it. A wink is as good as a nod to a blind hoss, ya dig.

Bar-B-Que pits smoked all night, derelict canines licked their chops, wagged their tails and looked for instant adoptions into the hearts of the owners of the pits. June nineteenth danced on the calendars of Americas contented and discontented souls. Denial of the facts has never lessened the validity of the facts. The date mentioned above is a re-occurring moment in time. However, important today, it is still just a moment and unfortunately moments are eternally temporary.

At four and a quarter in the a.m. four locations in or around the Houston area erupted into explosions simultaneously. Victor's three clubs all went into flames, explosions ripped the small establishments inside and out. The conflagration licked at the air hungrily and voraciously. Sirens wailed, the ululations echoed loudly and made the audience of birds as nervous as a long-tailed cat at a square dance. They chirped and skittered about, watching the flames watch them forever and ever.

In Dayton, a three-bedroom home exploded and was consumed by flames. Oasiym Serengeti, now an investigative reporter was sitting at home transfixed on his 80-gallon salt-water fish tank. Jamie Sires with her sexy ass strolled across his 65" television on ESPN. The mute prevented her voice from invading his manufactured solitude.

The police scanner squawked mundane matters ...

Two phone calls had him thinking ... His computer sat on the sofa beside him, the screen saver dancing a redundant repetition. Printed files were strewn willy-nilly about the floor.

Names ...

Places ...

Dates ...

The first call came from Yancy Mordecai, mentor and friend. A man who had risked everything to save him from the system and himself. A man he loved.

The second call from a Houston detective. He was as indifferent to this man and his struggle as a fish was to a raincoat.

But Yancy had called, nothing for 10 years then a call.

After leaving the FBI he discovered a passion for writing, a gift born of death should come a life set right.

Research yielded Vail Akbar; a man wronged. Daphane Keye, a woman untethered by the trauma of losing a child. Iyanna; a child snatched from loving parents. Kidnapped.

Fajr ... Candance ...

If laughs were dollars, if chuckles were quarters, and if smiles were pennies, Qasiym would at the moment be flat broke. Outside, a waifish wind growled, scratched on the windows and raised mournful howls to the eaves.

His phone rang, and was ignored.

The police scanner burst into commotion, and was equally ignored. He was thinking so hard that wax should have blown out his ears with the velocity of bullets. Mosquito swarms of questions buzzed through his mind, their bites more ruinous and frustrating than a monastery full of celibates.

The police scanner went crazy and immediately caught his attention.

An explosion ... a nightclub called 'Tangueray' ... Luck. didn't favor amateurs.

Luck didn't favor the hesitant either. Action.

Timing. Timing was equally important in ballet and gunplay. 'Tangueray' ... Qasiym didn't believe in coincidences. Life was a tapestry with patterns to be discerned if you looked for them. Then, not five minutes later ... a second fire was reported, it piqued his interest. Then two more fires were reported, not even two minutes after that. He was all in, something was jumping. He got on the horn and got the addresses, maybe we were under attack by some terrorist. Maybe the KKK had studded up for the nineteenth. News stations had already been dispatched to the locations. After snatching up his tape recorder, he killed the lights and bailed.

At four-foe-five in the a.m., Paul was woken up by the vibrations of his cell phone against the nightstand. He hit the button and silenced the irritating noise, rolled over and snuggled close to Yadira. He was having an intimate conversation with sleep, he rushed to re-engage with the topic.

At four-foe-nine in the a.m., the phone began tapping out Morse Code across the polished pine top of the nightstand again. Paul reached blindly for the irritating contraption and silenced it again. Yadira shifted, buried her buttocks deeper into Paul's crotch. He wrapped his hands around her waist and the conversation resumed.

At four-five-foe in the a.m., the vibrating phone finally got its message across. Slowly raising from the bed, he answered. "Hello," he whispered sleepily into his cellular phone.

❖   ❖   ❖

With the first pick ... pick ... pick ... in the 2016 ... 16 ... 16 ... N.B.A ... Draft, the Dallas Mavericks select Vail Akbar ... from the ... University of Houston ... Houston ... Houston. Vail jumped up, eyes protuberant, perspiration misted his solid athletic frame.

"What is it baby?" Daphane asked softly.

"Nothing but a nightmare." Sunlight streamed through the curtains and radiant beams fell on the bed. Daphane moved and her near naked softness caressed his skin. He stroked her hip and looked at his watch, it was a quarter past seven. He slapped Daphane on the rump.

"Ow! Quit it Vail!"

"Get yo' butt up, I'm hungry."

"I'm not your wife, I don't have to cook for you." His large hand came down on her soft lush buttocks again. "Damn Vail that shit hurts. You have heavy hands nig ... boy."

"Get up then," he whined.

"No," she stated adamantly. This time Vail sunk his teeth into her bottom. "Oww! Owww! Okay baby I'm up."

Vail held his grip and spoke between his teeth. "You gone cook!" It was guttural and barely understandable.

"Yeah baby!" she cried out. "Mama gone cook." She laughed.

"You love me?" he asked.

"I'm gone fart boy if you don't let go."

"You better not. Do you love me?" He bit down harder.

"Ow, hell no!" she exclaimed. He started shaking like a Pitt Bull and growling. "Yeah! Yeah! Ow ow ow I love you baby." He released her and flipped her onto her back and crawled between her thighs and anxiously found her lips. They kissed passionately, as the kiss broke Daphane locked onto Vail's bottom lip with her teeth. "Yeah potna," she spoke through her teeth this time. "Apologize!"

He tried to speak with her holding onto his bottom lip. It sounded like he was a year old again. "I thorry."

"Who's gonna cook?" she demanded.

"Ae' onalds," he replied.

Then, "Do you love me Mr. Akbar?" She released his lip so his reply could be completely understandable.

"All day long baby, and twice as much on Sunday."

They showered together and made love, feeding their carnal appetite first. It was surreal outside and just too damn beautiful to stay inside. Daphane slipped into a pale blue spandex short set that was a bit too tight and a mite too revealing. Her nipples and the soft juncture at the bottom of her tummy protruded lewdly and the jouncing movement of her ass at every step she took would have made a man with a broken back come on a pogo stick to watch her walk. When she exited the bathroom, Vail smiled. "That's cute baby, now go get dressed so we can go."

She laughed, "I am dressed."

Vail nodded his head, "Okay." Then stood and began removing his leather belt from his designer shorts. She ran back in the bathroom with a giggle and a buttock seductive hip rocking gait. When she exited the second time she had on complimentary shorts with the same spandex top, however she had added a sports bra beneath it, you could no longer see her nipples. Vail was watching the news, Daphane walked behind him and gazed at the vivid pictures on the screen. There were reporters talking about the four explosions that destroyed three clubs and one residential home in Dayton. Authorities had deduced that the fires were obviously deliberate, but outside of that, they were baffled. The interviewer was speaking with a tall blond-haired man in front of a smoldering home. Bystanders ducked in and out of the camera's eye.

"I know him," Daphane said tensely.

"Who is he?" Vail inquired.

"Mr. Holmes, the manager of the Tangueray."

"That's the joint Puckett asked you 'bout." She nodded.

They finished watching the news together and chatted. Vail called Puckett at home. The phone rang three times before a deep groggy voice came on the other end. "Yeah?"

"Good morning, Detective," Vail said.

"Who dis?" was Puckett's reply.

"Vail, I assume you don't know what's jumpin'."

"No." He bolted upright and eyed his clock. It read nine and a dime. "What happened?"

"The club you asked Daph about, the Tangueray, was burned to the ground about five this morning. Some other clubs and this man ..." Puckett heard him say something to Daphane. "... Holmes's house was bar-b -qued too this morning."

Vail heard water running in the background. "Where you get all this, the news?"

"Uh-huh."

"Y'all alright?"

"Just suckaduckin', maintaining minus the complaining."

"I had him Vail, had him and let him slip through my fingers.

"They're on top of their business. But I'll get your daughter back."

Vail did not want Daphane to become depressed again. She tried to pretend to be strong and unaffected by all that was trans- piring around them. Last night after they made love, she figured he was plum tuckered out, she cried like a baby. With his back to her, he silently allowed tears to wonder like nomads down his face and congregate on the cotton pillow. "Just stay up Detective, cause laying it down isn't an option. Me and Daph are going to move around a little bit today, get a little sun, alright."

"Cool, just be careful."

"Already!" He hung up. "Come on lets jet pumpkin."

When Vail opened the door, a light skinned brother with curly hair was in the act of taping a letter to the door. He stared at Vail and Vail stared at him, with remarkable cool he handed Vail the letter. "Comes from someone who's gonna help you. You can help her by not including the cops."

"How you find us?" Vail asked stoically. Daphane stood behind Vail and looked at the boy.

"I'm not the killers, just a messenger with a message." He pointed at the letter.

Daphane found her voice and asked shakily, "Do you have my ..." Her voice broke, "... my baby?"

Jerald dropped his head, "No ma'am."

"But you know who does?"

He nodded his head. "These are some serious people; I risked my neck coming here. They're dangerous, serious people," he repeated glancing around nervously.

Vail asked again, "How did you find us?"

"Been watching you since you were a freshman. Kind of figured you'd show up at the gym sooner or later. I got to move around Vail, you saw the news, Victor's done pissed someone off." He turned and walked away. Vail shut the door, looked at the envelope. Daphane had tears in her eyes. Vail opened the letter and started to read:

Iyanna is fine. If you receive this letter just know that I'm going to try and help. I'm only fourteen, in the same position as Iyanna really. I know you're worried, but she's fine. I wanted to send Jerald to the police but he's afraid. Plus, I have my own reasons for not going to the police. If I'm not able to get us out of here by Saturday night I will get this address to you. Sunday is the day I believe they are going to move her. I know we're somewhere in Sugarland. Stay hopeful.

Kenya Khaliyd

CHAPTER 26

Paul sat in the study with Victor and explained what happened. The lassitude he felt was overwhelming. The events of the morning were incomprehensible; someone had completely destroyed all three clubs and his home. After he finished speaking, the silence was thick, difficult to breathe, difficult to walk through, just difficult. The antique clock ticked, and ticked and ticked. "How could someone know the location of all three clubs and my house?" He was furious.

Victor steepled his fingers under his chin. It was not quite ten yet. "Go ahead and speak with the laws, fill out the paperwork, and avoid being followed back here." Victor was silent then. "Paul, keep this quiet as far as the women are concerned."

"Uh ... yeah, alright. You know who's behind this?"

Victor was upset but still in control, still in control. "I have a theory."

Paul fumed. "I want to take care of it!"

"Nothing impetuous is necessary; first thing's first, handle the police, the reporters, then ..." He rose and strolled toward the window, "... we'll take care of the latter issue."

"Alright, let me go."

As Paul shut the doors to the study, the phone rang. "Victor speaking."

A smooth voice cut through the clear phone lines. "You know you fucked up, huh?"

"Yes, I'm beginning to get the distinct impression. Truly it was unintentional and I'm apologetic, are we even now?"

"I'm thinking about that now, starting to feel really religious. That eye for an eye type thing. Too bad Mr. Holmes wasn't home."

"Mr. Guthfield, you knew he wasn't home, let's not play games. Surely you and I are businessmen, it's unnecessary for us to act like Philistines." Victor paused, "Uh ..." thinking carefully because he wanted his phraseology perfect, "... you are a very articulate connoisseur, that much I've gathered from your vast knowledge of me and my operations. Can we not reasonably reach an understanding without further bloodshed?" Victor's glib efficiency was on the verge of phenomenal.

The line was silent, Diamond thought, yeah, this mark is scared. "What do you have in mind?"

"Unfortunately, Mr. Guthfield, that is the question I intended to ask you. How can I place a value on your loss?"

At the other end Diamond's attitude changed. Victor's smooth oratory had completely taken him off guard. In Diamond's line of reasoning, you blow up the man's house and three clubs; count 'em one, two, three clubs. More than a hundred thousand dollars in damages and you expect the average human being to be pissed off. You expect threats and ill-intended promises to be thrown around. Anything to fuel your anger, anything but this. "Half a million," Diamond said quixotically.

"When? Where?" Victor crooned in the phone.

Diamond was flabbergasted. "There's a Mickey D's at Texas and Fannin downtown. I'll meet you there at ..." He paused, "... three o'clock."

"Thank you, Mr. Guthfield."

"It's nothing, later."

"Later it is." The line went dead. The minute the phone hit its cradle it rang again. "Victor speaking." It was Decker.

Puckett had taken a nice hot bath. He was miserably hungover. He was unsuccessful in finding a local news station on his fishing expedition. All he encountered was talk shows; Jerry Springer 'Your Mans My Woman.' imagine that. A few sitcoms; Charmed, Law and Order SVU. Abruptly he cut the tube off, walked past his answering machine. The light was blinking indicating he had some messages. Just before he depressed the button that would rewind his messages, the phone started ringing. "Hello."

"Hi daddy."

"Hey sweetheart, how's my baby?"

"I'm fine, just missing you. Mama's cooking, said since it's a holiday you can come by."

"Aw honey, daddy would love to come by, but I'm really tied down right now. How about you and me getting together this weekend?"

"You promise?" She sounded disappointed.

"Promise. You still love your old man?"

"Forever and a day."

"I love you too, be good ya heah."

"Always, bye daddy."

"Bye baby." For the moment checking his messages had slipped his mind. His thoughts were now on his eleven-year-old daughter Krystal. He wandered toward the door; he had not seen her in almost three weeks, that was inexcusable. Looking at his watch, it was ten twenty-one. He snatched up his attaché case and exited the house. He wanted to meet Decker, check into the fires, speak with Paul Holmes and in between it all surprise his daughter. Shit, he thought, all I need now is the cape.

Puckett drove slowly, you could smell the excitement in the air. His suburban street was in full swing, cars being washed, lawns being mowed. Corey sat on a brand-new bike purchased no doubt from the money that was awarded them in a settlement. Last settlement, they bought a car. Corey had been hit three times. The first settlement paid for the house. Puckett half expected to hear his mama, now perched on the porch, yell, "Now baby! Run now! There goes a Jaguar." Corey would bungee jump in front of the car and BAM! Instant paycheck, then she would buy herself a new husband. Puckett felt safe, he was only driving a Buick, but still he watched Corey. Natasha and her ten daughters were loading up into a Dodge minivan. All looking crazy, sexy, cool in denim shorts and yellow t- shirts a bit too tight and a mite too high. But hey, they went to church every Sunday.

The station was buzzing with activity, it was just one of those days. His desk was cluttered with papers which he ignored. Twenty or so uniformed officers cluttered the conference room and listened while the lieutenant talked and wrote on the chalkboard. Ten minutes later they dispersed and Puckett approached lieutenant Kareem. "Good morning, Detective."

"Back at'cha lieutenant." They shared a firm handshake. "What happened this morning?"

Kareem was not certain he knew what Puckett was talking about. This was Houston, the fourth largest city in the United States. A lot happened every morning. "Be more specific."

"Oh," Puckett said with a smile. "I'm sorry. The fires." Kareem ran down all that he knew. Puckett learned who had spoken with Mr. Holmes and inquired about Decker.

Privately he briefed the Captain about what he suspected of Paul and Yadira Holmes and their connection with Shane. He could not place Shane in Phoenix, not directly anyway. The only inkling of information that hinted to Shane being in Phoenix was the white BMW. "Puckett," the Captain began tersely, "you have nothing concrete, nothing solid on these people. All you have is guess work and circumstantial evidence. I'm lenient, this is your first case as a detective. However, you cannot continue to chase ghosts and trudge around here like a bohemian. Get me something I can use, or just ask for a transfer to another case." Puckett felt like he was eighteen and had just been lectured by his father. He made a gesture to speak but the captain cut him off. "Shit or get off the pot. It's that simple."

Despondent as hell, he left the station. He had gotten a hotel address to where Paul was staying, so he was headed there. Forced to acknowledge how little tangible information he really had was embarrassing, if nothing else.

CHAPTER 27

Adib played chauffer for Xavier the morning of the nineteenth. He was up at 8:00 a.m., so by 11:00 a.m., he had successfully stolen forty winks, taken his car to the Detail Shop Accessories Plus and paid a visit to a car dealership where he rented a 2016 Jaguar, Silver of course. He forced himself to ingest some Folger's coffee, which he hated, but coming off a rough night into what promised to be a full eventful day, he needed it.

Adib was Muslim for real. That may seem strange to say, but he was one of those brothers who in the middle of a hulley gulley basketball game, would look at his watch and run off the court headed for his car. After retrieving his prayer rug, right there he would pray. His stepfather had money. An only child, his mom spoiled him thoroughly, thus explaining the Cadillac Escalade. He was a no-nonsense type of brother that was easy to be around because he was not trying to be something he was not. He was paper sack brown, six foot even with user-friendly face and a mockingly crooked smile. To know him was to love him. Xavier and Adib had known each other since knee-high days, back to diapers and pacifiers. Xavier's uncle dated Adib's mom back in the game, when his biological father was chasing greener pastures and ducking responsibility. A.I.D.S. blew his ass up and he died when Adib was eleven. His mom had been with Step, Xavier's uncle at the time. Step was a seasonal lover; he had a phobia of long commitment. However, his philanderers' ways made this situation ripe for Adib's stepfather. An astute and austere Muslim entrepreneur and philanthropist. He was good for Adib and his mom. Fathers do make a difference and two parent homes are a blessing. Xavier missed having a biological father around, but he was blessed to have his mother around during the most vital year of his life. She schooled him thoroughly before she fell off. Gus did not believe in luck, only skill. Bugeye believed in prayers and blessings. Xavier had gathered a balance and learned to utilize both schools of thought. He adopted people like Gus, Bugeye and even Tao Sung, then merged all their best qualities into one, creating the ultimate father figure. His loyalty to his mother was innate. He had watched her care for Vianna and just realized, never in a lifetime plus could he ever thank her enough. Never could he remember the bottles that were repeatedly washed, sterilized and warmed. He could never recall all the diapers she had changed. The attention she must have given him at his most vulnerable point. 'Thank you' just seems so shallow, inept, inadequate. Maybe there was not a language in existence that could in essence pinpoint the magnitude of his feelings. Maybe there was and he just had not heard it yet. Maybe.

Xavier pulled in the clubhouse apartments at precisely twelve forty-one. He had called earlier to inform Bugeye and Gus to be ready. They were all going to spend the day in Clinton Park. Tao Sung said he would be there with his family. Adib had been coerced to bring himself and his family. Nellie, Bernadine and Vianna were headed toward the park already with containers of food, coolers of alcoholic beverages and sodas sitting on ice.

"Whoa-ho!" Bugeye exclaimed when the Jag sailed in front of their doorstep.

"Xavier, where do you get such wonderful toys?" That was Gus, as always, his usual jocose self.

Xavier smiled. "What's da deal, you old cats ready?"

"We stay ready, to keep from getting ready," Bugeye retorted. They loaded a cooler full of Hennessey, beer and soda in the trunk, along with a medium size tent and lawn chairs. Gus was loaded into the front seat, its plush leather interior squeaked as he adjusted himself. Bugeye closed up the wheel chair and packed it away in the trunk.

"Bring yo' ass heah woman!" a heavyset man yelled at a big boned yellow hammer in a hundred dollars' worth of weave and mile long Lee press on nails.

"You will be shittin' a baby before I come back!" she shouted over her shoulder. Promptly hopped into a vanilla-colored Geo Storm and turned a few corners at a dangerous speed.

"Must be P.M.S.," Xavier said to Gus amusingly.

Gus and Bugeye shared a knowing glance. "Naw X, mo' likely it's U.P.S," Gus stated.

Xavier looked confused, then Bugeye added, "They or she delivered mo' than the mail this morning." Xavier just smiled.

In Route to Clinton Park, Xavier detoured to St. Joseph's Hospital. It was a little after one. Xavier had chosen some Roca Wear gear to wear; grey and yellow short set. Same black and yellow Nike air max, black socks, with a black and yellow Gramblin State University cap twisted sideways on his head. When they entered the hospital, the cool air got intimate with their skin. Beauty of the week runner ups modeled their white uniforms. The antiseptic odor worked the hallways like a priest. At the reception desk he asked for Deshawn Lowe's room. Much to his relief she had been removed from I.C.U. and placed in a room.

Xavier tapped lightly on a door that seconds later was opened by Denise. "Hey Xavier." She wrapped her skinny arms around his waist and laid her head on his chest.

"Hey pretty eyes." He had ordered fifty small teddy bears of various colors to be sent to her room with a note that said:

How about a game of chess? Signed Xavier.

Deshawn was awake, pallid but functional. "Hey," she whispered and made a weak attempt to smile. He stood over her and rubbed her forehead, then cheeks; her lips were dry and her eyes swollen.

"You still look beautiful, what's your secret?"

This time she did smile. "Good friends," was her whispered reply, then "What' s up with all the bears?"

"I needed someone to protect you in my absence. It was either lions, tigers or bears."

Deshawn smiled, then winced when she said, "Oh my!" Mrs. Lowe laughed at their play on words. "Thank you, Xavier," Deshawn said rubbing his hand.

"Don't thank me, thank the Man upstairs." He squeezed her hand. "Do me a favor though."

"Anything." She squeezed his hand back.

"Pick your company a little better. If it don't fit, don't force it, there's someone out there for you. You're too intelligent and too beautiful to settle for anything less."

He left, but promised to return. Bugeye and Gus had waited in the lobby and by the time Xavier made it downstairs they had a swarm of nurses gathered and were playing three card Monty. Xavier just laughed. A white girl with more curves than a 'S' in Levi shorts and a flannel tank top asked him, "Is that your dad?" Referring to Gus.

Xavier looked at Gus, grinning from ear to ear while manipulating the cards expertly, then back at the sun-tanned face with pretty grey opals and straight white teeth. "Yeah, one of 'em."

It was after two when they made it to the park and if you have never seen Clinton Park on June nineteenth, it is difficult to describe. People are scattered to and fro like a million skittles or M & M's. Inside the basketball court a large stage is erected and the DJ's play energetic music. Tents are set up against the canopy of trees, hundreds of perfumes mingle conductively with hundreds of different aromas from food, nature and musk. A sweet musk. Laughter assailed the ears and danced with the music; kids ran, screamed and cried. Females decked in colorful tight, colorful loose, colorful lewd and colorful modest clothing; wore colorful lipstick and tasteful smiles. The male folk had jazzed up also, braids tightened down, Afro's fluffed up, curls activated and bald fades faded within less than an inch of error. The minute, no the second after Xavier exited the car he knew beyond a shadow of a doubt he would be all day locating Shai and his family. He just shook his head, removed his cellular phone and placed a call.

"Whoa-ho, now this is a festival," Bugeye exclaimed. Being so close to the parking lot, the music was deafening. The SOS Band bellowed an old school jam through the huge speakers.

Xavier looked across the vast canopy of trees, tents, cars and people. Bugeye and Gus were already in the trunk at the refreshment. He dug into the ice and pulled out a Hawaiian Punch.

The music and sights entertained them for the next few minutes. Sung showed up shortly after with his wife Soili and daughter Zen. Xavier saw her before she saw him. She looked radiant in charcoal grey silk shorts that came to her knees and molded to her firm shapely thighs every time the wind blew. A matching silk half shirt that hugged her bosom kind of salaciously. Her flat cornbread colored stomach looked prominent and lissome. He noticed for the first time that she was slightly pigeon-toed, not much, just a little. She wore this grayish looking lipstick, fingernail and toenail polish that matched her outfit. Her hair was more Toni Braxton than Halle Berry today. Either way, she was holding it down. Xavier walked up to her, "You got something on your face, some candy or something." She ran her hand over her face.

"Right here." Xavier pointed.

She repeated the gesture. "Did I get it?" she asked.

"Nah, here ... let me." He leaned over, took her bottom lip into his mouth and sucked on it. "Oh, my bad! That isn't candy, it's your lip, but it tastes like candy."

She grinned, poked out her bottom lip. "Here, you can eat it."

He laughed. "Nah, mama said don't ever eat anything that's gonna get up and walk away."

She smiled that smile and kissed him. "You're late."

"Been busy baby."

"Who's car?" She pointed to the Jag.

"I rented it this morning, my car's getting cleaned. A lot of blood." After introductions to Tao Sung and his family, she hopped in the Jag and stood up out of the sun roof. They drove their cars back to the spot, she giggled, pointed and gave animated directions. Standing up out of the sun roof like that she received some icy, envious glares from other females, while some fellas eyed her like a Cyclops. All about them, there was plenty of jaw jumping and slack jacking.

The first thing Xavier saw was the pearl white Cadillac Escalade. Bernadine looked like she was eighteen again in a blue denim tennis get-up. Her succulent legs drew more attention than the Watergate Scandal. Nellie's dress mode was motherly and Vianna's cute. Company was energetic and vivacious, everything but languid. Dominoes struck like thunder claps on the top of the erected tables. Another table was put up for spades, wisk and gin rummy. Some just lazed in lawn chairs and soaked up their festive surrounding. Coincidentally, Prophet stumbled upon them and after Pam slapped him across the back of his head, they started talking. Her personality, Colgate smile and milk chocolate suit wrapped in a similar outfit as Shai's, just small variations, satisfied his need for attention. Xavier was just able to get his attention long enough to get incoherent instructions to his mother.

On the search for his aunt, Jackie, Shai and Vianna tagged along. His love for Jackie could not be measured, from her he learned resiliency. She used to smoke, but her love for her child made her quit cold turkey. Not many folks could accomplish that feat. He marveled at her strength, tried to copycat her practical, prudent ways. Her and his mom had drifted apart, they were once tighter than two toes on top of each other. But for some to maintain sobriety you have to stay away from the negative influences (i.e., The Product) and in all actuality as long as Nellie smoked, she was a negative influence. It was a hard pill to swallow, but reality has always presented problems for some, remedies for others.

When Xavier was about fourteen, he had this crush on a little girl. Takka was her name. He was taking her to homecoming and needed forty-five dollars for a mum. He did not have the money and Jackie probably did not have the money either, not for a mum. Nevertheless, she bought it, then that Friday she escorted him to school. He would never forget walking down the hallway full of kids with his aunt. She wanted to meet this high school girl worth forty-five dollars of her money. Takka was at her locker when Xavier, his aunt and the crowd gathered. "Hey," Jackie said. "I'm his aunt, I just wanted to meet the young lady he's spending all his money on." Takka spoke, smiled coyly. More things were said that have been lost due to a sufficient lapse of time, but the important part was remembered— the walk. Yeah, Jackie was his practical aunt, Rhonda his business minded aunt, Gail the beauty queen aunt, Nicole his chaste aunt and mama, well, she gave him the game. It is amazing how Grandma raised all these diverse personalities. She was an extraordinary woman. Grandma was one of those women you want to write a book about but just cannot find the right words.

Xavier introduced Shai to Jackie, they chatted. It was a sweet exchange, so sweet it could have sent a diabetic into a coma fifty feet away.

CHAPTER 28

At two o'clock the blistering heat circled like a vulture, but on a day like this nothing could stop the ball from rolling. The condos were a beehive of activity, music, movement and modeling. Females airbrushed into existence with calculated precision in every coquettish wink, flirtatious tongue bite, lip licking goo-goo eyed facial wooing ogle, hip jutting side glance teeth sucking smack! A perfect equation with a lot of variables. $E=MC2$, oh really! An object in motion stays in motion, if you say so. Everything was so fluid it kind of made you wanna buy a vowel.

Diamond Slim, Big Cash, Dollar Bill, Kilo, Redd Dirt, G-Slim and Sideline Redd exited the condo with sho-nuff mugs, steel grills that kryptonite couldn't touch and headed for the parking lot. They would travel in two cars, Diamond's Lexus and Dollar Bill's Infinity. There was a red Iroc parked next to Diamond's Lexus, a white male in tattered overalls had his head buried under the hood, another white male dragging a large tool box from the trunk. Diamond hit his remote and the alarm chirped. "We'll follow you Diamond," Big Cash stated.

It happened fast, too damn fast. Timothy rose from under the hood and two muffled shots spoke volumes. Cash went down and Dollar Bill followed, both dead before they hit the ground. Concurrently Kenneth dropped Kilo and Redd Dirt in similar fashion. Somebody screamed in the parking lot. Could have been male or female, maybe both. Diamond fell to the ground struggling with his expensive jacket trying to free his small derringer. Sideline had pulled his pistol and pointed, Kenneth shot his foot out, knocking Redd's arm into the air. The forty-four barked viciously and landed on the concrete in an audible clang. Kenneth aimed his pistol but Redd was too close and seized Kenneth's hand. The silence-capped pistol whispered into the air. Kenneth shot his hand out in an 'X' fashion, catching Sideline Redd in the throat. When Redd clenched at his crushed larynx wheezing horribly in pain, without hesitation Kenneth reached out and twisted Redd's neck. A sicken snap ended the confrontation.

G-Slim had managed to put a 357 slug into Timothy's torso at the same time Timothy threw not one, but two knives at G-Slim; landing one in his throat and one in the heart. G-Slim's last thought was, the guy must have a vest. Diamond laid in his urine, terrified and crying. He didn't present a pretty picture, pathetic barely began to touch it, ugly would have been better. Revolting kind of said it all. Diamond kept thinking, he should have expected this, a madman often thinks way ahead of a sane man. All this had taken place in less than ninety seconds. Kenneth stood over Diamond, bystanders peeped from around corners or curtained windows. "I'm sorry, I'm sorry," Diamond cried.

Kenneth leaned down. "Don't cry, playa, I ain't gonna kill ya," he whispered. "Mr. Pierce wanted to renegotiate his verbal contract."

Timothy walked behind Diamond, leaned into his ear and whispered, "You know you fucked up, huh?"

Diamond was nodding his head tearfully, pitifully, when the pistol in Kenneth's hand whispered two final times. "Okay, I lied, sue me." Both Timothy and Kenneth's watches started beeping, time was up. They jumped into the Iroc and drove off slowly.

Qasiym Serengeti started doing his homework early. The four fires this morning' Paul Holmes background, that's who, according to paperwork, owned the three clubs and the house in Dayton. He had already spoken with Mr. Holmes, whose incoherent expletives, stammering and light switch like desultory demeanor successfully left more questions than answers. It was while listening to the hushed murmurs of some fellow colleagues that most of his earlier notions collapsed. The plot thickened and the quandary climbed several degrees on the scales. To Qasiym, the oldest child of a family of two, the chase, he could taste it. He overheard his colleagues discussing a similar explosion. and fire the day before, the home of a Judge that was murdered in his car with a prostitute the same day. He ran a check on the Judge and drew a complete blank. The prostitute however, was a little different. She had a well-known pimp. Qasiym thought maybe he knew something and would help a brotha out.

That's exactly where Qasiym was headed when reports of a multiple homicide came over his radio. He thought he misunderstood the address, but it was repeated several times over the police radio. At the light he had ample time to comprehend lucidly that the address mentioned and his destination were one and the same, Burningbush Lane.

By the time he got there, a throng of people were being held back by yellow tape. Reporters shouted redundant and trite questions. The dull hum of mixed murmurs emitted from the onlookers. It was hot, but there was a steady breeze. A channel 2 news crew were pestering the locals while a helicopter circled noisily, taking aerial photos. Police cars, an ambulance, the van from the medical examiners and a car from the Homicide Bureau were at the scene. Qasiym noticed forensic experts walking on cotton around the bodies. Blood cooked by the heat had turned black and looked like fresh oil stains. The nineteenth was shaping up to be one helluva day. There was a huge black man speaking to a small swarthy and tense looking man in Gucci loafers, Dockers and an oxford-blue shirt. His time-clawed face was blank as the back of a shovel. His name was Saddiq. No middle or last name, just Saddiq. No Mr.'s, sirs or other titles, just plain old Saddiq. Qasiym knew him to be an ex-FBI agent in his seventies and was now a homicide captain since leaving the Bureau ten years ago. Qasiym had bumped heads with him on several occasions. After flashing his I.D. to several officers, he parked himself in front of the large man and Saddiq. "Qasiym," Saddiq said without rancor.

"Saddiq," was Qasiym's Xeroxed reply. "What brings you out this way?"

"Answering a call." He extended a hand to Puckett.

Saddiq turned to Puckett. "Detective Puckett, this is Qasiym Serengeti, investigative reporter. Qasiym, Detective Puckett."

Courtesies were exchanged, Qasiym learned that six men were killed, the seventh was in critical condition. Paramedics didn't quite understand how he was still breathing. His neck was definitely broken and his larynx appeared to have been fractured. His pulse was faint, but amazingly he was alive. Witnesses gave about ten different descriptions of the two assailants. Allegedly it happened too fast, less than two minutes. Saddiq said it was a professional job, no one could kill six men and put the seventh on death's doorstep inside of two minutes, but professionals. Qasiym listened. Abruptly Saddiq excused himself to attend to some urgent affair.

"What's going on Detective?" Qasiym prodded.

"Can't figure it, just can't figure it," Puckett said listlessly.

Qasiym studied the detective, liked what he saw and made a quick decision. "You know Detective, there was a judge murdered yesterday in a similar fashion." Puckett met Qasiym's eyes straight on. "But ..." Qasiym continued, "... what interested me the most was that the Judge was with a prostitute. Her pimp, Andrew Guthfield lives at this address."

Puckett's mouth flew open, his esoteric knowledge, case wise was deeper than Qasiym, so he understood the ramification of Guthfield being killed. His connection with the prostitute and her connection with the Judge. Qasiym was nodding his head in a 'yeah potna' fashion. "Mr. Qasiym, I think we should talk."

Qasiym looked at his watch. "You had lunch?"

"Nope, follow me. I know just the house."

Qasiym's eyebrows went up. "My ex-wife's" Puckett explained. "I'm multitasking today, gotta see my little girl. Might as well kill three birds with one stone. Eat, talk and see my little girl, plus if I bring company, she won't start no static. "You game?"

Qasiym grinned, "Let's play."

Patty packed her things, trapped mentally inside by deep thoughts and occasionally beckoned back from her utopia by the movement of her own reflection in the mirror. The eyes in the mirror stared at her; there were questions there. However, some questions bring forth some of the most unpleasant answers or most adamant denials. So sometimes they were better left un-asked and unanswered. This entire pathetic scene had never been intriguing or pleasant. She thought often of the child she had given up or more correctly, sold to Victor; it had been a little girl. She hated Victor with a passion, felt as though he had given her an ultimatum instead of choice when Pebble introduced her to him. She was young and naive, paying dearly for her mistakes.

Although Victor and Paul tried to act normal, she caught the evening news which spoke avidly about the explosions and fires which destroyed three clubs and a residential home in Dayton. She couldn't believe that someone had retaliated on Victor so brazenly. Timothy and Kenneth were the epitome of chaos. She had witnessed the destruction they were capable of in Detroit. They only stayed in Detroit a month; some personal vendetta Victor had with the Italian Mafia. Somebody would pay for the destruction of the clubs, but who? There was a light rap on the door. She slid her suitcase on the other side of the bed to the floor concealing it from the doorway. Carefully she inspected herself before strolling to the door and swinging it open. "Hey Boo!" the husky male voice said softly.

"Hey baby, why aren't you out enjoying the day?" She snaked her arms around his neck and drew his lips to hers. He backed her into the room and shut the door. Last night she had divulged the fact of her pregnancy and his response was positive, solidifying her love for him. That's just how some relationships are, going through the hours, days, weeks and sometimes years, waiting for that special defining moment. The one incident that's so monumental in its significance, it either makes, brakes, shakes or solidifies the doubt, the faith, the hatred or the love.

"I was going to head to Juneteenth Fair with Vatly and Dominique, but I didn't want to leave you by your lonesome. You hungry?"

"Kinda, this morning sickness is killing me."

"Let's run and get something to eat."

"Can't, I have to watch the kids. Everyone else is out and about, so I'm stuck."

"I'm 'ma run and grab us some bar-b-que links, potato salad and pie, o-ite. I won't be long." A mischievous grin covered his face. "What color are they?" he asked.

She smiled. "None-ya!"

"Are they lace, French cut, bikini or G-string?" he asked as he wrapped his arm around her waist and kneaded her willowy buttocks.

"Why don't you hurry back so you can play detective and investigate?"

"Show you right." He kissed her a final time and bolted for the door. Patty pulled her suitcase from the floor and resumed packing.

Chapter 29

The jocular atmosphere excited everyone. The roar of the massive rides as they moved swiftly on their track was overpowering. The smell of cotton candy touched you here and there, now and then, disappearing then resurfacing in the only vehicle supplied to it, the wind.

Kenya had donned a purple form fitting gingham and Jami wore Guess shorts and shirt. Vatly had chosen baggy khaki Bermuda shorts and a tan shirt. The surprise of the evening was Dominique in her demure floral sundress and matching sandals. She and Vatly had talked for three hours on the phone last night. That was when he invited her to join them. The evening was in full swing, they rode the rides, visited several games, and ate up everything in sight. It was fun, a lot of smiling and laughing. "This place is fabulous!" Dominique exclaimed. This was her first trip to Juneteenth Fair. Jami agreed wholeheartedly. A young brother close to Kenya's age was undaunted by Vatly's presence and approached Kenya.

"Excuse me lil' sista, I really don't wanna step like a klutz and fumble the pill, so I'm willing to get out tha game and parley on the sideline with you if it's cool." Kenya smiled, even blushed a little. He had on a Philadelphia 76'ers jersey with the number 'three' on it, and some Allen Iverson's shoes on. He held out his hand, "I'm Chill." Vatly just watched the exchange, Dominique likewise.

Kenya shook his hand. "I'm Kenya. This is my little sister Jami, our uncle Vatly and his wife." Kenya gave Vatly and Dominique a mischievous grin.

"What's poppin'?" Chill sang directly at Vatly, Dominique and Jami. Kenya liked him immediately. He was fly and confident.

Vatly asked, "Who you here with playa?"

"My older brothas 'round dis camp somewhere chasing boppers."

"Why aren't you chasing boppers?"

Chill grinned broadly, "I'm a young prince en route to becoming a king one day, nothing less than a queen can satisfy my taste."

"Where's your castle prince?" Kenya inquired.

Chill took in her smile, thought to himself, she's cute! "It's constructed to perfection in the blueprint in my mind. If you remove your shoes, I'll give you a grand tour of every room."

Kenya laughed, so did Vatly and Dominique. Jami was unimpressed. The line moved steadily toward the next ride. Dominique was tickled pink by the young brother's creative nature. "How old are you?" she asked.

"Twelve and one, that's thirteen where I come from."

A woman in yellow hot pants stood off to their left. She was a little overly endowed in the posterior region and every movement of her hips made her buttocks shift and undulate in the thin material. Vatly caught Chill's eyes surveying her goods and intentionally put him on the spot.

"I see you looking at it, can you handle all that?" The girls who were up to that point unaware looked around then back at Chill.

"I learned awhile back, there's Corona, then there's Heineken. I'm more of a Corona man myself, but that never stopped me from looking at the Heineken bottle while I'm at the liquor store."

Jami snorted with derision. Chill looked at her. "Damn half pint, I must've rubbed you the wrong way."

"I don't even know you," Jami said.

"You must jus hate black folks cuz bein' black is the only thing I did today that's still ah crime in America."

Jami dismissed him with a wave of her hand. Finally at the ticket booth the machine operator ushered people into their seats. Chill watched the Heineken bottle climb her pliant body into the narrow seat.

"C'mon." Kenya pulled at Chill's arm.

"Nah baby girl, I don't get on anything that's going to physically make me fly."

"I know you're not scared," Dominique joshed.

"Say, it's not a felony, is it?"

Vatly laughed. "Not yet."

The machine operator was moving everyone expeditiously to their seats. Kenya pulled Chill's hand. "C'mon, I won't let you fall."

"Yeah," Chill exclaimed. "You gone have me looking like Lois Lane in the first Superman, where he flies up and catches her. You'll be Superman." He dropped his voice a few octaves. "I got 'cha, and I'll be Lois asking," he removed the bass from his voice, "Who you got?"

She smiled. "Come on Kenya!" Jami called out.

"Go ahead," Chill said. "I'm gonna stay parked right heah."

"Vatly, I'm going to wait here with Chill," Kenya shouted. Panic constricted his heart for a second. He did not want to separate; the crowd was too big.

"Alright, don't get lost," he said.

Jami shot Chill a 150-degree glare that singed his eyebrows and melted his sneakers to the asphalt. "I believe you betta check tha top of ya sista's head when she goes to sleep tonight," Chill said.

Kenya didn't understand. "What?"

"She might have 666 for a birthmark."

Chill and Kenya walked to an area where they could see Vatly, Dominique and Jami once they exited the ride. Chill purchased some ice cream cones, another Heineken bottle passed by, and he checked it out. Kenya conversed with Chill in an affable manner about really nothing in particular. They were still conversing when someone started shouting his name.

"Chill! Chill! Lookout Chill! I see ya playa!" Kenya spun around to see two brothers approaching. The younger of the two was molesting her with his eyes and congratulating Chill.

"I've been sucka duckin' yo' ass all day cuz of the kiddie stunts you do to embarrass ah brother. Please rise like smoke and evaporate!" Chill exclaimed rigidly.

"Aw lil chump, kill the frontin'," was Aaron's reply.

"What's up lil bit?" Dink said to Kenya. "Any more at home like you?"

"Yeah, but she's jail bait!" Kenya stated.

"Shit you look like you too old for my brotha. What's your numbers?" Aaron asked.

She studied Aaron then said, "Fourteen."

Chill looked at his brother. "Aaron why don't you chill man?" They dialogued, Kenya listened momentarily enthralled by these ghetto souljas, their lingo and rough ridah attitude. Kimberly, Kenya's mom had gone through great lengths to keep away from the ghettos and their product. They attended private schools that were majority white; the blacks that were there were mannered and refined. Kenya's daddy cruising through her veins and being around these brothers made her feel at home, safe and secure. They seemed so much different. The crowd thickened, the noise climbed the decibel scale and the heat peaked and climaxed even in the shade. The combination of it all successfully stole Kenya's attention from the ride.

When Vatly stepped from the ride his eyes immediately undressed the area in search for Kenya. Panic is a weak description for what he felt when he did not see her anywhere. His heart pounded; a thin sheen of perspiration formed on his brow. "Damn!"

"What is it?" Dominique asked.

"Kenya, do you see her?"

Dominique ran her eyes over the crowd. "No, I don't see her."

"I knew we should not have separated. Jami, do you see your sister?"

"No, I don't see her." They exited the gate and walked right past Kenya and Chill, shielded by Dink, Aaron and an assortment of others were strolling by. Vatly's apprehension began mounting. Victor would kill him if that girl escaped and went to the police. He had to find her. A security guard walking with two police officers, pointed directly at him. Vatly went rigid, almost bolted when they broke into a sprint. To his relief the officers ran right past him, a youngsta in white took off running and the chase was on.

Dominique suggested they back track; she was convinced that Kenya would not intentionally get lost, maybe they just missed her. Chill was the one who noticed them as they came into view from the opposite direction. The white girl in the floral sundress was built like a sista. She had legs like a stallion and was hard to miss. "Lookout Vat!" Chill yelled. Vatly swiveled at hearing his name and instant relief surged through him as he stared into Kenya's golden pools.

"Vail! Vail! Lookout nigga!" Dink called out.

Vatly and Kenya turned in the direction Dink was looking in. When Vatly turned his attention to Kenya, she was looking at him knowingly.

"Hey Vail!" Aaron yelled.

Vail heard his name and pivoted several times trying to locate the source. Daphane said, "Over there." She pointed. "Who are they?"

"I don't remember their names. They were at Xavier's apartments." Daphane's short, seductive sashay matched Vail's long graceful stride as they approached the little group. Vatly's heart was having a helluva day. Right now, it was racing like a snare drum in free meter.

"Uh … let's move around Kenya, uh, you know it's about that time." Kenya and Dominique noticed Vatly's nervousness.

"Hey," Chill handed Kenya a piece of paper. "Holla at me sometime."

"You got that comin'," Kenya said.

The first person Vail noticed was the succulent youth in the purple gingham, smooth mahogany skin and stunning golden eyes.

"Hold up, Vat!" Dink said. "Let me introduce you to the next NBA all-star. Look, this is Vail Akbar, U of H hired killer representin' the city to the fullest. What's ya girl's name? I neva got it."

"Daphane." She volunteered the information herself. "Who are you?"

"Oh, I am Dink, my brothers Aaron and Chill."

Vail was interested in what the little girl was looking at so intently. His six feet six inches frame towered over them. He had a blue teddy bear in his hand, Daphane had a pink one. He squatted so he could be eye to eye with the little one. "Hey, beautiful, what's your name?"

Jami smiled. "Jamilyah Khaliyd."

"Why don't you take this?" He squeezed her bi-ceps. "It's too heavy for me and your muscles look bigger than mines."

Jami wrapped her little arms around the huge teddy bear. "Thanks, Vail."

He touched her nose. "No sweat lil one. What's your name?" he said to Kenya.

"Kenya Khaliyd."

Daphane, who was only partially paying attention immediately looked at the young girl. Vail's stomach fluttered, his eyes left Kenya for a moment and went to Vatly and Dominique. He motioned for Daphane to give him the other teddy bear.

"Chill, I'm disappointed with you. A sister this beautiful shouldn't be walking around empty handed." He handed Kenya the bear. "Do you know me?" he asked in a playful manner.

Kenya said, "Yeah, your U of H's hired killer representin' the city to the fullest."

Everybody laughed. "You want my autograph?" he asked.

"Do you want mines?" she retorted.

Vail laughed. "Yeah, let me have it. I can easily believe you'll be the next Tyra Banks, Mary J. Blidge or Halle Berry."

She smiled again, "Well I could be the first Kenya Khaliyd. Instead of your autograph, give me your shoes so I can hawk 'em for a couple of mill when you blow up."

"I have athlete's feet, ask Daph," Vail said.

"It's alright, I want to sell them, not smell them," Kenya said humorously.

"Alright, dig this here. Give me a rain check on the shoe blast. This ground ain't so sanitary." Vail took out the blank envelope with the letter inside that Jerald had given him. He looked at Vatly. "I hope you don't mind me getting your daughter's autograph."

Through Vatly's paranoia he said, "Oh, she's my niece."

"Uncle Vatly, can I get a pen?" Kenya crooned.

Dominique went inside her purse at the same time Chill went into his pocket. Chill beat Dominique, so Kenya used his pen.

Kenya signed, Kenya Iyanna Khaliyd. Then handed Vail the envelope. Daphane was at a loss for words. Out of all these people how could they run into this little girl. She thought about the parable that had hung over her aunt's floor model television ever since she was a kid, 'Footprints in the Sand.' God is always helping us, sometimes we're just too damn blind to recognize and appreciate the help.

Vatly hastily moved them toward the exit and to the parking lot. It was a little after seven; they had been there since twelve, plus Dominique had a plane to catch at ten thirty. He was constantly looking over his shoulders, certain that someone was following them. Patty's words continued to nag him. The events of the day had scared him. That was the second time he had been face to face with that brother. He feared the third meeting, if there was one, would prove to be disastrous. He made four phone calls when he made it home. The first call was to the airport, his second call was to the police station where he spoke to Detective Bailey, the slim Caucasian he had spoken with before. He informed him that he was headed home, back to East St. Louis. His third call was to Dominique, to tell her he would see her in Mexico within the month, that he had to go home first to East St. Louis. He had to confront some demons; he had run long enough. His fourth call was to Victor's line in the study. As he expected,

Patty's clear voice cut through the haze and tension that had plagued him since they left the Astrodome.

"Patty?"

"Yeah ... that you Shane?"

"Yeah, ran into that kid and his girl today at the Astrodome."

"What kid?"

"Iyanna's mother and father. Just subtle signs telling me it's definitely that time. I'm going home first, then flyin' to Mexico."

Patty smiled at her end of the phone. "I'm proud of you Shane, I thought you'd let greed hold you. You're getting good."

"No, you're already the best. If'n I get ah chance to call you fuh sho I will."

"Yous betta, dats whut frinz su'pose ta do." Patty paused; the line sizzled. "I love you, Shane."

"Ditto Violet. Ditto."

CHAPTER 30

Nellie exhausted herself while at the park. She screamed and yelled enthusiastically on the domino table. She and Bernadine went undefeated even, smoking Bugeye and Gus. She ate heartily and just all around had a nice time. Shai's little boy Nathan was enamored of Nellie and was about to fight with Bugeye over a Pepsi she had asked for. Daylight waned and a descending sun painted the sky burnt orange. The trees grew in healthy profusion, it was peaceful and serene. As they packed and prepared to leave, there was some urgency to Nellie's movements. The day had been a success, but she wanted to get home. The dependency she had controlled all day was now calling her in full force. Xavier had left about thirty minutes ago to take Bugeye and Gus home. She and Bernadine would be leaving in Bernadine's beige Honda Accord. "Ms. Joyce, we really enjoyed ourselves. We can't wait another year before we get back together," Nellie said while hugging the other woman. After the embrace Ms. Joyce moved her sturdy frame effortlessly, tucking things here and there.

"Baby y'all will always be welcome in my home, we'll set something up. I have to cook for the fourth anyway, so y'all come then, alright."

Nathan and Vianna were dragging a cooler full of melting ice and surviving sodas. "Dump the ice Nathan," Shai called.

Bernadine strolled off with some fella she met, promising to be right back. In response to Ms. Joyce's invitation Nellie said, "Yeah we're going to do that." And threw her arm around Shai. "Looks like this is going to be my daughter-in-law."

"They need to hurry up and do whatever they're going to do, so she can get out of my house."

Nellie laughed. Shai exclaimed, "Mama!"

"Chile I gots to find me a man, I needs yo' yellow ass gone so I can take care of my business. I done got old and being quiet is getting harder and harder to do."

Shai laughed along with Nellie, then turned her lips up. "Huh ... nasty old lady."

"Baby, I refuse to go all the way to Jamaica just to get my groove back. Nathan wasn't thought into existence and neither were you."

Nathan heard his name and looked up. Vianna looked drained and ready to collapse. "Come on baby." Nellie lifted her into her arms, "Let's go home." She was exhausted and her clothes had been ruffled and soiled during the day's events.

"Nellie, tell your son to call me when he gets in," Shai implored.

"Alright." Nellie agreed. Then yelled into darkness. "Bernadine!"

The darkness answered, "Quit yelling my name, Stank!"

"Well bring your purple ass on!" she shouted back.

❖ ❖ ❖

Bernadine's mission had been clear since her return. Already she and Nellie had talked effusively about getting the monkey off her back. Lights of passing cars illuminated their features momentarily, then slipped back into darkness. The sound of the wind slipping through a crack in the window whispered its own tune. Tony Rich Project crooned 'No Body Knows' on the radio, and the Honda Accord bounced smoothly toward their destination.

Bernadine made a stop at her mother's in Sunnyside, daughterly dropping off some food and left beverages from the outing, chatted sparingly then loaded back up en route to Nellie's apartment. Before reaching their destination, they made a stop at the Circle K on Reed Road to pick up a pack of Newport's. She pulled in beside a blue Range Rover and Black Lincoln Navigator. Vianna was somehow re- energized and sprang from the vehicle in a vivacious gait. In all her excitement she bumped into a short Asian-looking man with huge glasses, protruding front teeth and an oversized suit. "Vianna watch where you're going!" Nellie shouted.

Nellie picked her baby up and dusted off her bottom. "I'm sorry." Nellie apologized for Vianna.

The man pushed his glasses up on his face. "It's quite alright." he said.

Bernadine watched two other men, both with sandy brown hair and decked in grey pinstriped Armani suits and silk Hermes ties. The Lincoln Navigator's ignition turned over which made Nellie peer inside the automobile for the first time. Through the richly tinted windows she made a solitary silhouette. The two young men in the suits loaded into the Range Rover and the short Asian climbed into the backseat of the Lincoln. Both vehicles exited the parking lot into darkness of Reed Road. Nellie, Bernadine and Vianna entered the store. Nellie needed some alcohol, Bernadine some Newport's and Vianna was undecided, but was sure she would see something she wanted.

They kind of just went through the motions after realizing the name of the little girl signed on the back of the envelope. Empowered with hope at first, they tried to follow them but the task seemed virtually impossible. Not only did the immense crowd enter into the conspiracy with the perpetrators, but so did everything else. It just appeared as though some elaborate scheme had been unmasked. Traffic entered the equation. At first, they had to relocate the black BMW because they were parked so far apart. Every time Vail tried to close the distance between them, a stray vehicle would drift into their path. As the level of interference increased, it became imminent that they were headed toward a rendezvous with disappointment. Really, they lost the black BMW before the chase even begun.

Feeling like a victim hurt. Feeling helpless and hapless is like oppression, and oppression is worse than death. Vail mentally chewed on various things while the dark yellow line of the freeway continued to disappear beneath the jeep. His despondentness melted his fortitude like candle wax. The voices in his head refused to hush. They would attack nosily then recede into some distant place. They would touch him like a fragrance he was fond of and used to wearing. Silly arbitrary questions surfaced like submarines or great white sharks. He thought of being rich one day—then questioned if he would rather be lucky than rich. It's true that some things are worse than death. Some things force our minds to escape beyond this world into void where ordinary men become more than themselves and momentarily shed their morality as a useless encumbrance. But then these men return, however reluctantly to face some horror of ordinary reality. Reality had been chin checking him since this nightmarish ordeal begun, and the only thing worse than hanging from gallows is sitting with your neck inside of a guillotine. You can hear the blade on its way down, there's always the moment right before death that the epiphany is most painful. In many ways death and moments of immense physical or mental pain are synonymous, only difference is one is nonnegotiably final. Martin Luther king, Jr. said, "There comes a time when the cup of endurance runs over and men are no longer willing to be plunged into the abyss of despair." Vail was at this point, his cup had runneth over.

"Are you going to wait until she sends another letter?" Daphane asked. She too had neared that point blank stage. Vail said nothing, just strangled the steering wheel and punished the accelerator. The Jeep surged forward with uncontested power on the grainy asphalt. "Vail slow down." Daphane's voice slid around him, through him and kept on going to wherever lost words go. Vail exited the freeway, headed downtown and came to a hard stop at the light. "Where we going?" She tried again.

Vail looked into her soft beseeching brown eyes and they beckoned for a reasonable response. "To the police station," was his reasonable response.

Vail was not certain what he expected to find, who he expected to see or what quick fix was sought after by this hasty move, but he was here nevertheless. Police walked aimlessly throughout the police station. The sterile ambiance only added to Vail's indecisiveness. At the desk he asked for Detective Puckett, gave his name then found a seat and waited. Fifteen minutes ebbed by before a slim, pale detective with pits in his face emerged from the back and waved for Vail and Daphane to come on back. They spent another thirty-five minutes speaking with the man who identified himself as Detective Bailey. Vail did not divulge any information, he only wanted to speak with Puckett. He informed Vail that Detective Puckett had been paged, but no response as of yet.

It was while Vail and Daphane were leaving the station that Vail saw him standing near a vending machine. There was no mistaking him for anyone, but who he was. Vail broke away from Daphane and sprinted toward Decker. Someone yelled at Vail. Decker spun, but it was too late. Vail's six-foot six inch, two-hundred-dred- and thirty-five-pound solid frame, plus momentum struck Decker with such force it vaulted him at least six feet and into the vending machine with a thunderous bang. Decker tried to recover but Vail's massive brawny fist pounded him. All he could do was ball up and listen to the youth's disgruntled cries, "Where's my baby you filthy sonovabitch! Where is she?"

Police converged on Vail like a veracious pool of piranha. Some were yelling 'freeze' with their weapons drawn, while others tried to restrain Vail. One officer raised the butt of his firearm with intentions to strike Vail. Daphane did not know what all this was about, but she was in like Flynn—down like four flat tires. She hiked up her dress and did the twenty or so feet in about 2 seconds flat, leaped into the pack like a bantam weight banshee, chunking nothing but overs and unders H-town style. The melee was brought under control swiftly as seven officers restrained Vail and three held Daphane. Captains, lieutenants and other ranking officials poured into the lobby area. Decker was slow to get up, but he found his feet shakily. He snarled at Vail, rubbed his swelling lip and approached him menacingly. He was poised to strike him when a deep husky voice broke into all the confusion with startling clarity. "If he hits him, y'all better let him go so he can defend himself."

Everyone faced the piercing voice of Detective Puckett, who was standing next to Qasiym Serengeti.

It was a little after eight, Puckett was en route to the station when his phone began blowing up. He and Qasiym had spoken extensively and compared notes. What Puckett supplied had opened things up for him tremendously. His decisive and incisively analytical mind ran in crisscross pattern, connected dots and organized a surge of hormones to his hypothalamus. His first thought after hearing all of this was this Victor character, whoever he was, had Andrew Guthfield killed. Why? Because Andrew Guthfield burned down his clubs. Why? Because Victor killed his prostitute who was in the wrong place at the wrong time. Why? Because Andrew put her into the Judge's soup because he obviously suspected Victor of something. Victor! Victor! Victor! The only reason they had the name was because of Vail. Maybe it was a fictitious name. Qasiym spun the entire equation in his mind like a giant strobe light. There of course was Paul Holmes, his name was on everything, the clubs and the house. Just one problem. Qasiym had his ex-girlfriend at the bank run a check on Paul's finances. He had some money but not the type he should have, considering he owns three lucrative establishments. Where was the money? Mathematics were simple: 2+2=4. But something was not adding up, maybe Paul was a flunkie, maybe?

Sitting across from Vail and Daphane as Puckett spoke with him, Qasiym studied the youngstas. He listened as Vail reiterated how he came upon the letter. Then the mysterious meeting at Juneteenth Fair, and the brother Vatly. Daphane sat as though she had been completely defeated and listened as Vail explained to Qasiym how Decker played into all of this. She stayed poised and ladylike but knowing that Vail had withheld this tidbit of information cut deeply, and the shit hurt. Yeah, it hurt.

The issue with Decker had been defused, and as expected Decker pretended, he had never seen Vail a day in his life, and feigned complete ignorance to all the allegations. Qasiym gave him thumbs up, it was an impressive showing. The man definitely belonged in Hollywood. They were about to disperse when Detective Bailey stuck his head in the door. "Puc, you got another one. Possible homicide and kidnapping off of Reed Road."

"How long ago?"

"Just came over the radio. Ambulances have already been dispatched along with patrol units."

"Shit, Qasiym can you make sure they get out of here safely and meet me at the hospital."

"Bet. Let's get outta'heah," he said to Vail and Daphane.

Once out of the station Daphane's walk had more attitude than a pit bull. Vail reached out to grab her arm, she spun too quick to be clocked and slapped Vail solidly. Qasiym winced because he felt that from where he was at. She tried a second slower version of the first but Vail's reflexes were on point now, he caught her hand. She swung the other one and like a bat catcher for the Astros, he made a great catch. Qasiym just watched in silence. His mother use to get spanked on a regular, so domestic violence was not alien to him. Daphane was struggling when Vail pulled her into his chest. "Daph, I'm sorry."

He squeezed her tightly. Through her sobs she choked out, "You should have told me they set you up! You should have told me. All this time I'm thinking I'm in this alone, that they thought I was the weak link in this relationship but ... but they went at you too."

"You're right," he said soothingly. "You're right baby, I should have shared that with you." He rubbed her hair. "It was just so damn unbelievable and embarrassing."

"Vail, all I'm asking for is a chance." She looked up into his eyes. "Give me a chance to be strong for you ... sometime."

Qasiym saw them to the hotel room, then headed for St. Joseph's Hospital. Vail and Daphane's relationship impressed him. Vail's brazen courage to attack a police officer in their own lobby. Then Daphane's fortitude to help out the way she did. Times like these always showed a couple exactly what they were working with. In his mind he switched lanes—where was Paul at four o'clock this morning when his house was toasted? He told the police he was at his girlfriend's house. Qasiym could buy that but ... how come they did not have his girlfriend's name and number. Plus, math was simple: 4+4=8, right? Something did not add up. What? Common sense, deductive reasoning told him what was Paul Holmes doing at the Westin Galleria Hotel at two hundred and eighty dollars a night? What type of girlfriend would not be sympathetic to your house being toasted and offer you a bed? There's another house, but where? Qasiym took his notebook off the dashboard. The address to the Anatole was there along with a number. He bet himself that Paul would not be there. No one checked into a two hundred and eighty dollar a night hotel when you have a girlfriend in the same city, unless it was a front, a cover up for another address. Qasiym questioned why would a rather normal club owner need a secret address, unless he was hiding something. Hiding what? Children. If this hotel suite is just a dummy address as he expects, he would move on from there.

Qasiym made it to the hotel ten minutes after nine. The clerk was a fortyish, tanned buxom vixen with a root beer colored mane and eyes to match, professionally polite and cordial. She buzzed Mr. Holmes' room several times. "I'm sorry Mr. Qasiym, no one's answering. Would you like to leave a message?" She smiled, straight white teeth, crow's feet at the corners of her eyes. It was a nice smile, pretty face. Her name tag read Charlotte.

"No thank you Charlotte. I'll call him later?"

She smiled again, "Sure."

"Where are the pay phones?"

She pointed to the left, Qasiym spotted them. During his short walk to the payphones, he noticed the huge chandeliers sparkling overhead. The expensive air of the place and for a minute he thought he saw Steve Smith from the Atlanta Hawks.

At the phones he pulled out his notebook and dialed the number Paul had given to the police earlier that day. The phone rang twice before Paul picked up.

"Hello."

"Mr. Holmes?"

"Yeah?"

"This is Qasiym Serengeti. I spoke with you this morning. Had a few more questions. Would it be a problem if I dropped by your suite to talk with you?"

"Can't this wait until morning?"

"Yes, uh ... I have some information that could be valuable to you. Uh ... where are you now?"

"I'm at the Westin Galleria. This will have to wait."

"I'm not far from the Westin, I could be there inside thirty minutes."

"Now's not cool, it's been a long, stressful day. I'll see you tomorrow." He paused, "Uh ... at ten, is that cool?"

"You like it, I love it. See you then." He hung up. Qasiym graduated number four in his class. This did not mean he was smart, but it did mean he was a long, long way from being dumb.

CHAPTER 31

Xavier entered his apartment complex at nine thirty exactly. Clue sat out front with Dink while he applied his trade. Chill sat at the foot of the stairs playing Tetris on Nintendo Gameboy. Aaron and some other young hardheads bobbed their heads as Tupac invented his own gospel in 'Heaven Ain't Hard to Find.' Little orange lights emitted from the group as they surreptitiously inhaled chronic squares, only breaking the routine to guzzle greedily from a forty-ounce bottle. Chill looked into the oncoming lights of the Jag as it approached and the glowing red eyes of a cat beneath the stairs making his presence known. It seemed odd to Xavier to see Chill set aside from the pack, maybe something was bothering him. Exiting the vehicle, the smell of marijuana hung thickly in the air, he made a pantomime gesture as if pulling a curtain back. "What's up cousin?" he asked.

"Ain't nothin' big timer. Where's ya shortie at?" "She's at home."

Chill eyed the Jag. "Damn shame you rollin' big Jag like that on newborns. You need some twankies."

Xavier looked at the automobile, then back at Chill. "Lookout cousin, that ..." He pointed at the car, "is bullshit. Trivial. I'm the same brotha with it as I am without it. Don't get caught up in the hype cause it ain't shit." Chill dropped his head, so Xavier asked, "How come you're not over there with your boys?"

"I'm divorcing the scene playa. Tired of those baller blockin' ass niggas. I dig yo' G-code X, you never tell ah nigga nothin' wrong. Sometime I think about getting' slugged up and stackin' ends so I can high beam, you know?" He stood up. "... Just put on the soulja rags and step out like a stunna. Then I think about how low-profile low key and casual you mob, plain jane and shit and still get mo' respect than a lil' bit."

Xavier smiled, "I'm plain jane, huh?"

"You know what I mean. Yo' G-code be bling sometime, but never bling bling! But still, it's cool, ya dig?"

"Yeah, lil homie, I dig."

"Then it's dug!" Chill retorted.

Xavier also noticed Chill was sober. "You're not blowin' tonight?"

Chill looked at his brother. "Nah, I divorced that bitch too." A thoughtful expression passed over his face. "How's Honey?"

"She's alright. Why don't you go see her?"

"No wheels," Chill said despondently.

"Excuses are like assholes, everyone has 'em and they all stink!" Xavier said acerbically. "What's wrong with Metro?" he added just as sharply.

"What hospital?" Chill asked.

"St. Joseph, sixth floor, room 618."

Chill looked at his watch, it was nine forty-five. "Yeah, I'm 'ma bounce, just wanna holla at her."

"Alright," Xavier said tapping him on the shoulder.

"Alright," Chill responded as he headed toward the bus stop. Xavier was at his door, had just stuck his key in the door when Chill called him. "Yeah?"

"Sometime ... when you get some time, can you take me to that Muslim place you be going to?"

Xavier looked at him thoughtfully, then nodded his head slowly. "Yeah, you got that."

Chill smiled, "Alright."

He smiled back, "Alright."

Before Xavier even got the door open good his phone was hollering like a little girl. He accepted the call on the third ill-tempered shrill. "Hello."

Rhonda did not give any specifics, just told Xavier to come to the emergency room at St. Joseph's Hospital. Something about his mama getting in an accident. He stopped at the bus stop and lifted Chill, since he was headed in that direction anyway. His heart pounded heavily in his chest.

"What's up X-man?" Chill asked.

"Just got a call. Said my t-lady had an accident." They rode the rest of the way in silence. Upon reaching the hospital, Chill asked Xavier did he want him to hang around, but Xavier sent him on up to the sixth floor.

He saw his aunt speaking with a burly black man, her eyes were red and puffy. She saw him and approached him in slow, monitored steps. Hugging him tightly, her short stout frame demanded support and some comforting. "Oh Masai!" She cried into the crook between his neck and shoulder.

"What happened?" Xavier inquired.

"Someone kidnapped Vianna and killed your mama's friend," she said into his shirt, but he still understood.

It just took another few seconds for it to register that he was definitely here; at a hospital and this little yellow woman crying on his shoulder was indeed his aunt. "Who?" he heard himself say. He felt detached, hearing his voice and at the same time it sounded foreign. Detective Puckett introduced himself and gave Xavier some brief sketchy details. From it all he learned that Bernadine Wilson, the woman he had known since he could remember was dead. D.O.A. from a gunshot wound to the chest. She had just gotten her life together, now someone had taken it.

Dark thoughts entered his line of reasoning. He blamed God for her death because He allowed it to happen. He tricked her into believing that changing her life would guarantee her some time to live. A red haze descended over his eyes; tears knocked like the laws but Xavier had placed a master lock on that emotion. He listened as the Detective explained to him that his little sister, his soul inspiration for living had been kidnapped. Stolen, Xavier tried to comprehend this, the red film in his mind darkened. Now the Detective was telling him that his mother had received a concussion, was unconscious when they found her, but had regained consciousness.

Just yesterday Deshawn gets shot, Solo gets killed, now Bernadine's gone, Vianna's gone and his mother injured. "Where's my mama?" was all he said.

"Are you going to be alright?" Rhonda asked.

He looked at her like she no longer existed. "Where's my mama?" he asked again.

Rhonda grabbed his shoulders. "Xavier, are you going to be alright?"

He released a cynical laugh. "You ask that question like it's multiple choice, do I really have options! Where's my mama?"

Detective Baily was speaking to Nellie Dean, her tears were unrestrained, they fell and fell. Sobs racked her body, she coughed and choked. When Xavier entered the room and saw his mother's head bandaged up and her emotionally hysterical state, his heart broke in two, almost literally.

"Xavier," she cried and held out her arms to him. "I'm so sorry ... I ... I ... I'm ... He sat on the bed and she climbed into his lap like a baby and cried and cried and cried. "... I'm sorry, I couldn't do anything," she whined.

"You didn't do anything to be sorry about mama."

"They took my baby ... ooohhh, my baby!" Xavier rocked her consolingly. "Bernadine's dead ... she ... sh ... sh ... she's gone. She tried to fight them, it it's my fault!" she screamed and a nurse entered the room.

"I'm gonna get her something," the nurse said.

Nellie screamed. "My baby! My Baby! I thought they wanted money; they wanted my baby!"

Xavier whispered in her ear, "Mama please calm down. Please." He held her tightly. The nurse entered the room again, injected something into the I.V.

"Xavier, get my baby back."

"I will, mama, I will. Just calm down." Whatever the nurse put into the I.V. started working immediately and Nellie drifted off to sleep right there in his arms. Xavier laid her in the bed, covered her up and leaned over to kiss her lips before he left the room.

Back in the lobby, his aunt and the detective spoke with a light- skinned brother in a nice suit and braids. His aunt tried to speak with him but he kept walking toward the exit. The detective grabbed his arms and Xavier spun into a defensive stance, hands up and fist balled. His aunt yelled, "Xavier Masai Dean!" People were looking at them. He met her eyes and lowered his hands.

Puckett's hands were up, palms facing out in surrender. "Whoa, kid, take it easy. I just want to talk."

Xavier looked at him. "We don't have anything to talk about. Find my sista, that's what you do." He turned and walked out. His aunt called after him, or did she, he was not sure. A lot of sounds familiar and foreign rolled off of his back and fell to the polished hospital floor. He heard her and did not, his thoughts spun like a cyclone, volatile and capaciously.

When he stepped through the automatic hospital doors, it was unusually cool for a June night. The wind blew echoes of laughter from the years following close behind. The sharp wind egged him on, even issued a simple warning; he must calm down and move forward. Then it started raining; it was not an angry rain, but quiet and warm to his cheek. One he did not mind standing in, one that stopped as abruptly as it had begun, leaving the earth's perfume to occupy the air after it had gone. At home he showered and changed.

The phone kept yelling, but he offered no relief.

Do slippers really count? Dope and liquor are they like 'happy' in a bottle? They're the ultimate escape from reality. You get to float, everybody else has to walk. D-Bar was kind of hype. There was a lot of the usual. Stimulating, hair raising temperature rising females in clothing that made you say 'Damn' or 'Hmm.' Xavier floated on tequila, other mixed drinks and Bacardi Rum. He watched silently the fabric and flesh of shapely females doing athletic movements on the dance floor. The music activated the melanin and infused everyone with an insurmountable dosage of enthusiasm and energy. Fat Pat 'Trunks Be Poppin' was moving the throng of bodies that twisted, shook, wiggled and bounced with impeccable timely rhythm. He flooded his body with the intoxicating fluid with reckless abandon and looked for an escape route from everything and nothing at all.

He did not see them, he felt them. Slowly raising his head from the table and his glass, grinning drunkenly, he chortled.

"It's a small world huh, hero?" the biggest of them quipped.

Xavier looked up at him and laughed again, dropped his head to his glass and lifted it to his lips. 'Rich As Fuck' by Lil Wayne crooned through the speakers causing bodies to melt together in the dim lighting. The guy slapped the glass from his lips, sent it flying to the floor and crashing inaudibly under the loud music. People turned to look and stare. "What's so muthafuckin' funny, bitch! At your apartment you thought you did something when you broke my boy jaw and smoked Solo. Now me and my boys are about to fuck ya ass up." Xavier dropped his head on the table, the guy from the apartment pushed his head up violently. "Get yo' bitch ass up!" Xavier just looked at him, by this time a small crowd had gathered.

Some women yelled, "Leave him alone!"

The ringleader swung and like a stealthy panther, Xavier leaned, stood and grabbed his attacker's shirt, using his weight and his own momentum slammed his face into the table. There were two knuckleheads with him. At the same time, he was pulling the first guy over the table, he rose with a 9-mm Glock in his right hand and without hesitation he shot the brother to his left in the leg sending him to the floor screaming. The other brother went for the gun, but Xavier caught him in the cheek with the butt of the gun in a wicked backhanded swing, opening the man's flesh into a deep bloody gash. Then brought the butt of the gun down on the bridge of his nose in a downward swing that broke his nose under the pressure and sent the man to the floor cradling his face.

A shocked silence fell over the club. "Uh-oh!" Xavier exclaimed to the one from the apartments. All eyes were on Xavier. The man was forced to lay face down on the table while Xavier crammed the barrel of the gun into his ear. "Uh-oh!" he said again. "I'm gonna fuck you up bitch!" he mocked.

"Now who's the bitch?" he slurred. The man started crying, begging and apologizing. "Nal, potna, you's a dead muthafucka.

Save your tears for hell because there's more sympathy there. You have no idea how fucked up my night's been or what's going through my head." Siren's wailing was still distant. "Holla at cha' stupid!" He was depressing the trigger when he heard his name.

"Xavier." It was calm. "Xavier." He turned to see the light-skinned brotha with the braids from the hospital. Xavier pointed at him, shaking his head. "Uh-uh cousin, you can't save him. I was minding my own, they started fuckin' with me. Tha nigga gots to go so I'm' not always looking over my shoulder." He was about to pull the trigger when someone else called his name, a female this time. Her voice was smooth as water, sweet as molasses and caressed his pain like an anesthetic.

She had stood there throughout the whole ordeal, had noticed him earlier during the night, but he looked depressed so she kept her distance. At first, she was shocked at what he had just done to two of the three men. Sometimes you can feel someone else's pain like it is your own. Up until the moment he spoke she did not know, but afterward she felt it.

Xavier stared into her wise soul piercing black eyes and saw his reflection. She wore a purple long sleeve silk shirt with cuts in the sleeves and purple tailored slacks. Her jet-black hair laid on her shoulders. "Xavier, what's wrong?"

He pointed at the man, "It's not me, it's them," he said thickly.

She walked up on him and rubbed his face. "That's not what I asked you. What's wrong baby?"

The liquor spoke for him, nothing but bottled truth poured from his lips. "Just hurtin', feeling helpless. A lot on my mind."

"Give me the gun and let's get out of here." He looked at the gun like he forgot he had it, and gingerly handed her the weapon.

Qasiym chose to follow Xavier. No one understands another black man's pain like another black man that's been through pain. The girl handed him the gun, they spoke briefly and he told her to get Xavier out of there before the laws came. He asked the crowd, "Anyone see what happened here?" People murmured and started to walk off. The D.J. started the music and Qasiym spoke with the three brothers. "What happened here?"

They looked at each other, then the ringleader hesitantly said, "I don't know."

Qasiym said, "Me neither, but if anything happens to that boy, I will." He flashed his reporter's shield.

One guy had a flesh wound on the thigh, the other needed stitches in his cheek and his nose was broken but he would live. Qasiym thought about Xavier. He had disabled three men in ten seconds and he was drunk. "I'd hate to see that boy mad and sober," Qasiym said to himself. Sometimes you never know how good you are until someone pushes you. Xavier was good, he thought to himself.

I know what you are thinking because it is the way the story has been written, but things are not always as they seem. Ruby Lashawn Vincent is the girl in your high school and mine that everyone knew; all the teachers, all the students, even the secretaries, cooks and janitors. I know you kinda figured she was just a mishappen ghetto hood rat and project ho, that just bopped and bounced her way off the welfare truck. You know, stuck on section eight, dilapidated HUD homes, food stamps and WIC card dependent that got touched up more than a Metro pole. On top of that, you thought she was ugly as sin, trapped in special education classes and rode the little yellow bus to school. I know that is what you thought, but this picture is not depicted with those negative colors.

Ruby was five foot nine inches, one hundred and forty pounds with one of those West Indies complexions, long hair and the most discerning black eyes to date. She was pretty, not the classical beauty, but pretty. She was the type of woman you took home to mama immediately and without preamble, not because of how she looked, but because of her charismatic imposing aura and the things she said. She was not the girl in your dreams, but could easily fill your heart. That is what made Ruby special, she was real. We never marry the woman of our dreams, never. We marry the women in our hearts.

In Junior High school, Ruby was the captain of the basketball team, captain of the volleyball team and a track standout. In just two years of high school Ruby made captain of the cheerleader squad, her tenth-grade year. Her junior year, she led the varsity basketball team to the finals averaging 23.3 points a game. In the championship game, down by three with 2.5 seconds left in the game, she dropped a three pointer on two defenders at the buzzer and sent the game into overtime. With 1.7 seconds left in overtime, she was on the free throw line, game tied, shooting two, she missed the first shot. Then with a stadium full of positive and negative hurrahing, she shot and missed the second shot. The referee called a lane violation on the defending team, that gave Ruby another shot. She shot again amid all the hoopla and found nothing but the bottom of the net. They won the championship by one point. Ruby finished with 27 points, 12 assist, 10 rebounds, 4 steals and no turn-overs. The cheerleader squad wanted her back, the basketball coaches prayed she would return her senior year. Volley ball and track coaches were vying for her attention also. She told them all that this summer and her senior year, she would learn to play tennis.

Ruby achieved a national merit achievement, PHI Beta Kappa outstanding Academic Award. She had won academic excellence in Spanish, geometry, science and was captain of the math team. Ruby was the national honor society vice president, Washington University book award winner, Spanish honor society, student government president and she participated in Houston's Academic Decathlon. Not all at once, but in only three years of high school. She was predicted to graduate number one in her class. Oh, and every Sunday she was in church, she could also sing.

Xavier could not remember when or how their odd relationship begun, was it pre-k? Kindergarten? Maybe elementary? However, whenever, it was understood that they disliked each other. In just about twelve years they had never said a kind word to each other, or was it thirteen?

Ruby drove Xavier home from the club in his Jag with the intentions of putting him to bed and calling her mama to pick her up. However, the liquor provided Xavier with the courage to give voice to feelings and emotions that had been locked away for so long. Sitting at the foot of his bed with Ruby standing between his legs he rested his forehead on her stomach with his hands dangling loose around the back of her knees. Her hands cupped and stroked the back of his head. It must have been her words that picked the lock on his emotions because he did not recall giving her the key. Ironically just as her comforting words opened his locks, his ineffable and effusive disclosure completely disarmed her and shattered her defense mechanisms to smithereens. The alcohol acted like a mild anesthesia, it numbed the pain; real and imaginary. The only light filtering into the room was that created by the moonlight as it came through the bedroom window bathing the room in a soft blueish hue.

He spoke about all that happened within the last couple of days. For some women to witness a man's obvious strength and character in their most vulnerable moments in life is a profound experience. Their innate proclivity is to support and comfort. Some women had an uncanny ability to suppress their own needs, desires, and pain; then metamorphosize into this giant sponge that absorbed all the poison ingested and inflicted by society. They cure the ailments that modern medicine had never, and will never cure. They were the catalyst behind powerful, unbelievably intelligent men.

With tears, Xavier found some sobriety and silence. His nose was stopped up and running at the same time. He felt some embarrassment, not a lot, just some. Surprisingly there was more relief than anything. A slight chortle escaped his lips. "I'm glad the lights are off because I know this can't be pretty." He rubbed his hands over his face. "I guess I'll never hear the end of this," he said. He felt her stomach shake as air escaped in a rush from inside laughter. She picked his chin up with her index finger so their eyes could find and focus on one another in the semi-darkness.

"Xavier," she said in a sincere and serious tone, "I been knowing you were a punk."

He smiled, she smiled back. "Don't tell nobody," he said.

She touched his nose. "It'll be our secret."

He dropped his head. "Damn, what am I going to do?"

"Xavier, you're not a quitter. A bend in the road is not the end of the road unless you fail to make the turn. Keep your head up and have faith. With faith there's possibility. With possibility, there's motivation." She picked his head up again. "Xavier, with motivation there's perseverance and accomplishment. Ignore all this negativity that's designed to break your spirit and keep your head up, because if you don't that's the first step towards giving up." She stroked his richly melaninated cheek. He reached up and grabbed her hand. She pulled it away suddenly flushed. Xavier stood awkwardly, still reeling from the effects of the drink. They stood extremely close to one another; he inhaled her fragrance. Became aware of her delicate femininity, while she at once acknowledged his masculinity.

"That's Sands of the Sable, right?" She nodded in the dark-ness. "My grandma used to wear it." His hands went to her waist, she tried to step back but he held firm.

"I better go," she managed.

"Dance with me Ruby, one dance."

"Xavier, there isn't any music."

"Sing then, I heard you once at school. Sing and dance with me."

Ruby hesitated, her mind and sound judgment were screaming at her to leave, but her heart and soul demanded she stay. Finish something that her heart and soul had conceived too many years ago. She was not a little girl anymore and could not continue to address her attraction to Xavier the way she had been. Her fear of Xavier kept her away from him. Inside the crooked spirals of this existence, the same element, circumstances and condition that made you laugh could make you cry. Nothing as shyster or sinister as the smile that's a frown upside down. Just a love so intense it hurts just as much to keep as to let it go. Damned if you do, damned if you do not. A woman knows; knows, like she knew the back of her hands, the men that are available to her for a season, reason and a lifetime. Try as they may to defy the reality of it all and fool heartedly attempt to tame and mold the former two for the latter. You cannot trick or cheat the heart or the soul, no matter how good you are. It's not happening. Superwomen are human too. It is how life evens things out.

Ruby knew long ago she could only rent Xavier, then suffer the heartache induced when the lease ran out. She refused to set herself up for failure, to lose something she knew she could never possess in the first place. To lose something that was never lost to begin with. Something that moved through life gradually serving its purpose and moving with the natural order of things. She understood that his presence in her life was only for a reason ... in her youth, that reason had not been realized yet, but truth be told there was no guarantee that the reason would ever be disclosed to her. Not tonight, not fifty years from now. The opportunity would probably never present itself ever again for her to move lucid dreams that had stalked her from fantasy to reality.

She laid her head in his chest, listened to the beat of his heart and Shirley Murdock surfaced and dominated her mind. Then Ruby Lashawn Vincent gave life to the song 'As We Lay' in that little room on Southmore and Scott, in Third Ward. They danced to her sultry voice, clung to one another like a stingy man holds money. Somewhere before the song was complete, Xavier found her lips in a hungry and insistent kiss. She moaned when he gripped her soft buttocks and pulled her to his growing erection. She felt him run through her body in the form of trimmers and slivers of intense erotic sensations. Her fingers slithered up inside of his shirt and caressed his hard muscular torso, then pulled the shirt over his head and momentarily separated their lips. "Is this what you want?" she asked in that moment.

"Yes," he whispered.

"Okay." She found his lips, his tongue and drank greedily from the nectar he offered. She felt his hand massage her small hand size breast through her shirt and pushed her back with urgency and desire. Something hard hit her tailbone, it shook and the sound of small objects falling over could be heard. She felt him put his hands under her round supple butt and lift her gently onto the dresser top. He stood between her legs and worked with the buttons of her blouse, while their tongues wrote music together. Her blouse was off, then the bra, his tongue found her sensitive erect nipples and loved them tenderly. She sighed. "Oh ... oh," arched her back, "Ah ... mmm." The rickety dresser shook while he sucked on her neck, leaving evidence of his zealous lust. With great dexterity she undid his belt buckle and pants, they fell to the floor around his ankles. He kicked out of them. Abruptly she stopped him. "Xavier, wait." Her voice was husky and winded, sweat coated her body and her stomach rose and fell erratically.

Xavier backed up; his tented boxers were undeniable evidence of his desire. "What is it, you alright?" he asked.

"Yeah," she said as she dismounted the dresser and slipped out of her pants. Her black lace panties stood out darker than the night, so did her dark garden when she removed the panties. The moonlight bathed her firm, young, athletic physique and made her look like an ethereal pixie. Her proud protuberant breast and taunt nipples caught the light and held it. He removed his shorts, she stood there like a frightened kitten. His approach was slow, his kiss on her lips was soft, slow and sensual. His hard tool dug into her thigh, she touched it tentatively, before sitting on the bed and scooting up toward the headboard while watching him crawl on his hands and knees between her upraised knees. Xavier licked her stomach, slid his fingers over her warm sex. He found her breast, her neck, her lips. Slid his hands under her satiny buttocks, she felt him stab impatiently at her soft moist center. "Mmm," she moaned, placed her hands on his chest. "Xavier," she said, her voice heavy with emotions, "don't fuck me ... make love to me, like I'm yours." She pulled his head to her and kissed him with all the passion she had. She felt him move into her body slow and easily, but with commanding power. She felt him move deeply through her, rotating and gyrating with sensually deliberate, emotionally orchestrated movements. She wanted to scream it felt so good. Holding him tightly she passionately and vocally matched his body stirring, soul pleasing rhythm. Ruby made no attempt to conceal her mounting pleasure. Her vocal murmurs excited him; her strong legs stretched out on either side of him.

"Oh! Let it go Xavier!"

He lifted himself to his hands, sweat dripped from his face and she put her hands on his sweaty chest. "Ughhh!" he whispered. He grinded hard against her undulating graceful hips while she writhed and wiggled with the pleasure of miniature orgasmic convulsions ripping through her body with unexpected potency. His swollen member seemed ubiquitous, touching everything at once.

"Uh ... uh ... ohhh ..." she gasped. He stayed with her, stayed at her, stayed inside her, hitting all the rights spots with precision, angle and precise pressure. She felt it coming and knew it would be big. She closed her eyes and bit her bottom lip. "Ummm!" She sighed as she experienced an orgasm that shook her like a major earthquake and would ... not ... stop ... "Ohhh my gawd, what are you doing?" Her vaginal muscle contracted, toes curled, fingernails bit into the mattress and her hips lost motions as Xavier buried himself deeply into her warm yielding flesh and lost his seed.

"Mmmgghh," he cried as the strong contraction of her vaginal muscles squeezed him and drained him.

"Give it to me baby, just let it go," she whispered.

And he did, she took everything he had and did not need. All his pain, frustration, aggravation, hidden complexes and insecurities. When he rolled over a deep calming nirvana descended upon him.

Several minutes had passed since she felt the hot fulfilling rush of Xavier's living essence. He had rolled over and pulled her close to him, cuddled close to her in the spoon fashion. Her body was still feeling waves of orgasmic contractions, tears eased down her face as all her nerves and emotions fought for control. At some point she felt a peace unlike anything she had known before and dosed off. She found a sleep in his arms that she knew would only come once. Maybe she had stolen this night, maybe he had given it to her. Drunk or not, it was over and done with, hers forever to keep; to hold and reflect upon. Sometimes the real thing is better than any dream.

At about 4:00 a.m. she awoke, Xavier's hand was on her breast. She moved and he called her name in his sleep. She dressed and used the phone to call her mom. They talked for thirty minutes or so; her mother was her sister, best friend, father and confidant. She already knew about the infamous Xavier Dean. She worried about her baby, heard the tears in her voice. Ruby did most of the talking, told her mama she now knew the difference between having sex and making love. Before hanging up she gave her mother the address and told her to come pick her up. While she waited for her mother, she sat in a brown leather chair and watched Xavier sleep. He said her name twice in his sleep; it made her smile. Maybe she was wrong, maybe he was her lifetime. Maybe she could hold him, maybe.

CHAPTER 32

Inside the study, the French provincial armoire sat to the left. The 65-inch flat screen sat next to it. The news had been broadcasting all day on all local news stations about the events of the day. The earlier fires and six deaths, with the seventh in critical condition, not expected to make it. Victor sat in his large leather chair, staring at the images on the television and sipping Christalle. Victor loved his study, the professional air and the impeccable cherry wood bookshelves. The hand-tooled, leather-bound volumes of Encyclopedias from Hemmingway's short stories that were not there for reading. Victor hardly read, but they looked damn good. He lifted a slender Mountain Davidoff Cadet from a humidor on the oak end table. He did not smoke either, but hey, it looked suave, poised and controlled. It looked damn good. The louvered windows opened to the canopy of trees on display. Yes, he loved this room, his private getaway.

He was slightly agitated about the fiasco at the police department with Decker, then with the total events of the day he had stayed in this room. Inadvertently seeking the solace it brought: Fuck·it, he thought. Twenty-seven or twenty-eight hours from now this shit was dead and stanking!

One by one they gathered into the study for a final run through. It was late, Paul and Yadira had returned from the airport. Dominique and the twins were on their way.

"Where is Vatly? Didn't someone inform him?" Victor asked.

"I called, there was no answer, left a message," Paul replied.

Victor released a gust of wind from his lungs. Surveying the other eyes in the room. "Well ...?"

"Well what?" Patty said as she entered the room in a soft green Christian Lacroix that clung and hung in all the right places. She wore make-up that accentuated her violet eyes and her hair was laid and styled. Everyone was caught off guard; eyes bulged; mouths hung open.

Timothy said, "Who the hell are you?"

"Yeah?" Kenneth exclaimed. "What did you do with Patty?"

She smiled with a mischievousness unlike her, then winked. "I am Patty, the real Patty!"

Victor glowered from behind his desk, rubbed his forehead with his bandana, pushed his glasses up and squeezed the bridge of his nose. "Where is Vatly?" he asked Patty.

She dug inside her pockets and turned them inside out, then hunched her shoulders. Timothy smiled. Victor shot him a penetrating glare. Timothy undaunted, reciprocated Victor's stare, equally penetrating and continued to smile. This unnerved Victor slightly.

Victor went through the protocol and procedure; how he expected things to go tomorrow. There were a few questions and the meeting went fairly smooth. Right before they dispersed, Victor asked Kenneth to go by Vatly's place, try and locate him. Then asked Yadira and Patty to follow him to the nursery.

The little girl's mettle surprised and impressed Victor immensely. She cried only during the incident. Since then she had said absolutely nothing. Victor knew the moment he saw her at the store that she was perfect. The woman that was killed was unavoidable. She exited the vehicle in an aggressive manner, and Paul overreacted. The other, female seemed disoriented from the impact. Shit happens, Victor thought.

"Where did you get her, Victor?" Yadira asked.

"Why did you get her?" Patty asked, unable to hide the disgust in her voice. Eww, she hated him. Her cheerful disposition from only moments ago dissipated, her blood boiled. "This shit was unnecessary!" The wry expression on her face spoke volumes.

"She completes the order, we were short one," Victor said insouciantly.

"Your bullshit shenanigans are gonna fuck shit up! Why man?"

Victor ignored her, walked toward the little girl, and bent at the waist: "What's your name baby?"

Vianna took in her surroundings. "I'm not your baby!" Victor tried to touch her, she stepped back. Victor tried to touch her again and Vianna swung at his face.

"Whoa!" Victor exclaimed as he dodged her young aggressive attempt. "Aggressive, isn't she?"

Patty kneeled in front of Vianna. "Honey, my name is Patty. What's yours?"

Vianna's young mind tried desperately to decipher if the woman was friend or foe. She needed a friend; her bravado was slipping into the dark cavern of fear by the second. Her eyes watered and voice trembled when she said. "Zav-ya gon come git me."

"Who's Zav-ya?" Patty asked sympathetically.

"My brotha. An ... an ... and he gon be pissed off and get you!" She pointed her small finger at Victor. He smiled. Her resolve evaporated and tears fell from her eyes. She never once took her eyes from Victor. "Zav-ya gon git you. I gon tell, you hurt my mama and Berdeen." She allowed Patty to wipe her eyes. Patty hugged her and tried to get her name in between sobs, but all she could hear was, "Zav-ya ... Zav-ya ... Zav-ya."

At two o'clock in the a.m. Patty walked to the surveillance room in a flimsy white night gown that came only to her hips. Matching white panties could be seen peeking from underneath the shirt, exposing the darkness from the mass of pubic hair visible through the thin lacy fabric. The surveillance men, Bobby and Chet, turned casually when the door slid open. Chet was leaning back in his chair, feet propped up reading a John Grisham novel, looked and clumsily fell to the floor. Bobby's eyes took in Patty's outfit, or lack thereof, and rocketed to his feet. Patty giggled dingbatishly. "Damn, Patty, what gives!" Bobby said.

"Just bringing you boys something to drink, some mimosa." For the first time since she entered the room, their eyes left her intoxicatingly intoning body and settled on the tray she carried. She handed each a cup. "A toast fellas," she said, "To all good things coming to an end." Chet was still staring at the seductive knot between her legs. "Chet, you can't drink staring down there," Patty admonished.

"Oh ... uh ... um, yeah. Right. Okay." He put the cup to his thin lips then swallowed hard.

"Well fellas y'all drink up so I can get this stuff back to the kitchen." They obediently did as she asked.

"Preciate it Pat!" Bobby said. "Do you need some help finding your room?" he asked flirtatiously.

She smiled, tiptoed and kissed Bobby on the cheek. Then leaned over and kissed Chet. "That's very sweet of you, Bobby, I think." Her smile turned mischievous. "But no thanks, I'll find my way." With an ostensible twist of her narrow hips, that both men could not tear their eyes from, she left the room. After the door closed, Bobby and Chet returned their attention back to the screens. Both thinking, damn.

At two forty-five in the a.m., when Patty slipped her head into the room, both men were sound asleep, snoring loudly. She smiled.

❖ ❖ ❖

It was late when Detective Puckett pulled into his driveway. Few lights shown in the neighboring houses. The street lights illuminated the asphalt unaided by the black sky overhead. It was so silent; it was almost eerie. Where were the crickets, the moon or the stars? Just felt like an immense black blanket had been draped across the heavens.

After cutting off the engine, he did not exit the vehicle immediately, no. Just sat there with his head resting on the steering wheel. His mind overloaded with too many dry scenarios, wet solutions also. Intangible ideas that continued to slip from his grasp. He felt listless and frustrated. What now, was the question that repeatedly surfaced and resonated inside his mind. His own ineptness depressed him also. Seemed like the more he heaved and hoed toward a viable solution and conclusion to this drama, the fickler the circumstances heaved-hoed against him. Figures. Momentarily, his thoughts drifted to his little girl and his ex-wife, the visit he paid them was pleasant. He had almost forgotten just how good his ex-wife could cook. There was hope. The marriage was dead, sure ... right. But there was still hope; SEX. She was a good woman; mother, wife and friend. Good. His daughter was ecstatic when he showed up unexpectantly, made him feel good. He had been fucking up so much, it felt good to do something right, he thought. Maybe he would surprise them tomorrow, maybe take them out to eat. Maybe put forth some assiduous efforts to mend things. He was getting old, just did not feel right coming to an empty house and empty bed. No, it just did not feel right when there was an alternative. Tomorrow, maybe.

His peripheral caught the shimmering reflection of the gold of his neighbors' Mercedes Benz as it silently pulled in under the car port next to him. She is no more than five foot one with a sepia-colored complexion and enough curves to make a coke bottle envious; no chilluns, lucrative career. Nuh, nuh, nuh. He watched her nubile voluptuousness exit the Mercedes. Apparently, she had spent her June nineteenth at the beach because she had on an indigo bikini top that strained to hold her heavy breasts, and some denim shorts unbuttoned at the top to slightly expose her indigo bikini bottoms. He figured this was as appropriate of a time as any to make his presence known. Her delectable derrière was still facing him when he exited the car. Leaning over the hood he carefully observed her benedictions. "Hello, Clinique," he rattled off in his rumbling bass.

Startled, she spun clutching her chest. "Shit, Darrell, you scared the hell out of me!"

"In a neighborhood like this, scared of what?"

"Any neighborhood, anywhere doesn't guarantee safety."

"Can I help you with your things? Looks like you could use a big strong man."

She flashed him one of those Jet beauty of the week smiles. "I'll pass on the big strong man, just let me borrow your hands."

He held up his hands. "Alright, where do you want 'em?" She pointed into the backseat at a huge box. "Isn't there anything smaller, softer, I can carry?"

"Darrell, I don't have any pets and my legs are working fine. Thanks anyway." He hoisted the box from the backseat and followed her to the front door. With flitting alacrity, she opened the door. A soft feminine scent walked out, sat down and started having a picnic on his nose. "You can set that down over there." She pointed to a vacant spot on his left. He noticed that her home was decorated in soft mauve and lavender leather sofas. Mahogany Lacquer ottomans, solid oak end tables with beige plush carpet. It was beautiful.

"Damn, you hooked this up," Puckett said. She gave a bland smile,

"Yes ... this is me."

"What do you do, Clinique?"

"Interior Designer." Still that bland smile.

"Well ... uh ... uh, I guess I'm 'ma go."

"Thanks for bringing the box for me."

"No problem, anything for a woman with your attributes."

She sighed, put her hands on her hips. "That's a sexist compliment. It amazes me how you brothas always expect some ass, but you can't recognize a sister for anything but these ..." She cupped her breasts in both hands and shook them. "... among other things. But's it's all good, it's expected." She pinned him with cynical, but beautiful soft brown eyes.

Instantly he felt uncomfortable, shifted his weight from foot to foot. "I ... uh ... ooohkay." He rubbed his chin and pointed at the door. "I'ma go."

Puckett exited the door and was well on his way to his front door when she called him. "Lookout Blackman!" He turned, half expecting to see her wielding a forty-five automatic with infrared siting screaming 'respect muthafucka!' Instead, she gave him her bland smile. "Thanks. No hard feelings, it's been a long exhausting day. I've been poked and prodded at all day like a choice sirloin steak. I'm just tired."

"It's cool," Puckett said. "No sweat, you right though."

"Goodnight," she said.

"Goodnight," Puckett replied.

Entering his dismal home to the empty thick musty air was a drastic change from Clinique's home. The dull hum of his ice box greeted him along with the phone.

"Hello."

"I see you finally made it home." It was Qasiym.

"I just crawled through the door. What's up?"

"I have a major idea. Been doing a little studying. We can use Diamond Slim blowin' those clubs up to our advantage. Just making sure you made it home also. Get up early so we can handle up."

"I gotcha. I'm up at seven already." "Bet," Qasiym exclaimed.

The message light was blinking up at him when he returned the receiver to its cradle. While thumbing through the mail he depressed the button to rewind. Puckett walked to look out of his window at the lighted window next door. The machine clicked loudly as it reached the end of the tape, then beeped.

The explosion shook the entire block. Puckett, standing near the window was conscious of the explosion and felt himself being elevated and thrown through the window by the impact.

Clinique was walking from the bathroom, clad in only indigo bikini bottoms. She had just started running the water for her bath including jasmine oil for the pleasant scent. She was humming along with the Isley Brother tune playing on the sterco when the explosion shook her home. The window facing Puckett's house exploded, hurling Darrell head first through her window and depositing him onto her plush carpet. She screamed and scuttled backwards in fright until she identified exactly what had just come through her window.

Puckett, somewhere in mid-flight from his home to Clinique's was certain he was dead. The swirling flames came after him and licked his clothes. Pain rapaciously engulfed his limbs, legs, neck and back. His skin burned; his eyes throbbed behind their lids. During his kamikaze flight to death and subsequent crash through Clinique's window, he screamed a strident bellow. He must have lost consciousness because when he opened his eye Clinique stood there with her hands over her mouth in indigo panties. He smiled, tried to raise up; failed and listlessly fell and lost consciousness. Within those precious moments he thought, damn she is beautiful, nice legs, awesome breasts. Then, of Krystal, his daughter, death had found him before he could change.

Clinique noticed that Puckett was smoking after her initial shock. She watched Puckett's glassy gaze travel her body, grinned kittenishly, then collapsed. Smothering the flames that danced on his clothing, she observed through her window the flames completely consuming his home. Clinique placed her hands on his chest, but did not feel anything. Next, she put her ear where his heart was supposed to be, it was faint, but it was there.

It could be said that Clinique saved Puckett's life. His overactive imagination led him to the window attempting to see if he could catch a glimpse of a silhouette or something from Clinique's window. Being thrown from the window saved him. Neighbors exited their homes disheveled and disoriented, standing by watching the flames. The darkness overhead rumbled and then opened only slightly; a light rain started to dampen the earth.

That smell wafted across the senses, you know that smell, the one that lets you know, well ... it's raining.

CHAPTER 33

Without struggle there is no progress, so everyone is adapting to the struggle. Contrary to popular belief there is an alternative to living; dying. Choices are simple, sink or swim. It is either live inside those guidelines or exist outside of them. Existing is not living, there is a difference. There is a mind field of malignant vices, ever-present. Insidiously offering yet another decision, ultimatums, that in some deleterious way will jeopardize and impact your reality. No matter how niggled you become, you are going to miss something, it is human nature.

Xavier opened his eyes, what? Thirty, forty minutes ago, somewhere in between there, the iridescent morning sunlight soaked into the room pellucidly and assertively, resting on the furniture without permission. A chee-chee bird landed on the windowsill and chirped loudly. Xavier felt languid, his head pounded and his tongue felt like leather in his mouth. So, this is what a hangover feels like, he thought. He laid there remembering ... every move was a Herculean task, so he elected to just lie still. His entire bed smelled like Sands of Sable. Her perfume refused to let him pretend it was a dream. "Damn!" He drove his fist into the mattress and instantly regretted· it when the bed shook. Of all people, Ruby. "Shai, I'm so sorry." Xavier was running down at least a hundred excuses, viable, understandable and acceptable excuses. Maybe he just would not tell her, yeah! That's a winner, just don't tell her he decided after he mentally chewed and digested everything that made sense, but at this particular moment, for some reason, nothing made any damn sense at all. He optimistically opted to run some fatuous propositions, just to see how they tumbled down the stairway of his conscious, but she did not deserve this bullshit. Really, he felt he was supposed to be the exception to the rule. Then Ruby, what about her? Men are muthafuckas, just cannot seem to get shit straight no matter what. Always allowing the dick to confuse and complicate, otherwise simple shit.

He finally forced himself to roll over and look at the digital clock at his bedside, seven-oh-five. His head continued to pound, suddenly his stomach rolled and he raced to the bathroom falling to his knees and vomited. Amazingly, his head slightly cleared, the lassitude ebbed slowly ... *a bend in the road is not the end of the road unless you fail to make the turn* ... Ruby's words reverberated resolutely off the walls of his mind ... *keep your head up Xavier and have faith ... perseverance, there is accomplishment* ... there was nothing duplicit in her actions. He recalled her trying to leave. He wanted what happened to happen. Why? Xavier attempted to be pragmatic and rational, but it just was not happening. Best bet was to get it out in the open while their relationship was young. He pulled his toothbrush from the holder while he drummed a steady stream of urine in the toilet, shook twice and flushed. Crest toothpaste would deal with his leather tongue and brief bout with halitosis. He was stroking his ivory towers when he stopped in midstroke ... wondering ... did I have oral sex with her? Nah! I don't get down, not yet anyway. However, his mind was still partially draped in a flimsy haze. Alcohol will definitely bring the freak out in you. 'Shai ... Shai ... Shai, damn!' He chunked his toothbrush at his reflection in the mirror. It made a dull clink, ricocheted and hit him in the forehead before falling in the toilet. "Shit!" Leaning over the bathtub, he began to run some bath water. Flushed the toilet again and walked back to his bedroom. Vigorously pulling the sheets from the bed, he thought about the man he shot. He was no killer, but he was willing if ah nigga kept pushing him. Momentarily the light-skinned brotha leaped into his train of thought, then Ruby's soothing voice.

... Xavier, what's wrong, baby ... baby ... He rubbed his eyes until he saw stars.

... Don't fuck ... me ... make love to me like I'm yours ... He literally shook his head trying to dislodge her words, her image, her period from his mind. He loved Shai, didn't he? It was just sex, do not make it any more than that, just sex. Shit, at seventeen he should be happier than two punks in a dick factory, about knocking off two sexy, fine women in one week. Images of his aunts flooded his conscious. No, that was not him, he was raised better than that. The phone began to ring. "Hello."

"Hey baby, you up? Are you okay?" Her voice was loaded with concern.

"Yeah, I'm cool. What's da deal?" Phone in hand he walked into the bathroom to shut off the water.

"Prophet told Pam, she called me." She paused. "How's Nellie? Want some company?" she asked. He hesitated; the silence stretched. "Xavier?"

"Yeah, I'm here. Shai, do you love me?"

"You know I do, why are you asking me that?"

"Yeah, come on over, I need some company. Plus, we need to talk."

"What is it, Xavier?" She could hear it in his voice. Something new, something she had never heard before. Was it doubt, or fear?

"Are you comin'?" His voice held a note of restrained anxiety, he paused this time. "Shai?"

"What?" she whispered.

"Are you comin'?" he whispered back.

"Yeah, but I really don't need any bullshit, Xavier."

"We'll talk when you get here, alright?" There was no re-sponse. "Alright?" he said with more conviction.

"Yeah," she said.

"Shai."

"What?"

"I love you."

"I love you too." She continued to whisper.

"Later."

"Okay." She hung up the phone.

The shower kind of revitalized him, kind of. He entertained more insults aimed at himself. More criticizing of his behavior as he donned Hilfiger shorts and blue and white Jordans minus a shirt. Vianna had an assortment of toys laying haphazardly around the apartment. Her little dolls were strolled about with the arms, necks and legs twisted awkwardly on their plastic bod-ies. Xavier felt more than a twinge of guilt, about the situation. Maybe berating oneself was sacrilegious. "I don't feel sorry for myself because it's against my religion," he said out loud. Maybe he would tell her he was considering becoming Muslim and ... and they believe in Polygamy. Maybe.

There was mail carelessly skewed on the end table. Bills ... bills ... bills, then a letter from his uncle. Xavier read it swiftly, his un-cle thanked him for the ends, informed him that Shai was on his list. The white folks this, the white folks that, blah ... blah ... blah, love Step. He folded the letter and placed it back in the envelope. His mind escaped him momentarily, he simply drifted. Vianna was she alright? Had they hurt her? How could he possibly get her back? Shit, if the police could not find her, how in the hell could he? A knock at the door made him glance at his watch. Oh, okay. Right, he thought, nodding his head to himself. He traipsed the short distance from the table to the door. When he opened it, the first thing he saw was a diminutive Shai pointing a huge fifty caliber double action Desert Eagle at him. Immediately he ducked sideways just as the cannon of a gun discharged noisily. Quickly, he grabbed her hand and spun her around.

"Lemmegomuthafucka!" she exclaimed.

Xavier was still holding the envelope when the insistent rapping on the door broke through his trance like reverie. He shook his head, sighed and glanced at his watch, oh. Right, he thought nodding his head, "I'm tripping."

The door squeaked as it opened, the sunlight raced in and made him squeeze his eyes tight. Shai stood inside the doorway with a tight pinched expression. God, she was beautiful. Her emerald eyes sparkled up at him. Her breast rose steadily with her breathing. She also had on Hilfiger shorts, sandy brown matching shirt and brown Karl Kani boots. He leaned over to kiss her and she lifted her lips to him; he touched them lightly with his own. He smelled the aroma before looking down and noticing the Jack-In-The-Box bags. The heady aroma seeped through the bags and did the WWF with his senses. Shai sashayed into the apartment, yeah that is what she did, sashayed. Her hips rocked and swayed to her natural rhythm; an ancient music living a separate life inside of her.

All the curtains were drawn closed and all the lights off. All the way over here she kept trying to figure out what he had done. Her female intuition was telling her it was another woman. She prayed silently that he had not got anyone pregnant, some long lost baby mama. Anything else she could handle. Either way she had prepared herself to hear something disheartening. Now the argument with herself was—would she forgive him. She watched his swarthy frame move in a restrained feral alacrity. Her legs weakened and heat rushed into her loins. Forgive him ... If he is honest that has to be a plus. Anyone else would have snuck around behind her back, lied and made her look like a fool. His honesty had to be a plus, something to build on.

Briskly she set the bag on the table. "You hungry?" she asked. Still in motion she slid the curtains back and lifted the window. The idle sounds of early morning traffic climbed over the windowsill and into the room like an unwanted visitor.

"Yeah, I'm empty."

"Get some glasses," she ordered. He moved slowly, but efficiently. Placed the glasses on the table and muscled open the top on the apple juice she had brought while she separated the food. Everything complete, he plopped down in the seat next to her. She propped her elbows on the table and put her hands under her chin staring at him while he looked down at the eggs and cheese croissants. At the present he felt like a gopher halfway down a sidewinder's gullet. He did not want to be in this situation and he could not get out. "You look tired," she said softly.

"Hung over, that's all."

"When did you start drinking?"

"Last night, when I left the hospital. Saw mama damn near in shock, all bandaged up ... just ... just needed something to numb the feeling I felt."

"Why didn't you call me?"

"What could you do, feel sorry for me?"

Shai 'pursed her lips in an agitated gesture. "Nah, you're doing a good enough job of that your damn self. To be so smart, you're stupid. Relationships are partnerships, it's about sharing and not just orgasms! Niggas always wanna play hard." She jumped up from the table and paced the living room. "That tough shit will not make you a man, Xavier! As your woman, if you needed someone to feel sorry for you, then it was my damn job. Not another bitch!" She was talking to his back because he refused to turn around. "Damn Xavier, this lone ranger shit isn't gonna get it. So now you're gonna tell me that you got drunk and your dick forgot to stay loyal. Is that what you're telling me?" she shouted. He just sat there with his back to her. Shai felt more hurt than anger, but she masked it and plunged forward. "Look at me dammit. Be a damn man about it!" Xavier spun his chair and pinned her with exhausted weary looking eyes. "Thank you!" she said acerbically. Shai ran her fingers through her short hair, she felt jumpy, agitated and even a little apprehensive. More calmly than she intended she asked, "Who was she? Just some stray bitch, someone you knew, who?"

"Ruby."

Shai gave him a puzzling look. "The girl from Churches Chicken?"

Comprehension filled the blank, void expression that had moments ago covered her face. Xavier knew she would remember; women always remembered these kinds of things. How? They just did.

She snatched up her purse and rounded the table. An even mixture of anger, hurt and confusion was etched into her features when she looked at him. "It's all good." Her voice trembled, she felt her eyes get that burning sensation that usually precedes the tears, but she willed herself not to cry, not to break weak in front of him. "It's all good you know ... I'm use to this shit. In the end you're just another dumb ass nigga!" She watched him wince as her words bit into his ego.

She snatched the door open to leave. Just then a light-skinned brother was about to knock. "Oh! Excuse me is Xavier here?" he asked.

She gestured over her shoulder, "Yeah, his sorry ass is right there!" And stormed out the door.

Xavier stared at his croissants. He was going to just let her leave, you know—fuck it! Replace her ass—he was. That seemed like the logical thing to do, sensible you know ... fuck it! However, anything worth having is worth fighting for and sacrificing for. He had to drop his pride and keep it real. His thoughts raced to personify themselves, to materialize. To find foundation and solidify themselves. Yeah, he was wrong, but hell, growing up is about making mistakes. As she hurried out of the door, he slapped his hands down palms flat against the tabletop. The loud clasp echoed throughout the kitchen. "Shit!" he yelled. "I'm entitled to fuck up sometime!" He bolted from the table and shot around Qasiym. "Excuse me bro-man."

Shai was a third of the way down the stairs when she heard Xavier call her name. At first, she thought he was not going to come after her. It made a difference; it would make forgiving easier. It made a difference, still she ignored him, headed for her car.

"Shai!" She unlocked the door and swung it open, he slammed it shut. She turned to face him and he thought she was going to swing on him, but she did not. Instead, she just stood inches away from him breathing erratically, glaring at him hatefully. "Let's go." Xavier nodded his head toward the apartment.

"I'm going home Xavier." Her neck swiveled and her hands went to her hips. She peered into his eyes defiantly and noticed something that bordered on anger, but did not have its fire; that resembled sadness but lacked its depth.

"Nah, you're finsta take your ass up those stairs or I'm going to cause a scene dragging you up there. Your choice."

"You wouldn't do that!" she stated in an exasperated tone. "Wouldn't I?" he retorted.

"We're through talking Xavier."

"No, you're through, I haven't said shit yet!" He grabbed her arm and she jerked it away.

"I can walk on my own."

"Let's see." Then after shooting him a serious meanmug, she climbed the stairs slowly.

Xavier and Shai disappeared into his bedroom. Qasiym was left in the living room with the lukewarm egg and cheese croissants. "Lookout Xavier!" he called, "You gonna eat this man?"

"Nah bra, go ahead. Getcha eat on." "Right."

Shai leaned against the dresser with her arms folded underneath her breast. Xavier sat on the bed in front of her. "Shai I'm sorry. I know apologies ain't about shit, but ..." he rubbed his forehead, "... it's ... it's just that I messed up. You're all I've wanted since I met you. I want us to be together, work around, through or over this." He walked upon her and stared into her radiant green eyes. "I'm willing to except responsibility for my actions, I'm human. Last night the pressure got to me. I lost focus because I didn't have the solutions. I felt helpless and got out of character." His voice was full of emotions, but steady and strong. "I wish I could make you stay ... but I can't. I'm not too proud to ask you not to go. It's always been about you."

She ran her hand through her hair, bit her bottom lip and sighed heavily.

"Xavier it's not that simple."

"Isn't it?" He grabbed his shirt from the bed. "I don't wanna put this off on you, but look, you can plan a pretty picnic, but you can't predict the weather. If you love me like I love you then let's weather the storm. To me that's simple. I should have called you, but I've never been able to really depend on anything or anyone, but me." As he walked to the door he said, "Shai, I'd never intentionally disrespect or hurt you, never." And walked from the room, hurting inwardly—grim faced outwardly.

Qasiym had helped himself to the juice also. Actually, he was chewing on a mouthful and rummaging through the cabinets. "Oh ... um," he said around his mouthful. "Hot sauce?" Xavier smiled for the first time that morning and pointed to the cabinet on the left of Qaysiym, "'Preciate it. Want some ... it's good."

Xavier grinned, "Nah, nah, go ahead. Enjoy." Shai walked from the room and headed straight for the door. When she passed him, he reached out and grabbed her arm. "Ball is in your court," he said beseechingly. See, that is just how it was. He wanted Shai; no ifs, ands, or buts about it. All pride kicked to the curb; she was the combination that unlocked his locks. Before she could say anything, someone knocked on the door. "C'mon!" Xavier shouted. He looked at Shai, she looked at him ... seemed like minutes, but it was just wicked seconds that defied time.

The door opened, Vail and Daphane walked into the room. Vail took in Xavier's stern expression, then looked at Qasiym. "What's up Xavier? Heard 'bout your troubles. You alright?"

"Uh huh, I'm holdin' down, mainly because all other alternatives are macabre."

"What's up Shai?" Vail extended his curtesy her way. She said a curt, "Hey," intended for both of them.

"Ahem! "Qasiym cleared his throat. "It's good you kids know each other. Xavier, I called Vail and asked him to meet me here so we could talk. Why don't y'all sit down?" Shai had intended to exit stage left, but you know women, curiosity and cats. "First, I want to let you know I'm going to help you get your babies back, Vail, your daughter, Xavier, your sister." He reached into his bag which was behind him and removed a black 9-mm and tossed it back to Xavier. "Here's your toy. Next time you decide to shoot someone, be ready to go to jail. If that girl hadn't showed up when she did, you would have killed that boy. In prison you can't help anyone."

"He shot someone?" Shai questioned incredulously.

"Yep," Qasiym quipped. "Shot one, disfigured another and would have killed the third if ..."

"Ruby had not come along," Shai stated sadly.

"I guess that's her name. He was drunk and out of character but all of that's still unnecessary. We all hurt and suffer loss."

Shai stared at Xavier while the brother went on speaking, "My name is Qasiym Serengeti. I'm an investigative journalist, ex-FBI special agent, ex-marine special forces. I work out of the Struggla building and the H.E.R.O. Foundation. As of eleven forty-five last night, Detective Darrell Puckett was put into a coma when explosives went off inside his home. The rest of the H.P.D are confused as hell with their thumbs up their asses. I'm gonna blow shit wide open and I'm gonna give you the opportunity to help. Your loved ones were injured and I believe revenge is better than repentance."

Qasiym had been ostracized by many in the journalist society, the police and reporters. He was a spontaneous, unsystematic, unorthodox bohemian. A maverick that religiously avoided the Palaver method instituted by others. He operated on his own rules and guidelines. Stepped on a few toes and politicked his way to a pretty aggressive reputation. His motto was simple and comprehensive: Do the very best you know how, the very best you can; and keep doing it to the end. If the end brings you out right, what is said against me won't amount to anything. If the end brings you out wrong—persecution and oppression—which has never ceased, won't hurt you none.

"I haven't been to sleep all night, been researching. In 1965, in Chicago there was a child prostitution organization headed up by a Cydney Pierce. I know that an Andrew Guthfield was murdered yesterday by professional killers. I believe that Andrew was behind those clubs being blown up. I have a plan to find out where they're at because of those clubs being destroyed." He looked at his watch, it was ten minutes 'til nine, still early. "I'm going to let you know that these boys are serious business. They are already responsible for eight deaths and two injuries here in Houston. No telling how many other states. They're professional and they're dangerous. But if you listen to me, we'll crush this shit and make the ten o'clock news." He glanced at his watch again. "I have to go; I've chartered a helicopter and I have a meeting. I'll meet y'all back here at six. Any questions? Y'all in or out?"

Xavier, who had never sat down spoke first. "Let's wreck shop!"

Qasiym smiled. "Yeah ... I like you, man!" They looked at Vail.

He shrugged his shoulders, pursed his lips, "Shit, make me famous!"

Shai was standing akimbo, a picture of disapproval. "Excuse me, Mr. Qasiym," she began, unable to mask the mild irritation she felt. "What's wrong with just notifying the police and letting them do their job? Xavier and Vail could be killed."

Qasiym looked her squarely in the eyes. "I don't operate like that. I did the homework. I'm not going to let the glory boys get credit for my work. I'm giving these boys a chance to get off that helpless trip and do something." He picked up his attaché case. "True, they could be killed, but if you haven't found anything worth dying for, you're not really fit for living anyway." He walked to the door, looked at his watch. "I'll be back at six." The door closed behind him with a soft click.

Vail, Daphane, Shai and Xavier stood in the living room. The air had become thick and tense. Xavier removed the clip from the nine, ejected the bullet that was already chambered.

"Xavier, don't do anything stupid. This Rambo, Commando shit only works in the movies. Call the police before you get yourself hurt," Shai exclaimed.

Daphane fed in with Shai. "I'm with her, this gun-ho shit ain't even cool."

Xavier reloaded the 9-mm with a loud snap! "Bernadine's dead, my mother's bandaged up, and damn near had a nervous breakdown. To top it all off my lil sister's been snatched by some perverts. I'm going to get her or die trying."

Shai looked into his eyes and knew instantly that her attempts at reason were futile. She snatched up her purse and left, slamming the door behind her. Once on the road she could not hold back the tears any longer. They poured from her eyes, the road blurred, she sniffled and glanced into the mirror. 'Get yourself together girl,' she said to herself. Her mascara had been smeared and she looked like a wreck. She wanted to go to the hospital, maybe his mother could talk some sense into him. Maybe Bug-eye and Gus. Certainly, they could discourage Xavier from doing something so obviously stupid. The man said that these people were professional killers. The police, she would tell the police. She hurt inside about his infidelity, but he felt guilty also ... had to. He brought her the truth ... that, to her meant a lot. They could make it, she just had to sacrifice her pride. He was a good man, or would be soon. There was nothing perfunctory about her relationship. He was only seventeen, so young, so much room for growth. Patience, that is all she needed. He would atone and shine, she could feel it.

When Shai finally came to a stop, she was not at the hospital, the Jailhouse apartments or the police station. The red Honda pulled into the parking lot next to a grey Ford Taurus. Before she entered the Churches Chicken, she cleaned up her face.

Ruby saw Shai at the same time that Shai saw her. This time of the morning there were very few people in. The aroma of chicken was overwhelming, which is understandable. It was a chicken joint. Shai felt as though she was on a treadmill. The counter refused to get any closer no matter how many steps she took. Then she blinked and was standing right in front of the woman, nothing but the counter separating them.

"Tony," Ruby called to the back. "Come hold the counter for me." Ruby disappeared for a moment and reappeared beside Shai. "Would you like to sit down and talk?" Ruby asked without rancor.

Shai did not quite know what she expected, she was not looking for an embarrassing confrontation. She was not the violent type, so fighting was not even on the menu. Ruby's congenial attitude made things easier. Shai just wanted to peep her competition, get a better understanding of what she was up against. To discern concisely whether Xavier was worth fighting for, or just say fuck it and regardless of how difficult it would be, just replace him. Neither one of them said anything for several awkward minutes until Shai looked into Ruby's eyes and noticed that they both had identical looks; undeniably easy, identifiable expressions. "You love him, don't you?" Shai asked.

Ruby hesitated. "Ever since junior high, but he loves you."

"How can you say that after what he did last night?"

Ruby displayed a bland smile. "What's your name?" she asked.

"Shai."

"Well Shai, if he didn't, I doubt very seriously you and I would be having this conversation. If he wanted to, he could have kept me a secret and had all he could handle with both of us. I wouldn't know about you and you wouldn't know about me." Ruby glanced out of the window. "Him telling you is what makes Xavier, Xavier. Telling you took nuts and character. Not to mention a lot of love. I wish I could find someone to love me that much."

"And what was last night?" Shai inquired.

"Shai, he could barely walk, let alone think straight. You're a woman, so you understand when I say, I took advantage of him."

Shai sat up rigidly, her voice was stern when she spoke. "I'm gonna hold on to him, he's mines."

"I'm not gonna mess with him Shai. I'm not with a lot of drama. If I knew he was deeply involved with a sista of your character I would have never crossed that line."

There was little else to be said. Shai rose, looked Ruby over once more. "Thanks."

Ruby rose also, "No, thank you."

Shai left Churches not really understanding what they were thanking each other for. Maybe they were grateful that they could sit and talk to one another like women, respectfully. Neither became irate or emotional like on Jerry Springer, or some other syndicated talk show. Thankful that two rational black women could turn a potentially volatile situation into something feasible. That is something to be thankful for. Now all she had to do was locate the lesson. There is a message in suffering; temporary suffering would soon lead to full recovery. To live is to suffer, to survive is to find the message in suffering—the lesson. Her heart was heavy, it thumped loudly in her chest. The conversation had eased the tension, soothed her feverish nerves. Ruby's words echoed inside her mind and solidified the utopia that was settling in.

... I took advantage of him ... Barely walk, let alone think straight ... He loves you ... loves you ... The sun was out and about, heating things up. I ... I'd never intentionally disrespect you ... Tony Terry's 'When I'm With You' spilt from the speakers and she hummed along.

CHAPTER 34

The water felt vibrant, she released, allowing her thoughts to dance down long hallways that led to pleasant, yet painful memories. She moved slightly and watched the ripples run from her skin and bounce against the black porcelain tub. The tepid bubble bath smelled like jasmine, oily bubbles rode the thin hair on her arms and legs. Her fears had subsided slightly, the house had been mild pandemonium this morning. Patty, Jerald and Vatly were missing. Paul, Yadira and a few others were wary, expecting police and reporters to swarm the place any minute now. Her only fear was that she was helpless. Jerald had betrayed her, which was sad because it furthered her belief that there was no one she could trust. Escape now seemed like the fanciful and obsolete raving of a precious child. And that too ... was sad. So now she was stuck. There was no plan B, because she had not realized there would be a need for one. She and her sister would have to just make the best of the situation.

Kenya made her way to the basement rooms to speak with Amber. On many occasions she had sought Amber's advice. Now she just needed someone to tell her that everything would be alright. On her way down she passed Yadira, there was a pained, worried look on her face. It saddened her even further. The basement rooms were dull, drab rooms; molded, musty concrete that gave off a slightly rancid odor. They were actually cells and no one made any attempts to deter the fact. As Kenya entered the room, off to the right the television was at full throttle. The children ran around aimlessly occupying their time with toys of various make-ups. Valerie was propped up in her bed flipping through a People Magazine. Amber was sitting near a small walnut complexioned little girl with an obstinate expression on her face. Kenya immediately knew she was new here, but instead of looking like a frightened little girl as most did when they entered these rooms, she looked formidable and pissed. The acuity of Kenya's observation rocketed to the forefront of her mind and for the first time that morning she smiled. "Amber, who is this?" Kenya inquired.

"Vianna," Amber stated despondently. "You heard what happen?" she asked.

Kenya nodded. "Hey Vianna." Vianna shifted her eyes from the ruckus around her and settled them on Kenya.

"Who are you?" she said waspishly.

Kenya sat on the sofa next to Vianna. "My name is Kenya."

Vianna's voice trembled and squeaked out uncertain, "I'm going home."

"That's all she's been saying since she's been here," Amber said weakly.

Kenya shrugged her shoulders. "So, she's optimistic!" Kenya and Amber smiled at one another, but they understood that there was not anything remotely humorous about this.

Vianna noticed the smirk that passed between them and said more forcefully, more defiantly, "He's comin'!"

Kenya's eyes widened, "Who?" she asked.

"My brotha, he's comin' to git me!"

"Not unless he can fly," Amber said insouciantly.

Kenya shoved Amber playfully. "Quit it!" But she was thinking like Amber. He would need wings to get close to this place and wings to get away.

"I'll take you wit me," Vianna said. Kenya looked at Amber, Amber looked at Kenya, they looked at Vianna and she looked at them.

Victor had been in a piss poor mood ever since Paul woke him this morning. He had in a fit of rage ordered the surveillance men killed, he still felt no better. Truly he was slipping, how could a conspiracy of this magnitude go on right under his nose. How? Of course, he knew they would never find them, not today of course. He would just wait a couple of years after they had settled down and relaxed, then he would get some of his boys to find them and one- by-muthafuckin-one he would kill them.

Sitting in his huge leather chair seething with anger, hatred and contempt he let the telephone chime several times before he had the presence of mind to reach over and answer it. "Hello," he growled.

"Victor." He sat up rigidly at hearing the voice at the other end. It was Patty.

"Where the fuck are you?!" he shouted.

"I'm gone Victor, but I know you're a rotten sonofvabitch so I just want to let you know not to fuck with me. I just left my lawyer." She paused. "With instructions that in case I come up missing or dead, it's to be opened and given to the police. Victor everything is in that envelope that you know I know and then some. Photos, names, dates, et cetera, et cetera, et cetera. Just leave me alone, do whatever you are going to do, just leave me alone." The line went dead and Victor was left listening to the dial tone. And you want to know how he felt; you ever wake up and there's this person lying next to you that you brought home. Fact is when you wake up and they're still at your side, it is easier to convince yourself that the act you engaged in last night, whether induced by artificial stimulants or mental psychosis, was actually out of love or something similar. That someone simply made love to you and you to them. However, when you wake up and they are gone ... all hallucinations dissipate. Then reality huffs and puffs and blows all the fallacious delusions to smithereens and you realize you have just been fucked. Yeah, that is the difference, when they are there, it is love. When they are not, it's just a fucking.

So, when Victor replaced the phone back in its cradle that is how he felt, like he had just been fucked. A menacing scowl covered his face. Little Patty had outmaneuvered him at every turn. Calculated things to an uncanny precision. He smiled his ugly, crooked smile and thought, so that is how it is. His smile deepened, then a chortle grew into a light chuckle. When it was all said and done, it was a hysterical uncontrollable laughter.

Qasiym waited in the hotel lobby patiently; the clock read nine- thirty. He had already spoken with the receptionist and Mr. Holmes was not in. The lobby was plush, smelled like money, he thought. The poverty that he and his siblings were raised in, at the time it had not dawned on him that it was poverty. They had bold roaches that did not scatter when your turned on the lights at night. Instead, it seemed as though they would stare at you, waiting for you to get out of 'their' house. In school he would entertain his teachers and classmates. Once he told them that the mailman came in his house and asked for someone they did not know. They were about to tell him he had the wrong address when something pulling on his pant leg forced him to look down and there a huge cockroach with its paw extended indicating that it was his. His overwhelming character and humorous ways helped deter the fact that his dress code among other things were not up to par. He even had a joke for the dreaded lunch card.

Qasiym's mother was very abusive. They caught whopping's for anything, with anything at any time. He was learning to tie his shoes, his mother lost her patience after twenty minutes and went to slapping, punching and hitting him. He could not recall what he had done, but once or twice she had filled the tub with scalding water and threw him in the water. When she finally let him out; hurting, naked and terrified, she whupped him with an extension cord. He hated her then. His father's laziness was really his own fault. Okay, he was abusive also, but not toward the kids. Qasiym felt guilty at the pleasure he derived sometime when his father would jump on his mom. It was the only means of revenge he could get, even if it was done vicariously. What goes 'round, come 'round ... right? Then cocaine hit the scene and everything else took a backseat to their addiction.

His older brothers, now in the penitentiary, use to look after them when their parents were ripping and running the streets; sometimes disappearing as long as three days. His brothers use to hustle up food when their parents smoked up the government money. They were young also, just got caught up trying to let the ends justify the means. His father stopped smoking and ... well both of them quit, she relapsed. His father assumed responsibility for his children and maybe that is the only thing that saved him. He no longer hated his mother. In his maturity he felt sorry for her.

Paul entered the hotel at a quarter to ten, waling tersely with an annoyed expression on his livid face. A RuPaul look alike strolled kittenishly over to Qasiym. "Hello sweetie!" she smiled.

Qasiym took in her claw-like, blood red acrylic nails, mile long blonde weave and her Adam's apple, then smiled back. She extended a hand and offered the name: Jamesetta. He stood, avoided the outstretched hand and walked past Jamesetta with a cynical grin and grim hauteur. Jamesetta my ass, he thought. A real tawdry exotic looking sister passed him in black fishnet pantyhose and a fuchsia pink leather mini-dress with six-inch heels. She took in his casual attire, braids and slalomed past him. He shook his head and smiled. Now black folks are afraid of black folks. He thought about winking, but then he might get charged with sexual harassment. If you fart wrong in the new millennium you were subject to litigation. Someone somewhere will want two point five million dollars in punitive damages because you farted and caused complications to their respiratory system. A little boy about seven had a melba pear in his hand, Qasiym took it, bit into it and handed it back. The kid looked at him, then his pear, then back at him ... this time he winked. Kids cannot litigate. He headed out of the hotel, not really wanting to speak with Paul, just wanted to follow him. The chartered helicopter was twenty minutes away at a private airstrip. Already things were in motion that would delay Mr. Holmes' departure once he failed to show up for their meeting.

Paul entered the hotel, agitated beyond reason. He would not be here long. All he wanted to do was see this reporter/cop and move on. He wanted to get to his room before the interview started. A slim, nicely dressed black man headed in the opposite direction and bumped into him. "Oh, excuse me," Paul said.

"You okay?" the stranger replied.

Just then a pale, plump woman screamed as she passed Paul and slapped him. The unexpected blow made him stagger backwards into the slim stranger who caught him. "You alright man?" he asked. A security guard nearby noticed the commotion. Other people gawked and ogled blatantly. Paul was astonished.

"You pervert!" the woman exclaimed vehemently. "Don't you ever touch me again." Her chubby, ruddy cheeks were flushed.

Paul threw his hands up. "Lady, what are you talking about?"

Dramatically her fleshy hands went to her hips. "You know gotdamn well what I'm talking about!" she shouted.

The security officer approached briskly in an attempt to put a lid on all the ruckus. This was a big money hotel and scenes like this were unseemly. A frail, weathered looking man with pinched features moved between them. The security officer spoke, "Lady, are you bothering this gentleman?"

She looked at him contemptuously. Paul also looked at him. "Humph!" she gasped. "He's the one who molested me in broad daylight."

The security officer and Paul shared a fleeting glance at one another, then refocused on the irate female. "Excuse me miss, but this is a respectable place. If you would like to file a formal complaint, let's go to my office. Otherwise—"

The lady had turned her back on them and was headed for the door. "Fuck you!" she shouted. "And him too!"

Paul did not realize that his keys and his wallet were missing until he reached his room. Fuming silently, he stared at the ringing phone, then on its fifth ring he picked it up. "Hello!" he said with all the attitude he could muster.

"Mr. Holmes, Qasiym here. Look, something important has come up. We have a strong lead on who may have killed those hoods that were suspects in destroying your clubs. So, I'm on it."

Paul became nervous. "Exactly what are you saying?"

"I'm going to check out a lead, someone took some pictures."

"What! Uh ... okay then. So, you're not coming?"

"Can't do, sorry." Qasiym hung up.

Paul had just replaced the phone to its cradle when it chimed again. It was the receptionist telling him that his wallet and keys were found and turned in. He could pick them up on his way out. They would have to break camp early; someone had taken photos of Kenneth and Timothy. Then he relaxed; they had worn disguises. Still, maybe someone was giving anonymous tips. Patty, Jerald and Vatly instantly came to mind. This shit was getting sticky. After retrieving his keys and wallet, the valet came with his vehicle. He was unaware of the noisy helicopter that hovered miles above him.

Kenya was at the pool when the helicopter passed overhead. Initially, she paid no attention. She and Jami had begun eating breakfast out there. The morning elements were clean, calming and refreshing. The fastidious ambiance had only gained intensity, so it was a relief to be out of the house. Amber had informed her that today was the day, or tonight, rather. The helicopter passed over again, closer. Consequently, the thick hum of its engine made it impossible to ignore. Kenya and Jami shielded their eyes to peer up at the flying object.

Victor was looking out of the glass patio door of the kitchen at Kenya and Jami. He was aware of the helicopter. Preoccupation with the morning's events was a hefty distraction. Kenya, also, was a formidable distraction. Still, he noted the helicopter.

As expected, Jet, Tyler, and Naomi had arrived at the airport. Yadira had gone to pick them up. In Victor's line of business, you needed to keep certain people on call. He called Jet and Tyler after the incident with Timothy. Plus, more muscle never hurt, especially the way things had been unraveling. Jet and Tyler were mercenaries; aged and slower, but still pretty efficient. They had trained Timothy and Kenneth. Naomi, well, she was Asian and an all-purpose woman. The click of hard bottom shoes on the marble floor interrupted his thoughts. He turned to see Paul enter the kitchen. The look in his eyes alarmed Victor. "What is it?"

Nervously, Paul said, "I just spoke with a reporter that said there are witnesses who photographed Timothy and Kenneth."

A low groan escaped Victor's lips. He removed a purple handkerchief from his pocket and wiped his forehead, adjusted his glasses and coughed into his balled fist. Staring back out of the patio door into the sun, he watched the branches of the trees sway in a gentle breeze. "What reporter?"

"Uh ... Qasiym, Qasiym, Qasiym."

"I'll call Decker. Have you seen the news this morning?" Paul shook his head. "Our immediate worry is over. The cop's house was leveled last night. He's in critical condition right now. Without him, I'm certain their case will hit a wall. By the time he recovers, we'll be on a thousand-foot yacht in the Pacific drinking

Louis XIII Cognac at $1,355.00 a bottle." Victor's confident air eased Paul's tension. He rolled his neck and rotated his shoulders.

"Where's the boys?" Paul asked.

"Went to the ship channel to speak with the foreman. Can't afford any mistakes from here on out." His stare drifted back out to the pool where Kenya sat with her sister at the wood rimmed linoleum table, eating sourdough with orange juice. She was indeed a prize. He could see her draped in expensive silks, satin gowns, diamonds and pearls. She would be eternally grateful to him for rescuing her and sending her to the best of schools. Single-handedly he could, would in fact, put her on top of the world.

"... mistakes, right?" Paul uttered.

He was brought back to the here and now by Paul's voice, but did not catch what was said. "Yeah, that's important," Victor said. "Let's go get things ready. Naomi's coming with Jet and Tyler. Prepare the kids meal with the sodium pentothal. I've already told Decker to be in position at nine. Timothy has prepared the vans. I just want to run through things once more."

Paul followed Victor out of the door. "What about Patty, Vatly and Jerald?"

"There's nothing we can do about them right now, so let's just focus on things we still have control of," Victor said stoically.

"You got it," Paul replied.

CHAPTER 35

The summer evening was shaping up just as expected. The sun was in attendance making the air hot and arid. Bees attacked the assortment of flowers with festive fever, while the wind carried the scent of roses, dahlias and exhaust fumes through the air. Several family members and friends had dropped by to comfort and console, it wasn't pleasant, but necessary. Even the neighbor, a woman of fifty or so, a noted hypochondriac showed up wrapped to the nines, even in this balmy weather. She moved around and socialized, but refused to make any body contact with anyone. It took all kinds; his hootchy-kootchy cousin showed up with her usual razzle-dazzle Donna Karan and gossip. She was the epitome of hypocrisy, but still blood was thicker than water, water just taste better. She and Xavier had gotten caught playing 'mama' and 'daddy' or 'house' once and damn near had all the skin tore off their bones. That ass whuppin' scared the dickens out of her. So, while she was absolutely adamant about never trying to play 'house' with relatives anymore, it did not stop her from playing 'house' with anyone else. Thus, at twenty-one, she had four children by four different daddies. Some of the family snubbed her, but Xavier did not have the time or presence of mind to snub or judge anyone. He loved her all the same because after all, blood is thicker than water; water just tastes better. It was pleasant seeing so many of his relatives in one room at the same time. But sad, that tragedy is the only element it seemed that would kindle the love and loyalty that is supposed to be axiomatic.

It was somewhere inside three when Xavier stepped outside into the gummy air, it was stiflingly dry. Activity buzzed just like any other day, which was not unusual because for many, that is exactly what it was, just another day. He had intended to visit his mother at the hospital, but for some subconscious reason he had been avoiding the hospital all morning. To the most extreme point he felt like a failure today. Maybe because of this dilemma, maybe tomorrow he would feel different, less vulnerable. Maybe not, he was ambivalent toward it all. There was only one thing he was certain of, he would know tomorrow how he would feel, if he made it that far. At the light there was a moment of indecisiveness. If he turned left, it would take him to the hospital. If he turned right, he was fifteen minutes away from Ruby's apartments. Someone behind him blew their horn and without further preamble, he nosed into traffic.

The radio was on 1540 A.M., a classic oldies station. Just his luck, Lenny Wilkens was screaming about how he cried. Damn near made him want to cry. He rounded a few corners that were decorated with the regular wannabes, usetabes, gonnabes and never-were-or-will bes. The male and female gold diggers, then a few ballers with some gaudy bedazzling women sitting on their arms like a ventriloquist dummy. He even noticed a few people that did not even belong in the scene and they stuck out like a nun at a brothel. No matter how assiduously they tried to fit in, it just was not happening today ... maybe tomorrow. At the light of O.S.T. and Scott, a bad little sista was exiting the store owned by the Iranians. She made him think of Shai, maybe she would come around, she just needed some space and time to think. He had to go into tonight focused: there was not any room for error. Vienna's life could be depending on his performance. To this point he had never killed a man. He was not keen on doing it now, but what was his alternatives? Perhaps Shai was on point and he should just contact the police. "No!" He rubbed his forehead. "No. I gotta stay down," he said to himself. "I can do this. I ... CAN ... DO ... THIS!"

Ruby's apartments were modest. A weary, old gazebo set out front, freshly painted, but you could tell that the old paint was never removed and instead of a smooth finish, it was rough and tacky.

While slouching on the grass meridian, it still had a settling effect sitting beside two broad maples flanked by a wooden fence. To him it had seemed like it took forever to get here; endless streets and turns but ... the endless drive ended. A lot of grisly rubbernecking took place as the Jaguar sailed through the parking lot, and eased over the speed bumps. He was not certain what he would say at first, but slowly decisiveness was crystallizing his mind, giving him a place to breathe.

The door was opened by a middle aged, bronze colored woman with black lake water eyes, moose brown hair and a crooked, but alluring and arrogant mouth. Before he could speak, she accosted him. "Well ... the devil is handsome. Nice to finally meet you. Xavier, right?" That she knew him was slightly unnerving. She stepped aside. "Would you like to come in?"

"Yes ma'am." The apartment smelled like fried pork chops and Lysol.

"Ruby isn't here, but she's close by. Sit down, let's talk. Would you like anything to drink?"

"Ah, no ma'am."

"Boy, quit calling me ma'am. I'm young enough to be your girlfriend." She smiled, it eased him. "My name is Darlene. I figured I would meet you today, after I spoke with my daughter this morning. You wouldn't be half the man she says you are if you hadn't come, so I've been expecting you."

"I came out here because I'm confused. So, I kind of thought—"

"That Ruby had some answers that would make you feel better?" she interjected.

"Sound flaky, I know. Ruby and I have known each other, what … fourteen years. And we've never so much as smiled at one another. I thought she hated me, and I hated her. But you know I woke up this morning realizing that I've never hated her. I was under the influence and I just don't want to be thinking I forced her into anything." He looked into his hands to break eye contact.

"Xavier, I want to be a mother and say you were wrong. But I'm also ruby's friend, and as her friend I'm happy for her. Trust me, she needed last night more than anything. I look at you and see what she sees. It's just sad when two people belong together, but can't be together. You know?"

"Yeah, I know," he whispered.

"Rub's at Shawn's house. You can cut through the back." She pointed. "Shawn's house is right there."

Xavier looked at her. "You drive?"

She gave him a sardonic grin. "You pee standin' up?" she retorted.

He smiled, nodded his head and tossed her the keys. "Let's ride."

"You're lazy!" she claimed.

He held his index finger and thumb inches apart, "Just a little bit."

Ruby and Shawn were just shooting the basketball around when Xavier and Darlene braked at the curb. "Shawn, come ride with me girl!" Mrs. Vincent shouted.

"Nah, I wanna see this!" "Brang yo' ass on heah heifer."

"O-ite, O-ite. What's up Xavier?"

He nodded. Ruby stared at him with the ball on her hip. "What brought you out of your hole?" she said sarcastically.

He was not in the mood. "You." She shot him a two-handed pass with a lot of heat on it. He caught it with a snap. "What's your problem Ruby?" he asked vehemently.

"Niggas!" she said. "That's my problem."

He dropped his head and shook it. "Can we talk? Sensibly."

She looked at him. "Beat me, we talk. Lose and you walk."

"We're too old for this shit," he exclaimed.

"What are you afraid of Mr. X?"

Xavier studied her momentarily in her shorts and t-shirt, soooo sexy. He smiled. "Alright tuffie, let's ball." He returned her two- handed pass with enough heat on it to push her backward, then removed his shirt.

"Ladies first!" Ruby crooned and bounced him the ball.

He threw it back. "My mom told me never to be cruel to dumb animals. So, you take it out, going to six."

They bumped and tossed birds back and forth. Xavier continued to match her wit for wit. "What happened last night Ruby?" he asked while defending her.

"We fucked, nothing more, nothing less," was her acerbic reply.

"Bullshit!" Xavier exclaimed. "It was more than that and you know it!" Ruby scored three quick baskets on seventeen-foot jumpers. Before Xavier made two aggressive moves to the hole and dunked the second one on her. His third shot he missed from twenty-two feet out, but out jumped her for the rebound. Went between his legs, spun and did a Tommy Hawk dunk, coming down centimeters from her face.

"How come you never said anything?" he asked.

"How come you never said anything?" she mimicked him.

He handed her the ball. "Three tight." Then, "I didn't realize until last night."

"Too little, too late, huh?" she said. She went up by two; one in a sweet cross over stop, spin and pull up jumper that hit nothing but cotton. The other on a hesitation dribble, pull-up runner that he tipped but it still went in. She kissed him on the nose. "Five; three. Game point."

Xavier stole the rock and pulled up a jumper at the free throw line. "Five; four." Then he backed her down and did a turnaround fade away. "Five tight! Game point!" he said. Some neighborhood kids had gathered and were looking on. The Jaguar slid silently to the cub. Darlene and Shaw exited the car and watched.

"We made a mistake Ruby," Xavier said softly.

She mistakenly thought he was referring to last night. "That's your opinion."

He read her eyes. "I don't mean last night. I mean all those years of games."

"Too little, too late, huh?" she said.

"Is it?" he challenged.

She searched his eyes. "Yeah." Xavier beat Ruby on a spin move, then went strong to the rack. He was clear to lay it up or dunk it. Instead, he accidentally on purpose back rimmed a dunk. The ball shot high into the air. She rebounded, went left, crossed over right, stopped on a dime and pulled up a fade away that found nothing but the bottom of the net. "You lose!" she exclaimed.

"Nah, we both lost!" Ruby had seen Xavier play before. He was not college material, but he was adequate. She knew he missed that dunk on purpose. Sweaty and winded, he retrieved his shirt and headed for the car.

"Xavier!" Ruby called. He turned. "Thanks." He smiled. 'For what?"

"The game."

"Which one?" he asked.

"Both of them. It was fun, you know."

"Then I should be thanking you." He walked upon her so his voice was barely audible. "For saving my life last night, and teaching me how to accept defeat today."

"That's what friends are for, right?"

"Yeah," he said. "That's what friends are for. They give you wins when you need the excitement of victory. And hand you a loss when you need the humbling of defeat."

"I spoke with Shai," she said. Xavier's heart raced; guilt washed over his face. "Don't worry, she loves you. I told her that you are all hers. It was nice, real nice, but you're not my type. My man has to be able to beat me on this court, you just lost."

He smiled. "It was nice. Maybe someday I'll ask for a rematch."
She pursed her lips. "I'll be around." He did not know why,
but he leaned over and kissed her; nothing fancy, just his lips
touching hers.

She was the last person that he wanted to see. The combination of the pungent hospital antiseptic and Shai's icy stare made
him feel dirty. This was unavoidable. He was circumspect and
thoughtful tonight. His mother was propped up in the bed, and
fresh bandages donned her head. She looked better. Shai looked
better too.

"Hey baby," Nellie said.

"You feeling alright?" He could feel Shai's eyes on him. He
stepped in front of her and looked into her emerald deepness.
Reached out to touch the spot where her dimple would be if
she smiled. To his surprise, she did not move away. "What's up
chipmunk?"

"I'm fine."

Xavier was under the impression that Shai had told all that
warranted being told, so he stilled himself for the double team
he was certain to come.

CHAPTER 36

It was seven minutes after six. Vail had argued bitterly with Daphane, then made mad passionate love to her, argued again, then sexed one another down again before she cried herself to sleep. Now he was tired, but the anxiety of what he was about to do had slightly invigorated him; fear is a helluva aphrodisiac. Daphane feared for his safety—but hell—he feared for his safety. So, she had tried her damnedest to persuade him otherwise. Then used sex to try and cajole him into submission. Sex is a powerful negotiator if nothing else. Consequently, Iyanna was wherever she was because of him, so it was his responsibility to get her back. This cloak and dagger malarkey was not his cup of tea, but he trusted Xavier and obviously Xavier trusted in Qasiym as well as their chances for success. The drive to Southmore was slow, filled with a lot of thought, second guessing his actions. Maybe the police were needed. He chided himself, but that thought was not a coward notion. It was a realistic thought. By the time he turned into Southmore's big driveway, he was ready.

Xavier's Jag was parked under his window, a lone light shone. There was a black suburban next to it. With all the exuberance he could muster, he bounced up the stairs and rapped lightly on the wooden door. It was answered by Xavier. "What's up cousin?" Xavier asked.

"Just shaking 'em out," Vail replied. Vail noticed that both Qasiym and Xavier wore black bodysuits with black boots. He could not stop himself from thinking of Tom Cruise in 'Mission Impossible.'

"Your bag is over there. Get dressed and join us, we need to go over some things." That was Qasiym. Vail lifted the duffle bag, it was heavy. He studied the contents. A 9 mm Glock and four seventeen round clips. A black suit similar to theirs, body armor and some strange looking goggles along with other miscellaneous stuff. The weight and reality of what they were about to do descended on him. Could he kill a man? No. Maybe? No. He concluded.

There was a large blueprint spread across the table. Qasiym had made special marks and circled certain areas. After they were ready Qasiym went over the plans. "Okay fellas here's the deal. This is the house, it's a three-story brick structure." He pointed at several points on the blueprint. Vail was lost, so was Xavier but they listened all the same. "All this land belongs with the house. It's about forty acres. I've scouted the area and the house all day. There are surveillance cameras here." He pointed to certain points on the blueprint. "Here, here, and here. They've basically cornered things within four sections and a seventy-five yard minimum. I've attached a CT-380 sleeper on the transformer leading to the house. Once I hit it, it'll kill all power for sixty seconds. We have sixty seconds to get from here," he pointed again, "to here. Any questions so far?" Both boys shook their heads. "Good. We're going in on the east side, here. There is a maze of horse trails all along here." He slid his finger along a path on the blueprint. "All this will be the easy part. I've given both of you body armor, some night vision goggles and a CT- switch. The CT-380 is only a power delay relay. It can be used twice. The first relay will get us past the cameras. The second, in case of an emergency. Once inside, we locate Victor. Police will come running once gunfire is initiated. Our job is to get in, wrap things up and make the front-page news tomorrow morning."

"How many are there?' Vail asked.

Xavier appeared to be in deep meditation, stood still and studying the blueprint. Qasiym hit him in the shoulder. "Hey, you with us kid?"

Xavier turned his eyes on him, nodding his head. "Yeah ... how many?"

"Right," Qasiym said. "From what I could tell, only three that are dangerous; three white males. I believe there are some surveillance men and I saw a woman."

Xavier looked at his watch. "What time we leaving?"

Qasiym glanced at his time piece. "Now." It was six forty-five.

Xavier noticed the little red Honda sitting beside the Jaguar when he stepped from the apartment. He reflected back to the hospital where they barely said ten words to one another. "Just give me a minute." Qasiym tapped his watch, Xavier nodded. He stopped in front of Shai, brought his hand to her cheek where her dimple would surface when she smiled. "What are you doing here?"

She forced a smile. "Gotta see my man off to war. It's the American way. Right?"

"I'm gonna be alright Shai."

"It sounds good Xavier. I just pray you're right." "Why didn't you tell my mom?"

She smiled for real this time. "You're a young man now, Xavier. I'm not going to run to your mother on you. That isn't going to help our relationship. I don't like what you're doing, but I'm going to stand behind you and your decision." She poked him in his side and grinned mischievously. "I'm down like whoa!"

Xavier smiled, leaned over and kissed her. She tasted like grape 'Now & Laters.' "Mm ... you taste good. Got anymore?"

"Uh huh. I'll give you some when you get back." He kissed her again before heading to the suburban. "Xavier." He turned.

"You cheat on me again, I'm 'ma cut it off." She moved her finger in a scissor-like motion and walked back upon him and began rubbing lipstick from his lips. "Okay?" He nodded.

"Please be careful."

He kissed her nose. "I will." Climbing into the suburban he was focused, functioning on all cylinders.

The ride was still until Qasiym broke the silence fifteen minutes into it. "I've never asked anyone to come with me, but I saw Vail at the police station battling the whole H.P.D. and it made me feel your aggression. You Xavier ... well, the hospital was one thing, the club was another, but you impressed me. I'm not telling you to kill anyone.

I'm not trying to turn you boys into killers, but neither can I promise that it'll be unavoidable. This is me; this is what I do. I investigate shit and solve it myself if I can. If you boys just get my back, we'll get in and out. If you have changed your mind, now's the time to say so." He looked over at Xavier.

"I'm in 'til it's over," Xavier said quietly.

Vail gave an uneasy grin. "Hell, make me famous baby!"

"I like you, man!" Qasiym exclaimed. They continued the ride with amiable chatter.

Qasiym pulled the suburban over to the shoulder of the road. It was black out, trees outlined in the moonlight, forming a menacing looking barrier. Qasiym produced a silver flask and pulled on it hard. "Hah! Ere' this always numbs the butterflies," Qasiym said.

"My butterflies are cool," Xavier said.

Vail took the flask and downed a healthy gulp. There were only two vests, which he made them wear. The guns loaded. Xavier had brought his Desert Eagle forty-five with infrared sighting and compact four-inch silencer. Slowly they entered the woods. Vision through the night vision goggles was new and strange to Xavier and Vail. It was an eerie green, but remarkably clear. Xavier instantly saw the wisdom of the goggles, no flashlights. The moon was bright, chittering insects talked that talk that no one understood, but always heard. It was 7:50 when they started quietly toward the house.

Kenya had pinned herself and Jami in the bedroom. The house was in total mayhem. Furniture being carted off; three new faces had arrived. Victor had been barking out orders all day. Without Patty, many of the younger children had cried until their eyes had swollen shut. She, along with Amber fought assiduously to maintain some order and peace; all to no avail. that was before the symmetrically polished Asiatic female with a delicate comeliness arrived. She was bright-eyed with an elegantly well-formed mouth, rosy cheeks and a small dainty nose. She was picturesque and if someone could be artistic, fashionable and chick in baggy faded jeans and a black Mickey Mouse shirt, she had pulled it off. Clapping her hands together twice, she brought the entire room into silence. Within a matter of seconds, the restive children became docile. Her smoky clipped tones were sleek and pleasant, charmingly wooing everything within earshot. She was called Naomi and within an hour after her arrival, most of the children had showered and were prepared for dinner.

Kenya exited stage left before they ate. Now in her room, she stood staring out of the window wishing for some freedom; her heart was heavy tonight. She had overheard a conversation between the two men as they went over a list. The children were not for prostitution. Victor had engineered a crafty exchange that would net him millions. Personal orders had been made by couples who could not have children; wealthy determined families. Surprisingly, American families that had purposely relocated to third world countries in preparation for the new children. Kenya just prayed that Iyanna would get a loving family. Amber and Valerie were going to two elderly couples, too feeble to completely fend for themselves. She experienced mixed feelings about that also. Happy that her friend would receive some relief from the constant ravishing of her young body. Disheartened that she was losing a real friend. She had to protect Jami, which was her top priority. If that meant eventually submitting to Victor, she would not resist. Had not her own mother made sacrifices to ensure that she and Jami had everything they needed. If not for the accident that had taken her life, it would have worked. She would manipulate Victor. That is the word Patty had used when she spoke to Kenya. Patty unexpectedly pulled her to the side one afternoon and told her in so many words that her beauty would always be a plus, if she understood how to utilize it. That Victor was a delusionary, overzealous fool and that his infatuation would make him weak, pliant and docile. She and her sister would never want for anything if she learned how to manipulate him. At the time Kenya did not understand the reason behind the chat shared between she and Patty. Now, in hindsight, she was grateful. She had convinced herself that she could do it.

Looking over her shoulder, she observed her little sister rolling in hysterical laughter while enthralled with the 'Martin' show. It was the episode where he was leading the exercise class. Kenya had to smile herself; Martin was a fool. It was 8:24, only six minutes until it went off. She focused her attention back out the window, at the bright moon as it slipped behind clouds. The twinkling stars refused to be hid this night. The aqua marine water in the pool was unsettled and rippled subtly by the light breeze; it was tranquil and sedative. Then the lights flickered once, twice and went out. Her heart lunged inside her breast as the room plunged into darkness. At that moment the moon slipped from behind cloud coverage and Kenya watched apprehensively as three solitary figures raced cat- like across the flat green landscape toward the house.

Victor, Timothy and Jet were in the main hallway going over last-minute plans to move the sleeping children in the vans. It was still early yet, but they wanted to be loaded and ready to go at nine. Naomi entered the hall, "What's the hold up?"

"We're ready when you're ready," Jet responded.

"Well, let's get this show on the road; it's already 8:24."

The lights flickered once, twice and went out. Timothy and Jet drew their firearms. "What the fuck!?" Jet exclaimed.

Victor's back slumped against the wall, his heart raced. Instantly sweat beaded his brow, he found it difficult to swallow. The abrupt silence inside the dark sounded so loud. The CB-radio on Jet's hip squawked loudly. "We just lost all visuals Jet! All visuals are zero!"

Naomi flicked a small flashlight and bathed the hall in its illumination. Don't panic, it's just a power outage. Victor, I know there's a generator."

"Uh ... ummm yeah, yes. ·It' s out back."

"Victor and I will go start the generator. Jet, you and Timo—" The lights flicked back on. "Ahhh ... se," Naomi sang. "No need to panic, let's just move and get things taken care of."

Timothy still had his pistol drawn. "I'm going to take a look around," he said.

"Take Paul or Tyler with you," Victor ordered. "Get Kenneth from upstairs. Let's start loading the kids. Decker will be here at nine."

Tyler sauntered down the stair. "Jet, it was a sixty," he said evenly.

"Huh?" Jet was a little lost.

"The lights were down approximately sixty seconds."

"You sure?" Jet asked.

"Positive!" Tyler said.

"Victor, we may have to abort. It's—" Jet began.

Timothy interjected abruptly. "What's this sixty second shit?"

Naomi answered. "CT-380, it's a power relay. Most notably known as a sleeper."

"Police?" Kenneth inquired.

"Not likely," Jet answered. "Cops don't get down like that." He turned his attention to Victor. "Do you have any other enemies?"

Victor looked at Jet like he had just asked the stupidest question in the world. Paul and Yadira were next to bounce down the stairs. "What's happening?"

"May have company," Naomi said. "Two-by-two we're going to sweep the premises. Kenneth and Timothy work front to back clockwise. Jet and Tyler back to front clockwise also." She looked at her watch. It was 8:27. "We've wasted two minutes. For someone who knows what they're doing, that's a lot of time. We'll meet back here in ten minutes, set ya watches."

The combination of fear, plus adrenaline was making Vail heady. A thin mist of perspiration coated his face as they trekked through the wooded area. Qasiym had been correct; there were plenty of wide well-traveled trails all the way through. The moon played peek- a-boo as it dipped behind passing clouds, causing the bush and trees to lose their deep green and become black and ominous. Insects conversed until the crunch of dry leaves and twigs underfoot silenced them. After a twenty-minute hike, the huge house came into view a little more than a hundred yards away. Lights shone brightly in several windows. A humungous tent stood out back against the night. The lights from the pool stretched up into the darkness.

So, this was it. Vail's courage bloomed. THIS WAS IT! Qasiym was near the perimeter of the trees. "Okay fellas, there's your babies. Look over there." He pointed. "That little red light is a monitor. Over there ..." He indicated another red dot in the darkness. "... is another one. Along that wall of the house is three rooms. We check all three and penetrate the house in the empty one." He looked at his watch. "It's 8:22:45, any questions?" They both shook their heads. "Okay. I'm going to trigger the device. At 8:25:00, the lights will come back up. We gotta clear this area in sixty seconds." Again, he regarded his watch. "Ready?" At 8:23:59, he flipped the switch.

The lights flickered once, twice and went out. Right before the lights went out, on the third floor, Xavier saw a lone figure staring out of the huge picture window. The darkness closed in everywhere. The moon which had previously been stuck came free brazenly the second the lights went out. However, they were already running at full throttle. Vail with his long, strong, athletic strides left Qasiym and Xavier. They were halfway there, no snags, no trouble. Vail hit a hole and fell. Qasiym and Xavier were several feet behind him and saw him fall. Something prevented him from getting up. Then they saw what Vail saw. Eyes swollen in terror, he looked into the cold black eyes of a rattlesnake, not a good arm's length away. Neither one moved. Vail neglected to breathe. "Shit!" Qasiym said and looked at his watch, 8:24:27, thirty-three seconds.

"Don't move, I'm going to get his attention," Qasiym instructed. Suddenly a swishing sound filled the silence and the snake's head disappeared.

Qasiym looked at Xavier. "Wh ... where ya ... never mind." 8:24:34.

"Let's go, twenty-six seconds!" Xavier's Desert Eagle with infrared sighting insured one thing. No missing tonight. They were running at full speed toward the house again. Ten yards away the lights flickered, they dived dramatically for the cover of the house.

Out of breath, sweaty and half paranoid Vail laid in the grass. "I think I peed on myself."

"Don't sweat it, we've all been there before," Xavier stated evenly, but with a little repartee.

"Yeah, but we were younger," Qasiym added keen wittedly. They shared a smile that eased the tension. Vail stood and patted his pants. No, he had not peed on himself. His goggles had fallen so he picked them up, peered through them and got a bearing on his surroundings. Everything glowed green. It was neat, Vail thought. Qasiym was peering into the first bedroom window.

Xavier was just looking around when he thought he caught a sliver of light in his peripheral vision. Maybe it was his imagination, he thought. Instinctively, he moved in that direction. Qasiym set to work on the window with a glass cutter. Vail watched and listened as Qasiym explained the process. There was not any security wiring, which puzzled Qasiym. On a home like this, it was expected. Once the window was open, he looked inside searching for motion detectors, heat sensors or laser trip lines. Nothing, nadda, zilch.

Xavier was looking around the corner of the house. Not exactly thirty yards away the beam of a flashlight played over the ground. He then ran to the other end of the house and glanced around the corner. There was not a light, but something told him that someone was out there.

"What's up, Xavier?" Vail asked.

"Shhh." He slipped on his goggles and instantly saw two figures silently making their way through the darkness. Unlike the other two, they wore black and the pistols were at the ready. "We've got company. Two from that end, two from this end."

"Wait a minute, that's four." Vail looked at Qasiym.

"What?" Qasiym said in response to Vail's wary stare.

"You said there were only three!" he whispered.

"What!" It wasn't a question. "Nigga, you betta git yo' ass through that window," he whispered urgently. Four ... they could handle four. Nope, four was not good.

Vail hoisted himself over the windowsill and jumped quietly to the padded floor. He could not have known the moment he landed on the plush carpet beneath the window, he triggered a silent alarm in the surveillance room. The floor beneath the bottom level windows was electronically monitored.

"Come on, Xavier," Qasiym called. With smooth athletic efficiency Xavier was on the window sill and into the room alongside Vail. Just as quickly Qasiym was up and in.

❖   ❖   ❖

Vance was flipping through a People magazine, periodically peeking at the ten or so black and white monitors situated in front of him. They had gone down, but it was no more than a minute, nothing big could happen in such a short period of time. He was cool, but since then, everyone else was paranoid. Ripping and running, barking orders and sticking their noses into the surveillance room to say something to Victor. Everything looked okay. Right now, Victor was watching Timothy and Kenneth on one monitor, then Tyler and Jet on the other as they circled the grounds. Victor flipped switches that zoomed in and backed off, still nothing. Paul and Naomi spoke with him intermediately through ear mics.

The red light in room three, bottom floor began to blink; flickering persistently. Several things happened to Victor at once. First, he lost his color, his mouth went dry and he lost his faculty of speech as he watched the blinking light. Someone was inside the house. Vance sprang to his feet, staring unbelievably at the busy light for a second before he spoke into his mic connected to everyone on patrol. "We've been breached," he said solemnly. "East end, room three."

Inside that strange minute of darkness, a number of things went through her mind. She was remarkably calm, she noted. Real calm. It lasted no longer than a minute, but it seemed so much longer. You know time plays with you like that. Sometime moving too slow, sometimes moving too fast. But no matter what, you can never speed it up or slow it down. Jami bolted from where she was perched comfortably on the bed trapped by the boob-tube, to stand next to Kenya, at the large picture window. Kenya held her little sister, and when the endless minute of darkness ended, so did her calmness, as the weight of her ideas crashed recklessly into the realm of reality inside the new light, which was not really a new light, it was the same old light. That was the problem; it would always be the same old light, unless she did something about it. Her heart pounded rebelliously in her chest because she was about to do something. What exactly, had not been mapped out yet. She slipped her sundress over her head and threw it on the bed. At the closet, she pulled a pair of blue jeans from the rack.

Jami asked, "Where are you going?"

"I'm gonna get us out of here." Her voice was unsteady. "Just stay here and watch T.V., I'll be back."

"Nooooo Kenya!" Jami cried. "I'm coming with you."

"No Jami, stay here, I'll be back." Jami was adamant; she removed her dress and went to the closet to get her some jeans. Kenya pushed Jami into the closet and slammed the door. Jami began beating and yelling but no one would hear her, they were on the third floor. Everyone was downstairs. "Shut up Jami!" Kenya stretched her arm out and pulled the chair to the vanity chest to prop it under the door knob. Jami continued to yell and pound on the door. "Let me out Kenya! Let me out! I wanna go with you, PLEEEASEEE," she cried. "Don't leave meee!"

"I'll be back Jami, it's too dangerous. I'll be back, I promise." She put her Jordan's on her feet, then snatched a black DKNY shirt up and pulled it over her head.

The back stairwell, she guessed would be empty. From the angle they were coming from she could only speculate that they would end up somewhere near the three bedrooms used to store all the clothes and medicines for the kids. Jerald had once told her that no one could enter the house without the security room being notified. She had asked how, but every time he gave her information his hands became bolder and bolder despite her protest. So, she gave up. But his evasive remarks lead her to believe him. Maybe she could get to them before Victor did. Maybe. By the time she had descended the three flights of stairs, a light sheen of sweat was riding her brow. She passed Yadira, but her back was to Kenya, so she was able to slide quietly by unnoticed. Afraid and nervous, her burning legs had to take a backseat to her determination and focus. She was determined to seize this opportunity. If that is what this was. It is better to be prepared and not have the opportunity, than to have the opportunity and not be prepared. She was ready, or so she believed.

Timothy, Kenneth, Jet and Tyler split up. Timothy and Kenneth would take the window. Jet and Tyler would head to the back door and cover the hall. They would trap them.

Decker was minutes from the house when a report of a disturbance was issued through the radio. He noted the address and when he did get to the house, he continued on past it headed for the freeway.

He did not look, just reacted. When the door opened, impetuously, Vail started shooting. Qasiym and Xavier also were taken by surprise, they swung, aimed, but did not fire. Vail's gun had barked four times before Xavier could seize his hand.

When Kenya opened the door, she was not certain it was the right room, then a gun exploded. She saw movement and dove for the floor as bullets whizzed over her head knocking chunks from the wood and sheetrock. Kenya covered her head and buried her face into the carpet. Her resolve cracked, but did not shatter.

"Wait!" Xavier yelled at Vail.

Qasiym felt the trouble more than saw the glimmer caused by the moonlight that was reflected off of a chrome barrel. He shoved Vail and Xavier to his left while he dived right, maybe a fraction of a second before the window exploded and silent predator sizzled through the air putting holes everywhere. The girl laying on the floor stared at Qasiym. He stared at her. "C'mon." She gestured. He nodded.

"Follow the girl!" he yelled. "I gotcha covered on GO." One deep breath and he sprang to his feet firing both pistols in his hand. "Go, NOW! NOW! NOW!"

Xavier lifted Vail and they ran toward the door, and in the same fluid movement he lifted the girl from the floor and pushed her out of the doorway. Aiming the 9-mm toward the window, "Come on Q. Now!" he shouted and started shooting. After Qasiym passed Xavier, he slammed the door.

"Whew! So much for surprises." Qasiym sighed.

Xavier was looking at their position. They were sitting ducks in the middle of a hallway that opened at both ends.

"Kenya," Vail mouthed as he recognized the little girl.

Qasiym and Xavier looked at them in confusion. "Y'all know each other?" Xavier asked.

"Yeah, we've met. It's a long story," Vail said.

"We'd love to hear it, but not right now." That was Qasiym. "How many are there?" He continued speaking to Kenya.

"Six," she said without preamble, then added, "That you have to worry about."

"We have to get out of this hallway. Which way Kenya?" Xavier asked.

"To where?"

Xavier looked to Qasiym. "To Victor!" Qasiym said. She pointed to her left.

Just as they rounded the corner that would take them to Victor's study, Jet came from nowhere. The cold steel touched Vail's temple, whispered, then heat and blood sprayed mist-like into Xavier's face. Tyler attacked exactly when Jet did. He lunged and shot at Qasiym. However, Qasiym was not where he was supposed to be. Tyler lunged and shot at nothing but the air.

Victor was already contemplating to just leave and accept this as a loss. Too much had happened. Was happening. It was time to go, unless ... unless Jet and Tyler could contain the trouble. The report of gunfire from some point in the house was loud and unrelenting. "Vance," Victor said solemnly. "Call everyone in. Tell them to abort and let's evacuate! It's over."

What saved Qasiym's life, it would sound arrogant to say instincts, it would also be false. Could say luck, but in so many ways that would be neglecting the presence of God. What it was though, was a barrette. He had stopped, bent over and picked up a barrette, just as Jet pulled the trigger. Vail, in turn paused, looked sideways to see what Qasiym was doing. Hell, there could be an ambush or trap anywhere and he was picking shit up off the floor. Then piercing heat streaked across his temple. To his right a guy dressed in black jumped up from the shadows. The bullet that was supposed to be lodged in his brain, struck the other guy in the shoulder and blood splattered into Xavier's face.

From the middle, Xavier pushed Kenya backwards. He only had a matter of seconds to get a grip on the situation. Vail was in trouble, Qasiym could handle his own, or so he hoped.

The boy turning his head the second he pulled the trigger surprised Jet. Seeing the bullet hit Tyler, put him off guard, but he recovered in time to see the darker, shorter boy bringing up a larger caliber weapon to the ready. He threw his left foot out, like lightning and kicked the gun. It discharged loudly in the hallway, tumbled into the air and landed in the girl's lap. Xavier was more than a little stunned. Jet seized this opportunity to point his weapon at Xavier, but Vail grabbed his hand. Jet shot his elbow into Vail's midsection. "Uh!" Twisted funnily and brought Vail's long form over his shoulder and flipped him to the floor on his back, simultaneously shooting the heel of his foot out and connecting solidly in Xavier's stomach. The power in Jet's kick elevated Xavier and sent him to the floor.

"Mmmgghh!" Jet yelled as he tried to wrestle his gun away from Vail, who was stretched out on the floor.

He kicked him in the stomach. "Ugh!" Vail exclaimed in pain.

Xavier was back on his feet, executed a jump kick with all power he could muster to Jet's midsection. "Ah!" That was Jet. He released Vail and the gun, turned on Xavier swinging a wild backhand and menacing growl. Xavier ducked and threw a punch into Jet's midsection that Jet blocked. Jet threw a kick that was blocked. Xavier was unable to defend the two-handed lunge into his chest hurling him into the wall. Then Jet fell into him, blood slipping from his lips before sliding to his knees and collapsing to the floor. Behind him Vail stood clutching Jet's gun, his hands trembling. Xavier nodded his head at Vail, a silent 'thanks.' Vail nodded back, returning a silent 'yeah.'

Qasiym was in a fight for his life. The bullet wound to the man's shoulder had not slowed him at all. Already Tyler had gone after his eyes twice, his throat twice and kept him on defense the entire time. Thank goodness he had defense. Tyler threw a roundhouse that Qasiym ducked from, then shot a kick that Qasiym dodged, but there was no relief, Tyler's attack continued. Out of nowhere he produced a knife and slashed Qasiym across the stomach. Reflexively he curled his abdomen away from the blade but could not escape the blade completely. He felt the heat sear across his stomach. Now he was pissed. When Tyler swung the blade at his throat, Qasiym stepped aggressively into the blow and caught Tyler's wrist; twisted and broke it with a sickening snap. Tyler howled in pain, but he was cut short as Qasiym spun and smashed his elbow into Tyler's larynx, crushing it. Tyler and Jet both found the floor about the same time. All three men stood breathing heavily, tired and sweaty. From Kenya's corner she watched in stunned silence, but she was glad they had made it.

CHAPTER 37

Victor stood in the study with Naomi, Yadira, Joey, Timothy and Kenneth. Vance had called everyone in on the mission more than three minutes ago, but Jet and Tyler had not shown as of yet. Tension in the room was thick as gumbo. Whoever these guys were, they were good if they stopped Jet and Tyler. Victor walked over to what looked like a floor model television with a built-in radio on top. However, when he raised the top, it was a bomb, it was last resort. He began to type an entry code while everyone in the room listened as the keys chirped. Naomi was first to realize exactly what it was.

"Victor, what are you doing?" she asked waspishly.

"All is lost, Naomi, it's time to go. You know there can be no evidence," replied evenly.

"What about the kids, Victor?" she shouted. "What about the fuckin' kids!"

Vacuously, Victor looked at Naomi and almost mechanically he responded "They're evidence."

"No way man, this is some sick shit! All those kids, they're just babies." Victor ignored her and continued to set the timer on the bomb. It was seventy pounds of C4-plastic explosives. It would level this house and the basement rooms would never be found.

"Paul, Yadira," Naomi pleaded. "Don't do this."

Victor's cell phone started ringing; he picked it up and spoke into it. Seconds later he hung up. "That was Decker. Gunfire has been reported by the neighbors. The police will be here soon."

Yadira looked at Naomi, "I can't go to prison Naomi," she cried.

"Paul," Victor snapped. "You and Kenneth go get the vans ready. Yadira, Naomi go empty my safe in the office." He tossed them the keys. "I'm setting this thing for twelve minutes, that's plenty of time. We'll meet in the driveway."

Jet and Tyler were professionals. If they had not shown up, it was understood they would not be showing up. Timothy was following Victor up the stairs. "Victor, where are we headed?" Timothy asked.

"I need to get Kenya." He discovered that the room was empty, Victor's heart plummeted. He called her name, but she was gone, that he could painfully see. He stood staring into the empty room; Timothy turned to leave. "Where are you going?" Victor snapped.

"I'm getting the fuck out of here," Timothy retorted angrily.

"No! We must find Kenya."

Timothy frowned. "You find her." Then headed downstairs. Once Victor realized he was alone he instantly became frightened, jittery and nervous. His eyes bulged, darted left to right. What if they are up here? He turned and ran after Timothy.

The house had gone completely still while Kenya was leading them to the study. Xavier noticed the sheer size of the place, and their progress was slow to avoid another ambush. It was when they rounded the corner off the kitchen that they saw four people in the hall speaking in hushed tones. Victor saw them come around the corner and spun, alerting Timothy, Paul and, Naomi. Not quite twenty feet away Qasiym, Xavier, Vail and Kenya all ducked back behind the wall. Victor spoke, "Vail, you surprise me boy! But here's another mission for you. Ponder this boy, in nine minutes this house is going up in smoke. You can (A) chase me. (B) try to save your daughter. or (C) none of the above. See I win again."

Xavier started thinking overtime. "Kenya, where are the kids at?"

"Downstairs," she answered. Xavier peeked around the corner and they were gone. "He's lying," Vail said.

"Maybe," Qasiym said.

The sounds of vehicles leaving at high speed could be heard, then: "He's not lying." Startled, Qasiym and Xavier drew down on the unexpected intruder. She raised her hands. "You can stand there pointing your guns or you can help me try and disarm the bomb. Matter of fact, if you're gonna shoot you better go ahead." She turned and walked into the study. Naomi had seen many things, been involved with a lot of bad people. She had even killed before. But she was a mother and as a mother, she could not let those children die. So, at the last minute she jumped from the van and ran back inside to help. That was the least she could do, but selling children on the black market to deprived families and murdering children were different. It was different.

They all gathered inside the study looking at the red digital numbers tick backwards. Victor had not lied; it was just now hitting the nine-minute mark. Vail and Xavier looked at Qasiym. "Can you stop this thing?" Qasiym asked Naomi.

She shrugged her shoulders, "I was hoping you knew how."

Time was ticking. "Fuck it!" Xavier exclaimed. "Let's just get the kids outta here. Eight minutes is a long time, where are they?"

Kenya led them to the room full of sleeping children. Xavier immediately scanned the room for Vianna. Damn, it was at least twenty kids in here, he just shook his head. Then Vianna stood up on the other side of the room and started crying when she saw Xavier. Her big brother. "Lookout, I'm gonna start calling you cry baby," he said.

She smiled through her tears as she made her way to him.

Kenya said, "So you're Zav-ya?" He looked at Kenya. "Yeah."

"She said you were coming."

Naomi added, "She wouldn't eat, that's why she isn't asleep."

Vail located Iyanna and lifted her into his arms, she started crying. He smiled. Kenya was trying to wake some of the children, but they did not budge.

"We're going to have to pack them out of here," Naomi said.

Qasiym immediately grabbed two of the children, one in each arm and ran from the room. They had less than six minutes. Naomi followed suit, Xavier picked up two of the sleeping children and ran from the house with Vianna close at his heels. Vail picked up a little girl along with Iyanna in his hand and started out. Kenya tried to wake Amber, but she did not move. The ululation of sirens could be heard in the distance. She picked up a little boy they called C.J. and ran outside with the others. Qasiym was on his way back in. It had taken about ninety seconds to put them in a safe distance from the house. There were still ten kids left, he picked up two more. Xavier was right behind, lifted Amber from her bed. She was a big girl, he lumbered up the stairs and out of the basement rooms. Vail grabbed Valerie and tossed her over his shoulder while grabbing a little girl by the back of her clothes, she was six or so. His strong athletic body toted them slowly. Valerie was heavy but, on his shoulders, his legs were handling most of the weight. Naomi grabbed two more and headed back up the stairs and out of the door. When Kenya entered the room, there were only three kids left. She picked up Keasha and trotted up and out. Qasiym exited the house with the final two children. Tired and sweaty, Xavier was leaning in front of Vianna, Vail was holding Iyanna. Naomi? Well, she was nowhere, gone.

Police were turning into the driveway with their sirens blaring and lights flashing. The moon had slipped out of view and this was the scene when Xavier heard Vail yell, "Kenya Noooo!"

Things seemed to move in slow motion as he turned to see Kenya running back towards the house.

"Qasiym, how much time is left?" Xavier asked.

Qasiym looked at his watch and shook his head. Honestly, it was like a slow-motion picture, you have to imagine it. The words dribbled from Qasiym's lips like a Screw tape. "Ahh 'bout siiixxx-ty- twwooo-seeecoonds." Xavier sprinted as fast as his legs would take him. He could catch her before she reached the house. He knew he could, he had to.

Kenya had just sat Keasha down. The kids were strolled in the yard, unbelievably still asleep. It was dark, the police had arrived with red flashing lights. She was tired; her legs were hurting from running up and down those stairs. Then she remembered. The weight of it descended on her like thick fog and she almost fainted. Jami! She had put Jami in the closet. In all the excitement, she had forgotten about her sister. She did not think, she just ran. How much time was left? Could she make it? She could make it, she had to make it. She ran as fast as her legs would take her. At the porch something, no someone grabbed her by the waist. She spun and swung at this person. Xavier ducked.

"What are you doing?" She heard him ask. She was crying and inches from hysterical when she screamed.

"My sister! Xavier my sister's in there!"

The slow motion kicked in again. Xavier grimaced, shook his head and looked at his watch all at the same time. If Qasiym was right, there was less than forty seconds. This was stupid, insane and suicidal. This was a bitch! He glanced back at Vianna and thought, they better spell my name right. He did all this in that slowed down second, it seemed longer but it only took him a second. If you have not found something worth dying for, life ain't worth living. "Where?" Was all he said.

Kenya turned and sprinted up the steps that led into the house. He followed her up three flights of stairs and into her bedroom.

She flung open the closet door and pulled Jami from the closet. Her face was tear stained and her nose was running. To Kenya she looked simply beautiful. Xavier looked at his watch, he guessed maybe less than fifteen seconds. They would never make it. Then he saw the large window and the woods outside. This was the side that the pool was on, wasn't it? Looking out into the night he saw the aquamarine glow from the pool lights shining brightly below, and water rippling subtly from a light breeze. Xavier hoisted the single sofa over his head and heaved it through the window. "Kenya, there isn't much time left. Run and jump, the pool's down there!" She looked at him, disheveled, sweaty, and red eyed and beautiful. Bit down on her bottom lip, ran and leaped out of the window. "Come on sweetheart!" He lifted Jami into his arms, ran and leaped into the night. The house exploded a second before he left the ledge and the force pushed him forward. Xavier felt the heat on his back, and he was airborne. Jami damn near blew his eardrum out, because she was screaming so loud, but it was alright because he was flying.

When the house exploded without Xavier and Kenya coming through the door Qasiym and Vail were crushed. Qasiym could not understand why he had gone back inside the house in the first place. That was stupid. The yard was full of police, the explosion would bring reporters. In a matter of minutes this place would be a circus. "Vail, let's go!"

The police would want to talk, but he could not stand the delay because he had to get Victor. He knew where they were going, he knew. Several minutes after the explosion, the flames were still licking at the darkness hungrily when Qasiym saw three bodies coming from behind the destruction. He squinted to see better. The moon broke free again and from the walk he could tell it was Xavier. He smiled and nodded to himself. When they were next to each other, he noticed they were soaking wet. "I like you man! Really!" Qasiym said affectionately.

They smiled and hugged. "Thanks," Xavier said.

"Nah, thank you."

Vail sauntered over with Vianna by his side, Iyanna safe in his arms. "Hey black man, lil bit heah was worried 'bout cha."

Xavier put his hand on her head; "You wasn't worried, were you?"

She shook her head. "I knew you were coming."

"How you get outta ther?" Vail asked.

Xavier looked back at the burning inferno, then at Vail. "We flew, didn't we Kenya?"

She smiled, put her arm around Xavier's waist and said, "Just like Mike."

Vail smiled. Qasiym said, "I like her too man!"

CHAPTER 38

If you are not careful, you could get lost. If you are not careful. You ever just paid attention to the hum of the vehicle as it travels over the road? Watching that yellow line disappear beneath the front of the vehicle in trite succession. It was 11:05 P.M. C.P.S. had placed the children in a shelter until things could be sorted out. It had been impossible to wrestle away from the Sugarland Police Department, well almost impossible. Helicopters, reporters and fire engines put in appearances. It was mayhem at its finest.

Qasiym dropped Vail off first. It was good and Daphane was full of tears, happy tears that spoke her elation. All tears are salty, but some are bittersweet. Vail almost cried when he saw his parents and his sister exit the hotel room with Daphane. It's impossible to explain, so just understand it was all good. Iyanna was home just as healthy, if not healthier. Vail's only question was, what about Victor? Qasiym told him it would be taken care of. By now the news would be flashing photos of Paul and Yadira.

They did not have any photos of Victor, Timothy and Kenneth, nor any knowledge of Vance.

Qasiym had phoned Detective Bailey and told him what he expected before leaving the rubble in Sugarland. He would meet them. You must think like criminals, to understand the criminal mind. So that's how Qasiym's mind had been clicking ever since Victor left out of there. Darrell Puckett's gone, or out of the equation. He thought, if I'm Victor I would breathe easier because Puckett was no longer a factor. Where would I go if I was Victor? Where wouldn't anyone look until a plan could be formulated?

He pulled in front of Xavier's apartment. To Qasiym and Xavier's surprise Shai's car was still in the parking lot. "You have a down ass sister on yo' side," Qasiym whispered.

"Yeah, even a garbage can gets lucky sometime," Xavier retorted. Vianna had slept in Xavier's arms all the way over. She still slept as he exited the suburban and shut the door.

It was a question he continued to ask himself over and over again. The more adamant he became to just crush it like Styrofoam and forget it, the more resilient it became. Unanswered whys continued to crystallize in his mind. It was a peripheral jumble of ideas that led to questions. Questions that led to more questions, that led to more questions. Last night he was about to make love to his girl in the privacy of his own home. He had just got off the phone with Puckett and told him to meet him in the morning. His lady was situated wantonly across their queen size bed. The curtains were closed, the room dark and smelled of sweet-scented soap and lotions his lady had used. His erection was towering, he was ready for this. She was an airline attendant and had just returned from a week-long layover. Just when he was crawling between her ebony pillars of pliant flesh, he lost his erection. Rolled over and said out loud, "Why did Victor kill the Judge?" His lady was thoroughly perplexed. He questioned himself out loud just so she would know it was not anything directly related to her that had zapped his zeal for the carnal deed. "I mean ..." he said out loud to himself, "... he killed the Judge, right?" Qasiym was a driven man. An obstinate obsessive compulsive. He would latch on to a case with the tenacity of a badger and would not let it rest. She did not know diddlysquat about this particular case. She had just flown back in from Boston six hours ago and was in dire straits for some sex, but it was apparent that it was not forthcoming while he was stuck in this mental dilemma. This behavior had proven very pernicious in his other relationships, but she played her role. He dealt with her job and frequent trips, she dealt with this. It was an equal give and take.

"See, I can't figure out why you kill someone with the power of a Judge that's obviously on your side." He shook his head. "Okay, then there's the prostitute he was with. And the issue with the pimp. You with me?" he asked. Of course, she wasn't, but she nodded flittingly. "Then you risk what must be a million-dollar operation to enact some revenge on a pimp because he blew up some cheap ass clubs that were only a front anyway." She nodded and he shook his head.

"No. This is a guy who has moved through at least seven different states. Getting away with this for years. He was smarter than that, had to be. So, let's say he killed the Judge because he knew something." He looked at her and she shrugged her shoulders noncommittally. It made her heavy breasts shake, they were exposed because, of course, she was still sitting up in the bed naked next to him. His eyes traveled the acreage of her jouncing bosom, kindled momentarily, then returned to his nonviolent diatribe. "Then he must have told the prostitute something that she told the pimp, so Victor had to kill him. So, what did the Judge know, what did he tell her?" He leaned over and kissed. "I'm sorry baby, I have to go back to the office."

It was there, researching the Judge that Qasiym discovered that Judge Willow use to be a trial lawyer in Chicago. Puckett had told him this. Did he know? Among Willow's cases as a trial lawyer, he had represented a Cydney Pierce. A Vietnam veteran that had started a child pornography and prostitution ring with two other fellas. He learned that the states key witness was a Vietnamese girl by the name of Mylon Pierce. What blew his wig back was not only was she his wife, she was a minor and she was pregnant. Although the records did not say so, he was willing to bet his life that she had a son and named him Victor Pierce.

It was there in the morning when he pulled up to 1313 Burningbush Lane Condominiums. They looked the same as they had yesterday evening, minus the police and dead bodies. It was an unreasonable hour, sure. Right. He was not even sure if anyone would be here, but this address was the end to it all. After six rings of the doorbell and no response, not stirrings inside that he could detect, he turned to leave. So that was it. He could go home and make love to his woman. A lot of questions had been answered. He knew why the Judge had been killed. Just as he was starting to walk away from the door, the workings on the locks began to click, the door creaked open and not one, not two, but four scantily dressed females stood in the doorway with macabre who the fuck are you— what the fuck do you want expressions on their faces. He wrestled his eyes from their alluring lush physiques and once again thought of his baby at home alone. He cleared his throat and spoke to their icy stares. "My name is Qasiym. I'm an investigative reporter among other things ... um ... I'm going after the man that ... uh ... well he's responsible for having Andrew Guthfield killed." He spoke slowly and with each carefully placed word the ice in their stares melted.

"I'm kind of in between a rock and a hard place. I know that Mr. Guthfield and Ms. Brimha were killed by the same people. Ms. Brimha was ... uh in some type of relationship with the Judge. He told her something that was worth killing for. What I need to know is, did she share something with any of you?" A non-descriptive expression crossed their faces as they looked from him to one another.

They invited him into the plush apartment where they talked for a brief time. They did not know anything beneficial. He had settled back in his car when Babydoll stepped to the driver's side window. She told him if anyone knew anything it would be Sideline Redd, but he was in a coma. She just wanted to tell him. His gaze fell on her backside as she sashayed back into the apartment. Once again, he wanted to go home, he needed some loving. The man was in a damn coma for Christ's sake! This was the end of the road, time to go home.

He was really talking to himself. Listening to himself. What end is dead, what door is closed, what road has no turning to a man piss- desperate. "I can catch him Sideline, I know I can."

He had been sitting in the room for thirty minutes listening to himself talk. Then the machines started beeping, the whatchamacallit went to jumping erratically. Every machine in the room was doing the damn fool. Qasiym was on his feet looking guilty as hell, thinking he had just killed the man. Sideline Redd's eyes were fluttering sporadically. Two nurses rushed in and with professional acumen brought everything under control. When he looked again at Redd's face, his eyes were open; intense and lucid.

The suburban pulled alongside the unmarked police unit. A swat van loomed nearby. Surveillance men were positioned. "You were right," Detective Bailey said banally.

See, at home with his girl the operative word that triggered everything was privacy. Adult prostitutes could take you in an alley, in a car, in a sleazy motel, anywhere. Victor, however would deal with powerful perverted adults and innocent children. There would have to be privacy. So, the question was, where was it? A place where even if the kids yelled and screamed, no one would hear them. Sideline Redd told Qasiym about a home Victor owned in Rosharon, Texas. It was thirty minutes from Houston, close and convenient.

The scene that they found was almost beyond description. Blood was everywhere. Victor had been shot with a large caliber weapon too many times to count in the face. Paul was in no better condition. The only woman in the room matched the description of Yadira Holmes. Her head was twisted awkwardly. Qasiym deduced that her neck had been broken. "Who done this?" Baily asked.

"The kids," Qasiym said despondently.

Timothy and Kenneth must have come to understand that the police would be looking for Paul, Yadira and Victor. If they took care of them no one could ever find them. Qasiym shook his head knowing they were gone. No pictures, no fingerprints, nothing. He smiled and repeated, "The kids."

CHAPTER 39

The living room was a beehive of activity, shouts, yelling and playful hurrahing. This was 2016, April. Sugarland, Texas. When Xavier brought his mom out to this house and finally convinced her that it really was hers, the expression she wore was priceless. Since checking out of that hospital she had not touched any more drugs. Losing Bernadine the way she had was painful. With Xavier's money and Tao Sung's professional acumen she started a catering company that was flourishing under her care. She had gained so much weight in the last eight months, but it was good weight. Xavier, Shai and Nathan bunched together on the love seat watching the game. Daphane and Iyanna were sitting on the single sofa also watching the game. Kenya, Jami and Vianna were stretched out on the thick plush carpet dropping more popcorn than eating. Xavier had gone to visit Kenya at a shelter. He liked Kenya, you know. She had encountered a lot of hard knocks in her young life, they had talked. So now Nellie was in the process of legally adopting her and

Jami. Qasiym was also making things easier. Lately he was in demand from talk shows, magazines, authors, etc. ... etc. ...

Xavier and Shai lived together in Northshore, engaged to be married. Everyone was here tonight watching the game. Gus and Bugeye sandwiched Nellie on the couch. Adib, Moophisey and Puckett were sitting at the bar. Qasiym was a busy man so he declined.

Puckett tracked Vatly down and found him in St. Louis. Vatly found his father dead. His stepmom slash lover and his son living alone. Even after he ran away, he had never stopped loving her, so thoughts of Dominique quickly evaporated. He was arrested at home, with Amber and Valerie as witnesses. He was looking at a life sentence. Vatly was asking for some leniency if he testified against Officer Decker and aided them in finding Timothy, Kenneth and Vance. They never brought up Patty's name so neither did he. However, they did want Shamiria and Yolanda. Also made comments about the twins, but he played dumb.

The game was the university of Houston and Duke in the NCAA finals. Vail and Prophet had taken them there. Duke was the number one seed. U of H had surprised everyone because they were number eight. Prophet struggled early on in the season. RaRa 'The Rock' had been hurt half the season, but Vail played like a man possessed all year long. Averaging 26 points and 13 rebounds a game.

So, this was the game they were watching. Duke was up by 11 at the half. Vail was struggling, 2-11 shooting with 3 fouls. RaRa, Prophet and the bench were trying to hold on, but it was only getting worse. With ten minutes left, down by 15, Vail checked back into the game. The living room had gone silent because the home team was losing. The commentators announced that Vail had put on 'the wrist bands.' One had Daphane's name embroidered into it, the other had Iyanna's. Earlier in the year, he had given an interviewer a statement about how he only wore them when he was struggling. The cameras zoomed in as the sports announcer spoke about the wrist bands. The fans were on their feet shouting, stomping and clapping. The camera men flashed to Vail's parents and his sister.

The ten minutes of that game was unbelievable. Vail came out and dropped two threes back-to-back. Prophet drove and gave a no look pass to the low post. RaRa spun into the goal and tried a dunk, was fouled but it was not called, the ball back rimmed and flew into the air. Vail came from nowhere, snagged the rebound over several players and dunked the ball ferociously. He came down yelling and beating his chest. That earned him a technical foul. Daphane jumped up from the couch wiggling her delectable hips. "Ah! That's my baby!" she shouted.

The room erupted into laughter. The crowd was really into it. Down by 9 with plenty of time. Duke missed the technical shot. On their next attempt to score, a Duke player penetrated smoothly, went up but RaRa, was crunk and blocked the shot. Prophet got the loose ball and headed a three-an-one break. He made a sweet move and had the lane but in Reggie Miller fashion instead of going forward, he stepped backwards behind the three-point line and pulled up. The shot blew the nets up! Now he yelled and pounded his chest while throwing Vail a wicked grin and a wink. The crowd jumped to their feet yelling and beating their chest. The whistle had blown, the ref teched Prophet. They were down by six pending the technical shot. Down by seven and with the ball, Staley passed to Roy at the top of the key. Roy lobbed an ally-oop to RaRa that he flushed with authority, then hung on the rim and yelled before dropping to the floor and beating his chest while facing the fans. The whistle blew, the tech issued and the coach called a time out. They were down by four with six minutes left. Plenty of time.

Down the stretch Staley hit a huge bucket. Roy snagged some crucial boards. Duke had a hired killer that came down and dropped a three pointer. Vail came down and off a feed from RaRa answered it with a three of his own. He had seventeen points. The same Duke player put up an acrobatic shot that went in and drew the foul on Vail, he had four fouls. Prophet came down and sent a pass to Vail driving the lane. He was double teamed, he sent it to Roy in the corner who rotated it to a wide-open Prophet behind the arch. Prophet sent the shot off and was fouled as he fell to the floor. The shot found nothing but the bottom of the net. Instead of yelling, the whole U of H squad put their fingers to their lips and "Shhh!" the crowd. Dukes' killer drove, stopped and popped an 18-foot rainbow that ripped through the nets leaving ten seconds on the clock. They were down by two, time out was called.

Now Xavier was later told that the play was drawn up for Prophet to get the ball from RaRa who was taking it out. Roy was to set a screen for Vail, who would swing into the paint. Prophet was to hit Vail in the paint for the turn around eight-foot jumper. That was the way it was drawn up, however things do not always go as planned. On RaRa's inbound pass it was brilliantly deflected into the air. Roy found wings and skied for the rebound. In all the chaos the only player open was Staley or at least that was the only player he saw with the same color jersey. Staley received the pass with two seconds on the clock. Hesitantly and without any other choice, he launched the three pointer. It looked good, everyone held their breath and watched the ball roll in the air toward the goal. It back rimmed and flew behind the backboard. The horn sounded.

No one had noticed Staley laying on the ground, or that the referee had called a foul. Staley would get three free throws. Right before he was to shoot, Vail whispered something in his ear. Remarkably Staley, a sixty percent free throw shooter hit all three free throws and U of H won by one.

Everyone wanted to know what Vail had told Staley, but neither would tell anyone. Years would pass before Vail confided to Xavier, "I told him I once knew a man who flew out of a burning house, and he could do it too. Just jump, have no fear and he could fly."

✦ 360 ✦

EPILOGUE

Ruby left Houston four months after beating Xavier in that basketball game, moved to Dallas with an aunt. She graduated and attended Xavier University on a full Academic Scholarship, but she excelled in basketball. The day she was drafted by the Houston Comets, she appeared in a Jet, along with other outstanding black female draftees. Xavier would see her in the Jet, with her five-year- old son Reivax Jaeshall Vincent. The boy kind of favored him but he was not convinced until he looked at the boy's name. 'Reivax' was Xavier spelled backwards.

Qasiym won the Pulitzer he so longed for. Married and settled down. That success bug that had been eating away at him all his life finally acquiesced its hold on him. He started a sports magazine called 'Talent.' Had two children and was living life at a moderate pace. Life could be good if you learned how to be good to yourself.

On Southmore and Scott, on the roof Chill stood looking over the rubbish. The trees, the grimy freeway and glimpses of downtown. The sun was on its way down, he loved the color it casted into the sky as it descended and all the cars passed through its golden glow. It was about time for Maghrib. Yeah, he had become Muslim. Xavier, Shai, Kenya and Jami also accepted Islam. Nellie was the only one bucking. Chill, now Hamzah, spread his prayer rug, seated himself with his Qur'an and began to read:

"In the name of Allah, most gracious, most merciful. Because Allah will never change the grace which he hath bestowed on a people until they change what is in their (own) soul: And verily Allah is he who heareth and knoweth (all things)."

ABOUT THE AUTHOR

✦

Shakur is a native Houstonian from Clinton Park, Texas. He attended Galena Park High School and went on to become a safety supervisor for numerous chemical plants in and around Houston. One job took him to Utah, a place he grew to love in a short period of time and relocated his family there.

Shakur has been married for 21 years and have four beautiful children. He is an aspiring screenwriter with several completed full-length screenplays.

He is also the editor of the book FROM IGNORANCE TO ISLAM: Transformative Stories of Change From Brothers Deep In The Cave.

Soon to be released. And Another Sunset II Unintended Consequences scheduled to be released in the summer of '22.

Stay Blessed, and Allah knows best.